PRAISE FOR C

'A knockout new talent you should read immediately.'

—Lee Child

'It really had me gripped.'
  —Marian Keyes, international bestselling author of *Grown Ups*

'The definition of an utterly absorbing page-turner. Richly drawn-out characters, a compelling plot, and a finale that will keep you guessing.'
  —John Marrs, bestselling author of
  What Lies Between Us and *The One*

'A real nailbiter of a thriller that gets darker and more twisted with every page. If you liked *What You Did*, you'll love *The Push*.'
—Erin Kelly, *Sunday Times* bestselling author of *He Said/She Said*

'Absorbing, timely, and beautifully written, *What You Did* is a superior psychological thriller from a major talent.'
  —Mark Edwards, bestselling author of
  The Retreat and *Here To Stay*

'I loved this story. The flesh-and-blood characters, dry wit, and brilliant plotting are every bit as enjoyable as *Big Little Lies*.'
  —Louise Candlish, bestselling author of
  Our House and *The Other Passenger*

'A perfectly plotted murder mystery that had me hooked from the first page. Twisty domestic suspense that's perfect for fans of *Big Little Lies*.'
  —Lisa Gray, bestselling author of the Jessica Shaw series

'I haven't flown through a book so quickly in a very long time. It delivers on every single level.'
  —Caz Frear, bestselling author of the DC Cat Kinsella series

'What a nail-biting, just-one-more-page-I-can't-put-it-down roller coaster of suspense!'
  —Steph Broadribb, author of *Deep Down Dead*

'Smart, sassy, and satisfyingly twisty.'
  —Sarah Hilary, author of the DI Marnie Rome series

'Huge fun with some very dark moments and brilliantly awful characters. Excellent, twisty plotting.'
  —Harriet Tyce, author of *Blood Orange*

'A brilliantly observed and compelling thriller.'
  —Anna Mazzola, author of *The Story Keeper*

'A roller-coaster read, full of thrills and one spectacular spill!'
  —Liz Nugent, bestselling author of *Skin Deep*

'*What You Did* is a triumph, a gripping story of the secrets and lies that can underpin even the closest friendships. Put some time aside – this is one you'll want to read in a single sitting.'
  —Kevin Wignall, bestselling author of *A Death In Sweden* and *The Traitor's Story*

'Hitting the rare sweet spot between a satisfying read and a real page-turner, this brilliantly written book deserves to fly high.'
  —Cass Green, bestselling author of *In A Cottage In A Wood*

LET
ME IN

ALSO BY CLAIRE McGOWAN

Fiction

The Fall
What You Did
The Other Wife
The Push
I Know You
Are You Awake?

Non-fiction

The Vanishing Triangle

Paula Maguire series

The Lost
The Dead Ground
The Silent Dead
A Savage Hunger
Blood Tide
The Killing House

Literary Fiction

This Could Be Us

Writing as Eva Woods

LET
ME IN

CLAIRE
McGOWAN

THOMAS & MERCER

Published by Thomas & Mercer, Seattle

www.apub.com

Amazon, the Amazon logo, and Thomas & Mercer are trademarks of Amazon.com, Inc., or its affiliates.

ISBN-13: 9781542035392
eISBN: 9781542035408

Cover design by Whitefox, Heike Schüssler
Cover image: ©Dave Wall / Arcangel; ©Polina Korzun / Arcangel; ©Katarzyna Mierzwinska / Arcangel; ©HAYKIRDI / Getty; ©Giulia Fiori Photography / Getty

Printed in the United States of America

LET
ME IN

Prologue

I never met my mother.

That's something I used to tell people, although of course it isn't true. Everyone has met their mother, if only for the first painful moments when you're struggling out of her. Even mine had to push me from her body and into the cold air, though her arms were chained to the bed throughout, and she wasn't allowed even a second to hold me after. As soon I landed in the world, red and wet and screaming, I was rushed from the room, and as soon as she could stand up my mother was taken back to her cell and the door was locked. She couldn't see me, or touch me, kiss my new-minted forehead. She couldn't say goodbye – barely even hello. After nine months inside her, I was whisked away, as if I had to be saved from her, as if her very breath on my newborn face might have corrupted me. As if my own mother was the worst danger I would ever face.

Helen

My mother's vase got broken on the day of the move. It wasn't worth much – a piece of green Murano glass she'd got on her honeymoon in Venice, pretty enough in a common way – but to me it was a symbol. That this move was inauspicious, that we were wrong to leave the safe anonymity of London and transplant to the country. People think you can hide in the country, where it's isolated, but they are very wrong. In the country, there are always eyes on you.

It was the movers who broke it. George had organised them, which I'd been surprised and grateful for, though really there was no other choice. I worked till 10 p.m. on the day before we left, the hospital squeezing me hard for every minute. A final check-up, a final chart, a last broken arm, one more rash on a baby. And I felt squeezed, like a lemon popping pips all over the place. George had handled everything for the move, in fact, as I put in a succession of late nights and came home in the middle of the night, exhausted, ready only to fall into bed. Sometimes I slept at the hospital, like a junior doctor instead of the consultant I was, trying and failing to clear the never-ending backlog of cases from Covid, lumps ignored, heart attacks left too long, broken limbs walked about on. People were afraid of hospitals now, as they had been in the old days. They were once again places of death.

On that last day, I cleared out my locker and handed back my staff pass, surprised to find something like sorrow in my throat as I said goodbye to the nurses, the receptionist with the nose ring, the sarcastic, trustworthy doctors, with whom I'd forged bonds like fighters in a war over the past two years. I'd been in medicine since I was twenty-five, almost thirteen years now, and I didn't know who I would be without it. But hopefully George was right, and the move would be good for us. I pictured waking up with natural light, stepping into the garden with my coffee cradled in both hands, raising my face to the sky with a contented sigh. But then I would think about how I wasn't going to be working, at least not until I figured out what I wanted to do instead of medicine, and my stomach would flip over. How would we manage? We'd paid for the new house already, so we were mortgage-free, but there would be bills and renovations, and I was used to dropping fifty pounds on a face cream or jumper if I needed retail therapy. Not that there would be any nice shops in the depths of the countryside, outside of the bougie tourist traps – if eighteen-year-old me knew I was moving back to the West Country, she would have thought I'd lost my mind.

Look at your cute flat! There are cinemas and more branches of the Body Shop than you could ever visit. Have you gone insane, Helen?

Maybe I had. But I knew George was right, we needed a change. Needed something, anyway. The hunt for a new job, the non-stop rejection and loss he faced every day, it was gouging away at my husband until I hardly knew him. So I'd let him handle the move, the packing up of our flat, giving notice to the landlord and the utilities, changing addresses, redirecting post, all that grind of relocation. It seemed crazy, but I'd never even seen the house we were moving to. George had found it as part of an auction sale, and it had never been listed online. He'd shown me some blurry photos from his trips down, but I'd been too busy at work to take any time off, or really even to think about it. I seemed to only have the energy to work, sleep, and sometimes shower, and my thoughts were narrow, blurred around the edges.

In the end George had declared it would be a surprise for me. A sign that I trusted him to find us a house I would like. It hadn't been easy, with my control-freak tendencies. Lou thought it was desperately romantic, like in a rom com, where a man hands you a set of keys and tells you, *I've bought us a house, darling.* I'd peppered him with questions about its energy ratings, the potential for dry rot and subsidence, the need for parking and a village within walking distance, until George became huffy and said I didn't trust him. And it was true, I didn't, at least not in matters of organisation. But I was trying. I'd signed off on a house and all I knew was I was moving to somewhere in Cornwall, not too far from my mother in Devon. It was old, he said. Pretty. Yes, he had got a survey.

I was up at five on the day of the move, worrying in the half-light over money and the future, while George snored beside me. Had we made a terrible mistake? What if I hated the countryside – what if the house wasn't liveable, and we didn't have the money to fix it? What if the locals resented us for inflating property prices? When the movers came at eight, my heart sank further. Typical George, he had cut costs by going on some task-bidding website, and we'd ended up with two scruffy guys in a dilapidated van. I wasn't sure everything was going to fit, and it had been such a stress getting parking permits for the van, which you had to go through the council for. Our snippy upstairs neighbour, Ken of Ken and Gloria, was down like a shot, making sure the van didn't scratch his Beemer. 'Moving out, are you?'

'Yes. Sorry for the hassle, we'll be off in an hour or two.'

'Just watch the paint in the staircase.' Ken was chair of the building board, because of course he was. At least I wouldn't have to listen to him blowing his nose through the paper-thin walls any more. My stress levels were up to eight (George says they start at three and extend, well, to infinity) as the guys bumped our lovely mid-century furniture into walls and doors. There were at least three chips and scuffs on the staircase walls already. They humped our boxes, poorly packed by George, with a lack of expertise that told me they hadn't done this before.

'Please be careful,' I kept saying, aware that I was the middle-class bitch in the Boden jumper. But I felt justified, if even more stressed, when the bottom of one box gave way and its contents rained down on the floorboards with a loud shattering sound. 'Stop!' I stepped over it, kneeling to pick up fragments of green glass. Mum's vase. It was only a cheap thing, but I felt tears come to my eyes. I hated this, the mess and chaos and uncertainty. For a moment I even wished I was back at the hospital, where chaos came in and I smoothed it out, called for instruments and consults and bandages and they appeared just as I asked.

'Sorry love,' muttered the older of the guys, who had a cigarette dangling from his mouth. George was in the doorway, holding his signed and framed copy of *Aladdin Sane*. That wouldn't get broken, of course.

'Careful, you'll cut yourself,' he said, seeing the bits of glass in my hands.

'They've broken Mum's vase. You didn't put it in bubble wrap? Newspaper even?'

He shrugged. 'I couldn't find any.' I could feel my annoyance build. This was why I ended up doing everything, because he would do it badly, and it would be twice as much work for me after all. I couldn't believe I'd let him pick the house. What kind of a dump was I heading to? It was an incredible bargain, he'd said, so much so that we could buy it for cash – was that perhaps because it was falling to pieces?

All the way in the car, inching through West London, I told myself I was lucky. We were going to a beautiful place, and we'd been able to afford a house, a large house. Even between us, it would have been years before we could buy a house in London. I only had so much time in my day; I was already working as hard as humanly possible. I needed a break from medicine. And with Mum the way she was, I really should move back nearer her. She kept saying not to – or communicating it as best she could, rather – but the guilt was getting too much for me. With Covid and work, I'd only seen her twice in the last two years, and then she'd got ill and so many things were lost for good. All the visits I'd put off till after the pandemic, all the activities and outings, it was too late for most of them already.

The sun came up as we hit the M4 and began the long, long journey west. We lost sight of the van immediately, and I didn't know if we'd get there first or they would, but I tried to tell myself it didn't matter. I had to stop obsessing over small details. I'd spent my life wound tight, taking care of everything, covering every track, and in the end I'd made a terrible mistake anyway and someone was dead. All my vigilance and planning had prevented nothing. So I had to let things go. I had to live a little. I tried counting my breaths, the way I'd learned in the meditation class Lou had dragged me to – in for four, out for eight. But I could still feel the fuzz of my heart in my chest, the weight of worry pulling me down. What were we doing? As London sank behind us, so did my spirits. Driving west in this way, it felt like turning back towards the past, to things I'd done my best to run from.

Later I would see I had been right to be upset about the vase, that it really was a bad omen. Because after we locked the flat up, the floors empty and dusty where our furniture had sat, and dropped the key with the estate agent on the high street, and left London for good, everything went downhill with a speed I have still not fully understood. The vase, it turned out, was only the first of many things to break.

◆ ◆ ◆

I don't remember much about the trip down. George can't bear service stations, with their over-priced Starbucks and screaming kids, and always wants to seek out an interesting or quirky place to stop instead, even if it's miles off the motorway and doesn't have any loos. I don't care personally; I'd rather get the journey over with. But I was being accommodating, so we drove into Glastonbury (adding an extra forty minutes to our trip) and stopped at a tea shop with chintzy tables and vintage crockery. George spread a thick layer of clotted cream on his scone, and I wondered if the move would encourage him to start exercising again. 'Can you feel the ley lines?' he said, through jam.

'What?' I'd scoured the menu for something that wasn't pure sugar or white carbs, and having failed, was picking at some buttered crumpets. The feeling of dread still dogged me, and I could see nothing charming among the shops hawking dreamcatchers and Tarot cards.

'Glastonbury. It's built on ley lines, that's why they have all these shops with crystals and whatnot.'

'You don't actually believe that?' I stared at him over my cup of tea. George and I had always sneered about such things. Sometimes he would read me horoscopes out of the paper, but would change them and speak in a spooky Mystic Meg voice that had me in stitches. *Today, beware of the colour red, if it comes in sirens, and if you recently committed a serious crime . . . Your lucky cell number is four, and your lucky offence is GBH . . .*

He hadn't made jokes like that for a while now – I missed them.

'Well, no. I've been reading up on it is all. The *occult.*' He said that last word with some embarrassment.

'Er, why?'

8

'There's a big tradition of witchcraft where we're going, you know. I just wanted to learn about our new home.'

I forced a smile. He was excited about this move; that should have been enough for me. And he really had done it all himself, since I'd been working non-stop while trying to deal with my own trauma. I hadn't had more than a week off, or a gap between jobs, since I was twenty-four, and my hand kept twitching for my work phone, like a phantom limb. I wondered how long it would be before I stopped gasping awake, convinced I had missed a 6 a.m. ward round or forgotten to file paperwork, or that a patient wasn't crashing on another floor, and I was too late to save them because I'd fallen asleep for five minutes. George said I had PTJS – post-traumatic job stress.

After lunch he wanted to look in the shops, but I nudged him on. 'Come on, we need to get there before dark. Since when do you like all this stuff anyway?'

He shrugged. 'I think it's interesting. What people believe in. I don't believe it myself, but I'm interested that they do, if you see what I mean.'

The occult has always unsettled me, for reasons I don't quite understand. Mum has a deep aversion to anything other-worldly – she wouldn't even watch the Harry Potter films. Maybe I'd picked it up from her. I dragged George away, reluctant, and soon we were on the road for the last leg. He insisted on driving, so I could have a rest. 'And a surprise,' he added, pulling away in second gear as I winced at the grinding of the engine.

'You really aren't going to tell me where we're going?' I could google the name of the town now I had a little time at last.

'You've come this far, my love. Why not be surprised?'

I don't like being surprised. But I had organised every aspect of our lives for years, and this seemed important to him. I tried to talk myself out of the dread with pure logic. So what if I didn't like the house? We could change it. Or at an absolute pinch, fix it and sell it on. It had been quite a bargain, I was sure we'd sell it for more. And what if it was entirely uninhabitable? Well, then we'd – there was probably a hotel or B & B somewhere. Not that we had much money left after paying for the house.

'Are you thinking about how you're going to change the house if you don't like it?' He caught my eye in the mirror.

I smiled weakly. He knew me too well. 'Maybe.'

He reached for my hand, his slightly greasy with the Doritos he'd been snacking on for the last ten miles. 'Look, if you hate it, we can move, I promise. I just . . . wanted to take care of things for you. And I really think it's a cool place.'

'Alright.'

I sat still and continued deep breathing as we passed through Dorset and Devon, then kept on going past Exeter. Cornwall, at last.

He smiled over at me. 'Here we go. The *Guardian* reader's dream, right?'

Moving to Cornwall had never been my dream, but I could hardly explain to George that the entire county held a weight for my family. After all, it was a big place. All the same I couldn't believe I was going to live down here again. Leaving the West Country, moving to a big city, had always been such a key part of my sense of self. I told myself it wasn't forever. Maybe just until – well, just until something changed. Mum got better or . . . didn't get better. Until there was someone in the back seat, perhaps, asking for sweets and were we there yet. I put that thought aside, as the familiar end-of-journey feeling started to develop – desperate to get out and stretch my legs, but also slightly dreading having to move from my warm seat, the long night of shifting and unpacking that would ensue, the chaos of arrival. Not knowing if anything worked – the cooker, the shower, the electricity. George said the house had been empty for a while. I tried to catch hold of his buoyant, excited feeling, but failed.

Soon, the motorway evaporated as we drove along, narrowing to B roads, magical names like Zennor and Redruth and St Buryan. The house must be right at the end of Cornwall. Hard to get to. Not actually all that close to Mum in Devon – it would still be a two-hour drive. But nearer than London, certainly. I exclaimed when I caught my first glance of the sea, a flat silver with shining patches of sun. George smiled again. 'Can you believe it? We're moving to the seaside. We're *those* twats!'

'I've always wanted to be those twats.'

I tried to calm my nerves about seeing the house soon. How bad could it be, really? Even George wouldn't have bought something with a hole in the roof or infested with pigeons. *Would he?* I'd just have to steel myself to live there until we could paint and redecorate, and it would all be fine. We turned off onto even smaller roads, lanes with trees growing gnarled overhead, shrouding us from sunlight. Narrow enough that sometimes two cars couldn't get by, and you had to pull over and let each other pass with a little wave. That would never happen in London. Finally, I saw a sign for a village – Little Hollow, half a mile. The name struck some kind of chord in me. 'Is that where the house is? Little Hollow?' It was vaguely sinister.

'Yeah. We should be almost there.'

He drove us through the village – a huddle of pubs and shops leading down to a small cove of yellow sand and grey water. No chi-chi coffee places in sight. After that the satnav gave up, taking us up a winding, pockmarked hill that tested the suspension of our 2009 Golf. We'd maybe have to get a Jeep – I was sure this place would flood or be snowed in come winter. Then we turned a corner and there it was. Gateposts, and behind them, up a gravel drive, a fairy-tale house, two storeys of grey stone, large bay windows, the frames painted green, faded from the years. Ivy up the front. Gingerbread fretwork around the eaves, a long chain bellpull by the front door. Carved into the lintel were the numbers *1724*. So old. This was it. This was my new house. I took a deep breath.

It was pretty, and secluded, surrounded by trees and a large overgrown lawn sloping most of the way down the hill at the back. Much bigger than I'd imagined, after our two-bed in London, where the second room wouldn't have held anyone bigger than a child. No obvious damage or holes or pigeons. Yes, I should have been happy, but the strange feeling was back, the one I'd had when I saw the name *Little Hollow* on the sign. A feeling like I'd left the hob on or my straighteners plugged in or something like that.

'Welcome home,' said George, stopping the car, then groaned. 'Sorry, that was so cheesy. Only guys in films can pull off lines like that.'

As I got out, feeling the cramp in my legs, trainers crunching on the gravel, I gazed up at my new home and I suddenly knew what it was, this feeling I couldn't shake, the dread that had been clawing my insides all day. It didn't make any sense, and I had no idea how or when, but I was sure of it.

I had seen this house before.

It couldn't be. Cornwall was a big place, full of houses. It must just be déjà vu, my brain trying to make sense of an unfamiliar situation. Or I'd been to a similar house sometime in the past. All the same, I felt goosebumps on my arms as I stretched my tired muscles and we shook the long journey off ourselves. 'So, here it is,' said George. 'Our new home. Hope you don't hate it.'

Home. Would I ever think of this alien house that way? I had never even been inside it (had I? Why was it so familiar if not?) and it seemed crazy I was going to live here now. 'Where are the movers?'

He rolled his eyes, looking up from his phone. 'They got lost a few villages back, they'll be a while.'

I bit my lip to stop myself berating him about choosing the cheapest, most rubbish option, without checking reviews or references. It was just so hard, once you started, not to criticise and carp all day long, and I had resolved to be different here. 'Well, we can take a look. You've got the key?' It had been couriered to us in London the week before, all the paperwork handled by a solicitor somewhere down here. It was an old-fashioned one, wrought iron on a scuffed wooden paddle. No other keys or fobs. He shrugged at my quizzical look. 'The place is old. No one's lived here in years.'

'And you're sure there's not a reason for that?' My head had gone straight to dry rot, rising damp . . .

'No reason. I got it checked out, remember? It needs modernisation but I promise there's nothing wrong with it.'

'We really got all this for less than two hundred grand?' We had saved up over the years for our own place, and got some money from George's parents, so it seemed to make sense to buy outright. The thought of no rent or mortgage eased my worries about giving up my job, a little at least.

He shrugged. 'It's cheap outside London. And it's not one of the trendy villages.'

The key stuck in the lock, turning with a squeak and a grunt from George. I added WD40 to the lengthy shopping list I'd started keeping in my head. He walked in ahead of me, not having to stoop to get under the low lintel. He was a middling man in so many ways. Middling height, just a few inches taller than me, middling weight – he'd put some on since losing his job. At thirty-four, almost three years younger than me, he sometimes described himself as middle-aged, though he seemed boyish to me still. A full head of hair, in need of a cut, lockdown beard also needing a trim, glasses smeared with grease as they always were. But how I loved him. It made my heart hurt sometimes still, after so many years. His fraying jeans, the unfashionable cut of them, his Sonic Youth T-shirt, stained with Dorito crumbs. All of it precious to me. Was that why I'd followed him here to the end of the country, to a house I'd never seen, but that I somehow recognised all the same?

As the door opened, I found myself thinking – *inside here, there's green wallpaper.* And when I stepped into the shuttered cool of the house, there it was, though faded and dirty – green wallpaper, a pattern of white flowers on it. I stretched out my hand to it but didn't touch it. George misinterpreted my confused expression. 'We can change all this. Just look at the bones of it.'

What a strange phrase. *The bones of it.* Déjà vu is so odd, isn't it? I knew that it was just the brain's way of making sense of things, but at the same time I felt so strongly I had been here before. It was all familiar. The staircase going up, the carved wooden banisters and crown mouldings on the ceilings. I knew the house had been built in the eighteenth century, by a tin-mining family who'd lost everything when that industry collapsed. It did have good bones, as he said. Solid wood floors and panelled walls, the top half papered in the green pattern I had somehow anticipated. That could come down. Cobwebbed but beautiful glass ceiling lights. Large fireplaces in the living and dining rooms, filled with twigs and dead leaves. The chimneys would need to be swept, as there were likely birds nesting in them. The tiny kitchen tacked on to the living room, dark and pokey, would also need modernising. We could maybe knock through, make it all light and open plan, pale tones, big windows. I hated the chipped 1970s cupboards, the ancient fridge and cooker, and when I opened a cupboard door, hanging off its hinges, I saw it was full of large jars, swimming in dark liquid. Pickles or something maybe. My stomach heaved – that would all have to go. 'It'll need a lot done to it.'

George was holding his phone up, looking for a signal. 'Whatever you want. You don't hate it then?'

'Well – no. It's pretty awesome.' I'd always wanted a house with history, not a new-build thrown up in the eighties for as little money as possible. But why was it so familiar? I couldn't have been here before, surely. It was too much of a coincidence. If I could get a minute to myself, and some phone signal, I could perhaps look up Little Hollow and see why the name meant something to me. Or I could ask Mum, I suppose, but it would upset her too much to talk about Cornwall, and it wasn't as if she'd be able to answer me. I didn't even know what she thought of us moving back here.

George coughed behind me. 'This is going to set off your asthma,' I said. 'Be sure to keep your inhaler nearby.' It's hard, as a doctor, not to view your loved ones as patients, to try and heal them where you can.

He waved away my concern. 'I'm fine. But do you like it?'

Just then we heard heavy tyres on gravel, and an ominous crash. The movers had arrived. George and I looked at each other and ran outside, to find that the van had knocked down the gatepost.

It was after midnight by the time we sank into a hastily built flat-pack bed I could see was all wrong for this house. We'd have to find something antique, not this Ikea chipboard. George had not thought to pack the bedding somewhere easy to find, of course, so I'd had to open every box with a knife until I located it. I itched to scrub every inch of the house, crusted in the dust and grime of decades, but it would have to wait. Downstairs was a cyclone of cardboard and bubble wrap, and I had no idea where anything was, not spoons or plates or teabags or George's toothbrush. I had of course packed mine in my handbag, along with essential toiletries, and I'd had to let him use it when he couldn't find his. It seemed gross, though we'd been married for five years, together for seventeen. Hard to take in, sometimes. My parents had been together for so much less time than that – they married in their early twenties, and Dad was dead before their fifth anniversary. George's are verging on their fiftieth now, Ruth and Gerald, Mr and Mrs Middle England that they are. He was vague about how much they'd given us for the house, and I felt ashamed, even though that's what middle-class parents do. By contrast I'd always made my own way in the world, ever since I was a teenager and got my first job in the local Spar. For the past ten years I'd been trying to give Mum money, though she wouldn't accept it.

George fell asleep right away, as he always did, like someone jumping off a roof, flat on his back and snoring. I nudged his head a few times to stop it, but I couldn't sleep anyway. The moon cut right in through the thin old curtains, and it was so quiet after the city, a deep and penetrating silence like one I'd rarely known. I took my useless phone off charge and went to the window, looking out over our new drive, the dark trees surrounding us. What were they? I'd learn that kind of thing now I lived in the countryside, now I wasn't a doctor any more. I keyed *Little Hollow* into the phone, but Google slid to a blank screen. There wasn't enough reception here for 4G, and it would take weeks to get the internet installed. I wished I could just look the place up and set my mind at ease that there wasn't a particular reason the name stood out to me. It would have to wait.

I moved the curtain to try and block the brightness. The moon was like a searchlight in the clear sky, reflecting off the sea in the distance. And there it was – a shadow, on the edge of the trees. My breath died in my throat. Was it a person? Watching us, lurking in our garden? As I stared, frozen with my hands on the curtain, the shape blurred and merged with the trees. Whoever it was, they were gone.

◆ ◆ ◆

It's hard in the bright morning to remember your fears from the dark. I woke up dry-eyed, scrunched into a ball at the side of the bed. George was gone, and I could hear music from downstairs. We hadn't unpacked the speakers yet so he must be playing it out of his phone, whistling along. I sat up, looked fruitlessly for my slippers in the pile of Ikea bags and suitcases dumped in the corner of the room, settled for some flip-flips, and slapped my way downstairs. The stairs were wide and bare, dust gathered in the corners. We'd need a runner. The carving on the banisters was beautiful; it would look great when it was all cleaned up and oiled. But I felt daunted by the scale of the task, and still haunted by the strangeness of it all. Something about the entrance hall, the living room and the staircase going up, I just kept thinking I'd seen it before.

George was in the kitchen, making a mess sawing through a fresh sourdough we'd picked up on the way down. 'Good morning, my beautiful wife!'

I winced. 'You're in an unusually good mood for a morning.' Normally he was still snoring when I left for the hospital at seven.

'I think this is going to be so good for us. New house, new start . . . all that.'

I knew what he meant, felt the tug somewhere wordless between us. 'I hope so.' I rubbed my eyes, feeling a sense of jet lag for London. 'I thought I saw someone last night. Outside, by the trees in the garden.'

George looked up. 'What?'

'Dunno. Like a black shape of a person. Creeped me out a bit, to be honest.'

He slapped a butter substitute on to the bread, licking his fingers. George is always so messy, so exuberant. Sometimes I wish I could be like that. 'Could it have been a hunter? The locals told me not to worry if we hear gunshots sometimes. People hunt in the woods here.'

'Hunt what?'

'God, I don't know. Rabbits? Bears?'

'Hmm. Well, they shouldn't be on our property, should they?' He smiled, and I nodded ruefully. 'Yes, I heard it. Sign me up for the Conservative Association now.' My tone was light, but I was thinking – hunting. Guns. Small dead things.

'It's been empty for decades, babe. They probably didn't know we'd moved in.'

I accepted the slice of bread and butter from him. It was chewy and fresh, delicious. 'We've got so much to do,' I mumbled through crumbs. If it was up to me I'd have got the movers to do it all, pack and unpack too, but George had wanted to save money. And since as of yesterday I no longer had a job, I supposed he was right. We ate our bread and drank tea standing up – he had boiled water on the gas hob, since the kettle was God knows where – and then we made a start on unpacking twenty years of belongings.

After several hours of organising that left me dusty, sweaty, sore-backed and cross, I called time. 'Come on, we need a break.' Looking about at the space, if anything it seemed worse than before.

'Just a second, I . . . ow! Christ.' George sucked his thumb after crushing it between the wall and the mid-century chest of drawers I loved so much. I could see it also didn't go with the house. 'God, that hurt.'

'Are you OK?'

'Yeah, yeah.'

George doesn't like me doctoring him, but I could see the skin was blackened with raised blood. *Don't freeze. It's just a small cut.*

Come on, get it together. All the same, the sight of an injury, even a tiny one, left me sweaty, rooted me to the spot.

'It's fine,' said George, shaking it off. Several drops of blood fell, staining the dusty floorboards.

'Oh dear.'

'Nothing like a blood sacrifice to begin our new life.'

George is always making stupid jokes like that, but today it upset me. 'Urgh, stop it. Go and wash it, this place is filthy. There's plasters in my handbag.'

'Yes, Dr Gillis. Sorry, Dr Gillis.' He rinsed his hand under the kitchen tap and wrapped the tea towel round it, so that would also now be bloodstained.

I said, 'Let's go to the village and find some lunch. Introduce ourselves, maybe. We've been in Cornwall for a whole day and I haven't been near the sea!'

'You're going to get so into that, aren't you. Dry robes, Wim Hof. A real wild-swimming twat.'

'It's the countryside, dude, there's nothing else to do.'

'True. Myself, I think I'll become a hiking twat. Gonna order a map pocket off Amazon and start boring on about Ordnance Survey.'

'Huh. Good luck getting Amazon all the way out here.'

We set off on foot, me still in flip-flops and the dusty jeans and T-shirt I'd worn all day. I hadn't even tried to shower yet, since the bathroom was filthy and I didn't know where the towels were. But the sun was high in the blue sky where we glimpsed it through the overhanging trees, the hedgerows chirped with little sparrows and waved with bluebells and cow parsley, blooming early in the relative warmth of Cornwall, and as we headed down the hill into the village, I could see the shimmer of the sea, today a deep navy and turquoise, and my heart lifted. We'd done the right thing, surely, despite all my weird forebodings – look how beautiful it was, and

I hadn't checked my emails once all day. No one had almost died on me, and I had slept past seven for the first time in years. In the sunlight, I could even explain away my feeling that I'd seen the place before. There must be dozens of villages like this in Cornwall, with houses just like ours.

The village was small, just a church, a post office, a pub called The Green Man, and a café advertising cream teas that seemed to be shut until May. The post office doubled as the village shop and was in a quaint stone building with plants in tubs around the door, the window filled with local fudge and beach toys. The bell rang cheerfully as we went in, my eyes adjusting to the dark and the low ceiling.

'Hi,' I called. There was a woman behind the counter, about sixty with very short iron-grey hair and glasses. 'Um . . . we just moved in so I wanted to say hello.'

She stared at me. 'Did you want to buy something?'

'Oh. Well, yes, probably, I'll just . . .' I edged away, confused by her hostility. Had I got this wrong, and people weren't friendly and chatty in villages? Maybe they thought we were annoying Down From London people, buying up all the houses. Which I suppose we were. But we hadn't bought a property for a second home, taken it from local people. We were actually moving here. 'We bought the house on the hill. The Gables?' That was the name on the rusted plaque by the gate. I felt it was a little pretentious to live in a house with a name, but most of them seemed to have one round here.

'Tresallicks',' she said, without looking at me, doing something with her till.

'Hmm?'

'Everyone here calls it Tresallicks'. The family name.'

'Oh, right. OK. I'm Helen, by the way, and this is George.' He was skulking by a display of shortbread. The woman didn't tell me her name or acknowledge I'd spoken, so I quickly gathered up an armful of things we needed, binbags and sliced ham and tomatoes, dumping them on the counter. In my embarrassment, I turned on George, hissing at him. 'Can you help? Pick something.'

He looked confused. 'I don't know what we need.'

'Well, everything.'

'There's a Sainsbury's in Penzance,' the woman said, ringing things up. Her fingers were stiff, arthritis probably. But it was no longer my job to notice things like that. 'Probably more in your line.'

'Oh, OK.'

She looked up, briefly, no warmth in her expression. 'Just so you know, that house of yours, people don't like to talk about it.'

'What? Why?'

She pursed her lips. 'Not for me to say. There's a history there, that's all. So I wouldn't go shouting that you live up there.'

I paid – they took cards at least – and almost ran out the door into the sun. My arms felt chilled from the interior. 'Well, that was weird. She was so unfriendly!'

George never cares if people are annoyed at him. 'Probably thinks we're tourists.'

'Why would she be so unfriendly to tourists though? And what did she mean about the house?'

'God knows. The locals think outsiders ruin little villages like this. Drive up prices, buy all the property.'

'How do you know that?'

'I spoke to people when I was down those times. In the pub.' He indicated it, as we were now standing outside. I was disappointed to see an old-man's pub, the kind with fruit machines and a lingering smell of smoke years after the ban. The sign read *The Green Man*, with a strange drawing of a leafy face. I'd imagined a gastropub with chalk boards announcing fresh fish specials.

'Well, you could have told me that before we moved here.'

He laughed, squeezed my arm, taking the bag of groceries from me. 'Don't be grumpy. They'll soon see we're not like the second-home brigade. Anyway, you're practically a local! Just make your Devon accent really pronounced, and whatever you do don't get into the great "cream first or jam first" scone debate. Lives have been lost for less.'

His mention of Devon reminded me. 'We should go and see Mum soon. Tomorrow.'

He nodded. 'Of course.'

'George – are you sure you looked into the house properly? Like there wasn't, I don't know, a horrible murder there or something?'

'Oh yeah, did I not mention all the horrible murders?'

I rolled my eyes. 'What did she mean then, that people don't like to talk about it?'

'Come on, Helz, she's a batty old lady with a stick up her bum about incomers. These places are full of old bad blood, it's nothing to do with us.'

I found that I was shaking a little. I'd anticipated fitting right into a lovely friendly village. Instead, it was almost deserted, bleak and cold in the wind, and as we walked off, I glanced back at the pub to see a man in the doorway, shirtsleeves up and a beer towel over one shoulder. He looked to be about sixty, and he caught my eye and went straight back inside.

'Not much here, is there?'

'That's kind of the idea of the countryside. We should head back now anyway, the builders will be here soon.'

'The builders?'

'Did I not say? I got someone to come to give a quote. For the renovations.'

I stared at him. 'Already?' We'd barely even moved in.

'You said you wanted me to handle it, my love. I handled it.'

'Right, it's just . . . we're hardly settled in yet.'

George started walking, the plastic bag of groceries (I should have brought a tote, I realised) slung over his arm. 'It's just a quote, Helz. May as well get started as soon as possible.' I hardly recognised this new, dynamic George. Maybe the move would be good for us after all. As we trudged back up the hill towards the house, I realised I still hadn't had a moment alone to google the place. Maybe tomorrow.

◆ ◆ ◆

'Can't be done, love.'

Two things I hate – being called *love* by random men, and being told things are impossible.

'Um, why?' I felt George shift behind me, no doubt uncomfortable with my tone, but the builder was seriously getting my back up. A sixty-something man, burly and red-faced in a paint-stained T-shirt, he had a pencil tucked behind his ear and a patronising manner. The kind of man who used to turn up at my A&E all the time with ominous chest pains. I could have diagnosed visceral abdominal fat, recommended he cut back on processed food and alcohol.

He pointed the pencil at the wall between the kitchen and living room. 'Load-bearing. You take that down, it could unsettle the whole foundations.'

I'd watched enough property shows in hospital waiting rooms to know this wasn't true. 'I'm sure there's a way to do it.'

'If you want to risk it.'

'I do. That kitchen is unbelievably dark and tiny, it has to go.' I still hadn't got up the courage to go through all the cupboards, with their weird array of jars. It reminded me unpleasantly of an anatomy lab.

He looked around him, scratching his head. 'You bought the place, you said?'

'Of course. Private sale.'

'Oh. It's just . . .'

'What?'

'Nothing. Surprised to see it go, that's all. Been sitting here years, this place has.'

'Right, so – it needs renovating, you can see that.' I didn't understand his reluctance to tear things down. 'It isn't listed, if that's what you're worried about, is it, George?' Surely the tacked-on kitchen could go, at the very least.

George was fiddling at his phone again, trying to get reception probably. 'Hm? No. So can you do it?'

He sucked air through his teeth. 'You have to have the wall down? Can't just refurb?'

'No. We have to have it down.'

'So you want the new kitchen, new bathroom, this wall down, pointing and redecorating, roof tiles . . . won't be cheap.'

'I'd like a quote for the work, at least. In writing.' I'd heard about cowboy builders with escalating costs, and this all seemed to be happening so fast. I wasn't entirely sure I wanted to stay in the house, even. But how could we sell? We'd lose a fortune flipping it so fast. I just needed to find out the place's history, shake this strange sense that I'd been here before. Discover why it might be that the villagers didn't like to talk about it.

'Alright then.' His tone implied I was crazy, but he'd humour me. 'I'll drop you over an estimate.'

'When could you start?' said George. I shot him a look – I wasn't convinced I wanted to go with this guy, if he was going to be so patronising.

'Next week, if you want. We had a big job fall through over Sennen way.'

'Great! Thanks, mate.'

'But we have to see the quote first,' I said, and saw the man raise his eyebrows at George in a way I did not like. *Stupid woman.* I'd grown up without a dad, and then gone into medicine, where women now outnumber men – I was always a little surprised when I encountered sexism in the wild.

George showed him out, trying to make manly chat about gutters, roughening his accent in a way I was sure he was unaware of. He came back in and saw my face. 'What?'

'Such a man of the people, *mate*. Why couldn't you back me up? That guy was annoying.'

'Babe, I tried ten other builders and every single one is booked up till next year, or else they never got back to me at all. Post-Covid boom, and all that. So if you want the work done, I think he's our man.'

'But why are *they* available? Sounds suss to me.'

'He had good reviews online.' George came up and took my elbows in his hands. 'Not everyone is untrustworthy, you know.'

He was right – I'm a suspicious person, always have been. It's not surprising, given my childhood, and they train us as doctors to always ask questions, be sceptical when our patients tell us they've quit drinking, or aren't looking for opioids, or have just walked into a door. But I have always, without reservation, trusted George not to lie to me, and it has never steered me wrong. 'Well, fine. But get a proper estimate, something in writing, OK?'

'I'm not an idiot, Helz,' he said, patiently, picking up the builder's abandoned tea mug, which had left a ring on the TV stand. 'Happy to go ahead, if the quote fits?'

'Well, how much can we afford?'

He shrugged. 'Seventy?'

It was an unsettling experience for me, not knowing how much money we had. I'd been so burnt out for the last two years, working so hard, all holidays cancelled, pulling double and even triple shifts as the patients just kept coming, that I had really lost the thread of our finances. The past six months were a kind of blur, where I'd been only dimly aware of George suggesting the move, making trips to Cornwall, showing me photos and bandying around vague figures. Had he mentioned the name of the village to me then? I had no idea. 'There's that much left over?'

'I told you, it's all fine.'

I really couldn't live for much longer with that filthy bathroom or terrifying kitchen, so dark and cramped only one person could fit in it. But if we started renovations, that meant we were staying. 'Alright then. See what number he comes back with.'

'Good.' He looked at the time on his phone. 'Well, I thought I might do some work this afternoon, if you don't mind carrying on here.'

'Work?' I almost said, *what work*, but stopped myself. This was a good thing. Writing had not come easily to George for a while now. Not since everything that happened.

'Yeah, you know. Got an idea for something.'

'That's exciting. Can you tell me what it is yet?'

He squirmed. 'Early days. You know how it is.'

'Yeah, I know. But just – is it an article, or something longer?'

'Something longer.'

Finally, the long-promised book. Well, that was the idea in moving here, that George could have the time and space to write one at last. And me, I would sort the house and tidy and clean and unpack, then figure out what I might want to do with my life that wasn't medicine. 'Great,' I said casually, not wanting to spook him. He's so easily put off from his work – I suppose that's the creative mindset. 'Can you write without the internet though?' I'd always prided myself on being the less phone-addicted of us, but having no Wi-Fi and extremely patchy reception was making me nervous.

What if someone was trying to get in touch – Mick, or Mum's home, or . . . well, that was just it. I had no job, and knew nobody in this place, so it wasn't likely anyone would be looking for me.

'Oh, I downloaded some stuff before we left.'

'Right. Well, sure, I can carry on here.' Though the piles of boxes and bubble-wrapped furniture were daunting, to say the least. It would have to be done, or we wouldn't have anywhere to sit or cook. We could only eat sandwiches for so many meals, although I was quite sure George would not agree with me. I listened to him bang upstairs on the bare steps, then heard him rustling around in the box room which was to be his office. I knew in about two seconds he would shout—

'Helz? Have you seen my laptop charger?'

I smiled to myself. I knew him so well, my husband, and that was comforting. I liked to know things, which was why moving unsettled me so. 'In the little suitcase,' I shouted. I'd packed it myself, knowing he would lose it if I didn't. I put my hands on my hips and surveyed the mess. It wouldn't get done unless I made a start.

First thing was to throw out those disgusting jars. I went into the kitchen – God, I hated those avocado-green units, chipped and coming away from the wall – and gingerly opened the door of one cupboard. I found the binbags in the living room and began to take down the jars and throw them out, ignoring recycling for the moment. They were stuffed with odd things, bits of plants and what looked like beetles in one. Who had lived here? The other strange thing was that all the cupboards were full. Dishes and glasses, old-fashioned ones in patterns I remembered from my childhood. Whoever had owned the house had for some reason left all their things behind. Maybe they'd died? I'd have loved to know the history of the place – perhaps George still had the specs somewhere, or there might be information online, if only I could get my phone to work. I pulled it from my jeans pocket again and waved it round the ceiling. Messages were getting through here and there, but a sustained google was not going to be possible yet.

I was up on a rickety chair removing the old chipped dishes from the cupboard when I heard something. A sort of fluttering that felt as if it was coming from the walls of the house. I got down off the chair, listening hard. There it was – a faint noise, a whir and a small crash.

'George?'

No answer. He'd have his headphones on and music blaring. I walked to the living room and paused to peer into the gloom of the chimney, in case there was a bird trapped, but could see nothing. I followed the sound out into the hall, and came to a halt outside a door beneath the stairs, which I hadn't really noticed before. Was it a loo? Probably not, though it could become one. The handle turned loosely, and with some forcing of the sticking door, I got it open. I was at the top of a staircase, leading down into the dark. A cellar? I hadn't even known we had one.

The lightbulb had gone, so I lit up my phone and descended, looking out for nails and splinters. The noise was coming from down here, and I soon saw what it was – there was a bird, struggling against the wall, its wing broken, eyes glassy. I stepped back at its frantic flapping – where had it even come from? There weren't any windows down here. It was a long, dark room, with a smaller white door at the end leading into a smaller room – the boiler, I guessed, from the clanking and warm air. Otherwise the cellar was full of junk: an old rusting pram, a bike, broken bits of furniture. A workbench along one wall with items on it, a pestle and mortar, a set of knives in a holder, a large leatherbound book. As I went closer, a strong green smell filled my nose, like must and growing things. What was this place? Something brushed my face and I jumped back, exclaiming – there were bundles of dried plants

28

hanging from the ceiling. Herbs, leaves, seed pods, most of which I couldn't identify.

None of this was going to help the poor bird. I could hardly chase it out, and it wouldn't survive without its wing being set. Maybe I could figure out how, if George would hold it still – oh! With a last final whoosh, and a cry that rang around the cellar, the bird flew straight at the wall, and hit it with a crack. Then it fell to the floor, motionless. I rushed over, heart in my mouth. It looked dead, poor thing. A magpie, glossy black and white, eyes now dull. I'd have to get George to move it before it rotted. *Why don't you do it yourself?* scolded my inner feminist. I couldn't explain. Since what had happened, I just couldn't face death any more. Even of a bird. Shining my phone around, I saw a hole in the plaster of the wall. Craning my head, I saw it extended up and towards daylight, which was probably how the bird had got in. We'd need to have the builder check that – I knew George wouldn't have paid for a proper survey.

Suddenly I just wanted out of there, so I left the bird where it was, and climbed back up to the light, shutting the door behind me. George could sort it out, since he'd wanted this place so badly. I found myself wondering about the previous owner, and what they had been doing with all that equipment down there.

We ate sandwiches again for dinner, with the cheap ham from the village shop, and fell into bed. George seemed absent-minded but happier than he'd been for a long time, and I could almost see the story taking shape in his head, whatever it was. He even sorted out the bird with just a brief roll of his eyes, after I declared I wasn't going down there again. We turned out the lights at ten and I tried to sleep, as his buzz-saw snore started up. I lay there thinking about the house, and how I could possibly have been here before, and what that meant, and how I could find out without upsetting George or Mum. I must have slept, because at some point my eyes shot open and I saw it was 3 a.m. I got up and went to the window, remembering the strange shadow from the night before. What had woken me? The cry of some animal, perhaps, or the wind in the trees, because as much as I strained my eyes out towards the dark garden, I couldn't see a thing.

◆ ◆ ◆

The next morning we drove to see Mum. I had been nervous since I woke up, snapping at George for leaving his shoes at the bottom of the stairs for me to fall over. 'Are you trying to kill me, is that it? I know I've still got that life insurance policy from work, but really, George.'

He came to me with his hands held out, conciliatory. 'Sorry, sorry, my love, there's just nowhere to put anything.' I calmed down, as I always did at his gentle mollifying tone. He rubbed the back of my neck as I brushed my hair in an old, tarnished mirror. 'It's going to be OK, babe.'

'It's just – I hate seeing her this way.'

'I know, I know.' George's parents are both disgustingly fit and healthy, always off climbing mountains and doing Pilates at the village hall. Whereas my father had died when I was two, and Mum – well. Mum didn't deserve what happened to her. No one could deserve that.

I'd been to the place she lived only once before, when we got her into it six months ago. I felt bad about how long it had taken me to come back, but work had been so crazy and it was a four-hour drive from London. Anyway, we'd moved now, so I could see her all the time. I hoped I would get used to it, and not wake up feeling sick and angry every time I had to go there. Angry that my mother, just sixty-five years old, was in an old folks' home. Sorry – rehabilitation facility. But we all knew she wasn't coming out.

I drove us east to Devon, a journey of almost two hours, all the while looking for the sea around every bend in the road. My phone was in the holder to give directions, but I couldn't risk googling anything about the house until I was alone. I wished I could text Lou, plug back into her flighty London ways, her non-stop chatter about nail bars and Ubers, a world away from my new home. The motorway was like motorways everywhere, featureless and grey. You couldn't see the sea at all for long periods of time, but then you'd turn and there it was again, re-emerging like hope. The facility was an old stately home on the outskirts of town, a cheerful sign announcing The Meadows. We parked in the car park, and I drew a deep, shuddering breath.

We'd moved Mum here after my emergency dash down the M4 that terrible night last autumn. A sudden stroke; found by Mick on the kitchen floor when he came back from work. The loss of all speech and the movement down the left side of her body. The doctors couldn't say if she'd ever talk again, but I knew she was still in there. It was cruel. I tried to put on a happy face like make-up. George held my hand as we crossed the tarmac, and I was glad to have him with me, as always. Inside it was more like a hospital than a care home. An antiseptic smell, glass screens and dispensers of hand sanitiser everywhere. We had to wear masks until we got into Mum's room. The floors squeaked. I hated it all.

There she was, in a chair by the window. Her hair, retaining the chestnut colour she'd put in it six months and two weeks ago, an inch of grey at the roots, was neatly brushed, and they'd dressed her in a pale pink cardigan and loose trousers. She needed help to get to the loo, which I knew she would absolutely hate. 'Hi, Mum.'

She turned her head as best she could, and smiled with one half of her face. She knew me. Maybe it would be easier if she didn't. I sat down and squeezed her cold, weak hands. 'How are you, Mum?' Hard to get out of the habit of asking questions, even when she couldn't answer. She waggled her head to indicate she was alright. As well as could be expected anyway.

George perched awkwardly on the bed. 'Hello, Peggy! Well, here we are. West Country residents – bet you never thought you'd see Helen back living here, eh? But I dragged her out of London.'

'Don't remind me,' I joked, or tried to joke. 'Haven't had a macchiato in two days, how will I cope?' We prattled on, trying to fill up the gaps in the conversation where she would have spoken. Mum patted my hand as if she wanted to ask something. There was a pad near her with words neatly printed on it – one of the carers had made it for her, perhaps. I held it out to her, and she pointed at the word *where*. 'Where's the house?' That made sense, she'd lived down here since I was a baby, so she would want to know exactly where it was. I'd told her only as much as I knew, in the awkward video calls the staff set up for us, where I was never sure if she could understand me – we were moving somewhere in Cornwall, where it would be easier to visit her. I hadn't known exactly where.

George answered before I could think how to phrase it. 'The house is called The Gables. Fancy, eh? In a village called Little Hollow. It's down near Penzance – oh dear!'

Mum had knocked over her plastic cup of water. I gasped as it soaked into my jeans, and George was up hunting for paper towels. A sound leaked from Mum's twisted mouth, a faint noise of distress. 'It's OK, Mum, it's just water. Is everything alright?'

'Here.' George was patting at me, bending down to dry my lap, but I was still looking at Mum over his head.

'Little Hollow – you know the name, Mum?' My heart was racing – it was risky to even ask her this with George here, but I had to know. She shook her head, as best she could. It was so frustrating, not being able to ask if she'd been trying to tell me something, or just knocked the water over at that same time. 'Because it seemed kind of familiar to me. Did we go there when I was little, some-thing like that?'

She just shook her head again. Oh, Mum. 'Alright, well – no harm done.' I stood up. 'I'll just go and dry my jeans. George can make you a cup of tea, maybe.' She had a kettle and teabags in the room, though there was no way she would be able to do it herself. I fled to the Ladies at the end of the corridor, bleach-smelling and with signs up about washing hands and wearing masks, a hundred little reminders that even if we called this place a home, it certainly wasn't one.

I sat on the loo and took out my phone. Typed in *Little Hollow, Cornwall*. A map reference, some walking websites. Impatient, I scrolled down the page.

And there it was. *Triple Murder in quiet Cornish village of Little Hollow*. My stomach lurched, and I closed my eyes, for a moment afraid I might throw up. So my strange suspicions about Little Hollow had been right – I had indeed been there before. In fact, I had lived five miles from there, until I was two. I'd known it was Cornwall we were moving to, of course, but it had never occurred to me that George would have found us a house in the exact same village. How could this be? Just a terrible coincidence? He didn't know the truth.

A knock at the door almost made me drop my phone. 'Helz?' His muffled voice. 'You OK?'

'Yes – fine! Is Mum alright?' I'd given her a nasty shock, with-out meaning to. I wished I could explain it all to her, that I hadn't known the name of the village before yesterday, but not with George here, I couldn't risk it.

'She's tired, I think.'

My heart sank at the thought of visiting her here for years. How could I keep talking to her like this, as if she was a baby or a dog, unable to answer? The place was the best I could find, but at the same time it was still a nursing home, it wasn't hers. And meanwhile we were stuck with a house that needed thousands of pounds of work, and which I now knew was disturbingly close to all the things about my childhood I'd tried hard to escape.

◆ ◆ ◆

I was dreaming. I was back in the cellar, and this time it was full of birds, dead and dying, their wings catching my face . . .

I sat bolt upright. Something had woken me – a hammering from downstairs, a sound like chipping wood. Someone was breaking in. The light was low outside, it was early still. Six o'clock, according to the clock on the bedside table. What was going on?

'George. George!' He was unmoving under the duvet. I shoved him. 'George!'

'Mmmm?'

'There's someone downstairs!'

'Mmmm.' He rolled over on to his face, and I sighed loudly. Fine, I would go down myself and face the burglar, or whoever it was. Groping around for my flip-flops, I pulled a hoody over the shorts and vest I slept in and went downstairs. I looked around for some kind of weapon, seizing a large golf umbrella. My head was full of hunters, the shadowy figure in the trees. What if they thought the place was empty still? Or the villagers had come to run us out or . . .

Two young men were unloading tools from a van on to my drive. 'Er, hello?'

One stared at my legs. 'Here to start the job.'

'What job?'

'The building job, love.'

I bristled. 'What are you talking about?' Then I saw the name on the van. Bob Marks. The builder who'd been here two days

34

ago. 'But – we never said we'd go ahead! We never even got his quote.'

The two men – boys, really – just continued to unload. 'He told us to get down here and make a start.'

'Well, that's insane. Also, it's six in the morning! You aren't going to start at that time every day, surely.'

'Building hours,' said the other, who sounded Eastern European. 'Is not early for us.'

I sighed deeply. 'Can you get him on the phone? Your boss? We need to sort this out.' Now that I'd learned my déjà vu was likely real, that I had in fact been to Little Hollow before, I wasn't sure I could stay here. The moment they started work, we'd have to pay them. They muttered among themselves, and the Eastern European one eventually got Bob on the phone. I could only hear his side of the conversation.

'Boss, she say no quote yet . . . she say not expecting . . . OK . . . yes, I tell her. I tell her that.' I hugged my arms around myself, very aware that I wasn't wearing any underwear. Eventually he said, 'He come. Bob come now.'

'Oh. How long?'

He shrugged. 'Twenty minutes, maybe.'

No point in going back to bed then. I went inside and put the kettle on, hating the way I had to dig through boxes to find a mug. We needed to sort this place out, it was a tip. How could we start building work when we hadn't even unpacked? Had George perhaps told the builder we could go ahead, without asking me? Should he even have asked me? Mum was always telling me – or she had, when she could speak – that I wore the trousers too much in our marriage. That I emasculated George. I'd asked him a few times if he felt that way and he'd laughed himself silly. But maybe he did. Maybe that was why he'd wanted to handle the house move himself.

I was drinking my tea – the milk already on the turn from the old, failing fridge – and grumpily unpacking glasses when Bob turned up, with a great crunch of gravel. I noticed he drove a Merc; nice for him. All those profits from clueless middle-class people. He knocked on the back door and walked right into the kitchen, cramming into the small space with me. I backed away with my mug, into the living room. I was aware I probably should have offered tea to the builder boys, but I was too cross.

Bob said, 'What's this then, love? The boys said you wouldn't let them start.'

'We didn't actually ask you to take on the job. I wanted a written estimate first, if you remember.'

Bob's eyes went wide. 'I don't know what to tell you, love. You want the work done?'

'Well, yes, but . . .'

'And we're here to do it. I mean, I can give you something on paper if that's what you *really* want.'

'Well, it is, yes.' Was that crazy? We didn't do anything in my job without a purchase order signed in triplicate – was he really proposing to start a fifty-grand job with just a verbal agreement? Which, by the way, we hadn't made either. 'How would you even know our budget otherwise?'

'Your fella told me. He about?' My blood boiled. Right, because of course he wanted to talk to the man.

'He's asleep. Because it's basically night-time still.'

Bob chuckled at that, and rolled his eyes. 'You don't want us starting so early, is that it, love?'

'Not at six, no.' Again, was I mad? Was that normal?

'Alright. So the lads are here now, and I'm dragged away. You want this done or not?' I thought of George saying he'd tried ten other builders and got nothing. And this lot were here, and willing, if a bit annoying. And the kitchen really was barely functional. Even if we re-sold the house right away, we'd add value by fixing it up.

I was still bewildered though. 'But – don't you need to know what we want doing?'

'You already told us. Rip this out, new kitchen, new bathroom, yeah? This wall down?' He slapped it with his meaty hand.

'Well, yes. But we haven't picked units or anything yet.'

'There's a showroom by the motorway. Don't take long. Since we're here now, we might as well make a start.'

'But . . . we'll have no kitchen at all then.'

He rolled his eyes again, not even trying to hide it. 'That's what happens when you get it re-done, love. Least for a week or two. You wash the dishes in the bath, yeah? And plug your cooker in next door – look, it's just electric.' He indicated where the grimy seventies unit was plugged in, not even attached to the wall.

'Well . . . OK then.'

'We can make a start?'

'I . . . I suppose so. I'd better check with George.'

'You do that, love.' His tone was so patronising it set my teeth on edge.

I went back upstairs, acutely aware of their eyes on me in my tiny pyjama shorts, and shook George awake with more force this time. He was in a pit of hair and blankets. 'Ummmm, Christ, Helen, what is it?'

'The builders. Are here.'

'Eh?'

'Did you tell them they could start today?'

'No! I mean, I might have said as long as they sent the estimate or something, if the price was right.'

'Well, they haven't. They've just shown up, at six in the morning, ready to knock down our kitchen.'

He sat up, feeling for his glasses. 'Well, hear me out – is this maybe a good thing? At least they're here. You know what it's like getting people to turn up.' We'd heard tales of woe from our friends Sam and Karl last year, whose builder had vanished, taking thirty grand of their savings with him.

'You want to just let them go ahead? No checks, no due diligence?' I hadn't even had the chance to google him or find any reviews.

'We do need it done.'

'We haven't even unpacked! I don't know where the lemon squeezer is!' I didn't know why I'd fixed on that as the one thing I couldn't find, but I saw George hide a smile.

'It'll all get messed up again anyway. This way we can just . . . do it. Get it over with. And I promise to squeeze all and any lemons you might need, in the meantime.'

I sighed heavily. 'You have to talk to them. Tell them not before eight, and make sure they understand seventy grand is absolutely the top limit, OK? No VAT or anything on top.' Assuming Bob's cowboy operation even paid tax.

'Yes, boss,' he said, and he said it mildly, but I thought of my mother's warning all the same.

◆ ◆ ◆

I'd hoped we might have a little time to settle in before our lives dissolved into dust and chaos, but it wasn't to be. By lunchtime that day, the two lads, whose names were Borak and Ciaran, had knocked down the wall between the kitchen and living room with sledgehammers, ripped out the sink, and torn off several cupboards. It was astonishing, the speed of destruction compared to the painstaking work of building up. I couldn't regret the old, chipped cupboards or the dark, pokey space, but we now had nowhere to cook, and I wasn't sure Deliveroo existed in darkest Cornwall.

Around one, I had resigned myself to lunching off the packet of crackers George had stashed in his office – a bad habit I insist encourages ants – when some shouts came from downstairs. I was upstairs rearranging the bathroom, wincing at every crash from below. I'd attempted a shower, but the water alternated between freezing and boiling, and I still felt dirty all over.

'Hello?' It was Ciaran, the younger and skinnier of the builders. He didn't look more than eighteen.

'What is it?' I went out to the top of the stairs.

'Eh, you should come down.' I looked at the door of George's study, shut firm, the tinny sound of music leaking out. I should have been glad he was working at last, but I resented having to do all the unpacking. I clattered down the bare, dirty stairs. The two boys were standing beside what used to be the wall between the kitchen and living room, now a gaping cavity, grey insulation sticking out from it like an old man's beard. The kitchen had been erected so badly the walls weren't flush, and I could see shards of daylight. I felt a stab of alarm – I hadn't realised they would actually open the wall up to the outside. 'We found this,' said Ciaran, sounding embarrassed.

They moved away as I came forward, and I saw Borak cross himself. What? On the floor was a small piece of cloth. I stooped down. 'Do not touch!' Borak barked, then looked surprised at himself. 'Er – I think you should not, madam.'

Maybe there was asbestos or something. But this house was too old, wasn't it? Squatting down, I peered at what they'd found. It was a doll, with a sacking-cloth body, a crudely drawn face, and what looked suspiciously like human hair, fair and faded, sewn on its head. And stuck through the body were four large nails.

I looked up at the lads, wondering if they were messing with me. 'This was in the wall?'

Ciaran cleared his throat. 'You get them in old houses sometimes, round these parts.'

'What is it?'

'A poppet. Like – for magic. Bad magic.' He sounded embarrassed saying it.

'So what, like some kind of voodoo doll?'

'Witchcraft,' said Borak, who had backed away almost to the window. 'Is witchcraft.'

I'm not a superstitious person, I never have been. When girls at school squealed over Ouija boards, I read up on the phenomenon of mass hysteria. I never even looked at my horoscope. But all the same, staring down at the thing that had been in my wall, I felt a cold shudder run through me.

'Should you be touching it?' I said. George shot me a look as he turned the poppet over in his hands, examining it, and I backtracked. 'I mean, it's dirty. There were probably mice living in there.'

'It's just a piece of cloth, Helz.'

'And *human hair.*'

'Well, yeah, they used to make kids' dolls with human hair. They still make wigs with it – Lou's hair extensions, where do you think they're from? Uighur women in Chinese re-education camps, most likely.'

I deflected George from his political soapbox. 'You don't think it's weird? Like, really, really weird and creepy?' The builders had left not long after finding the poppet, muttering something about 'needing parts'. I thought they were spooked, and couldn't believe

I had let my house be knocked down by two kids who were afraid of dolls.

'Well, yeah – but it's fascinating. You know there's a real history of witchcraft in these parts – dolls like this were used for ill-wishing. If you buried it in someone's garden it meant you wanted them to suffer. Or it was a way to deflect evil and throw it back on someone. They must have put it in when the kitchen extension went up.'

'Ugh, George! We live here now.'

'I know, it's so cool. You wouldn't get that in our eighties jerry-build in London.'

I didn't agree. 'I'm worried the builders won't finish the job now. They seemed really frightened.'

'They're just kids. Even the big one, he's probably like fifteen years younger than us.'

It was time to broach the subject of how we had ended up here, the same village I'd lived near as a child. 'George, seriously, how much do you know about the history of this house? Did you do any research before you put the offer in?'

He set the poppet down on the table. 'Some. It goes back to the 1700s.'

'But – do you know who had it last? Like why was it sitting empty all that time?' This was dangerous territory, but I had to know. Otherwise I might never sleep again.

'I don't know – no one's lived here since the eighties, I don't think. Maybe too expensive for the area? I dunno.' George was moving back to the stairs.

'Where are you going?' I snapped.

His bushy eyebrows shot up. 'I was working. You know, this find could make an interesting piece for one of the Sundays – how we bought a haunted house in the country.'

'Don't say that.'

'Come on, Helz! You're the most sceptical person I know. Surely you're not scared.'

'I know, but – this is real. I mean, the ill-wish behind it. The evil intent.' That was genuine enough, human malice. 'Will you at least get rid of that thing?'

'How – in the bin?'

'Bury it. Somewhere in the woods.'

'Are you serious?' He laughed. 'Are you trying to recreate *Pet Sematary*? Cos, spoiler alert, that didn't work out so well in the end.'

'I just – it doesn't seem right to put it in the bin.' And burning it felt a touch melodramatic.

George picked it up, rolling his eyes at me. 'Do we have a spade?'

'Of course we don't have a spade.' In London we'd barely had a window box.

'Then how . . .'

'Christ, I don't know. Use a big spoon. Please, just get rid of it.' And I thundered upstairs away from it, wondering why I felt so very off-kilter. It was this house. The house I was so sure I had been in before, so near to where I'd lived as a child.

I watched George from the upstairs window, stooping over in the garden in his T-shirt and jeans, despite the scudding rain. It was hard to imagine someone less at home in the outdoors, and yet he had moved us all the way here. It was strange – why hadn't I realised it was strange? He was scrabbling at the soil with what looked from a distance like my good ceramic salad spoon. The poppet lay beside him on the grass, blind eyes looking up at the sky. Soon, he gave up on the spoon and began digging with his fingers, then I saw him get down on his knees and begin pulling at something. Was there another object buried there – a tree root maybe? A stone? George stood up and held it to the light – a large jar, with dark liquid sloshing around in it.

42

◆ ◆ ◆

'What is it?'

We were standing on the porch, shivering. I didn't want the thing in the house. It was a large glass jar, similar to the ones in the kitchen, the kind with a screw-on lid, and inside was liquid with several items floating in it. Leaves, bark, and what looked like some small dead creature. A vole or a mouse maybe. 'No idea,' he said. His tone was curious, not afraid.

'I don't like it.' There was soil around its base, and I felt very strongly I wanted to hide it, along with the poppet. Hide everything.

'It's kind of cool. I think I've read about something like this – it's a witch bottle, maybe.'

'A what?' How did George suddenly know so much about witchcraft?

'For trapping evil spirits.'

'Christ. What is this place?'

He still seemed more interested than alarmed. 'I guess whoever lived here had an interest in the occult.'

'George!'

'Oh, come on, don't you find it a little bit interesting, at least?'

'No.' I was rubbing my goosefleshed arms. 'Can you just get rid of them, please?'

'God, alright. You're weirdly superstitious in Cornwall, you know?' I watched him carry it away, put it back into its dark hiding place in the ground. Try as I might, I couldn't seem to shake off the sense of foreboding. There were things in the walls, dying birds in the cellar, weird noises at night. The locals didn't want to talk about the house. And I had maybe been here before. None of it made sense.

43

I couldn't stay in the house as it was, with the busted-open wall leaking its stuffing, the creepy doll and jar in the garden. I could almost feel it, a pulse beating under the earth. I found my raincoat, a yellow waxed one like every middle-class woman in London seemed to own, and walked towards the village. My mind turned to the future, worrying away at it. What was I going to do for work? If George was actually writing a book, he might sell it, which would buy us some time. But what would I be, if I wasn't a doctor? If I didn't have people's lives in my hands? I had always been interested in mental health, and it seemed more needed than ever. I'd seen so many people at the hospital who could have avoided physical injury or suffering if they'd been helped with the pain inside earlier. Drinking and taking drugs to hide it, having risky sex. Getting into dangerous situations. Over-eating, under-eating. Hurting themselves. Maybe I could train in a different direction – take counselling courses – and do some good in that way. I didn't know if I wanted to give up helping people forever.

I had looked up some mental health courses before I left, in the snatched moments I had spare. It was clear that for all of them I'd have to undergo counselling myself, and provide professional references, and there was no way they wouldn't find out what had happened last year. Certainly there would be no avoiding it, digging it up, dealing with it. As if such a thing could even be dealt with.

A light but soaking rain was falling on me, and every house I passed seemed shuttered up for the season. I felt depressed, missing the buzz of London, how the streets were never quiet or dark. The sea was there down the hill, a dark teal under the grey sky, a tongue of sand. Even the post office was shut – it closed at three, apparently. But the pub was open, and so I pushed my way in, conscious of how people looked up at my presence. This place was such a rural cliché – weren't they used to strangers, even out of season? Or did they know who I was, what house I lived in?

44

Very awkward, I stood at the bar until the barmaid came over. She seemed young and friendly anyway, in her twenties perhaps, with frizzy blonde hair dyed pink in parts, and large, old-fashioned glasses. 'Hiya.'

'Oh, hi, I'm Helen. Just moved into the village.'

She nodded, as if confused as to why I was introducing myself. Maybe I had it all wrong and people didn't do that in villages. 'OK . . . did you want a drink?'

'Yes, please. Um, I'll have . . .' I didn't dare ask for a wine list. 'Gin and tonic please – diet if you have it.' It was early for a drink, but I supposed I didn't have a job now.

'Ice and lemon?'

'Yes, please.' She turned away to slice the lemon and I perched uncomfortably on a stool – I always think it should be illegal to make short people sit on them.

'So you've just moved to Little Hollow? Second home?'

Everyone was going to assume that. 'No, just the one home. It's The Gables?'

She frowned. 'Don't know that one.'

It was a small place, surely people knew what houses were on the market. 'Up on the hill, among the trees. Big old grey-stone place.' I remembered the hostile lady in the post office had used a different name. 'You might know it as Tresallicks'?'

Her eyebrows – strangely thick, as if drawn on by markers – shot up. 'Oh! That's . . . right, yeah. That's been empty years.'

'I know. We're fixing it up. Do you know anything about who used to own it?' I asked it casually, sipping the drink she'd passed me, enjoying the tart fizz of it. Day-drinking, a slippery slope.

'Oh, well – I always heard it was still in the same family, just standing empty.'

'What family is that? Are they still called Tresallick?' Surely it hadn't remained in their hands since the 1700s.

'Um, well . . . you bought the place, you said?'

'Yeah, why?'

'Well, it's just that doesn't make sense, because . . .'

The girl suddenly caught the eye of an older man who had appeared round the bar with the grizzled, tough look of people who spend their lives outside. He was maybe mid-sixties, greying but in good shape. I recognised him from our last trip to the village – he must be the landlord. 'Cara, why don't you go and clean the lines?' he said.

'Sorry, Uncle Martin,' she muttered, scuttling away. Uncle Martin looked at me. 'So you're the wife? Your husband was in here a few times, when he was down looking at the place.' Of course George would have gravitated to the pub.

'Do you know much about the house?'

He didn't answer for a moment, taking a cloth and wiping up the ring from my gin. 'The house . . . well, people don't like to talk about it here. Some places just have a history, you know.'

Same as the post-office lady had said. 'What history?' I was starting to feel the same chills again. Had I wandered on to the set of a low-budget horror film? Or was the house somehow connected to the murders? Neither name, The Gables or Tresallicks', meant anything to me. I could just about believe we had ended up in the village by accident, but not in a house that was also linked to the killings.

'You can find out easy enough,' he said. 'Best not to talk about it in public, that's all.'

I was bewildered, and not a little frightened. 'OK.'

He stepped back, changing his tone. 'Helen, did you say it was?'

'Helen Gillis.' It felt strange not to say *Dr Gillis*, as I had introduced myself to so many patients over the years.

'That a West Country accent I can hear?'

'Good ears. I grew up in Devon, actually.' Minus the two years I lived here, of course, but I wasn't about to tell him that.

'Oh, right, and you're back now. Husband's family from here too then?'

'Oh, no, he's from Reading. We wanted to move down to be nearer my mum.' Not that this was actually near. Which was also strange – why would George have chosen a place all the way out here?

'I see. Anything else I can get you there?'

'Um, no, I'm fine.' I had been hoping for a cosy, welcoming pub, maybe with an open fire. Instead, it was cold and smelled vaguely of chips and wet dog. An old man with a soaking sheepdog hunched at a side table, drinking a pint and reading the paper. Over in a corner a teenage couple who didn't look old enough to drink sat glued to their phones. That was it. I drained my gin, feeling the cold tingle in my sensitive molars, then stood up. On my way out, I saw the barmaid, Cara, skulking around the side of the pub with a vape pen.

'Oh, hi,' she said. 'Sorry about my uncle. He's nice, really, just super-grouchy.'

'That's OK. Listen, were you going to say something about the house just then? My house?'

'Um. You really don't know anything about it?'

'No. My husband sorted the purchase.' I didn't want her to think I was a bad feminist. 'I've been working so hard the last while – I'm a doctor. I was a doctor, I mean, all through Covid.'

'Ah right, yeah, that must have sucked. So you don't know who used to live there?'

'In my house? No. But we've found some things. Like . . . witchy things.'

I was expecting her to laugh, but she just nodded as if she'd expected it. 'Well, listen, I shouldn't say too much, but if you get a

47

chance, look the house up. I better get back in.' And she'd darted away before I had the chance to grill her any further.

At least I got a bit of reception at the brow of the hill, so after a bit of fruitless googling of *The Gables Little Hollow*, *The Gables former owner*, *The Gables Cornwall*, I dialled Lou's number. She answered after a few minutes, breathless. 'Hello?'

'Are you in the middle of something?'

She panted, 'Just a run. It's absolutely freezing out, so you've done me a favour.' Her breathing slowed, and I pictured her in her running gear, top-of-the-range Sweaty Betty and fancy cushioned trainers, her red hair held back by a woollen headband. Lou is always in motion, doing some sport or another, or taking a class, or going on another date that won't lead to anything. 'How's the sticks?'

'Meh. Right now, pouring and dead as a doornail.'

'Well, it's off season, isn't it? And the house?'

I sighed. 'Like a mausoleum. The builders have started already, at least.'

'That's good. God, it took me three months to get them to renovate my bathroom! Excuse after excuse.'

I didn't want to tell her about the poppet. Lou is the opposite of me, believes in everything from Tarot to tantra. 'Mm. It'll be nice when it's done – it's kind of Addams Family chic at the moment.'

'Aw, but George bought you a house in Cornwall! It's so romantic.'

'Well, he didn't buy me it, it's joint money.' Mostly mine, in fact.

'But still. I think it's sweet. And the village is gorgeous?'

I looked down the hill towards the sea, brightening in the distance, and the curves of the green hills and cliffs. 'I suppose.' I couldn't tell her about my strange connection to this place – it was just safer if no one knew, always had been. Even Lou, who's known me since university, has no idea about my past.

'It's going to be an adjustment, that's all. I bet you'll love it when it's all fixed up.'

'The locals are a bit *Deliverance* though. Not a friendly smile among them.' If this was a women's fiction book I would already have been invited to join a knitting circle and probably had a run-in with a grumpy but hot fisherman.

She laughed. 'Did you go into the Spar asking for Madagascan vanilla or something?'

'Huh. I guess my dreams of fitting right into a community were unrealistic.'

'It takes time is all. Most of these people never move away, so any incomers seem weird.'

'Urgh. Yeah. Anyway, tell me about you before I lose reception. Latest date?'

'Heart surgeon, who ironically seemed to have none of his own. Kept calling his ex "crazy" and moaning about child support.'

'Spring wedding then?'

She laughed, but without humour. 'It's not far off, that. Slim pickings. You're so lucky with your lovely George.' All my friends loved George, his enthusiasm, his intensively competitive trivia knowledge, his sense of fun.

'He seems happier here. Typing away in his study already.'

'That's great! Time to finally get that book done?'

'Who knows. I don't ask any more.'

'Is he doing better, do you think?' I could hear the concern in her voice. George and I liked to pretend everything was alright, but there was no hiding the fact that he'd had something close to a breakdown last year. Another reason I'd agreed to the move.

'I think he is, actually. Yeah.'

Her voice began to crackle. '. . . nail salon . . .'

'Lou, I'm losing you.'

'. . . hear me?'

'Nope, the reception is rubbish. Sorry. I'll email – come and stay when the place has walls and stuff!' She was gone.

I stood on the road, rain pattering on to my phone, and suddenly felt very alone. But I wasn't alone – George would be at home, and even if said home was currently dank and structurally unsound, at least I was loved. At least I had a house. I told myself how fortunate I was. If only we had the internet installed, I could look up the history of the place, calm the niggle of fear at the base of my neck. Doing my best with the intermittent 3G, waving my phone around as if that might make a difference, I googled poppets and witch jars, and found the details of a witchcraft museum about an hour away, in a place called Boscastle. It seemed they had a collection of the things. Quickly, before I could change my mind, I dropped them an email explaining what we'd found in the wall.

◆ ◆ ◆

I broached it with George over dinner that night. Since we had no kitchen, 'dinner' was instant noodles softened from the kettle, with a sprinkle of spinach in a concession to nutrition. George wolfed his down with every sign of enjoyment, noodles dangling from his mouth.

'Aren't you struggling with the lack of internet?' I asked. I was finding it hard myself.

He shrugged. 'The thing I'm working on is more . . . archive-based. Don't need Google.'

'But it's kind of annoying, isn't it? We can't stream TV, and the phone reception here is non-existent. When are they going to install it?'

'Maybe a week or so,' he mumbled through food. 'Anyway, you're always moaning I'm online too much.' George is a low-key Twitter addict, claiming he needs it for research and uncovering stories. I'm a bit more of a Luddite – I have my own reasons for not wanting to be findable. 'What do you want it for anyway? Gonna watch Netflix all day now you're a woman of leisure?'

'No,' I said, crossly swiping up his discarded packets of sauce. 'It's for this place. We'll need a ton of new things, furniture, kitchen stuff, you know . . . cushions. I was hoping to order things online.'

'Cushions.' He raised his eyebrows at me. 'That's our most pressing need here?'

I sighed. 'Never mind. I'm sure I can survive till next week.'

'I can act out scenes from *Emily in Paris* for you if you're really bored. OMG this croissant is TO DIE FOR!' He mimed snapping a selfie and pouting.

'Oh, shut up, Charles Dickens.' But he had made me smile, as he always could. Although my conversation with Cara had unnerved me, it had made me feel better to chat to Lou too, and I fell asleep more quickly than I had since we'd moved here. So it was disappointing to shoot awake again in the darkened bedroom, and see from the shadows moving over the floor that it was the middle of the night. I made the by now familiar trek to the window – we had to install blackout blinds asap – and peered out into the garden. I wasn't really expecting to see anything, so it was a nasty shock when I realised someone was standing there again, at the edge of our lawn. Yes, it was definitely a person, right by the treeline. One of the builders, coming to collect something? As the clouds scudded over the moon, I couldn't make out who it was, or if it was a man or a woman – they were tall, whoever it was – but I could see they were looking straight at our bedroom window. For a second our eyes almost met, and then a cloud dulled out the light. When it came back, the intruder was gone.

I woke up the next day to find the house freezing, my breath coming white over the duvet. The radiators were cold to the touch, and when I ran the tap in the bathroom the water was icy too.

'The bloody boiler's off!' I yelled to George, who shuffled in, sleepy-eyed. 'And it's after eight – are the builders even coming back?'

'I don't know.'

'Urgh. This is what they do, isn't it? Start the work then vanish for weeks.'

'I'll call them,' he said, through a mouthful of toothpaste, and I felt guilty. I was the one who wasn't working, it should be me who sorted these things. Since I couldn't face a cold shower, I got dressed and headed up to the brow of the hill. I knew George wouldn't share my worry about the figure in the woods who seemed to be watching us, so I'd decided I had to find out more about this house, and with no easy internet access, I resorted to more old-fashioned investigative means, and rang my mother-in-law. We were not especially close, Ruth and I. I texted her sometimes, usually thanking her for gifts or sycophantically asking for recipes, but rarely actually called. I found a fallen log to perch on. The village was spread out below me, the woods rich and green, the sea sparkling with patches of sunlight, white clouds flitting over. It wasn't bad, I supposed.

'Hello? Helen? Is everything alright?' An edge of worry in her voice. Why did that happen, that as people got older they thought every phone call was bad news? But then I remembered the call about Mum's stroke, and my stomach lurched. Sometimes it *was* bad news.

'Oh no, all fine. Well, the house is upside down, the walls are gaping, but you know, it's fine.'

'Oh dear. But you do like the house, I hope? I wasn't sure how you'd feel about it, but George said – well, I'm glad it all worked out.'

What did she mean? 'I like it, of course. It'll be lovely when it's finished.' I had a feeling I would be saying that a lot in the coming months. 'Though it's going to cost an arm and a leg.'

'You've still got your savings though, to do it up?' She lowered her voice a bit, as if talking about cash was uncouth. I hoped she didn't think I was fishing for more.

'Of course! Well, some of them. Most went on the house, of course.'

'On the house?' She sounded confused.

'Yes, the asking price, you know.' We had bought in cash, as George was worried his flat-lined earnings from the past two years, as well as me giving up my job, might affect our getting a mortgage.

'Right, but . . .' She trailed off.

'What's the matter?'

'Oh, nothing. Nothing. You said . . . the asking price?'

'Yes, I think it was just under two hundred, that's what George said.' What was she confused about? Maybe George had told them it was less? Or more? But I couldn't think why he would do that. 'Anyway, we're so grateful for your support, and there'll be plenty left to do it up, no problem at all.'

'I'm glad.' She still sounded worried.

'Did George tell you where the house is?' I risked. 'The name of the village?' Would it even mean anything to her? I didn't know how much she knew. This was risky behaviour from me. I had been safe for so many years I was growing complacent.

Ruth paused. 'Is something wrong, Helen?'

'Oh no, no. Just . . . trying to get to the bottom of it, I suppose.'

'There's nothing to get to the bottom of, dear. It's just a house, and he thought you would like it. If you need more on the renovation budget, I'm sure we could—'

'No, no, no, we're totally fine. All good here.'

'Right. Well, I'm sorry, dear, but I have to run out to yoga now. Do come up and see us when you need a break. Bye!'

I sat there, looking at the dead phone. That was strange. Everything she said made sense, even if it was odd, but something in the way she'd said it had caught at me. As if she was surprised, as if something about the house sale had disturbed her. Had George told them something different? I wished I could just ask him, but of course I couldn't. I stood up, brushing moss off my jeans. Was there a way to find out who'd owned a house before you? There had to be.

The answer came to me as I contemplated going back to the house – a library. With no internet and the house torn to pieces, everything I needed would be there.

I went home to get the car, finding the place quiet but for sounds of frantic typing from upstairs. The library was about five miles away, in a slightly larger market town by the name of St Edwin. Part of me was intensely relieved to see open shops and cafés, a branch of Boots, a White Stuff even. As if I'd come back to civilisation, to sanity – I'd hardly seen anyone in days except the landlord and the barmaid and the surly builders. The library was in a Victorian red-brick building, a little shabby but cosy, with that kind of industrial school carpet on the floor, and shelves full of reassuring books. I told the librarian, a fortyish woman with a surprising undercut and a surf logo on her top, that I wanted to find out who had lived in my house before. She didn't seem to find this at all surprising, and I supposed I had amateur genealogists to thank for that. I learned that the census records were online, but only up to 1911, and I needed to know who'd owned the house after that. Electoral registers were another option, but those only went up to 1965. Otherwise I could try the Land Registry, but a quick google told me that former owners were not always listed on title deeds of houses. So it was surprisingly hard to find out who had once owned a place. Still, it was warm, a faintly dusty soporific air over all, and indeed there was a teenage boy asleep at a table in the next room, and the drift of a mother reading to a toddler in the kids' section. I smiled at them, tucking secret hopes into my heart.

Next, I checked my emails. Various London friends and colleagues getting in touch, making me homesick. A message from Sharon, the staff nurse in my old job, which I deleted unread. I couldn't think about anything to do with that, not now. I also had a message from the Witchcraft Museum, which I had to smile at slightly despite my anxiety – they were passing my inquiry on to a local expert who might be able to help me identify the strange objects we'd found at the house. Right after it was an email from that same person, who called herself Lisa McSweeney, *healer and herbalist*. She sounded enthusiastic, and encouraged me to come and see her – she lived a few miles outside of Little Hollow. It made me feel better that people were taking me seriously, in some obscure way.

I checked our joint bank account too, finding it as expected depleted, with just the renovation money left. Not surprising after we'd bought a house for cash, but still worrying. Then, after clicking a bit, and inputting my card details, I learned that, in 1911, and also in the 1960s, the house had been owned by a family called by the rather excellent name of Tresallick. That fitted with what Grumpy Shop Lady had said. But what of my odd feeling I'd been to the house before? I still hadn't been able to remember when or how, but it was perfectly plausible Mum had taken me there as a kid, if we'd lived locally for a while. An odd coincidence, but not so very unlikely in a place like this where everyone knew each other. What was strange was that George had bought us a house so near to where I grew up. That's what was giving me shivers of unease up and down my spine.

Tresallick. Such a pretty name, rolling off the tongue like foam off waves. But it told me nothing. Idly, I put it into Google, realising how very dependent I now was on the search engine to answer my every slight query. I typed in *Tresallick Little Hollow Cornwall*. To my surprise, there were several results. One stood out for me – an extract from something on Google Books, a tome called *Cornish Superstitions*.

> *A family from Little Hollow, near Penzance, were renowned witches who could reputedly produce love spells and ill-wishes for those who paid. One matriarch of the clan, Alanis Tresallick, was burned as a witch in the Assizes of 1778, and was said to have left a curse on the surrounding area.*

Sitting in the too-warm library, I went cold all over. It was all silly of course – witch hunts had been nothing more than an outlet for misogyny that didn't want women being healers or midwives – but I had found a poppet in my walls, after all. I'd found strange things in jars, preserved and pickled, dried herbs in the cellar. George had dug up a charm of some kind in the garden. I had to face the facts: I was living in a house full of witchcraft.

And that was too big a coincidence as well, wasn't it? The house had to be linked to the murders somehow. I was almost afraid to find out, but I pulled the keyboard towards me, and with a sense of calling down the fates, googled *Janna Edwards Little Hollow*.

There it was.

Janna Edwards is a convicted killer born in Little Hollow,
Cornwall. In 1987 she was found guilty of murdering
three people on the same day in October 1986, including
two children. Edwards is currently serving a fifty-year
sentence but has appealed against it several times.

And under the heading of parents – *Father, Robert Edwards,*
death unknown. Mother, Eve Tresallick, died 1987. Of course. Why
had this not occurred to me? The house had belonged to her mother's family, but she bore her father's name. Even clicking on the
Wikipedia link felt dangerous, the chance I might see something I
couldn't cope with, find out details I'd never wanted. I already knew
too much. Janna striding through the woods, her fair hair flying in
the wind. The knife in her hand. Her grip on his head, cutting his
throat like a pig. Her refusal to ever show remorse. *I had to do it,*
those were her words. That much I knew. And now I also knew I
was living in the house of the woman who had destroyed my family.
Of a murderer.

I could hear my breath coming over the hum of the computer,
and I closed my eyes tightly against the fluorescent lights. Nausea
rose in my throat, so much so I had to hang my head for a minute
and breathe deeply so I wouldn't be sick right there in the library.
This couldn't be. How had this happened? I'd known the house
was too good to be true, its price so exactly matching what we
had in savings, the ease of the purchase, so rapid I didn't have to
get involved at all. Had I even signed anything? Because there was
another possibility, wasn't there? Which would explain why Ruth
was so puzzled when I talked about buying the house. And why
Cara in the pub said she thought it had never gone out of the family. Maybe it never had. But if that was true it meant other things,
terrible things I didn't want to countenance. Lies I had never even
imagined.

I drove back home, taking extra care since I was so upset and jittery. Rain scudded on the windscreen, and I wanted to get on the M4 and drive all the way back to our cosy flat in Stoke Newington. But there were new people living in it now, a young couple in their late twenties, all big glasses and giant headphones. This house, haunted as it was, was my home now.

The place looked forbidding as I drove up to it. George hadn't put the lights on or pulled the curtains, so it was gloomy and unloved on this late March afternoon. How had I ever believed this house had been on the market? Whoever had owned it had not been here in years. As if they were unavoidably detained. In prison, for example.

I let myself in, feeling the chill of the place, the gaping holes in the kitchen, the dust over everything. The builders had left muddy footprints over the floorboards, McDonald's wrappers balled up in a corner. It felt like a violation, but I had a bigger one to worry about right now. I went upstairs. Behind George's door, I could hear a tinny sound, as if he was listening to something on his headphones. Not music, a video or podcast or something. I went into the spare room, where a mountain of boxes still awaited unpacking. Maybe there was some information about the house in there – if we'd bought it, there would be paperwork, wouldn't there? Contracts, surveys? George's admin was a mess of receipts and documents, jammed into a series of plastic folders. If I'd had time to organise the move, I would have insisted on searches and surveys and I would have recognised the name of the village immediately. But George had been strangely insistent he would do it all. Why? Just to be a helpful husband, while I was struggling to keep my head above water at work? Or for some darker reason?

I searched through endless boxes and cases, throwing things over my head in a kind of mania. I knew I'd have to clear it all up again, ten years' worth of bills and receipts and warranties for things we'd left behind in London, but I didn't care. There didn't seem to be anything at all related to a house purchase.

A noise from outside. George had opened his door. I had a second to choose – did I tell him what I suspected? Was there any chance he didn't know, that this was all some terrible misunderstanding? Of course it was possible. In the end my old instinct won out, the one that said he had to be protected. He poked his head in, looking at the devastation. Raised his bushy eyebrows. 'Is this your way of unpacking?'

'Sorry. I was just . . . looking for something.' I shuffled my leg over the documents to hide them. 'You don't know where the council tax bill is? We still have to tell them we moved.'

I knew he wouldn't. 'Absolutely no clue. Isn't it all online these days?'

'Yeah, maybe. I'll clear all this up. Are you working?'

'Mmm. What shall we do for dinner?' He meant, what would I provide for dinner.

'Well, the kitchen's even less functional than it was, if such a thing were possible. There's some pasta, I think. And a jar of pesto maybe.'

'Sounds good.' He withdrew his head. 'I'll do another hour or so.' The assumption that I would cook, sort it all out, was one I recognised from his periods of manic work. I was so used to it I didn't even mind, and indeed it was almost a relief to see it return. Besides, having a distracted creative husband meant I could hide all sorts of things, because he simply wouldn't notice. For the first time, however, I began to wonder if it worked both ways.

◆ ◆ ◆

There was only one other person I could think of to ask, since I was sure Ruth would tell me nothing over the phone and she was miles away in Reading. Every time I thought about it, my stomach clenched. The house must have been left to George, but why now? Maybe my in-laws had known about it for years and only just decided to give it to him – perhaps he had no idea of its history. But why then would he tell me we'd bought it? And where were our savings, if we hadn't spent them on the house?

That morning the builders had woken me up at the crack of seven. Me starting awake, heart pounding, while George didn't stir. I didn't even bother getting up to let them in – they had their own keys, I may as well let them get on with it. I hated feeling like I couldn't go downstairs in my own house, though the bathroom was at least functional. After a shower that was at best intermittently warm, I looked at my face in its old, spotted mirror, drawn with anxiety and lack of sleep. I hardly felt like the same person who'd left London less than a week before. From downstairs came the usual bangs and drills, setting my teeth on edge, but I was still startled to come out of the bathroom in just a small towel and see the face of a strange man staring in my landing window.

'Jesus!' I gave a yelp, and that at least woke George, who came out of the bedroom in his pants.

'What's wrong?'

I pointed shakily to the face, which through the old window looked all teeth and pallid skin.

'Hang on.' George went into the bedroom and threw the window open, called out of it. I couldn't hear what he was saying as I cowered in the hallway. He was back in a moment. 'It's OK, they're just working on the front of the house today. The pointing. Whatever pointing is.'

'How's he even up there?'

'He's climbed on to the porch to check the tiles.'

'On the slanted roof?'

'The slanted roof, Helz. I promise it's fine. Go and look when you've got some clothes on.' I did, after getting dressed hurriedly in the spare room, ignoring all the boxes and the cobwebs draped in corners. I had envisaged this room painted with ducks and teddies but that seemed miles away now. I couldn't imagine leaving a child to sleep alone in this spooky house. In *her* house.

Outside, a man was crawling along the roof of the porch, with its missing slates and askew gables.

'That can't be safe,' I called to George, who'd gone into his office, which was also at the front of the house.

'I know, I told him, but he says he's fine. Does it all the time.' The man was of indeterminate age, anywhere between twenty-five and forty-five, with a ratty fleece and the kind of skinny, weather-beaten face you get from serious indulgence in drugs and/or alcohol. I could have diagnosed some form of chronic malnutrition.

'What's he actually doing?'

'God, I don't know.' I saw that George was dressed now, in tracksuit bottoms and his university hoody. I hoped the builders wouldn't see it and think he was boasting about having gone to UCL. 'You're not showering?'

He shrugged. 'I want to get stuck into work. Anyway, the shower's a disaster.'

Normally, if George stopped washing, I worried, but this seemed like something else. An almost manic energy rather than depression. Was that something else I needed to worry about? He was thirty-four. It would have shown up by now, wouldn't it? Something like that? The depression we could handle, but bipolar disorder was in a whole different league.

I stared at him until he cocked his head, quizzical. 'What?'

Do you know whose house this is? Have you been lying to me? 'Nothing. Good luck with it. I'm going out. To see a witch.'

That caught his attention, as I'd known it would. 'Oh?'

'That's right, some local healer woman. I thought I'd ask them about the thing. The poppet, you know. You want to come?'

He sighed. 'Aw, man, I really do, but I better get on with this.' Whatever this was.

◆ ◆ ◆

The witch – sorry, healer – lived in a small hamlet further along the road to Land's End – just a few houses, a pottery shop and café, and a cold, clear river shrouded in thick green plants. I passed a few outdoorsy couples on the road, in anoraks and toting walking poles. I'd thought George and I might have some days out like this before I figured out what I wanted to do with the rest of my life. Climb hills, eat cream teas, drink shandy in pub gardens. I hadn't banked on him diving head-first into a new project. Apparently, the move had been a little too effective. But I shouldn't complain.

I had texted Lisa McSweeney the night before, hoping the message might squeak through if a bar of reception appeared, but I didn't get her reply until I left Little Hollow. As its name suggested, it was in some strange phone dip. It hardly seemed credible after years spent in London, but there were large parts of Cornwall that appeared to have no reception at all. She encouraged me to come round, sounding friendly and interested.

Lisa was in her forties, I guessed, dressed in a tie-dyed maxi dress with lots of silver jewellery and long, tangled hair. She lived in a new-build bungalow, which I hadn't expected, set in a beautiful, overgrown garden with a small hut at the end of it, hung with fairy lights. She followed my gaze over to it as she opened the door of the house. 'That's where I do treatments. Reiki, massage, that sort of thing.'

Maybe that was what she meant by healing. I had to keep an open mind, remember there was good clinical evidence for some of these things. Inside, the modern kitchen was full of drying herbs, copper pans, a block of wicked-looking knives, a stack of wrinkled books about healing, plants, Tarot and so on. She didn't offer me water or anything, eyes flickering over me. I hadn't brought a bag, just shoved my phone into my jeans pocket. 'You didn't bring it?'

'The poppet? Oh God no, we buried it.' I felt kind of stupid saying that. 'I was worried it was . . . dirty. Do you think it really was a poppet?' I clicked open my phone and showed her a picture of it. She stared at the screen intently. Somehow it was even more sinister seen like that, lying innocuously on my dining table, its button eyes blindly looking up.

'And those are nails stuck through it?' She sounded quite matter-of-fact.

'Yeah. And the hair, that's . . . I think it's human.'

'Hmm. Yes. Probably is, very common in these parts. Just meant someone wanted to curse the inhabitants – or the person living there wanted to repel evil spirits. It might have been pointed towards the house of someone they wanted to ill-wish.'

'Oh.' I'd hoped she'd tell me there was a more benign explanation. I reminded myself it was just fabric and hair crossed with iron. Evil existed, but it couldn't seep into my life. Could it?

'Can you tell me what house it is? It's years since we found one of these. It's old?'

'I think it was built in the 1700s. It's in Little Hollow. The Gables.'

'The Gables,' she repeated. 'That's funny, I know the village well, but not the house you mention.'

'I think the name is a recent one. It's the one on the hill, if you know it. With a green door.'

I heard her intake of breath. 'Oh! I know the one you mean. The Tresallick place.'

'That's right. We just bought it.' Not that I was entirely sure this was true.

'You bought it?'

'Um, yeah.' She was biting her lip, eyes staring at something in the distance.

'Is everything OK?'

'Helen, was it?'

'Helen, yes.'

'Hmm. How much do you know about the history of your house?'

'Not a lot, to be honest.' Just that it had belonged to a witch and murderer.

'Well. Look, it's maybe not my place to tell you. And if you don't believe in dark energies, it's just a house, right?'

'Did something happen there?' As far as I knew, it hadn't. But clearly there was a lot I didn't know.

'It's not so much what happened as who owned it. People can leave powerful traces.'

'Traces of what?'

I didn't want to know these things. Why was I asking? Whatever I found out could only unsettle my life, knock down its walls and rip up its foundations.

Lisa looked me in the eyes, and I saw hers were a bright hazel, a darker band around the pupils. 'Well, of evil.'

I tried to shrug it off. 'It was a long time ago. The house has been empty for decades, hasn't it?' It was just a house. Even if it had a strange connection to me, even if a killer had lived there, it was only bricks and mortar. 'I think I know what you mean. Are you saying she lived there, the woman who – you know, the murders?'

Her gaze was steady. 'You already know that she did, I think.'

'I – I read something. You think this was hers, this poppet?'

She shrugged. 'It could have been. People said her grandmother was a witch too – all the Tresallick women. Not her mother, she was always weak. But the rest of them.'

I wasn't sure why I'd come here. Was I hoping she'd tell me I was wrong, about all the things I was suspecting? 'OK. But it was a long time ago, wasn't it? People seem very upset by it still.'

She stepped back, crossing her arms over her stomach. 'You shouldn't have come here, Helen. You should leave Little Hollow while you still can.'

◆ ◆ ◆

Feeling profoundly shaken after that, I stopped in the nearest pub and drank half a shandy, ate a plate of chips smothered in ketchup. Lisa had refused to elaborate on what she meant by telling me I should leave the village, and had all but hustled me out the door. I told myself Lisa was clearly a little unhinged – she had to be if she believed in the occult. The fact was we had ended up living in the house of a murderer, someone who dabbled in spells and curses. Well, so what – I didn't believe in those things anyway, so they couldn't hurt me. I was more concerned about the murkiness around our purchase of the house. I'd taken my eye off the ball, the last few months – I'd been barely functioning outside of work – so it wouldn't be surprising if I'd missed some red flags. Because it couldn't just be a coincidence, could it, that we'd ended up with this, of all the houses in the world. Question was, did I really want to follow this thread all the way through the labyrinth? There were things in there I had not thought about in years – had not allowed myself to. Things I also did not want seeing the light of day.

On my way back into Little Hollow, I pulled the car off the road at a sign for a nature reserve. The Devil's Altar, they called it – a melodramatic name for what was just a rock in the middle of the woods. There was no one else about, no other cars in the small parking area by the side of the road. I shrugged my jacket on, and began to follow the dirt path into the trees. Nothing but birdsong and the breeze, the distant sound of traffic. Leaves underfoot, everything green and lush. The altar stone was in a small clearing, with a graffitied plaque explaining it might have had some pagan significance, cajoling visitors: 'don't change the place, let the place change you'. Cute. There were lots of sites like this around Penzance, stone circles and holy wells and ruined churches. There was no mention of the violent event that had taken place here, which I supposed was to be expected. It was just a large flat rock, its surface a smooth grey and white, surrounded by bluebells and primroses, peaceful in a patch of sun. The landscape had forgotten what happened here – maybe I could too.

When I got home, mind still mulling over my revelations, it took me a moment to realise things weren't right. There was an ambulance parked outside the house. I parked askew, heart in my mouth. The builders' van was there, Bob himself standing with a paramedic in a green overall, his burly arms folded. Where was George?

I dashed past them, rounding the ambulance. Someone was slumped on the gravel on the other side of the porch, a second paramedic working at them. Oh God. My old instinct would have been to run towards the trouble, as a doctor should, get down on my knees and try to help, but instead I froze again. The same problem, the reason I'd left my job. *What if I make it worse?*

And where was George? Had something happened? I'd been wrong that he was alright, I'd missed the signs? Or his asthma had succumbed to all the dust in the house? Oh God, after all these years of watching him . . .

There he was. Coming out of the house, safe and sound, in the same scuzzy outfit as when I left. I looked again at the body on the ground – of course, it was the builder. The man who'd been climbing on the roof earlier. The other two guys were there too, Ciaran and Borak, watching fearfully as the paramedic worked on their colleague. His limbs were twisted unnaturally.

I hunkered down beside him. 'What's his status?'

The paramedic, a young lad of no more than twenty, looked up. 'He's stable. We need to get him secured before we move him though.'

'There's a risk of spinal displacement – I don't see any bleeding?' He stared at me. 'I'm a doctor. Not locally.'

'No obvious bleeding. Think his spine took the worst of it, so no head injuries that we can see. Responded to stimulus.'

I'm a doctor, I had said. Not *I was a doctor*. And yet my body had betrayed me, rooted me to the spot when I should have rushed to help.

'Right. That's good.' So he would likely survive this, but he might not walk again, if the damage was severe. His spine would be swollen and inflamed for several days before they could tell. I made myself stand up and back away. 'What happened?' I hissed to George. I reached out and clutched his arm, needing to feel his warm, wiry body, alive and safe.

George was pale. 'Oh God, it was awful, Helz. He fell.'

'I said it wasn't safe!'

'I know. I know. I guess . . . one of the tiles slipped and he came off with it. I saw him kind of wobble for a minute – he almost got his balance – then . . . urgh.' George drew a deep shaky breath. 'Will he – be alright?'

'I don't know. He's alive, anyway. If he doesn't have head trauma, that's good.'

There was then a flurry of movement, and the paramedics lifted the man strapped to a stretcher, took him towards the ambulance. His face was grey, eyes closed. At least one of his legs looked broken. Bob shot me a look that was pure poison. He blamed us? But why?

I couldn't help myself calling out. 'I'm so sorry this happened. He just fell?'

Bob didn't meet my eyes. 'Your tiles were loose. You should have told us.'

'But – we didn't know! We hired you to fix all that.' I could feel George shift beside me and tried to moderate my tone. 'It's just a terrible accident. I did ask if it was safe.'

'You're saying this is *my* fault?' Bob's tone really shocked me. Cold, and mean. 'I don't take care of my workers, is that it?'

'No! It's no one's fault.'

'Because if there's fault to be discussed, we are on your property. No public liability insurance, I'll bet?'

I just stared at him. Could this be in some way our legal responsibility? Surely not. The man had been doing something dangerous, and he'd fallen.

'It was your ladder and all,' chipped in Ciaran, who'd come around to stand beside Bob. The other guy glared at me. I was taken aback at the sudden burst of malice – obviously they were upset, but why direct it at us?

This was unbelievable. The paramedics were glancing over as they secured the man into the ambulance. Did they blame me too?

'Look, everyone's upset, I'm sure. Let's just send all our best wishes to . . .' Oh God, I didn't even know his name.

Bob glared. 'Lukas. One of my best lads.'

'Well, let's just hope Lukas is alright. We can sort the rest out later.'

Bob made a sort of grunting noise, and he and the other two guys started throwing large kit bags into their van as the ambulance nosed off down the hill. They weren't putting the sirens on, so I hoped that was a good sign for Lukas. The builders also drove off after it, quite a bit faster, without saying goodbye. Wheels kicking up gravel like small nodes of spite.

I turned to George in disbelief. 'What was that? He's just being a twat, right? There's no way this could be our fault?'

George ran a hand through his hair, so it stood up. I could see he still hadn't showered. 'Um. I think I wrote a column about this once, on the money page. There are some circumstances where you can be liable, if people get injured on your property.'

'But he never mentioned we needed insurance! We never signed a single piece of paper – did we?' And that was crazy, now that I thought about it. This was what happened when I let George be in charge. We might be getting sued, then we'd lose the house we'd only just got and be back to square one. 'Are they even going to finish it now?' We had a hole in the wall and no kitchen. 'Did you . . . George, you didn't give them any money yet?'

He looked sheepish.

'George!'

'I had to! He needed to buy supplies, he said, pay the guys. We can't expect people to work before they get paid.'

'That's literally every job in the world. For God's sake.'

'Look, I don't think losing your temper's going to help. It is what it is.'

I've always hated that phrase. Last bastion of people who can't be bothered trying to change anything. 'We need to at least block up the wall, if they aren't going to come back.' It was incredible that people could take your money, do major damage to your house, then bugger off and not return. In any other business that would be called a crime, but with builders we actually had to beg them to do it for us.

'What with?' he asked.

I snapped, looking at his helpless face, the ink stains on his fingers, knowing he only wanted to be back writing, not sorting out the various disasters we were embroiled in. Not living in the real world. 'I don't care. Just find something, will you?'

He gaped at me. 'What's up with you?'

'I just . . . I don't like it here, George! The house is cold and horrible and dirty, the locals don't want us here, and . . .'

I don't know if you've told me the truth about how we got this place.

I made myself not say it. Gaps can open up, not just in houses, but between people. In the walls of your marriage, your love. Many times I had been exasperated by George, or even angered, but I had never before not trusted him. And I didn't want to start now. I had to find out more first.

◆ ◆ ◆

The next day I badgered George into texting for news of Lukas. 'Anything?'

He shook his head absent-mindedly. He'd brought his laptop to the breakfast table, and I itched to see what was on it, but that would violate one of the most deeply held agreements in our relationship.

I'd spent the night googling liability, and he was right, we were potentially at fault, especially as they'd used our ladder. I didn't know we even had a ladder. 'Great. So next thing we know we'll have a solicitor's letter, and they'll have taken our money and not finished the work.'

'We don't know that,' said George, not even looking up. 'I better go upstairs. Got stuff to do.'

He didn't ask what my plans were. I'd long grown used to the way I ceased to exist for George when he was deep in a project. Maybe that explained some of it. Safer, if you have things to hide, to have a husband who doesn't pay you too close attention.

As he shuffled to the stairs, laptop under his arm, I called after him, 'I might go over to Mum's again today. To the house.'

He turned, eyebrows raised. 'Isn't Mick there?'

'Well. Yeah. It's time to bury the hatchet, maybe, given how she is.' What an odd phrase that was, *bury the hatchet*. So brutal.

'I think that's good, Helz. You need to pull together in the tough times.'

Easy for him to say – his family was loving and close, or at least the family he knew about.

'I'll pick up some groceries on my way back.'

'OK.'

He didn't care much about food at the best of times, or at least only the most article-worthy innovations, a cereal café or a burger the size of a small dog. I'd have to watch his calorie intake or he'd lose too much weight, not that this had been a problem for some time now. I wished he would tell me something about his project, but knew better than to ask.

Visiting hours at Mum's home were until three each day, and it was close to two by the time I got there. No matter. I didn't imagine what I had to say would take very long. It was difficult to smile and nod at the staff, answer their polite enquiries about Mum's progress. I was sure they thought me very rude, but I was just too worried. About the builder, about the house, about George.

71

She was sitting in the same place by the window, eyes scanning the horizon as if she was looking for something. Or someone. I waited till the nurse had gone and stared at her. No words between us now. Her eyes were the same, blue and sharp, her hands twisted up on her lap like small dead creatures.

'Mum. You recognised the name of the village we've moved to, didn't you?'

Of course she said nothing, but she turned her face to the side.

'You knew what house it was, too. That's why you spilled the water. And I've been there before, haven't I? When I was a baby.'

A slow blink. *Yes*.

I was shaking. Everything I thought I'd known was crumbling. I had been barely two when I left Cornwall, it was a wonder I could remember it at all.

I faced my mother. I could not find the courage, even after all this time, to bring up the thing I had never told her. I'd rested safe in the knowledge that she could never know, there was no way she would even guess. But what if she had? 'I'm sorry, Mum. I had no idea what house it was until we got there. I guess it's just – some awful coincidence. George was looking for a cheap house in Cornwall, and it was empty all this time, so.' Would she believe that? It was just about plausible. If you didn't know what I knew, that was.

Silence between us. There was so much to say I had no idea where to start.

'Anyway, it's just – well, he doesn't need to know my connection to it.'

Mum's face was expressive, slack as it was. It said – *but* you *will know, Helen.*

And I did. And I also knew, deep down, that we couldn't have bought this house through sheer coincidence. No, there was only one explanation. We hadn't bought it at all, and that was why Ruth had been so evasive on the phone, why she thought we had more money than we did, why George had handled the sale himself. It was all a lie.

◆ ◆ ◆

Until her stroke, Mum had lived in a small house in a cul de sac outside Okehampton. Seventies bungalows, boxy gardens, the kind of street that could be anywhere in the country. Now, I parked outside and walked down the path, noticing how neat it all was, how suburban, the raked gravel and flowerbeds, and rang the bell, with its jaunty *bing-bong* sound. I knew he'd be in – he never went anywhere, except for the daily trip to the shops for the paper and groceries, and that was always at ten. Sure enough, his bulk appeared behind the frosted glass of the door, and he opened it to me.

'Helen!' He looked shocked to see me, as well he might.

'Hi, Mick. Can I come in?' I had always called him Mick, even when he'd asked me to say *Dad*. It wasn't his fault – he had tried. When he met Mum at the local pub, where he was calling the meat raffle, and married her, I'd been a truculent nine-year-old. Mick was pretty much the only father I'd ever known, but I couldn't let him be one. Some obscure loyalty to my real dad, maybe. Also why I kept using my old surname, not his name of Keown. Although I had been eighteen before I realised Gillis was not in fact my birth surname, that Mum had gone back to her maiden name when we moved to Devon.

I sat on the sofa while he made me tea. Mick had never done any cooking while Mum was herself, and I could see now he was living out of tins and the freezer. The milk was UHT. I braced myself as he came in with the tea. 'Look, the first thing I want to say is sorry. I shouldn't have said those things to you when Mum got ill – I know it was a hard time.'

He sat opposite me, the quintessential dad in his fleece and baggy jeans. Mick would have been a wonderful father, if I'd ever let him, if he and Mum had ever had any kids themselves. 'Well, that's OK, love. I know you were upset.'

I'd screamed at him in the corridor of the hospital. Why didn't he notice this was coming. Why hadn't he called the ambulance faster. 'I was . . . not thinking straight.' Afraid that I was about to lose the only parent I'd ever known.

'There's no way to predict these things, love. She was fine one minute, sitting there watching *Escape to the Chateau*, next thing she was on the kitchen floor, spilled her tea everywhere.'

I nodded, and we sat in silence for a moment, thinking of Mum no doubt, how clever she'd always been, how sharp, now silenced by the explosion that had gone off in her brain. 'Anyway, I'm sorry. It was a horrible time.'

'That's alright.' He cradled his cup awkwardly. 'How's the house, then?'

'Oh God, a disaster. We have these builders but I'm not sure they know what they're doing. They've left a massive hole in the wall.'

He shook his head in disapproval. Mick has never actually worked as a builder – he's an engineer by trade – but he's the kind of man who knows how to do practical things. He and George have very little common ground, but Mick always makes a point of reading his articles to have something to talk to him about. He's a good man. It was entirely on me that I'd never let him in. 'Listen, Mick, would you mind if I poked about? I still have a few things in the loft, I think. Seems a good time to move them to the house.'

'Course, love. I'll get them down for you, if you want?'

'Oh no, that's fine. Easier if I take a look at it up there. I'm sure Mum wouldn't want boxes everywhere!' We both maintained the facade that Mum was coming home again.

He made a big fuss of going for the pole and pulling the ladder down, climbing up to put the light on for me. 'Don't step between the struts now, you'll come right down!'

'I won't.' The loft was lit by a dim bulb, swinging from Mick's departure, casting crazy shadows over the walls. I knew exactly what I was looking for. A box that had once contained Tunnock's Teacakes, set against the far wall, now covered in a fine coat of dust, which I brushed off. It had been taped shut, but the years had dried and loosened it, and it opened easily.

A neat pile of newspaper clippings, yellowed with age. The headline on the first: MAN SLAIN IN CORNISH WOODS. The name of the woods was given, and the rock – the Devil's Altar. They hadn't named the nearest village, which was perhaps why I hadn't made the connection right away, but I knew now it was Little Hollow. The article had a picture of the entrance to a woodland path, the same path I'd taken the day before. Also the same path a man had gone down on a day in 1986, then walked deeper into the woods towards the famous rock, where he had been sitting drinking tea from a Thermos when a woman approached and slashed his throat, left his body there, spilling out blood on to the flat rock. The woman with the knife was Janna Edwards, a Tresallick on her mother's side, whose family had for generations owned the house I now lived in. And the man she murdered that day, cut his throat and left him to die, that man was Adam Jeffries.

My father.

George

My parents are predictable people. I could tell you exactly what they're going to order every time we go out to eat – no bread for Mum, who's convinced she's gluten intolerant, and whatever she thinks is least fattening. For Dad, nothing spicy or with garlic, ideally a plain chicken breast. My life with them had been like that too, predictable, safe, boring at times. I grew up in a semi on the outskirts of Reading, Dad was an accountant; Mum didn't work when I was little, then started helping out at my primary school and eventually became a teaching assistant. Every evening I'd sit between them on the sofa, drinking cups of tea and eating Club biscuits (Mum encouraged Dad and me to snack as much as we liked, it was only herself she policed). Being an artsy, moody teenager, I couldn't wait to get away from the suburbs. I started sending in gig reviews to the local paper while I was still at school, then did an English degree at UCL (I didn't get into Oxford, OK). After that, a journalism MA, where I picked up work experience on some music magazines (Mum and Dad paid my rent, as Helen likes to remind me), then I got a staff job on one of the nationals. An effortless rise through a tough business. Until it all went wrong.

As I said, my parents are predictable, their house a haven for me, where the wallpaper is always the same and they haven't switched teabag brands in twenty years (PG Tips). Where the biscuit tin is always full and Mum always washes my clothes for me overnight. So I was surprised, to say the least, when my parents suddenly revealed the existence of a house I had known nothing about, in rural Cornwall. It had been left to me, it seemed, and it came at exactly the right time. Not just for Helen, who was tearing herself in two wanting to be there for her mum but not abandon her job, the job that was slowly grinding her into dust, but also for me. For the past two years I had been watching my career, so carefully built, melt away like ice in the sun, and nothing I did, not pitches, not networking, not writing, seemed to make a bit of difference. Once I'd got over my initial shock of learning about the house, I realised the thing I had been looking for was this. I would try to turn a difficult discovery into a gift, and save my career as well.

Helen was easy to convince – she had no time to even think about buying a house, and here was one ready-made. She could give up her job, since there would be no mortgage to pay, as well as being closer to her mum. All during Covid, as I did nothing and felt totally useless, I had watched Helen become gaunt and pale, battling each day to save lives as if waist-deep in blood. This would be good for us – and if I needed to bend the truth a little to convince her to move out of London, it would be all with the best of intentions. I couldn't exactly tell her I had inherited the house, not yet anyway. I would explain it all to her in time. When the moment was right. I convinced myself it was just a small lie, one for both of our good. She would understand.

The first time I saw the house, I drove up alone as night was falling, long shadows cast by the trees around the house. They were cypresses, I thought, dark green, seeming to absorb the light. The house was big – two storeys plus cellar and attic, with a large garden. The paint, a deep moss green, was peeling from the doors and windows, and the slate roof and grey-stone walls were discoloured with lichen. But it was mine, and it was old, and it could be beautiful. I told myself it didn't matter whose house this had been, what its history was. I didn't believe in anything like that. It was just bricks.

Pushing aside the door took effort, silted up as it was with dead leaves and old post. I searched for a particular name among the letters, but there was nothing, only flyers and junk addressed TO THE HOMEOWNER. Well, that was me now. I was taking possession. What a strange word that was, with its double meaning. I walked the rooms, holding my breath for some reason. It was all dust and dirt, bits of broken furniture left behind. In the kitchen, 1970s units and strange jars in the cupboards. Helen would hate it, I knew, with her aversion to dirt and disorder. But I could convince her. It was a free house, and if we didn't get out of London soon it might be too late.

As I stood there in the large living room by the tiled fireplace, I felt a surge of optimism. Something good would come of this, the terrible revelations I'd learned about my past and my family, centred around this house. It seemed like a sign that my parents had told me now, if you believed in that kind of thing. It had come at the best possible time.

Since we moved in though, things hadn't gone well. As predicted, Helen seemed upset by the house, its dilapidation and dirt, and she wasn't happy about the builders, though I'd thought she'd be pleased that I found them so quickly. I hadn't wanted to tell her how hard it was to get anyone to work on the house – as soon as I said its name they would stop calling me back. Then there was the weird doll in the wall, the jar in the garden – she seemed more disturbed by these than I would have imagined. I just found it interesting, good colour for a future story, but she was so unsettled.

She'd even been asking questions about the house, how much I paid for it, that I really didn't like.

The morning after the builder's accident, Helen had gone out again, to visit her mother and stepdad. I knew something had been bothering her the last few days – surely it wasn't possible she'd found out the truth? It wasn't that well known a case, so even if she learned the name of the previous owner, she likely wouldn't make the connection. Or perhaps it was more well known around these parts, or maybe someone from the village had told her, or she'd googled it. Still, it was all a long time ago, and she wasn't a superstitious person, or at least she never had been. I told myself again I was doing this for her good – for our good.

The builder's accident had been horrible. I even saw it happen. As I sat in my new office – the Ikea desk barely reconstituted, and my office chair still with bubble wrap on the legs – I'd felt the story consume me. Worries about Helen, about the truth coming out, they all faded away, because I had an idea, and it was absorbing me like nothing had for a long time. It was a gift, really, that kind of creative focus, nothing but the words, no time to worry or angst about the past, the future. Just the story. But one thing I didn't like was being pulled out of that flow, which had evaded me for so many years. There was a noise outside. A scraping, as if a large bird had landed on the roof. Something larger than a bird. Irritated, I stood up and looked out the window. The man was up there again, doing something with the tiles on the porch roof. Did he have to make so much noise? I was regretting the efficiency of finding builders so fast, though I knew Helen wouldn't long put up with the kitchen and bathroom in their current state. That doll thing had really shaken her, though I had to admit it was the perfect opener for my book. *It was only a scrap of fabric and some button eyes. And, of course, the large nails driven through its smiling body. A poppet. A curse of kinds.* I typed a few more lines.

Another burst of noise. How could I work if it was going to be like this all the time? Drilling and hammering and the tinny pop music they played from their phones? I stood up again, and made sudden eye contact with the builder. I don't know what happened next – he seemed totally fine, balanced on the slant of the porch, as if he did it all the time. Then something crossed over his face, and he turned pale, and his body seemed to crumple. *He's going to fall!* I lurched forward, as if there was anything I could do from the window. And he fell, slowly, not even trying to stop himself, and hit the ground with a crunch that shook the items on my desk.

I ran to the window, as if I might somehow be able to catch him, only in time to watch him plummet, and the crumple of his body on the ground. Shaking, I took out my phone, as I heard the other two builders run to him, shouting. No reception. We were so isolated here that I couldn't even call for help.

Here was the idea. I had crashed and burned out of journalism, and as I saw it, there was only one way back. I had to write a book. Something timely, non-fiction, and hard-hitting, which ideally would propel me into the bestseller charts and the Sunday interview pages, from whence I could negotiate my way back to a columnist gig. Thousands of pounds to spew out the odd idea once a week. Aren't self-service checkouts droll? Isn't it awkward dealing with a cleaner? That kind of middle-class bullshit.

I didn't say it was going to be easy, this plan. Just that it was the only way. I'd spent almost a year looking for the idea, googling until my eyeballs burned, hours in the London Library researching, until I realised I couldn't afford the membership fees any more. Helen, by virtue of being run ragged and having no ounce of attention left for our finances, had left me to shepherd them for the past two years, and well, they weren't in the best of shape. It was a bit like the square of back garden she'd also assigned to me, now choked with weeds and one mouldy bench, stagnant water pooling in bits of rubbish the foxes dragged in. I'd been trying. I had even written the beginnings of several books, sample chapters and so many proposals I could have re-wallpapered this whole house with them. Literary scandals through the years. A biography of an obscure aristocrat who'd worked as a spy in the war. A biography of a grand Fleet Street editor, which would have been fascinating to me and perhaps ten other people in the UK media. A dozen different takes on modern music, modern film, mental health, Brexit. I'd sent these proposals off to more agents and editors than Helen knew, since I'd rather she thought I was lazy and depressed than a failure. One agent, a red-trousered type named Roland, had gone so far as to take me for a coffee, admitting he had enjoyed my pieces back when I was still getting commissioned. 'Such a shame for you, old chap. Bad luck, really.'

'I'm trying to make my way back, but it's hard.'

'Yes, it's tricky to be a white man these days. You can't say anything, can you? All they want are these "diverse" voices.' He did sour air quotes.

That, I baulked at, but I had said nothing, hating myself. 'So what do you . . . you think I've got a chance?' I hadn't told Helen about the meeting, but I'd spent the previous few days relieved and excited in equal measures. He would take me on, of course, or he wouldn't bother to meet me, surely. Things were going to turn around, and not a moment too soon.

He leaned back in his chair, hitching up the leg of his trousers to reveal jazzy socks. 'The thing is, if you do happen to be a white man, middle class, from the Home Counties, no sob stories or diversity, well – do people still want to hear your point of view?

Unless you have some really unique expertise. That chap with the geography books does very well.'

Did I have expertise? I'd been a typical journalist, equally fluent in music and film and politics and celebrity gossip. Nothing specialised enough to write a book about it. And then my parents had presented me with what was, depending on how you looked at it, a wonderful gift or a terrible curse. Either way, it was a story and that was what I needed. For it to work, we had to move into the house, and so we did, Helen surprisingly amenable to leaving London. I think she had simply given up, broken by years and years of working herself to the bone while I sat at home typing. Not to mention the secret hopes we weren't quite talking about, but which I knew she nurtured. Surely being out of London, being in the same place for longer than an hour a day, that would make a difference. But now we were here, and the strange happenings, the hostile locals, the cursed dolls in the wall, the slapdash builders, it was all getting to her. It was also very good copy. I just had to persuade her to stay.

The day after the accident, I waited till Helen had pulled the car out, and pushed back my chair, pulling on the stupid yellow raincoat she'd bought me, which couldn't have been more Stoke Newington if it was made from artisan cheese. I was still shaken from the memory of his fall, seeing it behind my eyes when I closed them, my own rush forward not quick enough to stop anything. I couldn't settle to write, so instead I would go and do some research. I ambled to the village, mooching around the quiet, shuttered-up streets before pushing open the door to the pub. Should Helen have seen me, she would only have thought I was drinking too much again. There are some advantages to being thought of as a dysfunctional idiot, which, to be fair, I often am.

Martin was behind the bar, watching the racing with a paper and the sound turned down. He nodded to me. No over-friend-liness here in Little Hollow. I'd met him a few times when I came down to view the house, but his warmth had in no way increased.

'Eh, half-pint, please.' Lunchtime drinking, just like the old days. Journalism used to be all chats in the pub and door-stepping in the rain, now it was clickbait and trawling Instagram. A half wouldn't hurt me. I hopped up on the stool and he grudgingly put the paper down.

'Your missus was in the other day.'

'Oh?'

'She's been asking about the house. Who owned it before and that.'

Ah. So that's what she was up to – trying to find out about the poppet, I imagined. 'Yeah?' I'd had to tell him that I knew the house's history, or I wouldn't have been able to do my research.

Martin glowered at me. 'She doesn't know.' It wasn't a question. 'Who lived there.'

'I didn't see the point of worrying her, no. It's just a house, after all, no matter who used to own it.'

'Not to us.' There was a quiet seam of bitterness in his voice. 'Not so long ago, for all that.'

'You're sure there's nothing more you can tell me? About . . . ?'

'I told you. I only moved to the village around then. Hardly knew her.'

'Well, it's ours now. We'll do it up, and that'll be nicer for the village than some old pile going to rack and ruin.'

'I hear one of Bob's lads took a fall from your roof.'

'Yeah, that was rough. They don't use harnesses, you know! Just leap up there.'

'Bob says the tiles were unstable.'

'It's an old house. Look, it's awful what happened, but I had to assume they knew what they were doing.'

He grunted. 'You want to be careful is all. Bob's making noises.'

'What kind of noises?'

'That maybe there's a liability issue. Few quid in it for him.'

'That's crazy.' Was this the next thing – the village would turn against us even further, convinced we'd hurt one of their own? The selfish Londoners, smashing the place up, like some latter-day Tom and Daisy Buchanan. *They were careless people.* But we weren't. Helen was the most careful person I know. Of course she would dig into the history of the house; it had been stupid of me to think she wouldn't. I'd forgotten that the blank, uncurious fug of the past two years was not her natural state, just the result of extreme burnout. But at the very worst she'd learn she was living in a murderer's house. There was no way she could find out how I'd actually got the place.

'Thing is,' said Martin, deceptively casual, 'that house never was for sale, that I knew of.'

'It was a private sale.'

'Don't think so. All the Tresallicks, they had to swear to their great-grandma it would never go out of the family. Wise woman, she was – witchy. They said she'd put all kinds of . . . spells, protections, on the place. They'd never have sold it.' He fixed me with a stare. He couldn't possibly know.

'Look, I'm just trying to protect my wife. She had a rough time of it during Covid. She worked on the resus wards, lost a lot of patients. I wanted to take her to a nice place, but I didn't want to upset her by telling her the house's back story.'

He unbent slightly. 'Heroes, they are, the lot of them.'

'I just didn't want to worry her. It's a nice house – or it has potential – and she wanted to be near her mum. She's actually from here, you know, Helen. Well, from Devon.' To show we weren't out-of-towners, not entirely, despite my Home Counties accent.

He looked suspicious. 'What was her maiden name again?'

Don't tell him. I realised, and I didn't know why, I shouldn't reveal any more about Helen. 'Eh, she doesn't have a maiden name, mate. She's a doctor, why would she take mine?'

He withdrew then, muttering something, no doubt about the terrible encroachment of feminism.

'Don't mind Uncle Martin, he's such a grump.' I looked up to see a young woman behind the bar, with pink streaks in her hair. 'Did I hear you've moved into Janna Edwards' old house? You're Helen's husband?'

'Er, yeah.'

'That's so cool, that you live there.'

I blinked – I hadn't expected that reaction. 'You think so?'

'Well, yeah. She was a bona fide witch, you know. The real deal.'

'But – a convicted killer also, so there's that.' I said it as if it meant nothing to me.

She narrowed her eyes as she wiped around the pumps. 'Only if you believe she did it.'

'Oh – is that – do people think she might be innocent?' My heart was beating fast. At first, when I'd learned the truth, I had wanted to believe this – a miscarriage of justice, a terrible mistake. But her conviction had been so absolute, with such a long sentence, that I didn't hope for long. And she had confessed, hadn't she?

'There's no real evidence, you know? No witnesses. And the dead girls – well, she wasn't even there at the time, she always said she had nothing to do with that. It's circumstantial, at best. I've been listening to podcasts about it.'

Aha, a true-crime fan. I would have scorned them at one stage, and yet here I was trying to write just such a book. 'And the witchy stuff, you believe in it?'

'Of course. I do it too. Well, I'm just a baby witch, but I'm getting more followers on WitchTok all the time. I'm @TheTraineeWiccan.' I looked at her blankly. 'You know, WitchTok, it's part of TikTok.'

I had only the haziest idea what TikTok was. 'Right, right.' An idea occurred to me. 'Listen – sorry, what's your name?'

'Cara.' Martin's niece, I assumed.

'You didn't grow up here?' Her accent sounded Scottish, not Cornish.

'Nah, but we came here all the time, then when I left school Uncle Martin said I could live here for a bit. He's my dad's brother.'

'So you know people round here.' Not being local, I sensed there was a limit to what people would tell me. I was also a bit of a slouch when it came to true crime, not to mention witchcraft. 'You wouldn't be interested in a bit of research work, would you, Cara? I'm writing a book, you see. About the case. I'm a journalist.'

She nodded enthusiastically. 'God, that would be great, it's so boring here off-season. I can send you some podcasts too.' She fished her phone from her baggy jeans and held it out. 'Put your number in there.'

'Um – OK.' I did so, wondering if it might look dodgy to her glowering uncle. She couldn't be more than twenty. 'You really think she was innocent – Janna?' I still felt a tingle saying her name out loud.

'I think there's evidence that suggests it. It's the oldest trick in the book, isn't it, accuse a woman of witchcraft just because she can crush up a few herbs. But really, no one can know what happened out there in the woods. She shouldn't have got *fifty years*, either way. Even if she did kill him.'

I agreed – the punishment seemed extreme. 'Well, thanks for the info. I'll drop you a line, and we can work out payment and that.'

'It must be soooo spooky living out there,' she said wistfully. 'We used to break in as kids, but we never got past the hallway. Everyone said she'd curse us, from beyond.'

'No no, it's just an old house.' I sensed Cara would lose her mind if I told her about the evil doll in the wall.

I drained the rest of my drink and headed out. What would Helen say, if she knew what I was doing? The idea of losing her, or even of damaging our marriage, made me feel sick. But some terrible part of me, that shard of ice Graham Greene talks about, was already thinking how to work in a strand to the book about 'and then my marriage began to crumble under the strain of the secrets'.

◆ ◆ ◆

I made my way through the village, such as it was, and stared mournfully at the little café, shut up for the winter. I could have murdered a cortado, but the nearest one was probably twenty miles away. Soon I had come to the shoreline, and there was nothing left to look at. As the wind howled around me and churned the grey sea, I sheltered in a bus stand and rang Andy. As his picture flashed on screen, I realised I should have changed his name in my phone. A few years ago he had decided to go by his actual one, which was Anoj, feeling that a Tamil name was no longer the roadblock it might have been to success in journalism. Indeed, Roland the agent would probably have said it was an advantage. But I had always known him as Andy, since we'd met doing our MAs at City University, and the habit was hard to break.

His face appeared on my screen, and I saw he was in a bustling coffee shop, Beats on his ears, a cool leather jacket draped around his lean frame, and I was almost viscerally jealous. Despite getting married, to the sexy and fun KC, and having baby Lola, Andy has never lost his cool. He still has all the new vinyl, goes to the hot clubs, and knows the best place to get whatever cuisine is newly in (Mongolian, according to his last piece for *GQ*). He has byline after byline and is one of the few journalists who earns enough for a zone-2 mortgage. KC runs a baby yoga business or something like that. Meanwhile Helen and I had spent years in a crumbling rented flat, and she was working herself to death. And there was no baby Lola for us, not after years of trying.

I tried to put my jealousy aside. After all, we had a house now, and maybe the rest would follow. 'Hiya, mate.'

'Where are you, a wind tunnel?' The breeze was whistling hard in my cheapo headphones. I wanted some Beats but Helen said they were ridiculous.

'May as well be. Weather's a bit brisk off-season.'

'How's the escape to the country?'

'Well, the house is a bit – it needs work. But I'm writing.'

'That's brilliant.' Andy, more than anyone, had witnessed my increasing desperation with my career. He was sympathetic, and he tried to help, but it was hard to offer comfort when you had exactly the thing the other person wanted. The jealousy had come between us, stretching out our friendship. Maybe distance would help. 'So is it a long-read or . . .'

'I'm thinking a book.' Andy had already published two books, one about the experience of being British-Asian, and one about the history of Britpop, which I was wildly jealous of. He'd got to hang out with Liam Gallagher for a whole afternoon. But I had something now, something big. No one in the world could write the book I was sitting on.

'That's great – what about?'

'Ummm, still working it out. Kind of a personal thing. Memoir-ish.'

'Yeah, yeah, good market for that.' He was probably thinking I meant another mental health memoir. How I stayed in bed for a full week until my wife told me I stank and needed to have a shower or she'd give me a sponge bath. How I applied to work as a Deliveroo rider and got turned down. But no, I had something better than that. 'What does Helen think?' he said.

'Yeahhh, I didn't tell her yet. It's sort of . . . about the house. Partly at least.'

'Aha! The old move to the country thing – comic?'

'Not really.' Tonally, this was going to be hard to square. 'Maybe a bit more . . . true crime.'

'Yeah?' He sounded baffled, as well he might. That was a lot of different things to cram into one book.

I could tell him. The entire story, all the things I was keeping from Helen. But I wasn't ready for his confusion, his judgement at the fact I'd lied to my wife. How he might look at me differently once he knew the truth. 'Have you heard of the Janna Edwards case at all?'

'Rings a bell, maybe.' Andy would never admit he hadn't heard of something. I could hear clicking and knew he'd be googling it on his laptop as we spoke. 'Oh right. Triple murder in Cornish village – is this your village?'

'Yeah. Little Hollow.'

'And is this – wait, is it something to do with the house?'

'It was her house.'

'No shit. You've bought the house of a murderer?'

'Yeah.' A lie, but I couldn't have him knowing what Helen didn't. 'You think there's a story there?'

'You mean, how you found out you'd accidentally bought a murderer's house, that sort of thing?'

'That's the idea.' And the rest, my own unique link to it.

'I take it it wasn't accidental though.'

'Well. No. But it's a better story if I just discover it.'

'Does *Helen* know?'

89

'Um. Not yet. Look, I didn't want to worry her. You know she's been struggling.'

'I know, I know. But – hm. OK, mate. I'm sure you know what you're doing. What's your angle – reopening the case? There's something there, like she didn't do it after all?'

I wished I was sure. 'God, I don't know. She confessed to the first murder, so probably she did do it. But she always said she didn't kill the girls. And the man – well, she must have killed him for a reason, I figure. You don't just wake up one day and decide to murder someone.'

'No. Suppose not.'

Andy sounded unsure, and I was beginning to wish I hadn't mentioned it. 'Also I thought I could link in, you know, what happened to me. A literal witch hunt, and the fact people said she was a witch.'

I could hear Andy pause.

'What?' I asked, irritated.

'Oh, nothing. It's just a lot to take in.'

'You don't think that would work?'

'Oh, it would work. It's just . . .'

'What?'

'Well, it's a tricky tone to get right. So you don't seem like you're . . . well, like you're denying her experience. Emylia. What happened.'

'But I am denying it! She totally misunderstood what I was saying.'

'Right, right. But do you think people will believe it?'

'I thought you believed it, at least.' My tone had grown frosty.

'Course I do. I just mean – the public. The media.'

Weren't we both part of the media? Or he was, at least. Was he saying he didn't trust my account of what happened?

He said, 'Look, mate, it's so great you're writing again. And this is a hell of a story. Really groundbreaking. I just don't want to see you get hurt again.'

I was annoyed – he'd rained on my parade, and made me doubt that this book would be the magic salvation I had hoped for. 'Right.'

'Sorry, mate, I just . . .'

'It's fine, it's fine, early days and all that. How's you anyway, how's the fam?' Urgh, I hated myself for saying *fam*.

'Brilliant. Lola took her first steps! And KC's doing so good in the business.' Andy is a real wife guy. Helen and I used to secretly screenshot some of his tweets to each other for a laugh. When she still had time to go on Twitter, that was. KC is an Instagram influencer, her feed a cascade of yoga poses, baby pictures, and inspirational quotes. Carefully arranged messy bun, tight leggings, love and light. Despite that, I'm fond of her. 'Helen doing OK with the move?' said Andy.

'She's . . . well. Struggling a bit without work maybe. The house is worse than she thought, I guess. But it's going to be amazing when it's done. The builders have already started.' Then knocked down our kitchen and left, but I wasn't going to tell him that. I had to put a gloss on it, if only to convince myself I'd done the right thing moving us, leaving our London life. I wished it was me in that cool coffee shop, writing up a piece on new nightlife trends that would be printed on glossy paper in a magazine in every newsagent's in the country. A picture byline. A cute kid. Everything he had. But there was enough to go around, wasn't there? I didn't need to begrudge him.

I didn't want to talk to Andy any more. 'Better go, mate, got to get back to it. And it's starting to rain here.'

'Well, it looks absolutely gorgeous. Better not show KC – she's been on at me for years to get a country place. Think she wants to churn her own butter or something.' He laughed. It would take a nuclear attack to get him out of zone 2; I used to think I was the same. It turned out there were lots of things I hadn't known about myself.

We said our goodbyes and I hung up, looking round the rainy, shut-up village with a deflated feeling. There was just so little life around the place. I'd imagined sessions in the pub, film nights at the village hall, maypole dancing or some crap like that. But out of season, it seemed like everyone withdrew into their homes and pulled the curtains and watched TV. And our TV wasn't plugged in or unpacked. I wondered where Helen was. Perhaps I should have gone with her to see Mick, it had been rough the last time they met. I needed to not neglect her – Helen had saved me more times than I could remember. Hopefully, with this move to the country, I might have returned the favour.

◆ ◆ ◆

Janna Edwards was born in a village called Little Hollow, in Cornwall, in 1956. Nothing in her early life indicated the notoriety she would come to. She took care of her mother, who suffered from MS, she worked in the local primary school as a teaching assistant, and in her spare time she made herbal potions to heal a variety of ailments, based on recipes learned from her grandmother, Alice Tresallick. There were never any Tresallick men, I was told by one villager. They just didn't last. Janna's father, the Edwards from her name, had been around long enough to marry her mother, Eve, but he'd run off when Janna was five, and everyone thought of Janna as a Tresallick woman. Strong, capable. She was said to be able to cure gout and insomnia, deliver babies and lambs, and could even offer spells for love. Revenge, some said, as well, though she didn't like to do it. Ill-wishing rebounds, she always said. She read the Tarot, she had crystals, she did full-moon rituals and cast horoscopes. Low-level witchiness of a kind that has once again become popular (check out WitchTok, if you want to feel a thousand years old). But when Janna went to prison for a triple murder, it all came out. Satanic rituals, screamed the papers. Blood sacrifice. Human offerings. Perhaps because Janna never gave a motive. She never said why she followed a man into the woods around Little Hollow, on a sunny Halloween in October, 1986, and slit his throat. The case has remained shrouded in mystery and rumour.

This book is going to change all that. And I hope, in the process, to illuminate how Janna Edwards, who everyone knew as a caring, practical, slightly other-worldly young woman, could have committed such brutal crimes.

Up in my office, I sat back from the Mac, realising I was breathing hard. It was a long time since words had flown from my fingers like this, and I could see a clear road ahead of me to proceed. I'd downloaded the trial transcripts before we left London, which had given me a list of possible interviewees. Now I'd met Cara, I could send her over the names of people I wanted to track down, and then I could focus on the actual words, the soul of the book. Cara's hints had sparked something in me, a complicated feeling I recognised as hope. The idea that not everyone condemned Janna, not everyone thought she'd done such terrible things. It was true she'd always said she didn't kill the girls – their deaths could have been an accident. But the other – the man with his throat cut? Was it possible she had a reason for murder? Self-defence, or something else? Or was there another explanation – there was someone she was shielding?

I found I was shaking with energy, excitement, agitation. Yes, it was painful stuff to write about, and my life was never going to be the same again if this did get published. I didn't know how Helen would react, and I imagined how I would plead my case: *I had to do this. I just needed to understand it.* It would dig up difficult memories for the locals too, things they had tried to forget. Perhaps we wouldn't be able to stay here, even. But I would cross all those bridges when I came to them; for now I just had to keep on writing.

> *Adam Jeffries was also not someone you'd expect to make headlines. A smart boy, born on the Kent coast, he had gone off to university in Bristol and then back to London to train as a teacher. He had married a girl there and soon been appointed headteacher of a primary school in Camden. That's where things get mysterious, though – he worked there for only one term before accepting a lower-paid job at the small primary school in Little Hollow. That was where his path crossed with that of Janna Edwards, the teaching assistant, a fateful conjunction that would lead to both their lives being destroyed.*

I stopped and took a swig of my now-cold instant coffee (the machine was still in a box somewhere) and wondered was I overplaying it a bit. Fateful conjunction? Oh well, I could always fix it later.

◆ ◆ ◆

The first time I met Helen, I didn't remember her. She likes to tease me about it, that she knew right away I was 'the one', and I didn't even recall it. I was very drunk, in my defence. It was at UCL, where she was studying medicine and I was reading English, so our paths really should not have crossed like they did. I was in the student union bar, having just won a debate about whether or not the UK should have taken part in the Iraq War. I'd won resoundingly, and if I'd not quite been carried from the chamber on people's shoulders, I had certainly been showered in applause, back slaps, and shots, from the leftie liberal students. Not that it made any difference what I thought, some chippy kid who wore an old army jacket and grew a Che Guevara beard and didn't see the irony in this – we were at war anyway. But the point is, I was hammered. Swaying vaguely in a corner to some Oasis, my debating partner Matt gone to the loo or to buy more shots or something. That's when she came up to me.

I remembered it later, when she jogged my memory, when I realised how significant the moment was for the rest of my life. A faint pressure on my arm as someone leaned past me to the bar. The brief softness of her breasts in a flannel shirt – Helen has always dressed down, even then. A cloud of red hair, minimal make-up, a smell of roses.

'George, isn't it?'

'Umm-hmm.' I could barely speak at this point, so according to Helen I just gave her finger-guns, dropping my plastic cup of beer in the process. She laughed. I remember that sound, clear and fresh as a bell.

'Like that, is it? Well, George – we'll talk another time.'

I ended the night throwing up in a flowerbed and losing my shoes – all in all, an excellent time. The next morning, I was in the canteen attempting to sober up before my 9 a.m. seminar on Chaucer, with two sausage-and-ketchup sandwiches and four coffees poured into a big metal travel mug, when someone came up and sat beside me. Cloudy red hair, smell of roses.

'Morning! How's the head?' I must have frowned in faint recognition because she laughed that same bell-like laugh. 'You don't remember me, do you?'

'I – maybe vaguely. Sorry, I was pissed.'

'And the man of the hour, apparently.'

That day she wore navy cords and a college sweatshirt. Most of the girls at uni were quite glamorous, with shiny hair and big eyelashes, so she kind of stood out to me. Like a statue of a saint, pale and solid, her hair a corona around her.

'I'm Helen, anyway.'

'George.'

'Well, I know *that*.' The way she said it, as if I was someone important, turned my heart over.

'What are you studying?' I asked her.

'I'm a medic. Got a nine a.m. lecture, so.' She was eating Bran Flakes and a banana. Always the health nut to my slob. I wondered then, and I wonder still, what she saw in me. 'You?' she asked.

'English. And yes, I've heard all the jokes about why does the English student not pull the curtains in the morning.'

'So they have something to do in the afternoon?'

'That's the one.'

Her laugh. I wanted to hear it all the time. Even in my sweaty-armpitted, greasy-mouthed, existential-horror hangover, she was lifting me up. She stood then, knocking back her tea in one gulp. 'Well. I have to go and chop up a body now.'

'Was it something I said, or . . . ?'

Another laugh. 'See you around, George.'

I had to see her again. It was a big university, it would be easy to miss her altogether, and suddenly I couldn't bear the thought. 'Wait – are you at the student union a lot or . . .'

She turned, holding her satchel of books, the light from the high windows falling on her hair. 'Sometimes. There's a lot of medical socials, you know. Lot of drinking. Keeps us busy.'

'There's a gig Friday. British Sea Power. I have tickets.' I was going to bring Matt, but screw him.

'Should I have heard of them? I don't have much time for music.'

I'd always thought I needed an indie girl who would spar with me over who was musically better, Oasis or Blur, sit on my shoulders at gigs, ring her eyes in dark liner and cry to Eliot Smith. Whereas Helen's appreciation of music basically ended with the Spice Girls. 'Well, I have two tickets. If they ever give you time off from grave-robbing.'

She smiled. At the time I didn't understand that smile, the slow, almost sad curve of it, and it would be a long, long time before I did. 'I don't know if it's a good idea.'

'Come on, what could go wrong? If you hate it you can leave after the first song, though heads up, that might be twenty minutes long.'

She nodded slowly. 'Alright. If you don't mind me not knowing any of the music.'

She was so beautiful to me then, so endlessly fascinating, and she still is. All of this was for her, even if she might not realise it right away.

◆ ◆ ◆

The day after she went to Devon, Helen was pale and withdrawn, said something about driving to Penzance to look at wallpaper. 'Should I go to the hospital as well, see Lukas?'

'Who?' My mind was elsewhere.

She shot me a look. 'The builder. Who fell off our roof.'

'Oh. I think not, to be honest. Don't think they'd want us round there. Also, it might be an admission of guilt or something?' I thought of what Martin had said.

She bit her lip. 'You really think they'll sue?'

'I hope not.'

'I'll have to ask Lou, see if she has any advice.'

Helen's best friend is a lawyer, though so scatterbrained it has always been a mystery to me how she manages to hold down a job. 'Good idea.' I didn't have space in my head to worry about the builders, though I felt bad about it, obviously, and relived a sick lurch every time I thought of how he'd fallen. Running to the window, always too late to stop it.

'Are you going out today?' She saw me pulling on my trainers.

'Yeah, just some research.'

'Oh.' Her eyes searched my face, as if looking for answers. She wouldn't ask about the book though, that much I knew.

Waving her off in the car, I headed down to the village again, glad of the dorky raincoat she'd made me buy. It may not have been Andy's cool distressed leather, but I would have frozen to death in that. The place was no livelier today – I spotted a few walkers shivering on the beach, one or two bravely eating ice creams from the pokey shop and post office, that surely couldn't sell enough boxes of fudge to keep going through the winter. I didn't imagine there was currently much call for buckets and spades either, though the cheerfully coloured windbreakers might come in handy. Such a very British concept, a screen to keep the gale off on the beach. In other countries they simply wouldn't go to the beach in such weather.

Since Helen had taken the car, I had to walk to the site of the murder. The last murder, I should say, if you included the two girls. Personally I thought that was a grey area, and Janna should never have been charged with those killings, where there was so much doubt around what happened, if the deaths were even deliberate or not. The actual murder, the throat-cutting, supposedly satanic one, that took place in the woods outside Little Hollow, perhaps a mile away from the village. Far enough to tramp in the intermittent rain and wind.

I entered the woods on to the marked footpath, quickly swallowed up by wet, dripping trees. A safe green haven, the only sounds the rain and the birds. But it hadn't been safe for Adam Jeffries, that Halloween evening in 1986. Of course, a lot had been made of the date too – Celtic feasts, sacrifices, Samhain. Myself, I think it was just a coincidence. It was the last Friday of term. Things had come to a head and needed to be dealt with. I tried to imagine how it had been for Janna, following him deeper and deeper into the trees. She had the knife with her, perhaps in her hand, perhaps strapped to her leg under her long swishy skirt – she had no bag and no jacket. Feeling it with each step. Solid, heavy, perhaps a little sore, but in a good way. A knife to cut her fear.

The woods were confusing, the paths poorly marked, and my phone didn't work at all, just showed a blue dot lost in a sea of white. I should have brought a compass. Not that I knew how to use a compass. I bet Helen did. She used to do Girl Guides as a kid, a fact I like to tease her about. Eventually, I spotted a very small brown sign with an arrow on it, and after following the leaf-mulched path for a few minutes, a clearing opened up. There it was. The Devil's Altar.

Of course, it was not really an altar. It was only a large, flat rock, and the 'ancient' carvings on the side were just Victorian graffiti, but it looked spooky in the low green light. Its smooth grey surface was slick with rain. That night, it had been slick with blood. The papers said she had tied him down, but she hadn't – there was nowhere to fasten ropes. She had simply drugged him, using her vast knowledge of plants. They'd found several compounds in his Thermos of tea, and it wasn't clear how they'd got in there, if she'd put a potion in that day at school, or slipped it in before the killing, while he wasn't looking, if they'd spent some time talking before she took out her knife. It was premeditated anyway. She had taken the knife with her, so she must have planned it. She had got him flat on the stone somehow, and she had cut his throat. He was dead within seconds.

The mutilations to his face and hands – that made less sense. It was possible some animals had got to him in the hours he'd lain there, while the police had to be called from Penzance, and the small local force tried to figure out what to do. Or perhaps she had marked him. She never said either way.

In the confusion after the murder, Adam Jeffries' wife was not contacted until almost eight that night at their home in a different hamlet five miles away, but she had not felt any concern, no inkling of the danger he was in. It had been a half-day at school, the last of term, and he had planned to camp in the woods. He loved the outdoors, often sleeping out on the moors and crags. Leaving her at home with their young daughter, who was two. Did she not mind his absences, Margaret Jeffries? The wife was a blank spot in my book, who would have to be filled in, assuming I could find out where she'd gone when she moved away from Little Hollow. A mystery, one of many, about the case.

I snapped to myself – I had been writing the book in my head again. It was good to feel so absorbed, but I suddenly realised I was miles from anywhere, all alone. That was when I heard the rustle. Something in the branches. Maybe a bird, maybe a deer. Maybe a person.

'Hello?' I called.

Nothing. Then an explosion of birds from a tree.

'Jesus!'

I stumbled back with sudden, stupid fear. It was just the countryside. No eyes watching from trees, no mysterious figurines hanging from branches. This wasn't *The Blair Witch Project* – there was a main road a twenty-minute walk away. Still, I could work this in, the powerful atmosphere of the place. I took my phone out and snapped a few pictures, vaguely thinking that if the book sold they might send a photographer to the scene. Was I getting ahead of myself? Probably, but it was good to have a taste of hope for the first time in a long time.

◆ ◆ ◆

The Devil's Altar was not the only crime scene in Little Hollow. The other place I had found by piecing together various reports in the local papers – I'd been right to keep up my newspaper archive subscription, though it was an expense – and looking at house sale records from around the time. Unsurprisingly, the Monkton parents had moved away right after it happened. Well, you would, wouldn't you? The site was an unassuming bungalow set in a small cul de sac outside the village. Pebble-dashed walls, wheelie bins in the gardens. Everyone thought a house in Cornwall meant some beautiful cottage with a woodburning stove, but there were a lot of ugly ones too. Number sixteen. I hovered on the street, surreptitiously snapping the odd picture. As I stood there, a woman came out with a child on a scooter. I didn't know much about kids, but it was a girl and maybe five or six. In a school uniform anyway, talking loudly about something Miss Crawford had done. My ears pricked up – I knew that was the new headteacher of the village school, the post Adam Jeffries had once held. I needed to talk to her next.

'Well, it sounds like he deserved it, if he pinched the girl,' said the mother, her eyes flicking to me. I thumbed through my phone as if looking for an address – maybe she'd think I was delivering a parcel. Or maybe this happened a lot, when you lived in a murder house. Perhaps they were well aware of the house's history and didn't care, or they didn't know a thing about it. She looked about thirty, not even born when these events unfolded. Time kicks dust over even the worst tragedies.

In the late eighties, number sixteen had been more run-down, the doors and windows still cheap PVC ones, the roof crumbling, garden untidy. The girls had gone to Grace Monkton's house that day because her parents both worked, Dad in a warehouse in Newlyn, Mum cleaning holiday lets, so the place was empty. The other girl, Lucy Fillane, she was a bit posher. Dad was a lawyer in St Ives. Mum didn't work. At the time Lucy died her mother was giving the two younger children their tea at the kitchen table, less than five hundred metres away. Lucy had said she was at Grace's, since they had a half-day off school, so her mother wasn't worried. It was a safe village. What could possibly happen there?

This would have taken place around the same time Jeffries' throat was being slit. The girls drank the potion – the poison – mixed in with orange squash, I believe Kia-Ora. To mask the bitterness, maybe. I wonder if they toasted each other, giggled a bit. Made a wish. There's no way to know, because by the time Grace's mother came home and searched the house for them, they were already dead. Mrs Monkton looked out of Grace's bedroom window and saw something white in the grass. It was her daughter's hand. The girls were stretched out like Romeo and Juliet, the glasses of orange and poison fallen from their hands.

The contents matched those of a bottle discarded near Adam Jeffries' body, and the compounds found in his Thermos. A brown medicinal bottle, labelled in neat writing – *To attract love and affection*. Janna's writing, it was soon determined. Her prints were all over the bottle. But how did the girls get hold of it, that was the crux of it. Janna maintained they had stolen it from her house when they came to visit her the week before. She worked at their

102

school, and the children were in the habit of playing in her large, overgrown garden. Had they drunk it by mistake, thinking it a fun prank? Or had someone given it to them? How then had the bottle ended up in the woods with Janna, with Adam? She must have taken it with her. It contained enough digitalis to kill ten grown men. Lucy and Grace were barely eleven, slight and delicate girls. They would have been dead within seconds. Was it a joint suicide? I don't think the police even considered this possibility. They were kids, with everything to live for. Most likely it was a game, a girlish hope that someone or someones would fall in love with them. They couldn't have known the danger. But as it was, their bodies were found just before Adam Jeffries was, and Janna Edwards was charged with their murder as well as his, which was why she was still in prison over thirty years later. The murder of two young children, the satanic aspects – this all stacked up against her. Even if it wasn't true.

I realised I had to get moving – there was a twitch of curtains from the house behind me, and I didn't want to rub people up the wrong way. Not yet, anyway. I set off to climb the huge hill home. To Janna's house.

Helen was there when I got back, and no sign of the builders. She was wearily sweeping the floor clear of a fresh layer of dust and dirt, as the inadequate tarpaulin they'd tacked over the wall billowed in the wind. It couldn't have been more than twelve degrees in the living room.

'Hi.'

She didn't ask where I'd been, and I didn't ask her. I had a sense we were both burrowing into the case, but from different angles. I couldn't tell her yet what I knew.

Then she surprised me by saying, 'George. Do you think we should move out?'

'Already?' I didn't understand. 'We just got here.'

She gestured to the wall. 'It's not exactly liveable like this, is it? It's freezing, the boiler only works some of the time . . . When are they going to fix it all?'

'I texted him, but . . .' I shrugged to indicate the silence of Bob the Builder. 'He's probably taken up with Lukas.'

'Well, that doesn't work. You'll have to call him, or even go round there. We can't live with a hole in the wall, not in this weather.'

'I could try boarding it up.' I could hear the dubious tone of my own voice. I doubted I'd be able to undertake such a task.

Helen just looked at me. 'I don't like it here, George. Even before they knocked the wall down, before the accident. It's . . . well, I heard in the village the house had kind of a spooky history.'

'Most old houses do,' I said casually, bending down with the dustpan to pick up her sweepings.

'Do they have voodoo dolls in the walls too? Some kind of, I don't know, laboratory in the cellar, birds getting in and dying? It's just . . . if it's going to be this much hassle, the rebuild, is it even worth it? Maybe we should sell up, cut our losses.'

If we sold the place it would definitely come out that I had been lying to Helen for months now.

I said, 'We'd lose a lot of money.' Helen did not like to waste money.

She shot me a look. 'Because you already paid the builders.'

'That's just how it works. I promise, I'll call him tomorrow. Go round there if he doesn't pick up. It'll be OK.' I just needed time to write the book. Another month or so and I'd have broken its back. I played a trump card then, and I knew it wasn't fair, but I did it anyway. 'I'm writing so well here, you know. It works for me.'

She nodded sadly. 'I can see that. It's just – I can't bear this dirt and disorder.'

'It's always like that when you renovate. Remember Pete and Mary? And now their place is beautiful. If you really hate Cornwall after it's done, we'll flip it, find somewhere else. Go back to London!'

She bit her lip. 'I should be about for Mum, I suppose. At least this is closer.'

'Right. How was she the other day?' I realised I had forgotten to ask.

'Oh, the same.'

'And Mick?'

'Yeah, he was – it was fine. We had a chat.'

'I'm glad.'

She sighed, resting the brush against the wall. 'I don't know what we can eat for dinner, with the kitchen in bits. I'm not even that hungry, I feel sick with all this chaos.'

'I could make us pasta, tuna, and mayonnaise? Ideally eaten straight out of the saucepan to save washing up? You used to love that.'

'Back in 2005, maybe,' she said, but she smiled, and I knew she was thinking of those early days when we first met, when we were so happy nothing else mattered.

Not that we got together right away, of course. She made me work for it, as I like to remind her. After our first date and the hours we spent talking in my room, I had waited to see her again with unseemly impatience, jumping a little every time I saw a girl with red hair around the university. Matt asked me what the hell was wrong with me. 'Love, my friend,' I'd said grandiosely.

'You've met this girl twice, mate.'

'Three times! Admittedly, I don't remember the first time, but there you go.'

He shook his head. 'Pathetic.' And I indeed felt a bit pathetic when Helen texted me to cancel our second date, claiming she had too much studying to do. I'd tried to laugh it off, but it made me morose. Why had she cancelled? Did she not feel something between us, like I did? Because I had always been sure about her, from that first moment.

Hoping to remind her of how I'd won her over back then, I put my arms round her waist and rested my head on her shoulder until she stopped sweeping. 'It's going to be alright, you know.'

'Our house has a hole in it.'

'I'll sort it. Please, just try and trust me, my love.'

I could feel her soften in my arms. But it wasn't fair, what I was asking, because why should she trust me when I was lying to her?

That night, I didn't sleep well, which wasn't like me. Usually I can sleep far too much, all day if I allow myself. But my mind was full with Janna, the house, the builder, the secrets I was keeping. Beside me, Helen was asleep, her face softened in rest, curled in on herself in a ball. I knew she hadn't been sleeping well either since we got here, so I was glad to see it.

The moon was bright. She'd been telling me we needed new curtains, maybe a blackout blind, but it was so far down the list of priorities I hadn't done anything about it. Perhaps I could get one and install it, show her I was a good husband. But I hadn't the faintest idea how to do such a thing.

I got up to pull the thin curtain over and that was when I saw them. Just like Helen had said, there was someone in the garden, watching us, at the edge of the lawn. I ducked back, my heart racing. It was a person, wasn't it? She hadn't imagined it. A dark shape among the trees that bordered our property. I should go out there and confront them, ask why they were spying on us. A disgruntled villager, maybe? Some local perv? I waited and waited, and eventually I realised I wasn't going to go out there. I was too much of

106

a coward to confront them, like with so many other things in my life. So I went back to bed.

I got up before Helen the next day, and locked myself in the office. I was worried she might see it in my face that I too was becoming afraid of the house. In the daylight, sun on the sea in the distance and the trees shaking off rain, it all seemed stupid. I just had to keep going with the book. My next mission was to go to the school, the one where both Janna and Adam Jeffries had worked. Where they'd met. Do you get a frisson, I wonder, when you meet your murderer for the first time? A sense that this person is going to be your doom? Of course you don't, but Janna might have believed it, with all her witchiness. The big question everyone asked, everyone assumed at the time was: were they having an affair? But Janna had always said, no, they weren't. She wanted his wife to know that they weren't. She even said this in court.

So why did she kill him then?

She never gave an answer to that, no motive, no defence, and so she was still in prison, almost thirty-six years on.

The school was very old and very small. In Janna's day it still had open fires, even in classes full of five-year-olds. For a while the school had almost closed, but a new influx of Londoners, seeking a better life, had swollen the ranks and now it was full again, with a hundred pupils, twice what it had in 1986. Adam Jeffries had been the head back then, teaching a combined class of ten- and eleven-year-olds, while the younger kids were taken by a Mrs Jenkins, long dead sadly, and a Miss Bodger, Susan Bodger, who had moved away not long after the murders. They had both given evidence at the trial, as had Nancy Dunne, the school secretary. I was doing my best to track Nancy and Susan down, along with Margaret Jeffries, or whatever she was called now. Janna had helped out in the school as a sort of floating support worker, since she had no formal qualifications. But she practically ran the place, several people had told the court.

I purposely went down at 3.45 p.m., when Helen had gone off for a walk, and when I judged the children would have left for the day but the teachers might be clearing up. In the eighties, there wasn't the same distrust of adults around children, but now people were on red alert for scruffy men hanging about outside playgrounds. I knocked on the glass-bubbled door of the school and saw a short corridor, hung with kids' paintings, and leading off it several small classrooms, mobiles hanging from the ceiling, tiny tables and chairs, bright yellow walls. A nice place. Hard to believe it could be associated with something so bad.

The door was opened by a woman in a cardigan and knee-length skirt. She was surprisingly young, about thirty perhaps, and mixed race, which I was also surprised to see in Cornwall, though I suppose I shouldn't have been.

'Yes?' That mixture of hostility and impatience that so often accompanies a lone adult in a children's space.

I explained I was writing a book about the murders, and had recently bought a house in the village. I watched her expression change – shut down, no intention of speaking to me at all – then warm up a fraction as she realised I actually lived here.

'Down from London?'

'Well, yes. But my wife is from here originally.'

The mention of a wife usually helped too. Wholesome, unthreatening. 'Right. Well, obviously I wasn't around when it happened, so I can't tell you much.'

'You didn't grow up here?'

'In Portsmouth. Moved here for teacher training and sort of couldn't leave.'

'Yes, I can see that, it's very beautiful. So is anyone around who might remember Janna – any of the kids from Grace and Lucy's class?'

She didn't flinch at the names – she was an outsider, after all, and it wouldn't mean as much to her. 'Mmm, I'm not sure. There are some old class photos up in the teachers' lounge – there were fewer children in those days, of course.'

'Can I sneak a look?'

'I suppose so. The school won't come off in a bad light in what you're writing?'

'Ah. So, it's actually all in the public domain – that means anybody can write whatever they want about the case. My concern is to make sure it doesn't hurt the village in any way. Or the school.' God, I still had it. That slippery journalist ability to lie on command. 'So can I . . . ?'

'Alright.'

'It's Miss Crawford, is it?'

'Irina, yes.' I wondered how a young woman like her got by in such a small, closed-off place. If she had a boyfriend or husband or someone. I tried not to think this, put it aside so it wouldn't show on my face. It wasn't safe to ask someone these things nowadays, as I knew only too well.

The teachers' lounge was a tiny room with space for four chairs and a microwave. On the walls were framed pictures of successive intakes of children, scrubbed up and smiling. Bigger groups now, but in the eighties there had only been ten, twelve to a year. I found the right one – 1986. There was a man posing at the end of a row, arms folded – Adam Jeffries. A good-looking man, with thick dark hair and blue eyes that pierced even from the sun-faded photograph. Three middle-aged women in the picture, dumpy in ill-fitting dresses. And on the end, fair hair shining even in the poorly executed shot – Janna Edwards. I caught my breath. She looked like a film star, taken off guard by the paparazzi perhaps. She wasn't smiling, and instead had a watchful, almost hunted look. A picture of the victim and the killer, and this had never leaked to the papers? It was perfect for my book. I leaned forward to read the names of the kids printed underneath. Grace Monkton. Lucy Fillane. I snapped a picture on my phone before the teacher could tell me not to, of the girls and the other eight pupils in the class. Surely some of them would still be around the area.

'Thanks! I'll let you get on, I'm sure you have a lot to do.'

'Alright.' She looked unsettled, as if she'd allowed me a liberty, but she wasn't quite sure what it was.

I paused for a moment in the corridor, and tried to imagine them walking over this same ground, standing in these rooms, those living, breathing people, one now long buried, one rotting in prison. In the warm, bright space, beside the 'kindness wall' that was so full of simple goodness and hope, I found that I could not.

I made my way back along the blustery road into town, turning my face from the wind that whipped the sea white. Another week here and I'd have sandblasted off my skin down to the epidermis. I really had to buy some proper outdoor gear, as Helen had suggested, but I was being stubborn, trying to hold on to my London self. Even though that man had died long ago, together with my career. But it was OK. I had a plan.

I'd discovered there was a café of sorts operating out of the village hall – urns and home-baked treats laid out on paper plates. I went in and took my laptop from my rucksack, though I could feel the disapproving and curious looks from the other clientele, mainly mothers with children. What is it about having offspring that makes people so high and mighty? And they'd better get used to

MacBooks if they wanted the remote-working revolution to bring life back to their dying village. All the same, looking at the babies, I couldn't help wondering. Would Helen be happy if we could have this too, after so many years? I wasn't sure I'd be much of a father, but she wanted it more than anything, I knew she did, though she'd never said. Perhaps it was time to get some help, though that would cost money we didn't have. Maybe if I sold the book. *When* I sold the book, I should think – that's what Andy would do. Manifest it all into existence, as KC was always urging him to do.

I paid for a tea in a plastic cup and a traybake studded with marshmallows. Helen would shake her head at the sugar, but I had to have some vices, and it was weeks since I'd had a drink. Well, a proper drink. The odd half in the pub didn't count, that was essential research. Pub landlords always know everything in a small village.

I enlarged the picture I'd taken at the school and began googling the names of the children one by one. All Anglo-Saxon names, mostly Cornish – it wasn't a diverse place in those days, but now I looked about me and saw several non-white faces. I found nothing at all online until one name on the list – Lisa McSweeney. There was a website for someone of the same name, who practised 'massage and reiki therapy', and she lived just outside Little Hollow. There was no information on the site, and no picture of her, but that must surely be the same Lisa who'd been at school with Grace and Lucy. The dead girls. A class of ten, and two of them gone – that must have caused terrible trauma among the survivors.

Caught up in excitement, I turned to WhatsApp. I saw Mum had sent me a message – *hello darling can you call when you get a minute, LOL xxx,* plus the sticking-out-tongue emoji that she had inexplicably embraced in her later years. I'd deal with that later. I dialled the number on Lisa McSweeney's website, earning myself a few more black looks from the café-goers, who seemed a right bunch of Luddites. Voicemail, the standard network one.

I stammered, 'Um, hi, Lisa, I'd love to make an appointment for, eh – back pain, I've got serious back pain. Could you text me sometime, maybe?'

I reeled off my number, even though she would have it from my call, and hung up before I realised I hadn't said my name. Oh, well.

To reward myself for my hard day's work, I ate my traybake in one bite, wiping chocolatey fingers off on the meagre napkin before positioning them over the keys and going back into the story. I consulted my plan – still had to find the wife, Mrs Jeffries, and persuade more people from the village to talk. If I could get hold of the policeman who'd arrested Janna, that would be good background colour – he'd lived somewhere round here. Then of course the big one, the interview I hadn't been able to face, even assuming she would talk to me – Janna herself. Did I have the guts to contact her? I honestly wasn't sure.

When I got home, I was feeling quite pleased with myself. The downstairs was still a disaster zone – wind blowing right through the wall, everything cold and dirty – but I could see the glow of light from upstairs, where Helen had set up a temporary living space in the spare room. She was good at things like that, making places seem welcoming. I remembered the first time I'd seen her university room, after months of trying, with its fairy lights and floral bedding – it hadn't even occurred to me to buy my own linen. It had taken me a bloody long time to see that room – after our first date, to the British Sea Power gig, Helen had backed off, and I hadn't seen her for another few weeks. Texts ignored, total silence.

I've always wondered if she had someone else on the go at the same time, though she swears not. I'm a persistent guy – you have to be, in journalism – but I'm not a creep. I was about to give up when she somehow came back to me. Sometimes I think about how easy it would have been to let it go, to never be with Helen, and it brings me out in a cold sweat.

Now she was on a big cushion on the floor with her phone, and I recognised the quick movement she made as what you do when you want to hide something on your screen from your partner. It can be innocuous – a gift for them, or a stupid clickbait article you're wasting time reading – or it can be something else. I'd caught a glimpse of what her screen said – Mental Health Courses – well, that was good, she was looking for what to do next in her career – but then why was her face so stricken?

'What is it?' I asked. 'Why do you look so . . . ?'

She'd found out. I had been waiting for this, the bolt of fear automatic. Oh God. I was already marshalling my excuses.

'Um . . . have you been on Twitter today?'

I relaxed a fraction. She wasn't angry at me, she was concerned for me. But wait, that meant something was wrong. 'No, why?'

'I . . . there's been an article. About – what happened.'

'What?' That must have been why Mum messaged. She had a Google Alert set up for me.

Helen held her phone out to me. 'I screenshotted it.' I took it, holding it awkwardly in front of me. It took ages to load, the reception terrible, as always. It was a piece in the *Guardian* about 'When Journalists Become the Story'. The guy who'd made up quotes from Bowie; the one who'd been murdered and dismembered – that seemed in poor taste; others who'd been taken hostage. And there was me. George Sanderson. *Hit the headlines in early 2020 when pop star Emylia (15 at the time) accused him of inappropriate behaviour in an interview.*

The wind was knocked from me. I handed the phone back before I dropped it. 'Oh.'

'Look, it's nothing, just a footnote in a longer piece.'

'How did you even . . . ?' Helen doesn't go on Twitter, of course, she's much too sensible.

'Someone sent me it. It's nothing. You and I know what really happened.'

I knew. But it didn't matter how much I protested I'd been joking, that I'd been referring to a British thing Emylia didn't understand, because she was from Bible Belt America, that she'd taken me out of context. She'd still gone public with it, complained in another interview about older male journalists asking her uncomfortable questions, and she had mentioned my paper by name, so everyone knew it was me. God, that day. Summoned into the office of my editor, finding him with the same look on his face Helen had now, only angrier, feeling my stomach plummet to my knees. The interview in a rival paper making its way round the internet, right at the height of Me Too. Other journalists, male and female, weighing in to say how awful I was. People I'd considered friends. Andy hadn't joined in, at least, but then he hadn't defended me publicly either. My disgrace, the loss of everything I'd built up for ten years. *Well, we can't send you on interviews now*, my editor said. And a journalist who can't do interviews isn't much use at all.

I'd gone home, picking up my satchel and jacket in a kind of daze. I didn't want to bother Helen at work, where she was probably busy saving lives. When she came home, many hours later, she found me sitting on the sofa, still holding the satchel. In shock. Opening up Twitter had felt like the most frightening thing I'd ever done, and sure enough I had a thousand notifications.

So stupid. A throwaway comment to a teenage girl – ironically about whether other men were sleazy to her, that 'countdown to legal' timer the *Sun* once ran on Emma Watson and so on – and she had misunderstood and I was now branded a pervert, an abuser. Lumped in with rapists and paedophiles. This was the modern world – you could climb and climb, but one tiny slip and you were plummeting to earth, and everyone else climbing with you just watching without stretching out a hand to save you. They would clamour to take your place, even.

Helen is not an online person. She hadn't reacted at first, made me explain it to her over and over, as I ranted and paced and even cried. It wasn't *fair*. That was what most got to me. I didn't deserve it. In the end she had nodded, and I saw she had weighed it up and believed me. I wasn't a secret sleaze, I was still her husband, who she trusted. Without that support, I couldn't have gone on, I truly believe that.

'So what do we do?' she'd said.

'God knows. I can't post a rebuttal, I'll just look petty.'

'Can you say it was taken out of context?'

'Yeah, but – well, it's out there now. People believe it, they're too lazy to question it or look up what really happened. And everyone's so bloody keen to show they're pro-women they're piling on to condemn me.'

'She's fifteen?' Helen was staring at a picture of Emylia, dressed up for an awards ceremony in make-up and jewels, looking at least twenty.

'It was just a bit of banter, that's all. I forgot bloody Americans have no sense of humour.'

Even as I blustered, a snake of doubt had slithered in. Was I wrong to say those things to her? Had I over-assumed her maturity, because of her poise and success and grown-up clothes? She was only fifteen, after all. I supported the Me Too movement, of course I did, I piled on to condemn whoever it was that had slipped up. Did that mean I really was guilty too, if the mob had now come for me?

115

Helen looked at me then, frank and appraising. 'I'll ask you this once. Do you swear to me there's nothing more to come out – no one else with a story about you, however small? Flirting, or touching, or . . . more "banter", as you call it?'

I stared at her. 'Helz, journalism runs on banter. I can't tell you everyone I've joked with in ten years!'

'But nothing like this.'

'I . . .' That was the worst part, I didn't even know. I was replaying every interaction I'd had over the course of my entire career. 'Not that I can think of.'

But she took a breath and stood up, as if deciding something. 'Alright. I'm on your side.' But the implication was there – *unless there's something else.* And there hadn't been, and maybe I could have pulled it back once everyone had forgotten, but then it was Covid, and lockdown, and journalism was falling apart, and since I'd been fired at exactly the wrong time it was that much harder to get back in. And now here it was, raked up again. The last thing I needed was to be in the news, at least before the book was finished.

Now, I felt something cool on the back of my neck – Helen had stood up and put her hand there, her healing hand. 'Come on. We're out of that world now. Who cares what people say on Twitter?'

But I had to care, unless I admitted I would never work in journalism again, and instead became a windsurfing instructor or something disgustingly outdoorsy. She was right to remind me that there was a world outside the London media bubble, however. That most people hereabouts would never even have heard of Emylia, let alone the journalist she'd accused of something vague. If my editor had liked me more, if I hadn't been so expensive and so bolshy, if he hadn't had a mate lined up for my job, he would have fought for me, maybe, and it would have blown over. As it was, he'd pried my fingers off the ledge I was hanging on to, and once you've fallen all the way down, it's so much harder to get back up there.

I buried my face in her shoulder now, breathing in the clean smell of her, shampoo and soap, and I realised from her warmth how distant she had been the last few days. I had to be careful, because if I lost Helen, there was no point to any of this. I needed to tell her the truth, but I also needed to finish the book, and find out what I could about the Janna Edwards case. Just a little longer with the balancing act. Just a few more lies and this would all be over.

◆ ◆ ◆

When we slept that night, Helen held me from behind, as if she knew I needed comfort. In the morning, the familiar sound of tyres on gravel, the shouts and bangs we had grown used to. The builders were here. Oddly, I was comforted by that too.

'Well, at least they're back.'

We weren't going to be stuck with a hole in the wall of our house. Did that mean they also weren't going to sue us?

Helen let out a long exhale, mumbling into her pillow. 'I was worried they'd leave us like that forever.'

I got up to peer through the curtains. 'Well, they're here, large as life and twice as noisy. Ciaran and whatshisface. No Bob.'

'Good. I hate Bob, patronising arse.'

'Imagine being a builder and calling yourself Bob. The man has no shame.'

Helen laughed faintly, still half-asleep. It was going to be alright.

Helen was now refusing to even speak to the builders, despite being in the same house as them all day. On my orders, I ambled down the stairs in my pants and T-shirt. I didn't even care now that they'd know I'd just gotten up. It was eight in the morning and I was a freelance writer – why on earth would I get up earlier when I didn't have to?

'Morning,' I said, yawning.

Ciaran was doing something with wet sludge on a trowel.

'Afternoon.' Very witty.

'Is your, em – your colleague, how is he?'

'Not so good,' said the other one – Borak, was that his name? – from the kitchen. 'In hospital.'

'I'm sorry to hear that.'

Was saying sorry legally dubious? They were here, so surely they couldn't also be planning to take us to court.

'Any chance you could look at the boiler while you're here? It only seems to work some of the time.'

Ciaran sighed. 'You need a new one, mate. It's nothing we've done.'

'It's just we have no hot water, like, half the time.'

He carried on slapping the sludge, said nothing. 'I'll have to ask Bob about the budget.'

I'd already paid them for parts and labour, so surely they had enough to sort things out for now. A stab of fear, that I had sunk so much money into this place and it was falling apart.

I went past Ciaran, looking for the coffee machine, which Helen had unpacked. It was plugged into the wall by the TV, already surrounded by brown drips. I supposed I should offer them a drink, but sod it, they were rude and I doubted they would appreciate my seven-pound roast from Columbia Road Market. As the machine whirred, I looked around me. The other builder was in the kitchen up a ladder, prying out the remaining cupboards. Well, that was good. We'd have to go and order a new kitchen soon, which would mean dipping into the savings we mostly didn't have any more. I would have to be clever about it, make sure I paid, that we chose a cheap one or ideally some kind of payment plan, or . . .

A loud curse in Polish from the kitchen. God, not another accident! I jumped, splashing coffee up my arm, and yelped.

Ciaran had gone running to see what was wrong, but the other man – Borak – was fine. He had leapt down from the ladder and backed all the way out of the kitchen into the living room, and he was saying something in rapid language. I met Ciaran's eyes – neither of us had a clue. Then he switched to English.

'Something on top. Top of cupboard. *Thing.*'

What thing? I went over to look. The kitchen had a crazy lopsided look now, the units pulled down and thrown to the ground, becoming trash. A gap between the cupboard and the sloping, uneven ceiling. And that was where he'd found it – the dried-out skin of what looked like a rabbit. Glassy eyes, stiff fur, still red with old blood. Honestly, what was this house? Dead things in the kitchen. A cellar full of dried herbs and stunned birds. Mysteries floating in jars, dolls in the walls – even I was starting to be a little spooked.

◆ ◆ ◆

When I got out of the shower – ice-cold – Lisa McSweeney had left me a slightly breathless voicemail, which I managed to listen to by leaning slightly out the window.

'Hi! So I'm based over at Calzean, it's just a tiny place along from Little Hollow. You can find it, I'm sure! Everyone has Google Maps these days, don't they? Anyway, yes, you probably saw my rates on the website, it's forty for the deep-tissue massage. And if you want to add on any reiki or crystal healing, we can discuss. Anyway! How's today at eleven, if you get this in time? You let me know. Text or call. Oh – it's Lisa, by the way.' Then she hung up, laughing.

Very odd. I had already decided Lisa might make an excellent character for the story – she was clearly a bit nuts, and she'd been taught by both Adam and Janna at the village school. She'd been in the same class as Lucy and Grace. So I texted back, accepting her offer of 11 a.m. for a massage.

◆ ◆ ◆

I came downstairs to find Helen picking through the wreckage left by the builders. They had knocked off already 'to get some parts'. I doubted we'd see them again that day, especially after the latest grisly find. I had quietly disposed of it in the outside bin, without telling Helen. There were lots of reasons it could have been up there. Janna planned to do some amateur taxidermy, or use it to make lucky rabbit's feet, who knew? She didn't exactly get time to plan her departure.

'I need the car, if that's OK.'

'Oh? How come?' Helen sighed, running her hands through her hair. 'Are they coming back today, the builders?'

'Not sure.'

'They've left it in such a mess. The sink is hanging half off the wall! What are we going to do?'

'I'll call them.' My standard response.

'You said you were going out.' She looked at me shrewdly, and I reminded myself I could not rely on my wife missing things, even when so distracted.

'Yeah, I'll do it before. What are you going to do today?'

'I was planning to try and clean up. But I'm not sure it's even worth it. Or go for a long walk on the beach. Not much else to do around here, is there?'

'I thought you wanted that. Peace and quiet.'

'I did. I do. It's just – people aren't very friendly, are they? I mean, I'm surprised by it. Every time I try to chat to the locals they just sort of shut me down, or don't even answer. That post-office woman, for example! She's so weird. And the pub landlord, I definitely don't feel welcome in there.'

'There's a little café in the village hall some mornings, you know. It's for mums, I think, but they wouldn't turn you out! They let me in, after all.'

Helen fell silent for a moment, and I felt the weight of it bow us briefly, standing in the dirty, rubble-strewn space that had been our living room. We hadn't talked about it for a while, but it was always there. The unspoken hope, that things would happen now we had more time. Now we slept in the same bed – now she actually made it home instead of crashing out on gurneys waiting for yet more patients to rush in, their life in her hands. Stress didn't help, as we knew very well. I reached for her again, squeezed her shoulder, and she smiled back at me. We didn't need to say it.

'Well, maybe I'll do that then. If I can fit it into my busy schedule.'

'Great. OK, shall I bring anything back for dinner?'

She shrugged. 'Whatever we can cook on two hobs. I'm still not very hungry.' She was pale again, and I hoped she wasn't getting ill.

I pretended to think about it. 'What about . . . some kind of Italian?'

She rolled her eyes. 'For a change.'

'*Pasta alla pesto de Sainsbury's?*'

'Sounds groundbreaking.'

'We could go mad and have the red pesto for once. Shake things up around here.'

Helen laughed. 'Just pick up a few bits and I'll sort it. I didn't marry you for your cooking skills, thank God, or we'd have been in the divorce courts long ago.'

As I drove out of Little Hollow on the narrow coastal road, I felt my spirits lift. The sun was bright on the sea, spots of silver and pewter, and the hedgerows flitted with little birds, bloomed with spring flowers. In my head I made a list of questions to ask Lisa, but I realised I was excited, because here was someone else who had met her in person. Janna Edwards. Everyone I spoke to added another shade to the picture I was building of this woman. Fair hair, impassive face, jailed at thirty for half her life. I glimpsed her shadow on the walls of my house, felt her breath at my neck, imagined her round each corner in the village. Some said she was a cold-blooded killer, a witch, a poisoner. Stealing the lives of two young girls, and a family man with a child. Others said she was kind, caring, clever, wasted in this village. A herbalist, not a poisoner, though the same thing can be a poison or a cure, depending on the context. Who was she really? Perhaps Lisa McSweeney would be able to tell me, or at least consult the crystals or something.

Lisa McSweeney was about ten years older than me, I judged. Mid-forties, but she looked good on it, with long highlighted brown hair and fresh skin. Perhaps it was her hippie ways that kept her young – her massage studio was full of yoga mats and balls, crystals, books about soul healing and tantra and Tarot. It smelled pleasantly of essential oils, which were billowing out in a cloud of steam from a lit-up diffuser. The studio was a tiny shed, hardly big enough for us both to stand up, at the end of her garden. I could hear the sea crashing a few yards away.

She was more efficient than I'd expected. She directed me to leave my clothes on a wicker chair and lie down with my face in the hole of the massage table, cover myself with a towel. I'd decided I might as well actually have the massage first, since I did have terrible neck pain from my ad hoc desk set-up.

She slipped out while I got into position, feeling oddly vulnerable. Then I heard the door click and her soft footsteps on the wooden floor. She'd put on some kind of white floaty robe with no arms, and I felt it brush over me, along with a cloud of more oils, lavender perhaps. Her voice was soothing.

'Alright, George, can you take three deep breaths for me, in and out.' I did so, while she started to press on my back. I was vaguely ashamed of the hair she'd find there, not to mention the love handles I'd gained during my two years of feeling sorry for myself on the sofa, while my wife worked herself to the bone.

She began to knead my shoulders, and I let out a little groan – I had actually needed this. But I still had to get the interview.

'You're local, are you?' I mumbled through tissue paper.

'That's right. Little Hollow, born and bred.'

'I just moved here. Bought a house in the village.' I wondered how many people knew by now that this wasn't true. That I hadn't *bought* it at all.

'Oh yes?' It wasn't really a question, but I pressed on.

'The Gables? Do you know it?'

Her fingers didn't falter. Strong fingers, surprisingly so. 'I think so, yes.'

'Janna Edwards' house.'

'I know that, yes.' Her hands moved up and down my spine, kneading so hard it made me gasp.

'You've been there?'

123

'Janna worked at my school. You probably know that.'

'You're about the right age, I guess.'

'Is that why you booked with me? To ask me questions?' She didn't stop working the whole time. Nor did she sound especially annoyed – more curious, if anything.

'Partly. I've been wondering about the house I bought. But also, my neck is a mess.'

'It really is.' She dug in harder and I let out a hissed breath. 'What have you been doing to it?'

'Sitting down for approximately my entire life. Typing non-stop. Never exercising. You know, the usual.'

'Have you considered a standing desk?'

God, the standing-desk lobby. Who wants to write on their feet? I'd have chosen a different job if sitting down all day wasn't my ideal state. 'Maybe once I get settled, yeah. We're still moving in.'

'You can ask me questions. I don't mind talking about Janna. After all, it happened. Pretending it didn't doesn't help anyone.'

Yes! I had picked this right – of course the hippie believed in openness and healing truth. Unlike the rest of the village, who just wanted to lie and obfuscate, not realising that this was the modern world, and information simply could not be contained any longer. 'And Grace and Lucy?' Speaking their names felt like a spell, or a prayer, in the hushed, scented room, darkened so I could barely see the floor through my face-hole.

'They were in my class, yes.'

'Your friends?'

I felt her shrug. 'We were all friends, I suppose. It was a very small class, just ten of us.'

'Anyone else still living in the area?'

'I think there's about four of us.' She pushed her elbow into my trapezius and I hissed.

'What do you think happened that day, Lisa?'

124

'What do you mean? You know what happened – everyone does.'

I wasn't sure that was true, but OK. 'Right, but . . . the poison. It was just an accident?'

She hesitated for the first time, a break in the rhythm of her fingers. 'Janna didn't mean for them to die, I'm sure. I think they stole it. They were always stealing things, and they'd hang about her house a lot. She told them not to, that it wasn't appropriate, but they were kind of obsessed with her, I suppose. The way girls are at that age. Her and Mr Jeffries, they were convinced there was some big romance between them.'

'But there wasn't?'

'He was married.' Lisa's voice had closed off, something in it that I couldn't read.

'So they just stole the bottle, drank it for a laugh?'

'They were always messing about. They probably thought it was a real love potion or something like that.'

'And Mr Jeffries – have you any idea why Janna would kill him?'

'I was ten years old, George. I had no clue why any of it happened. Suddenly my two friends were dead, and my teacher, and my other teacher had gone to prison.'

'Have you ever visited her?'

'Why would I do that?' Her tone was almost cold now. Even her hands felt colder against my skin. 'She was a convicted murderer, and I was a child. Anyway, it's far away, where she is. A few hours at least.'

'I just wondered if anyone had, from the village.'

Was it strange if not? This woman who had been so popular, so beloved locally, and they had abandoned her to her fate? Left her to rot in prison for nearly thirty-six years?

'Not that I know of. It's not something people want to remember.'

'Right.' It was getting hard to talk, lying down like this, and I was feeling mildly suffocated. I went quiet for a moment while she manipulated my arm in its socket. 'Thank you. That feels good.'

'You're very stiff.'

She seemed mollified by returning to the task in hand. And she was good, as far as I could tell. I don't go in for massage much, but it seemed to be working. Helen, as far as I know, has never in her entire life had a massage, or a facial, or even got her nails done. Low maintenance, that's my wife. I'm the highly strung one.

After another twenty minutes or so, Lisa pressed her hands on my back and asked me again to take three deep breaths, which seemed to mark the finale of the ritual.

'OK, George, that's the end of your treatment. Remember to drink plenty of water to flush out toxins, and I'll just pop out now and let you get dressed.'

With the obscure feeling I'd dropped the ball on this, I pulled my shirt on to my greasy, oil-saturated body, and got back into my jeans and shoes. When I pushed open the door, she was hunched on a stone bench in the corner of her garden, smoking a roll-up cigarette. There were lots of different flowers growing, and I wished I knew the names. It would set a better scene in the book if I could say, *Her garden grew with lavender and . . .* something. Whatever flowers were called. She looked different outside, raw and vulnerable, not the gentle-voiced therapist from the hut.

I looked her full in the eyes for the first time. 'I'm sorry for ambushing you. I did also need a massage.'

'Yeah, you really did. I've never seen a back so tense.' She exhaled smoke, and I caught its tinge on the salty air. 'Janna taught me how to garden, you know.'

'It looks good.' My eye was caught by a yellow flower with a dark heart. I'd no idea what it was, but it looked a little sinister. Janna had grown poisonous plants, too, of course.

'Herbs, healing plants, all of that, she started me on the road. She was very good to us, the girls at school. We could always go to her house if we had trouble at home, or if we needed a meal or a safe place. My father, he . . .' She stopped herself. 'Things were chaotic at home. Angry, shouting. She let me be with her, just quiet, digging in the soil, snipping off plants. It always smelled so good. She told me which ones to avoid, which ones helped.'

'You must have been surprised, when she did what she did? If she was always so nice?'

Another deep drag. 'But she did do it, didn't she? What's the use of trying to figure out why? It happened, and he's dead, and that's all there is to it.'

'What was he like? People tell me a lot about her, very contradictory stuff most of the time, but he's sort of a blank to me.'

She looked out to sea, a restless turquoise today. 'He was . . . well, like any man, I suppose. Some of the girls – Lucy and Grace – had crushes on him, they used to write his name on their books and giggle, that kind of thing. He was handsome, I guess. Tall.'

'And you?'

It was a rude question really, but she didn't react. She seemed to have gone somewhere far away in her head. 'No. No, I never had a crush on him. I was ten, like I said. And very young for my age.' Then a long moment went by, and she seemed to snap to herself, grinding out her cigarette against the bench. 'Right! That'll be forty pounds for the massage, please. I'll just get my card reader. Assuming you don't have cash, who does nowadays!' I watched her walk away, the cigarette butt carefully pinched in her hand, her white robe swishing, like some modern-day priestess, but one with PayPal and Rizlas.

On my way home, I stopped in the village to get the groceries, parking beside the war memorial. The place looked nicer today, with patches of sunshine, though a cold wind was still blowing. I dialled Mum's number as I walked to the shop, knowing that if I didn't call her soon her anxiety would only build, and eventually she'd ring Helen, and I didn't want that at all.

The line was crackly. 'Hi, Mum.'

'There you are, darling! We were starting to worry.'

'Sorry, we just have no reception at the house. It really is the sticks! And the internet's not in yet.' I should really get on that, chase it up. Soon I would need it for research.

'Did you see the . . . ?'

'The article? Yeah. It's fine, Mum. I was hardly even mentioned.'

'I'm just worried because . . .'

'I know. But it won't do any more damage than has already happened. Anyway, I'm not pitching articles right now. I'm working on a book.'

'Are you alright for money?'

I winced. The answer was, not really, but they'd already given us fifty grand. 'Yeah, yeah.'

'Helen called me last week.'

'She did?' Things were worse than I'd thought, if she'd resorted to ringing Mum.

'It was a bit confusing, George. She seemed to think we'd given you money to buy the house. And that you didn't have much of it left.'

'Oh?' Well, of course she thought that. I'd downright told her as much. How else to explain the two-hundred-grand gap in our finances, everything we'd saved to buy a house? 'Crossed wires, I suppose.'

'But you do have enough for the renovations?'

'Of course. That's what the fifty was for, which you kindly gave us.'

She still sounded worried. 'You had savings too, I thought? You'd been trying to buy a place for a while?'

'We did, but, Mum, I haven't worked in almost two years. London's expensive, you know that.'

Helen knew it too, but she had no idea of the real amount of debt I was in. The loans I had taken when commissions didn't come in. The credit cards I'd maxed out before I lost my job, sure that my rise through the ranks would always continue. The nights of drinking and dining with celebrities, chasing stories. I was far into the red even before I got fired.

Mum said, 'You haven't told her, have you? Who you inherited the house from.'

'Well, no. I just said a distant relative. I don't want to upset her. She's very fragile still, after what happened last year.'

'But won't she find out – won't the locals know who used to own the place?'

'Maybe. But the name wouldn't mean anything to her, would it? It was ages ago.'

A silence filled with worry and sorrow. 'Darling, I know it was all a shock, when we told you about the house. Maybe we should have done it sooner, but you always seemed – you never seemed to want to know. And you don't have to tell me if you decide to contact her. Janna. But I would be supportive of that, if you did. Whatever you decide to do is fine with Daddy and me.'

I closed my eyes. 'I know that, Mum. Thanks.' But it wasn't as easy as that, was it? Just to contact her. Just to open that channel up, when I hadn't even known she existed until a few months ago.

I saw someone waving at me from the door of the pub – Cara. Today her hair was somehow green. 'Mum, I've got to go. Talk to you soon.' I hung up and went over to the pub. 'Hiya.'

'I've got some information for you. Got time to come in?'

In the pub on yet another lunchtime? Well, she hadn't given me much choice, and it wasn't as if there was anywhere else to meet in the village. Inside was almost deserted, just the same old man with the dog, who gave me the same hostile look. Cara went back behind the counter. 'Want something?'

'I'm OK. Oh, go on then, just a half. What did you find out, then?'

She poured my drink, then consulted some notes on her phone. 'Well, no go on the police guy who arrested Janna, he's super-dead. Same with the early-years teacher from the school, she was old even then.'

'Yeah, I figured.'

'But the other teacher, Susan Bodger, I've got her phone number.'

I was actually impressed. 'How – the phone book?'

'What's a phone book? Kidding. No, one of the ladies from the knitting circle had it, I just asked around the village.'

'You're in a knitting circle?'

'Oh yeah, crafts are so soothing. Plus, it's a traditionally female art form that's often undervalued. Now the wife, Margaret Jeffries, I can't find anything on her so I'm thinking maybe she remarried. There's a way to look up marriage records apparently – you have to, like, go to some records office or a library.'

I felt a million years old talking to Cara, but she had got results. 'That's great, thank you.'

'I'll keep looking. There's a few more people I want to try and speak to. From the school and that, pupils, anyone who knew her.'

'Sounds good. Carry on.' I was barely listening – my mind was still chewing over what my mother had said, the warning that Helen probably already knew I had moved us into a murderer's house. As long as she didn't know why, it would be alright.

Back at the house, it was quiet and cold, no sign of Helen, and I had no idea where she might be. The distance between us was growing. As I went into the living room to make coffee, I heard a noise. A kind of banging and swooping, coming as if from under my feet. The cellar.

I went to the door, noticing that it was open – perhaps the builders had gone down there after all. I felt a stupid fear as I descended – it was so dark in there, smelling of old damp things. Was there another trapped bird – how on earth were they getting in? But as I turned in a circle, peering into the distant corners, I couldn't see any, and the strange noise had stopped.

◆ ◆ ◆

Helen shook me awake early the next morning. 'Umm?'

'There's no hot water or heat.' She sounded vaguely hysterical. 'The boiler must be out again. Did the builders even look at it?'

I fumbled for my glasses, remembering how quickly the builders had fled after finding the dead rabbit. The air in the room was chilly, unwelcoming. 'I don't know.'

'Well, you need to fix it. It's bad enough we have no kitchen, and a hole in the living room, but now we have no heat and I can't wash my hair!'

'Hey, hey, it's OK.'

'It's not OK!' I'd rarely seen Helen so upset. She flopped back on the bed, her red hair tangled, in the T-shirt and shorts she slept in. Her face was pale and crestfallen. 'George, I can't – I don't know if I can live here. Since we came I just – things haven't been the same.'

'What do you mean?' I tried to sound casual, but my heart was racing. Please, let her not know.

'Oh, everyone is just so strange and hostile, and your mum – I called your mum – she seemed really puzzled about the money they gave us to buy the place.'

Oh dear. 'Oh, you know Mum, always getting the wrong end of the stick. She is nearly seventy, Helz.'

'But – we don't know if you'll ever get a job again, or what I can even do next, and we need money to fix this place up. A lot of money.'

'I thought you were looking into mental health work.'

'But that costs money too. And – well, I'd have to tell them what happened last year. They'd make me do therapy.'

Privately, I didn't think that would be the worst thing, but since I'd always refused it myself I could hardly talk. 'Look, it's going to be OK. I'll call the builders – I'm sure it's easy enough to turn the boiler on. Maybe I can even work it out myself, bit of YouTube.'

Helen made a noise of disbelief. 'There's hardly any reception in this place. No phone reception, no internet, no hot water – we're basically in Victorian times.'

'OK, OK. Look, I'm getting really close with my book. Maybe I can send off a proposal soon, and who knows, it could sell on that, with a few chapters of text.'

She looked sceptical. 'Really?'

'Oh, yeah – it's how Andy sold his last one.'

'Hmm.' But that's Andy, she might have said, but didn't. I knew she was thinking it. 'George, do you promise me there's nothing about the house you haven't told me?'

Oh God. There were so many things I hadn't told her. I just needed a bit more time. 'I'm sorry, babe. I honestly thought you'd like the peace, and that we could fix it up nicely. It's always a nightmare with builders. One day we'll look back on this, as we sit in our lovely living room gazing out to the sea.'

Helen sighed deeply. 'Just get them to fix the boiler, OK? I honestly can't cope without a shower.' I wondered if she'd noticed I hadn't actually answered her question.

When we went downstairs, I shuffled over to the coffee machine to turn it on, while Helen went to the front door to get the post. After a few moments, I heard her exclaim.

'What?'

'I don't bloody believe this.'

'What's wrong?'

She came back in, pale and shaking, holding out a single sheet of paper and torn envelope. A letter, cheaply printed. I scanned it quickly, taking in the name of a local law firm. *Letter Before Action. This is in reference to an incident on your property where injury resulted to an employee of our client, Mr Robert Marks . . .* It was Bob the Builder. He was suing us after all, or threatening to.

Helen said, 'What the hell is that? It won't stand up in court, will it?'

'I don't know. Looks like he's just thrown some cash at a local solicitor to knock up a threatening letter. I doubt he'll actually sue us.'

'He's asking for ten grand compensation!' For injuries and loss of reputation to the company, apparently. Sounded like bollocks to me.

'He's just chancing his arm, Helz. It's fine.'

'It's not fine, George! At the very least they'll hardly come back and finish the job if they're suing us, will they!'

'I'll handle it.'

'When? How?' She was right. I kept telling her I would sort things out, and so far I had utterly failed to.

'I – let me talk to him.'

'When?'

'Now. I promise, I'll go up the hill right now and ring him.' Shoving my feet into Crocs, without so much as a sip of coffee, I went to find the patch of reception.

At the brow of the hill, I dialled Bob's number. I was cravenly a little relieved when it went to voicemail, and I left instructions for him to call me back. I aimed for a bemused tone, as if in my view we were all still friends and he couldn't possibly be threatening legal action. Next, I tried Nancy Dunne, the old school secretary, again to no answer. I left another voicemail, explaining who I was. Then I punched in Susan Bodger's number, not really expecting her to pick up – no one did nowadays.

'Hello?'

There she was. Her voice was crisp and impatient.

'Hello, Ms Bodger, is it?' Hell of a name, that.

'It's Miss. What do you want?'

'Um, well, my name is George Sanderson, and I'm a writer. I'm working on something about the Janna Edwards case, and I wondered if you might—'

She cut in. 'Why on earth would you write about that evil woman?'

'Oh – you think she's guilty then?'

'Do I think she's guilty? She was sentenced to fifty years in prison. She murdered a wonderful teacher, a father and husband, not to mention two little girls.'

'Yes, but—'

'There are no buts. I don't care what people say about evidence or witnesses. She was a wicked creature – I wouldn't go so far as to say a devil-worshipper, but not far off. She was a liar, a manipulator, a deceitful whore, really.'

I sucked in a breath – the word sounded so much worse in her cut-glass tones.

'I see.'

134

'Do not contact me further, Mr Sanderson. I never want to hear that woman's name again.' And she hung up.

It wasn't my first hang-up – Alex James had once put the phone down on me when I'd said something rude about cheese – but it jolted me. She had sounded so angry, as if the case was still alive for her. I suppose I'd grown used to the idea that maybe Janna was innocent, or at least partly innocent, of killing the girls, if nothing else – Cara seemed to think so, and Martin had been vague. Lisa McSweeney had suggested as much too. But now, for the first time, I got a sense of how most of the locals must feel. Of what they thought she had destroyed, the evil she had brought to their doors.

Just as I stood up to go – I still needed to wash and eat breakfast, and it was damp and cold at the side of the road – my phone pinged. Cara. *I got a hit!*

And she had. She'd gone to the library after all, and found Margaret Jeffries, on an electoral record from 1987. She had moved away after her husband was murdered, if it was the same Margaret, and looking at the date of birth, I was sure that it was. My hands started tingling as I typed, and my breath was coming shorter. I just needed an address, and after filling in my card details and paying a small amount, I had one. EX20 – the postcode meant nothing much to me, but I'd be able to drive there OK. People have no idea how easy they are to find. I imagined she had changed her name, remarried probably, but if she was still in this same house as 1987 I'd find her. If not, there was a chance whoever lived there now might have a forwarding address. As soon as I washed, I would go and seek her out.

Starting to walk, I typed back to Cara. *Well done!*

She replied straight away. *No problem. There's another lead too – I want to check it out a bit more before I say, but could be a huge one!*

She was so young, still finding excitement in these dark happenings, as if they could never touch or hurt her. Sadly for me, I knew better.

◆ ◆ ◆

Helen didn't even ask me where I was going that day. She seemed withdrawn, shutting herself into the bedroom to 'sort' it, a process that often seemed to result in more mess than she began with. She was doing something with socks, folding them in some odd way into the drawers of the new/old tallboy she'd found in an antiques shop.

'I'm taking the car, OK?'

'OK.' She looked up at me from where she was kneeling on the bare floorboards. We'd have to get a rug or something. 'George, do you . . .'

I waited. 'Do I what?' That same little trip-drum of fear in my heart. She would find out, sooner or later. Maybe she already had, but for some reason wasn't telling me.

'Oh, nothing. Bring back something for dinner, will you? I can't really go into the village shop again, the woman is so rude.'

'OK.' As I drove away, I was rehearsing the same speech I'd been planning to give her for weeks now. *Helz, I haven't been totally honest with you. I didn't buy this house at all. I inherited it. Who from? Well, here's the thing . . .*

That was where I always stalled. I could tell her I'd lied about buying the house, and maybe even answer her inevitable follow-up question about where the money had gone in that case, though it wouldn't be pretty. But I couldn't tell her how I had inherited this place. Who left it to me and why. Not until I understood more about the why myself, until I'd got my head round the case and what it meant for me. If there was a chance Janna Edwards wasn't guilty, well, that would change everything, and the terrible heaviness I'd felt since I learned about the house, perhaps it would lift. Helen would understand, wouldn't she?

The drive to Devon took almost two hours, and as I turned off the A30 I began to get a strange sense of déjà vu. I'd been here before, hadn't I? I recognised that BP garage, the little village with the pretty green, ducks in a pond. I understood more when the satnav guided me to a small cul de sac on the outside of Okehampton, pebble-dashed houses with low, huddled roofs. This was right near Helen's mother's house, the place my wife had grown up.

Was it a weird coincidence? There were a lot of similar housing developments in Devon, I supposed. I had never written to Helen's mum, of course, and Helen had driven whenever we came before, or we took the train before we could afford a car. I realised I couldn't actually have told you what their address was. But this looked like the same street. It rang a bell now – Carlton Close. I could picture Helen writing it on the envelope of a birthday card.

With a mounting sense of surreal fear, I parked and walked towards number twenty-four. Of course I recognised it.

This was Helen's mother's house.

Was it? Or just a really similar one? I was going mad. This didn't make any sense.

I rang the bell with trembling hands, and of course, of course I knew the person who opened it. Mick Keown, Helen's stepfather. It took him a second – we hadn't seen each other in a while, and I was out of context.

'George! What a surprise.'

Not as much of a surprise as it was for me. Because I had followed directions to the house of Margaret Jeffries, widow of the murder victim, and they had led me to my wife's old home. Her mother's house – and her name was Peggy! Peggy Keown! Why hadn't I seen it? – and there was only one conclusion to be drawn here.

My mother-in-law was Adam Jeffries' widow. And that meant my wife, my beloved, straight-as-a-die wife, who had never as far as I knew told a lie in her entire life – she was Adam Jeffries' daughter.

◆ ◆ ◆

I had to know. The time had finally come. After making an excuse to Mick that I'd been in the area and come to borrow a stepladder – all the way from Cornwall for a ladder! – I got back into the car and sat there for a moment. He had seemed to believe me, if only because he'd believe any mad thing an arty Londoner like me would do, such as drive a hundred miles for a fictional nearby interview. I lifted my phone from its holder, my hands shaking. I'd been putting this off for months – was I really going to just go there, in my old jeans and Wilco T-shirt? I wasn't on the visitors' list, and I had a vague feeling I would need to book one in advance. At least I could find out how to go about a visit. I should have done this sooner. There was no good way for it to happen, I realised.

I saw that Helen had sent me several messages, asking where I was. Well, let her wonder. I dialled the number for the prison.

The automated system asked me to state the name of the prisoner I was calling about. 'J-Janna,' I said, fumbling her name, the one that had been running through my head ever since I learned the truth. *Janna Janna Janna.* 'Edwards.'

Janna Edwards. Murderer, teacher, witch.

Janna Edwards, my mother.

Janna

Most people think that if you're convicted of murder, you're in prison for life. That isn't the case at all – life in the UK typically means fifteen years, and if you behave yourself you could be out sooner, in twelve years maybe. Then there are ways to bring the sentence down, make it not technically murder, even if you've killed someone — defences, they call them. Provocation, when someone pushes you so far you snap and aren't in control of your actions. If you didn't plan it – you didn't bring a weapon with you, for example. If you were temporarily mad or in some way out of your mind – diminished responsibility. If you were in fear of your life. In fact it's surprising how little time you can serve for a murder. It would almost make it worth doing. If you felt someone really had to die.

I was unlucky. When I was convicted of murder, I ended up with life, but closer to actual life than the fifteen years or so this normally means. Fifty years, so the intention was I would die in prison. When that happens to you, it's very, very hard to get out. But not impossible.

◆　◆　◆

My life divided quite neatly in two the year I turned thirty. There was before – living in Little Hollow, where I knew every man, woman, and child in the place, working at the school, making my medicines, looking after Mother. Then there was after – the same small prison cell I've been in for the past thirty-six years. Sometimes I look at the cream-painted ceiling of my cell, peeling and dingy, and imagine it's the rooftops of Florence, or the karsts of Rio de Janeiro, or the Eiffel Tower even. But it never is, it's always my cell in the prison on Salisbury Plain. I don't have a cellmate, I'm allowed a TV, and I work in the education department, so I suppose it could have been worse, but it isn't quite what I'd expected from life, as a young woman of thirty, in love for the first time and looking to the future.

For a long time I believed that my life bisected on the day of the murders, when the girls died. The worst day of my life to date, which was soon followed up by an even worse one, when I gave birth in shackles and they took my baby from the room before I could even hold him. But no, I think the split happened further back than that. I now believe the fateful moment, the crack in my future, occurred when I first met Adam Jeffries. I've had a lot of time to think it over, stuck in prison, and it's all very clear in my head. The day Adam Jeffries came to Little Hollow was the day my life as I knew it ended.

◆ ◆ ◆

Before the events of 1986, I'd lived a quiet life. One or two visits to London, a holiday in Spain with a schoolfriend, the Lake District on a school trip. If I'd known that was all I was going to get, I would have made the most of it. Taken lovers, lived in different cities. I would have liked to go to university, medical school, and I had the marks for it, but Mother needed me. She'd been virtually house-bound ever since I was a little girl, and I'd started helping my grand-mother with her care when I was eight. When I grew up, instead of becoming a doctor, as I might have liked – I always played hospitals with my dolls, never weddings like my friends did – I found work at the local primary school. Not even as a teacher, since I wasn't qualified. A classroom assistant. The rest of the time I visited the sick in the village, gave them my concoctions, and acted as a kind of unofficial therapist to the locals. People used to come to Granny with their problems, their miscarriages and broken hearts and swollen feet, and she would send them away with something in a bottle. After she died, when I was eighteen, I had taken over some of her practice. Did they work, people always want to know. The potions? Of course they did. Medicines are just chemical compounds, and that was what Granny made too, though she didn't know the technical names for things. Most of her recipes have a basis in evidence, and if a broken heart cannot be cured by a potion, perhaps it can by listening, by good advice, and most of all by hope. That was what she offered, and I tried to do the same.

I was thirty when Adam Jeffries took on the job of headteacher, after Mrs Critchley finally retired and moved to the South of France. She'd taught me, and it felt like a big shift in the rhythm of the village when the governors announced they would appoint some-one to the post from outside the local area. Fresh blood, they put it, and it came to have a meaning they could never have intended. I was unsettled by the change, and I suppose I was brooding on what I might do next. Turning thirty had focused my mind on my situation – unmarried, childless, living with my mother. I'd had so little *fun*, you see. I wanted more. I wanted to leave my home town, experience somewhere else. Be careful what you wish for, they say. These days I would give anything to see Little Hollow again, the yellow sand of the cove, the gorse on the coastal path, the swinging sign of the Green Man pub and Martin inside it.

The day Adam Jeffries arrived, I had led years five and six in a discussion of the themes in *The Iron Man* – not the superhero, the one by Ted Hughes. I remember it was a drowsy, hot day, the first week of school after the summer, the children restless and edgy, staring out of the window remembering long August days playing in the nearby woods and on the beach. Our new headteacher had delayed his start by a few days – a long-planned family holiday, they said, which seemed odd to me, but I accepted it – so I hadn't met him yet. We were all – myself, Nancy the school secretary, the sweet juniors teacher Mrs Jenkins, who was pushing sixty even then, and mealy-mouthed Susan Bodger, the other teacher in this tiny school – agog to see what he looked like.

I was on the verge of letting the kids go early to play in the balmy afternoon, when Nancy rapped on the door and marched straight in without waiting. The school was so small, barely four rooms really, that we were always on top of each other. And I was not a teacher, as I was so often reminded in a million small ways, even if I'd been taking the top two classes on my own for most of the previous year, as Mrs Critchley wound down.

'Janna, he's here,' Nancy stage-whispered, the kids' heads all whipping around.

I smiled at them. 'Alright, everyone, now, nice and quietly, close your books up and pile them on my desk.' Cue a stampede of ruffled pages and shuffling feet. 'Who's here?' I said to Nancy, who was red-faced with excitement. I didn't blame her – not much happened in Little Hollow to get excited about.

'The new head. Mr Jeffries! He dropped in for a visit.'

'I thought he didn't start till next week.'

'Well, he's here. Wants to look around, and Susan's already gone for the day. Dentist.' Susan would really have preferred to be called Miss Bodger by the school secretary, but Nancy was cowed by no one.

'Alright, I'll show him about. There's not much to look at, mind you, does he know that?'

I rarely saw Nancy shaken, not in the case of invasive nits we'd had the year before, not in the nasty business of Robin Matley's dad and his fists, not when a seagull flew into the staff lounge and had to be chased out with a broom. So when she stepped forward and giggled – giggled! – I was surprised. 'Oh, Janna. He's ever so handsome, he is. You'll see. Married, sadly.'

I had always distrusted handsome men. My father had been handsome, Mother said, and look where that had got us. All the same, when Adam Jeffries came into the classroom, stooping a little to fit through the low door, my body reacted despite myself. Treacherous. He was half a foot taller than me, a lean, strong body, with the muscles of someone who worked outdoors (he didn't, but was a regular hiker and cyclist, I would learn), sharp blue eyes, dark hair. There are some people whose faces just look right to you – I'm told it's a matter of symmetry, of familiarity, and of genetic compatibility. Whatever it was, he had one of those faces to me. The perfect alignment of chin and brow and nose. And that was even before he smiled at me, and I felt slightly winded, and understood the strange giddiness that had overtaken stern Nancy. 'Hello, you must be the famous Janna.'

'Famous?'

He took my hand – his grasp was strong, but didn't crush me. 'The place couldn't run without you, I'm told. Or without Nancy here.' Another giggle from her.

'You must be Mr Jeffries.' I pulled my hand back, unsettled.

'Oh, please, Adam. I'm sure we'll be like family here, in such a small school.' He gazed around him at the classroom. Allowed the run of it in the absence of a third teacher, I'd had the children fill it with autumn leaves, long trails of coloured paper hanging from the ceiling, birds' nests, pretty rocks from the beach. Not very tidy, but beautiful and interesting. 'What a display! So creative.'

I felt myself glow a little under his attention, and squashed it fast. I didn't trust that kind of reaction. Granny had always warned me against being ruled by my body, and I'd learned my lessons well. For the most part, anyway. 'Thank you. What was it you wanted to see? We only have the three rooms really, and the staffroom. It's a tiny place. You've come from London?' It seemed a strange thing to do, leave a role in a big school, where the salary would likely be double what it was here.

'Yes – got a bit tired of the hustle and bustle. I've always loved Cornwall.' His bright eyes shifted away, and I sensed there might be something. A reason for leaving, one that he didn't want me to know.

'You're living in the village?' I asked.

'A few miles away.'

'With your wife?' I'd spotted his wedding ring.

His eyes tightened for a micro-second. 'That's right. And our little girl. She's two.'

'Awww,' said Nancy, who was not normally a sentimental woman. 'She can join us here in a few years. What's her name?'

'Helen,' he said, but he was looking at me still. Appraising. And although I could not possibly have known I would eventually go to prison for Adam Jeffries' murder, I did already know by then that we would have trouble, the two of us. I just wasn't sure what kind.

◆　◆　◆

The next day I arrived at school slightly later than usual – Mother had had a bad night, and I'd fallen asleep after five, waiting for her to stop wailing and shaking. She called out for my father at times like that. *Robert, I'm sorry. Forgive me!* I'd long ago promised myself I would never call for a man like that. Never need one.

I felt sick and exhausted too as I dragged myself to work. I hadn't been able to eat any breakfast, as was becoming the norm these days, and I knew I was getting too thin. Maybe I was going the same way as Mother, a lonely, neurotic woman. Usually, the playground would be full of children when I got there, their parents dropping them off before going to work on the fishing boats or in the warehouses. In winter their breath puffs formed a warm cloud over the school as they played and shouted, never bothered by harsh weather. Today, I saw they had already gone into assembly, which was held in the biggest classroom, the one that had been mine for a brief time, the smaller children sitting cross-legged on the old wooden floor. But two girls remained outside, whispering together. The best of friends, inseparable: Grace Monkton and Lucy Fillane, both ten years old.

'Girls, shouldn't you be inside?'

I should be inside myself, of course. Mrs Critchley had always understood my situation with Mother, but perhaps the new head would not be so accommodating. In my experience men often seemed to believe that the dirty work of life, feeding children, changing beds, cleaning toilets, happened by magic.

Grace giggled. 'The new headmaster's here.'

'Yes, I know. I'm sure you'll want to make a good impression on him, so go inside.'

Lucy whispered something, and Grace, always her spokes-woman, said, 'Is it true he's married, miss?'

The children usually called me that, just miss. Not Miss Edwards, since I wasn't a teacher. I didn't mind if they called me Janna, though Nancy would pull them up for it.

'I don't think that's any of our business, girls.' I put my hand on the heavy safety-glass door of the school – it was an old build-ing, but had been a given a modern facelift ten years before, like a crone in a new wig.

Another giggle, rising up like bubbles. 'Miss. He brought in a *guitar*.'

I ignored this and strode inside, pushing open the door to my classroom, hearing the girls scurry behind me, loitering in the hall. They were almost eleven now, and would already be embarrassed to walk in late in front of the whole school, although it numbered only fifty children or so. Sure enough, Adam Jeffries was standing at the top of the room, playing an acoustic guitar and singing. It was one of our usual hymns, 'Make Me a Channel of Your Peace', but his interpretation was jazzy, folky. Mrs Jenkins was doing her best to falter along on the old piano, and I could see Susan was actually clapping, Nancy at the side, swaying along. It was as if the man had the whole school under his spell.

Today he wore suit trousers and a shirt and tie, the sleeves rolled up. His eyes were shut as he sang, and his voice rich and tuneful. A stab of something like irritation went through me. The entire front row, girls and boys aged from four to seven, were gaping at him, and at the back, the older girls, ten and eleven, were all whispering to each other. I recognised the same look that had been on Lucy and Grace's faces. Oh dear – we had a handsome headmaster, and now we were going to have a run of awkward crushes. It was so tender, that age, when you started to notice boys and men, but you hardly knew what to do with your feelings, your sudden sharp interest in what had the day before been annoying nuisances, making bad smells and throwing pencils. You didn't even know what to call it. That was what made the girls so very vulnerable.

I tiptoed forward to take my place beside Nancy, trying to be inconspicuous. The children parted for me, a Red Sea of little upturned faces, and my sandals seemed very loud on the bare wooden floor. Adam opened his eyes and stopped singing – Mrs Jenkins plonked on for a few notes more before realising.

'Sorry,' I whispered, but Adam glared at me briefly. He played another note or two, then stopped, as if the spell had been broken. He glanced at the clock.

'Now that Miss Edwards is here, I can see it's nearly a quarter past nine, so you'd better all get back to your classrooms. Years five and six, let's put the chairs and tables back. Quickly.'

'Yes, sir,' came the raggedy reply, followed by a chorus of squeaks and a babble of rising voices.

'QUIETLY,' barked Mr Jeffries, and the noises died down.

I saw Susan shoot me a look as she rounded up her class, and Nancy seemed slightly flustered, not meeting my eyes as she too went out, followed by Mrs Jenkins and her brood of small charges. Adam set the guitar against the wall and looked at me.

'I'm sorry,' I said, keeping my voice low so the kids wouldn't hear. 'I didn't mean to interrupt.'

'I was just finishing up.' He glanced at the clock again. 'Were you only coming in now, Janna? I'd like you here before nine, please. It isn't fair if Miss Bodger has to do playground duty alone.'

I could have said I was here every other day at eight, that I stayed past six many nights tidying and cleaning, hanging up the artwork the kids made, scribbled and fragile. But I had too much pride.

'Of course,' I said, making my tone even frostier than his. Imagining his skin turning blue and stiff from my words. Ill-wishing, my grandmother would have called it, and I did my best to avoid such things, though her books had plenty of charms and incantations. I've always thought ill-wishing just rebounds on the sender. 'It won't happen again.'

I turned and made my way to go to Susan's room – I helped her with Art on a Friday – but he called me back, looking up at my hanging leaves and dried flowers, the stones and birds' nests I had arranged throughout the room.

'Oh, Janna? I'd like all these hanging things to come down, asap. It's a fire hazard, didn't you know?'

◆ ◆ ◆

I was unsettled by the encounter, so much so that I did what I'd promised myself to swear off, and called into the pub on my way home from school. It was barely five, so quiet enough, football showing on the television, a few old soaks sitting in corners. Martin was behind the counter, doing a crossword. He looked up when he saw me.

'Distant objects formerly spent. Nine letters.'

I thought about it for a moment, hopping on to a stool. 'Far things. Farthings.'

'You're too good at this.' He inked the letters in, and I watched his hands, strong and shapely, freckles on the backs from being out in the sun. 'What can I get you?'

'Oh, just orange juice.' I've never been a big drinker. You can't, when you're sensitive to things.

He set the juice down and waved away payment.

'You'll never stay in business like that,' I joked. 'Giving out drinks to all and sundry.'

'You're hardly that,' he said shortly, not meeting my eyes.

'No Morag today?' I asked, trying to sound light. His wife was usually somewhere in the back.

'Ach no, she's . . . not feeling well.' I knew what that meant. Against my will, I knew her cycle as well as my own. 'So what brings you in?' he asked.

'Oh, it's the school. Have you met this new teacher yet? The head?'

He rolled his eyes. 'Pretty boy. Oh, he's been in alright. Introducing himself to everyone, even Alan.' Alan was an ancient fisherman who had never knowingly spoken to anyone in the pub, despite being in there every night of his life.

'You didn't like him?'

Martin was a good judge of character. He had something of it, the understanding. The sensitivity. It was usually more blunted in men. He'd told me about his grandmother from the Western Isles, who had 'the sight'.

He shrugged. 'Not my type of person. You've clashed with him already?'

He knew me too well. 'Oh, I was a bit late today and he made a fuss. Then he took down all my decorations. From the ceiling, you know. And he was singing. To the kids.'

'Did you call the police?' He raised his eyebrows.

'Ha ha. It's hard to explain, it was . . . something about him makes me uncomfortable. I can't say what it is. I just don't trust him.'

'You're usually right about these things, Janna.'

I was, and that was the problem. When you know something bad is going to happen but not how or why, what can you do about it? It was like being Cassandra, cursed to see the future come crashing down, and powerless to stop it. Animals are better at this than us. They don't ignore their bad feelings, the raised hairs on the back of the neck, the intuition we can easily explain not as witchy powers, but simply older senses we have forgotten about or don't quite understand. Senses that kept us alive in the wild, now dulled by civilisation. 'Yeah. But everyone else seems to love him. The kids, the teachers, even Nancy's under his spell.'

Spell. I had meant the word in its generic use, but it chimed with me awkwardly, like the note of a broken bell.

'He's popular with the ladies, that's clear. Heard them all squawking about him down the post office earlier. So handsome, so charming.'

Martin was handsome – to my eyes at least – but no one could call his dour directness charming. I was glad of it. I had always distrusted charm, not least because that word too has another meaning.

'What can I do about it? Tell me,' I asked.

He shrugged. 'Just keep an eye out. Maybe don't leave the kids alone with him.' At the time I didn't read much into it – just a catch-all warning, not seriously meant – but it was true that Martin had a touch of the sight too. Perhaps that was why we'd connected as we did, when he moved down here two years ago. 'You seen the wife yet?' he asked.

'No, they're living out in the country, aren't they?'

'The country' in this sense being anywhere outside of the heaving metropolis of Little Hollow, with its two streets, pub, post office, and church.

'Aye. But she comes to pick him up every day, waits at the shore-front for him in the car. He doesn't drive, for some reason.'

Interesting. Though I longed to stay and talk more to Martin, I knew I had already pushed my luck, so I finished my orange juice and went on my way.

◆ ◆ ◆

That night, Mother didn't feel well enough to sit up for dinner, so I brought her soup in bed, in the large cold room on the front of the house, with the two windows bisected by the porch roof. A branch of ivy was poking in through the glass of the window – the whole place needed work. We could have moved to a bungalow, one of the new ones in the village or even in the next town over, but neither of us would hear of it. This had been the Tresallick place for generations, and we wouldn't be the ones to let it go out of the family. Alone downstairs, I ate my usual lonely dinner – crackers and Cheddar. I couldn't seem to find enthusiasm for food, not by myself. Sometimes I would imagine having a husband opposite me, someone to ask about my day. I'd serve him a roast dinner, or spaghetti Bolognese. Or he'd cook for me – it was the eighties, after all. I would never have admitted it to myself, but part of me was waiting for Mother to be gone so I could start my life. It wasn't her fault, but I couldn't meet anyone when I had to empty her commode and feed her from a spoon.

Left to my own devices and smarting from my put-down earlier, I found myself turning to the Tarot. It was an old set, made of heavy embossed card, that had been in the family for years, and it was comforting to see their faces, touch their surfaces. I turned a three-card spread, to represent the past, the present, and the future. The cards gave me little comfort. The Hermit – that could have been me, alone but at peace. Next I turned over the Page of Swords – that could mean a cruel man, one who would wound and cut. Finally, the Ten of Swords, and that sent chills through me. It showed a man stuck with blades, and in the background the sea. I'd always thought the picture looked just like Little Hollow. This card could mean abrupt change, painful endings, turbulence. But in the end they were just cards, and for all my witchiness I knew they only showed me reflections of my own thoughts. Whatever I saw did not have to come to pass. It could always be changed.

In search of something else, wisdom I couldn't pull from my own mind, I descended to the cellar, and took Granny's book from the shelf where it lived. I had been afraid of it as a child – leather-bound, the pages stained as if with tea, smelling of must – and then as a teenager I had found it somewhat funny. The women in my family were witches! We had an actual spellbook! Now, aged thirty, I approached it with a sort of wary reverence. Really it was a herbal, a list of different recipes and home remedies. The kind of things people used to cure themselves before we had antibiotics. Maybe they worked, maybe they didn't. The section at the back was the spells that weren't for physical ailments but for problems like love sickness, grief, and even revenge. I'd always thought the spells were silly, but I found myself now turning to that section, which was written in the ornate copperplate writing of my great-grandmother, Granny's mother, a woman I had never met, but I'd lived in her shadow all my life anyway. I was named for her – Jennifer, she was, same name as on my birth certificate, but my father apparently had French Breton roots, hence Janna. It didn't seem fair he had decided both my names, when he'd been gone by the time I was five. Jennifer Tresallick might have been a very different person. One who could actually live in Paris, or Rio, or anywhere.

A spell against evil, I read. *Fill a jar with morning water.* Urine, in other words. *Add herbs and flowers, tansy if you can find it, rosemary for remembrance. A dried beetle or a small rodent.* It was a spell for protection, to be buried in your garden, so that ill luck could not find you and any bad wishes would be deflected. There were all kinds of charms and protections hidden round this place, in walls, in the garden, hanging up in the attic. Recalling the way Adam Jeffries had looked at me, I was sure that one more would not go amiss. So later that night, in the black dark that always surrounded the house, lit only by the moon on the sea in the distance, I buried the jar, and went to sleep with earth under my nails.

I suppose the next thing that happened was that Morag came to see me. Yes, Morag, Martin's wife. She had never fitted into the village like he had – people sometimes forgot he was a recent transplant, all the way down from Glasgow. He was just good at making himself belong. Morag, on the other hand – people found her accent difficult, and her facial expression was unfortunately sour no matter what mood she was in. Resting bitch face, it would later be called. She and I were not exactly close, so I was surprised, to say the least, to find her on my porch the next morning, before school. She had no children and worked in a pub, why would she be up so early?

'Hiya, Janna.' Not much warmth in her tone, and my stomach turned over. I straightened my spine.

'Morag. All alright? My mother's still asleep, I'm afraid.'

'Oh, that's no bother. I just needed to ask you something.'

'Yes?' She hesitated, and I understood. 'Come downstairs.'

To avoid disturbing Mother, I did most of my medicine work in the cellar, a spidery old place that smelled of soil and vegetables, where I remembered my grandfather potting bulbs. He had been a largely silent man, which was not exactly a matter of choice when you married a Tresallick woman, and he'd died when I was four. We walked into the house in silence, the tramp of Morag's sandals light on the floorboards. I opened the creaky door to the cellar, leaving it ajar since it was so dark down there, pulling on the string to light the one dim bulb.

Morag blinked around her, as well she might. It was a bit over-whelming, all the jars with things floating in them, the dried herbs hanging from the ceiling, the strong smell of lavender and sage.

'Are you having the same problems?' She'd been to me a few months back, for heavy and painful periods, and I'd sent her away with ginger, fennel, liquorice root.

'Aye. It's worse, really.' She sounded stiff, embarrassed.

'I'm sorry to hear that. Were you wanting to try the same things again?' I spoke carefully, feeling the jagged edges between us. 'Or something else?'

'I need to get pregnant,' she said in a rush. 'You know. Everyone knows, don't they? It's the talk of the village. That I can't.'

I said nothing, but it was true. Village gossip had wondered for years why they had no children, a young couple moving to a place like this.

'It's me, you know. He's fine. Me – well, it doesn't work like it should. I've tried and tried, and we don't have the money for that test-tube way you can try now. So. Is there anything you can do for me?'

I took down Granny's herbal, mostly to hide my face. It was dark in the cellar, the one bulb no match for the shadowy corners full of decades of Tresallick junk. Morag's face was all planes and shadows. 'Certainly there are herbs you can try, that might help. But if the problem is . . . well, if it's a physical thing, not hormones, say, well then, it's harder to . . . do anything.' I was embarrassed too. I reminded myself she was just a patient, like everyone else, in need of help. 'You know, it might take surgery or something.'

'Whatever you have. I'll try anything.'

I moved around the small space as she perched on a high stool, crushing herbs in my pestle, releasing dry, green smells, wrapping them up in brown paper. At the end, I handed her three packages. 'Make these into a tea and drink it every morning for the month. Leave it to brew for at least three minutes. If you don't like the taste, you can add honey.'

'I don't mind bitterness. If it works.' She took them, turning the little packets over in her hands. 'How much do I . . .'

'Oh, no. We're friends, aren't we?' We weren't, but Martin and I were. I sometimes took payment, if the person could afford it, if it felt right. But Morag – I owed her a certain debt, and I knew it. Maybe she did too, because she just nodded and put them into her handbag. I sensed she wasn't ready to leave yet. 'Do be careful with these – don't take any other medications with them, and don't exceed the dose I've written down there.'

Lightly, her face turned away as if reading the labels on my jars, she said, 'I heard you make love potions too!'

'Oh, that. It's mostly for show, you know. For tourists and young girls. If anything it can give a little boost of confidence, and sometimes that's all you need.' I'd kept up some of Granny's practices, and sometimes sold potions at fairs for extra cash, though I felt stupid doing it. It wasn't that they didn't work, exactly. It was more that it was hard to control the effects.

'What goes into it?' She sounded more serious now.

'Herbs, mostly. There's . . . kind of a method to it.' I didn't like to talk to just anyone about that side of my work. It was too open to misinterpretation.

'Like a spell?'

'You could call it that.'

She nodded. 'Well, maybe you would . . . let me know. If you make any.'

I was shocked. I shouldn't have been, but I was. 'It's a long process and . . .'

'I'll pay. Whatever it costs.'

I didn't know what to say to that. The last thing on earth I wanted to do was make a love potion for Morag Macrae. But I couldn't say no to her either. 'I'll let you know if I find time to do it. It needs certain ingredients that are hard to source.'

'Thanks.' She drew in a deep breath. 'Don't tell Martin, OK. About any of this.'

My heart turned over. *She knew.* 'Of course not,' I said, turning away, voice neutral as possible.

After that she left, and I sensed a greater lightness about her. As if she had transferred the weight of her worries to me, and I felt them like an iron collar resting on my shoulders. Alone in the cellar, I found myself leafing through the book and turning to the part about curses. How to hex someone so they'd bleed out through the eyes, and die within two days. How to kill their cows and poison their wells. How to sicken a child.

That's right – the women in my family, apart from poor Mother, might have helped people, but that didn't mean they were especially nice. Certainly you would not have wanted to cross them. I put the book away, troubled without quite knowing why.

◆ ◆ ◆

I used to not sleep well in prison. The absence of natural light had broken something deep inside me, my connection to the natural world, and I never knew when to wake up or close my eyes. I was always tired, but I couldn't rest. However, you can get used to anything, and thirty-six years later I just close my eyes and switch off when they tell me to, like the model prisoner I am. But things are changing now. I know he is out there, in the world, and that he must be finally aware of me. It's brought up all manner of unhelpful feelings. That he might be ashamed of me, for example. He will only have heard the official story of my terrible crimes, not what really happened. Above all, I wish I could tell him the truth, but of course I can't.

I was awake today before the alarm went off, the day beginning with its usual rattling of bars and shouts of the guards. Staring up at the same damp-marked ceiling that has been mine for years now. It was Magda, my favourite guard, who came to unlock me. She struggles with her weight but always puts on red lipstick, always does her hair nicely. It's an inspiration to the rest of us, not to give up hope. Not to stop trying.

'Up already, Janna?'

'Couldn't sleep.' I smiled at her. No sense in making enemies – it's just a job for her; it's not her fault I'm in here.

'Well, nip out to the showers now before it gets busy. There's new soap in today.'

'Bless you.' I started to gather my towel and spongebag.

'Not long now, is it?' she said, her voice kind.

'That's what they tell me.' I kept my tone casual – after all this time, I had learned not to get my hopes up. But it was true that things were shifting and changing, after being stuck for so long. That there was finally hope for me, a sliver of daylight opened up.

'Well, this might sound strange, but we'll miss you round here, Janna.'

I laughed. 'Not sure I can say the same, Magda, but thank you.'

She was right in a way, of course. Even if I do get what I have most longed for all these years, it will be a big adjustment. I will finally be able to see people face to face, and perhaps even right some of the wrongs that were done back in 1986.

The next important thing in my story is how I met Margaret Jeffries, Adam's wife. She was absent from the trial, trying to distance herself from me, and I understood it, but I wished we could have spoken one last time. Because what no one knew, what was never reported in the press, was that Margaret and I were friends, of a sort.

I met her after I'd been to the post office one day after school, having detoured to drop off a remedy to Barbara Walsh, who ran a small knitting business from a farm outside town. She'd been suffering from arthritis, and I had something that would make her fingers fly again. The post office had always been dingy, under-stocked, run by the world's rudest woman, Angie Carter. She was so violently opposed to the idea of tourism that I'd seen her literally make people cry when they wandered by in search of directions or ice creams or buckets and spades. It was a shame, because Little

Hollow could have been another Marazion if we'd only learned to let new people in. Maybe then, with a thriving economy and lively restaurants and hotels, rental cottages and nice shops, the events that took place would not have occurred. People will do terrible things when they feel cornered.

I'd gone to Angie's shop to buy some meat, which was about the only thing I couldn't get at home, unless I shot a rabbit in the woods, which I wasn't willing to do. I made most things myself in those days, stocks and teabags and sauces, and I grew my own vegetables – I suppose I was at the start of the environmental movement. Twenty years later I could have sold my soaps and candles for five pounds each in the local craft shops, but in the eighties this was seen as odd behaviour. Angie kept a small butchery counter in the post-office shop, the meat so flayed and red it turned my stomach. I'd been vegetarian most of my life, but the sicker Mother got, the fewer things she could eat. I had thought to make a bone broth, or a stew with meat, to try and give her strength. As I approached the post office, I saw a buggy parked outside, and in it a little girl, perhaps about two years old. She had a head of gingery curls, and was looking about the place with a curious, alert expression, a ratty stuffed dog clutched in her fists.

I couldn't help it. I stooped to smile at her. 'Hello, sweetheart. Where's your mummy, then?' She looked at me curiously, chewing on the ear of her dog.

If I had a child I wouldn't leave her outside shops. Even in a place as quiet as Little Hollow. Fighting an urge to stand guard, I jangled inside, where I heard Angie's sharp voice.

'You want what?'

Someone answered, a woman's voice, but too low to make out.

'Speak up, will you, I can't hear you.' I rolled my eyes. Angie was just so rude. It was one thing to be disagreeable to those of us

who'd lived here all our lives and knew her well, but not to strangers. We'd get a bad reputation as a village.

Slightly louder: 'I was wondering if you had nappy cream.'

'Oh no, we don't stock anything like that. You could go to the
big supermarket if you're after fancy things.'

I looked round the shelf I was standing behind to see a slight
woman with hair the colour of apricots, wearing a drab trench coat
and low navy heels. I knew instantly who this was – there weren't
many people in the village I didn't recognise. That must be her child
outside. Having decided it would be preferable after all to catch my
own meat if I was going to use it, I followed her out of the shop,
casting a judgemental backwards glare at Angie. The woman was
dejected-looking, her shoulders slumped.

'Don't mind Angie,' I said, catching up to her outside the shop
window, with its dusty display of old beach toys.

She jumped slightly. 'Oh! She was a bit . . . hostile, I thought.'

'She's like that to everyone. No excuse for it, but nothing personal either.'

'Thank you.'

Her face was pale, and she was very thin. Immediately I
thought of what herbs I would prepare for her given the chance, to
pep her up a bit – ginseng if I could get it, sage perhaps.

I smiled down at the baby. 'This must be your little girl?'

'Oh! Yes, this is Helen. Say hello, Helen.'

Helen just looked at me, her head cocked to one side.

'You know, I make a cream that works wonders for nappy rash.
Much better than the bought stuff, that's just full of chemicals.'

The woman looked confused.

'I make things like that, you see. I'm a herbalist. Well, I work
at the school too – with your husband.'

Even more confusion, and I remembered why people called me
a witch sometimes. I make leaps other don't, I suppose.

'I – sorry, I just guessed who you were. Since we don't see many new people round here.' How provincial it sounded.

'That's alright. Yes, I'm Margaret Jeffries. I'm just on my way to pick him up.'

'He doesn't drive?'

'Um, no, he – well, usually he cycles, but he hurt his shoulder a few months ago, so I've been driving him.'

This was before the revolution of men in Lycra on expensive bikes that cost more than a car, so it seemed somewhat eccentric of Adam to cycle the five miles between his house and school. Like me, he was ahead of his time in some ways.

'He's working late today?'

I had left school at four, already finding it less of a haven than it used to be, and he'd been in his classroom, tidying up or marking or something. I hadn't said goodbye, still feeling heart-sore at the denuded classroom, forlorn bits of tape the only sign left of my beautiful display. I needed to heal this breach between us somehow – you couldn't have bad feeling in a team as small as ours. Perhaps his wife would be a way in.

She glanced at the neat leather watch on her wrist. 'He should be finished now.'

'I'll walk with you. I need to get something from the classroom.'

I didn't, but again instinct told me to go with her. As if this fragile woman needed my protection somehow.

As we walked, her pushing Helen in the buggy, I learned a little about her, that she was from Kent, that the move to Cornwall from London had been sudden – she didn't say as much, but I could hear the words between the words too.

'We just thought, a new start. Why not?' A new start. Interesting. I wondered why they would need such a thing. 'Helen being so small, it seemed a good time to go. And the air here, it's so good, of course. Such a lovely village.'

I felt a stab of fear then for her – because Little Hollow was not always a lovely village. It was not always kind to outsiders.

I said, 'Listen, I'll make up that nappy cream for you, if you like. It's no trouble.'

'Alright. Thank you – it's Janna, isn't it?'

He must have mentioned me. 'That's right.'

We had now reached the school, which always seemed unnaturally quiet without the children. I could see the lights were still on, so Adam must be there. I opened the door and we walked down the corridor. I can remember how Margaret's heels echoed, alongside my quieter flat shoes. I can remember seeing the door to the classroom was shut but unlocked, then pushing it open and realising that the door of the storeroom – a little cupboard off the classroom, where we might store books, or make a cup of tea – was closed too.

Beside me, I felt Margaret falter, and her fear was almost a tangible thing in the room. Pushing down my own instincts, I strode forward and knocked on the door of the storeroom. I knew there was no lock on it, though we might have often wished there was, when the kids got too much for us. Without waiting, I opened it.

We didn't see anything. Not really. Just Adam Jeffries in there, sitting on a hard plastic chair, and on another, Lisa McSweeney, a girl from year six, who like Lucy and Grace was ten. Nothing awry, and they had books in front of them on their laps, but they both looked up with strange expressions. Lisa guilty, scared. Adam guilty, angry. He said, 'Janna, I'm working here. I'm giving Lisa some extra tutoring.'

'Your wife was looking for you.' I didn't even bother to moderate my tone.

He frowned and stood up. 'Margaret, I told you not to come here. There's no need to drag Helen in. I would have been out soon.'

'I know, I didn't . . . I wasn't going to.' She was twisting her hands like small, strangled rabbits.

Then he cleared his face, like someone shaking an Etch a Sketch, that toy the kids loved. The anger was replaced by his usual geniality. 'Lisa. I think that's all for today. Well done.'

She scurried off, casting a fearful glance at me. A skinny, nervous girl, often coming to school with the marks of her father's hands on her. Exactly the type who would blossom with some individual attention.

With the child gone, the three of us adults stood looking at each other. I knew I could say something, shatter the illusion that this was somehow alright. It was tissue-thin, but he could still plausibly say there was nothing untoward about him being in there alone, after hours, with a child. He held the bridge of his nose and sighed, as if I was the most annoying person in the world.

'I wish you hadn't interrupted, Janna. I'd finally got her to make sense of long division.'

I opened my mouth. *Say it!* Say something wasn't right, that he shouldn't have been in the tiny room with her, with the door shut, and why were they in there anyway and not the main classroom? The classroom with its large windows anyone could look through? But I didn't. I was afraid, and cowed by him, and I've had to live with the consequences of that ever since.

'Come on, let's go.'

He took his wife by the arm – could have been courteous, could have been controlling. She cast a look back over her shoulder, riddled with many emotions – guilt, shame, confusion – and they left.

I would have to lock up. Alone in the school, the silence and the settled chalk dust began to give me chills.

◆ ◆ ◆

Rita is my only friend in prison. Not that I would let myself trust anyone in here – I've seen too much of what people can do when desperate. I know she'd sell me out for some cigarettes or a day off her sentence, though Rita isn't getting out anytime soon. She smothered her newborn daughter in 1997, in the grip of postnatal psychosis, as they call it now, but that understanding came too late for her. She's only in her forties but looks older than me, I pride myself. I haven't given up. I was always sure I would get out one day, and I have unfinished business, after all, which tends to focus the mind. I never took up smoking, and I trade everything I have for extra conditioner, so my hair doesn't get coarse in the way of the other women. I don't bother with make-up, because who's going to see me, though I use face cream, waiting for the day when someone might. For the first time, I had started wishing I had some cosmetics too.

Rita, who has the cell next to mine, looked up in shock when I went in and made my request. 'You want *foundation*?'

'Yes. Or something like that.' I glanced at myself in her scuffed mirror and saw an old woman, wrinkled, with long grey hair. In my head I was still thirty-year-old Janna, slim and blonde, who had never worn make-up and not needed to. 'I just want to be presentable. For when I – see people.'

'You're really thinking they'll let you out, then?'

Rita may be broken but she isn't stupid. She keeps a picture of her daughter, the one she killed, tucked into the side of her mirror, and every year on the child's birthday she trades all her canteen items so she can bake a small cake in a mug, a match stuck in it in the absence of candles. People are rarely one thing or the other.

'I think so. I hope so.' I had no reason to hope, having been turned down many times before, but I did all the same.

'You'll look for your boy?'

'Of course.' I had not seen my son since the day they took him from me, wrenched from my bleeding body, and then they locked me up again, gave him to someone judged more worthy. She had written to me, the adoptive mother. A nice woman, by the sounds of it. She had offered to keep in touch, to tell him about me, as often happens in adoptions. But I hadn't wanted him to see me like this, in here. I had given him up, but never lost hope that I would one day get out and find him.

She brightened up so much she even turned off her TV, which was showing *This Morning*, the young presenter shiny with lip gloss and youth. 'Will you let me do a makeover?'

'Oh God. You have to call it that?'

'Please, Janna. I would love it so much – I still remember how.' Rita was a hairdresser before all this. Now, like all of us, she is nothing.

'Alright then. Nothing brassy! And no hair dye, I like it grey.' It was silver in fact, from the gold it had once been, and that pleased me. The moon and sun. Precious metals.

'Yes, yes.' I had made her day, if not her month. It was sad, how little we had learned to get by with, in here.

After the strange encounter in the storeroom, I didn't know what to do. Normally I would have asked Martin for advice, but I was aware I had been doing that too often. Since his wife had come to see me, I'd realised she thought the same, and so I had to keep my distance, however hard it was. In a small village, a rumour can start by a breath out of place. Instead, I tried to talk to Lisa at break-time. As always, she was huddled near the fence, not playing with the other girls. Lucy and Grace were doing their usual showy skipping, calling in the other girls to jump the long rope. *My mother says . . .*

'Not skipping with the girls?' I asked. Sometimes they would play with Lisa, like they might play with a toy. Other days they wouldn't.

She shrugged. She had a nervous habit of chewing her plaits, and I itched to push her hand away. I could see she had a ring of bruises round her wrist – John McSweeney was known to be quick with his fists, and I sympathised. I'd only been five when my father went, but I could still remember the feeling of cowering on the stairs, listening to him shout at my mother. The marks that would bloom on our skins in the morning.

'So Mr Jeffries has been giving you extra lessons.'

'Yes.' Her voice was weak.

'Is that what you want, Lisa? You wouldn't rather be out with your friends?' She shot me a look, and I felt ashamed. Lisa had no friends.

'Mr Jeffries says he'll help me pass the eleven-plus exam. Go to a good school.'

'That's kind of him.' I spoke carefully. 'And . . . you liked studying with him? You didn't feel, I don't know, bored, or scared?' Nowadays there are protocols for talking to children about such things. You would never be alone with one anyway. Back then, I was making it up for myself, and no doubt I got it all wrong.

'Scared?' She shook her head, making the soggy plaits fly. They were so tightly done I wondered if it hurt. Lisa's mother went to work at seven, housekeeping for a family over in Mousehole, and her father worked the fishing boats, out even earlier. 'He's helping me.' The youngest of the family, she was all too often left alone.

'Well, alright. Remember you can talk to me about anything. Anything at all.'

Then, perhaps resenting that Lisa had my attention, Lucy Fillane beckoned her over. 'I call Li-sa in, in!'

She jumped to it, flushed with pleasure, and ran off, tripping over the rope in her eagerness. I watched Lucy and Grace, both well-loved, well-fed girls, clever and confident, snigger at her clumsiness, and I wished the world were not so unfair.

I looked up to see Adam Jeffries in the door of the school, holding a steaming cup of coffee. His eyes were on me, and I felt my heart race, as if he could somehow have known what I'd said to Lisa. He called, 'Break-time's over now, children, come inside.'

It was five minutes too early, and they dragged themselves away from their footballs and skipping ropes with reluctant groans, forming into rough classroom groups. One boy, Bobby Jackson, hadn't heard the summons, and was still zooming around the far edge of the playground, pretending to be an aeroplane. Nowadays, Bobby would probably be diagnosed with ADHD, but back then he was just seen as naughty. I knew there was no malice in him, so I waved him over, as the other kids disappeared inside. 'Come on, Bobby, Mr Jeffries has called you.'

He came racing towards me. His face was red with exertion, a happy glow, and his jumper tied loosely round his waist. I loved this about the kids, their energy, their exuberance for life. 'Sorry, miss!'

'That's alright, in you go.'

Jeffries was still in the doorway, as if supervising me. Bobby raced past him, clumsy as a young puppy, and accidentally knocked the coffee cup so that a long stream of brown liquid stained Jeffries' white shirt. So nicely clean and ironed – Margaret's work, no doubt. He jumped back, exclaimed: 'Look where you're going, for God's sake!'

Bobby stopped. 'Oh, sorry, sir.'

'Sorry, sir, is it? You little brat.'

I was standing a few metres away still, but I saw it all happen clear as day – the headmaster stretched out his free hand, and cuffed the boy. Bobby looked stunned. I hurried over. 'Bobby, are you alright?' I put my arm around him, examining his face.

'Umm – yes, miss.' He was holding a hand to his cheek, which now showed a slap mark, and he looked more shocked than anything. Bobby was in Susan's class.

'Off you go. Miss Bodger will be looking for you.'

It was now just the two of us. I stared at Adam Jeffries. He'd hit a child. Slapped him round the face, and we simply didn't do that – even in the eighties this was so far from OK I didn't know where to start. I tried to find my voice, which was so weak and trembling I hated myself. 'He didn't – it was just an accident. Bobby is a little clumsy, that's all.'

He was still dabbing at the stain. 'It's not good enough. Everyone round here needs to learn a bit of discipline. Not just the children but the staff too.' And with that clear warning, he went inside.

◆ ◆ ◆

Later that day, we had a staff meeting. Once the children had gone off, the five of us gathered in the small teachers' lounge, where there were barely enough chairs for everyone. I couldn't meet Adam's eyes, and sat looking at the ground wondering how I could bring up my worries without angering him further.

Nancy had been droning on about permission forms for some school trip later in the year, and Susan highlighted the need for all students to be in their seats by five to nine every day. Personally, I didn't see what was wrong with some leeway – often, their parents were trying to get to work, or they might live several miles out in the countryside and have to walk. I've never understood the need to apply rules for the sake of rules.

As the conversation petered out, I sat forward and cleared my throat. 'Er – I just wanted to raise something, if I may.'

Jeffries flashed me a look.

'It's about – I think we should review our child protection procedures. You know – that we shouldn't ever be alone with the kids.'

'Well, of course we shouldn't,' said Susan crisply, looking at the clock and starting to gather her things. 'Does that even need to be discussed?'

'I'm talking about the matter of – eh, private lessons. Tuition.'

The three other women looked confused.

Adam Jeffries cut in. 'I believe Miss Edwards is referring to some extra help I've given one of the year six girls. I was hoping to help get them all up to a certain standard – I'm afraid it's been a little neglected while Mrs Critchley was – well, perhaps she was somewhat demob-happy, shall we say.' And I'd been the one to pick up the slack, hadn't I? I heard the slight implicit in his words.

'But we shouldn't – we aren't supposed to be alone with them. Isn't that right?'

He shrugged. 'Depends what we mean by alone. We're a very small school, with no spare classroom space, so I'm sure we've all used the storerooms on occasion for a quiet chat. Miss Bodger?'

Susan was nodding. 'I use mine to test their reading age.'

'Exactly. It's just what we have to do, Janna.' His tone was patronising, and I would have liked to say that there was a difference between what he'd been doing, and taking a child aside for a moment in a full classroom, with the door open.

'I know that, but I – after hours, though?'

He sighed. 'Some of these children have nowhere to go after school, if their parents are working. I feel it's safer they should be here, using the time wisely.'

'Susan? Do you – you think that's alright?' I appealed to her.

She wasn't really listening, she was putting her empty lunch-box, reeking of tuna, into her handbag, and she shot me a severe look, her eyebrows up in her low hairline. She would have liked me to call her Miss Bodger. 'Janna, I really don't think it's for you to interfere. After all, you're not a qualified teacher. And if Headmaster wants to give extra time to the children, well, that's very kind of him. Goodness knows some of them could do with it.'

Headmaster, that's what she always called him. It makes me sick to think of it now. 'Well – alright. I just wanted to check what our procedures are.'

'Very admirable, Janna.' His tone was bone-dry. 'I did see you hug a child earlier, also. That's something we should discourage as well.'

I couldn't think for a minute. 'You mean Bobby? But he was – he was upset.' *Because you hit him.*

'Regardless. If there are to be strict procedures, no one is above them.' Even Nancy was nodding as she took the minutes. I could see this too was going to be a dead end, and I wished I was the sort of person who could just give up, let things go, say it wasn't my problem. Unfortunately for all concerned, I was not.

'Come and work here,' said Martin, wiping sweat off his brow after he'd hefted a barrel up from the cellar. 'Seriously. Tell him to stuff his job, they don't appreciate you anyway up there.'

'You don't need an extra person.'

Anyway, working with Martin was a terrible idea. I shouldn't have let myself come into the pub at all, but I'd been feeling weak, upset by the events of the day.

'You want to slip him something in his tea. Sort him right out.' He winked at me.

'Ha ha. That's all I need – people already think I'm the local witch.' That reminded me. 'How's Morag?' She hadn't appeared from the back to peer at me suspiciously, as she normally did.

'Been a bit poorly. Throwing up and that.'

'Oh.' That could mean two things. My herbs had worked, and she was pregnant. Or else I'd made her sick with them. If taken with other things, there could sometimes be adverse reactions. I could hardly ask him about it, since I would never betray a woman's trust. 'I'm sorry to hear that. Forget what I said about Jeffries, OK? Maybe I'm wrong. Everyone else seems to like him.'

'You really think he was . . . up to something, with that girl?' I'd told Martin all about it, mostly to say it out loud and run my mind over the words, try to discover where the bad feeling was coming from.

'God, I don't know. I didn't see anything untoward. But she's a very vulnerable girl and he shouldn't have been alone with her.'

Martin leaned on the pumps, looking at me with affectionate exasperation. That look was too dangerous; I glanced away. 'Well, if anyone's not helpless, it's Janna Edwards. You have ways round this. I know you do.'

As I walked home, the wind tearing at my loose hair, I realised he was right. He had been joking about putting something in Jeffries' tea, but I could do it, couldn't I? Granny had given things to my father, when he still lived with us, to stop him lashing out. There were certainly herbs and plants, which, if made up in the right way, had the power to change situations. To turn hate around. Neutralise an angry person, make them docile, drowsy, amenable. I just had to figure out how to get Adam Jeffries to ingest them.

But no, that was crazy. I wasn't actually a witch, whatever people said, and I only acted to heal, only when asked. Of course I wasn't going to drug the headteacher.

That night, remembering my vow to myself in the village shop, I fashioned a rabbit trap, with a wooden stake and a loop of wire, like Granny had shown me years ago. As I pushed it into the earth, I spoke a charm of forgiveness, for the small, unsuspecting life I was about to snare.

◆ ◆ ◆

'You're sure you don't want this?' Rita fingered the pink plastic basket I used to carry my toiletries to the showers. Just a cheap thing, but we had so little in here that I knew she coveted it.

'Of course. I won't be taking anything with me when I get out.' Not that I even had much. A few books, some snacks, some personal items. I would distribute them all to my friends in here, such as they were.

'But Janna, you don't . . .' She stopped herself.

'I know it's not certain yet. But I will get out this time. I'm sure of it.'

She nodded. Rita has always been very accepting of my witchy ways. 'You do look nice.' I had let her pluck my eyebrows, put a colourful rinse through my hair, even show me some make-up tips. I would not emerge as a grizzled crone, when I'd come in here a beautiful young woman of thirty. 'What will you do? When you're out?'

'Oh, there's several people I need to look up. From the past.'

'Old friends?'

I smiled at myself in the small plastic mirror, my blue eyes sharp as ever. 'You could say that. A few friends. A few enemies. You know how it is.'

◆ ◆ ◆

It was a while before I saw Margaret Jeffries again – I think I'd scared her off, with that strange moment in the classroom. But a few days later I spotted her going into the post office again, girding herself no doubt. It was why Angie got away with being so rude – there was no other shop for miles around. I stepped faster, catching Margaret on the doorstep. Helen, in her buggy again, looked up and waved to me, twanging my heart with a sudden pain. She was wearing denim dungarees with little ducks sewn on to them.

'Braving it again?' I said to Margaret. 'Hello, Helen!' I reached to touch her hand, chubby and soft.

'Hello,' she said, shyly.

Margaret looked flushed to see me. 'I needed washing-up liquid. And the drive over to the big supermarket – well, it didn't seem worth it.'

'I made that ointment for you. For the baby.' I'd been carrying it around in my bag for days, hoping to run into her.

'That's kind of you.' She seemed uncertain, as well she might.

'You can ask any of the local mums, my nappy cream is better than anything on the market. No parabens or artificial chemicals – just soothing plants. Chamomile, calendula.'

'Well, alright then. Thank you. She is in a lot of pain with it, poor baby.' She stroked Helen's head of curls. 'We're working on potty training, but she still needs a nappy at night.'

I fished it out, in a little brown jar like most of my preparations, carefully labelled. Then I drew out another, all casual. 'I made this too – you mentioned Adam's injury, his bad shoulder. This is great for muscle release.' And it was – I hadn't lied.

'Oh. I don't know if he'd . . .'

'Oh God, I know what men are like, you have to force them to take care of themselves, don't you! But if nothing else works, and he doesn't want to be on strong painkillers, this is worth a shot.'

'What's in it?' She took the jars uncertainly.

'Herbs and plants. It has a numbing and relaxing effect – a bit like Deep Heat, but more effective. All natural.' I had tried several compounds – hops, easily obtainable, and valerian, which had a strong, bitter smell that wouldn't seem out of place in a lotion. Chasteberry, which I had a small dried stock of in the cellar. On top of this I had added a chemical called scopolamine. A strong alkaloid, derived from plants in the nightshade family, one of which was henbane. The witch's herb, it was sometimes known as. It had many useful applications – pain relief, anaesthesia, an intense plea-surable high, and it could even help with illnesses such as dementia. Like anything, it could be a cure or a poison. Most of these herbs would work better if taken orally, but I was afraid of causing too much damage. Of being caught. They were all rumoured to calm a man. Reduce certain urges. I hoped it might make Jeffries more docile, keep him away from the children while I worked out what to do, if I was even right in my suspicions. It was a long shot, but hopefully risked little.

'Thank you,' said Margaret, still looking unsure.

I wondered what the chances were he'd try it – slim, I guessed.

'Maybe don't say it was from me? I don't think he's my biggest fan!' I said it cheerfully, and she gave a faltering smile. He had talked about me at home, I deduced. A terrible thought occurred. 'Also – don't mix them up, whatever you do. This would be far too strong for a baby.'

A surge of fear. It was risky, what I was doing. Maybe even against the law. But I had to try something, and if it worked, it would ultimately be for the good of that baby too.

Margaret thanked me and went into the shop. I could see Angie staring out at me, her usual hostile glare, and I gave her a wave and a smile. I had to learn that you could get more things done that way.

When you're convicted of murder by poison, you're seen as the sneakiest and most reckless of killers. If you strangle or stab someone, you have to go right up to them, look in the whites of their eyes, see that they know that it's you killing them. Not so with poisoning. So yes, I admit, I did poison Adam Jeffries, in the sense that poisons are simply a matter of dosage. But I wasn't trying to kill him. Unfortunately, this distinction was quite hard to prove when it came down to it.

◆ ◆ ◆

I watched Jeffries for the next few days, alert for signs of the lotion working. He was a little subdued, perhaps. I noticed him rotating his shoulder a few times. Dangerous things, bikes.

School went on as normal, and I tried to keep out of his way as much as possible. Then, at the end of the week, around three o'clock, the children were running to the door, eager to go out and play, or home to be fed with biscuits and watch Gordon the Gopher. I was in the classroom helping Jeffries tidy up, putting away the books and craft materials. I felt restless and agitated, as if I needed to say something to try and push back the nameless fear I had in his presence. 'Is your shoulder OK, Mr Jeffries?'

He glanced at me. 'It's fine. I had an injury a few months back, that's all.'

'There are things you can take for it, you know. Herbal remedies.'

He was looking at me strangely, and I wondered if I had played my hand too soon. Would Margaret have told him the lotion was from me? Perhaps he could guess. 'I don't know about that. You can't be sure what's in things like that, can you? It could be anything.'

I bit my tongue. So he likely hadn't used the lotion, or perhaps she had never even given it to him. I was just cleaning the paintbrushes when I heard light footsteps in the hall, and realised Lisa was still there, walking up and down, glancing back into the classroom every few seconds. Jeffries saw me notice her. 'Lisa,' he called. 'Come on in.'

She came running in, her face flushed.

'I've been thinking, Lisa, it would be nice to gather up some decorations for the classroom. It's looking so bare.'

'Yes, sir, what kind of things?'

He looked at me as he spoke. 'Autumn leaves, maybe some berries, some nice rocks and feathers, that kind of thing?' Exactly like my display, which he had destroyed. 'Maybe you can look for some over the weekend.'

I said nothing. I shut the cupboard door and turned the key.

'Oh, and I found this, Lisa. I thought you might like it.' From the corner of my eye, I saw him hand her something. A small rock, shaped vaguely like a heart.

'Oh, thank you, sir! For me?'

'For you. And next week we'll carry on with our lessons, OK?' He put his rucksack on and picked up his keys. 'Good evening, Janna. You'll lock up?'

'Of course, Headmaster.' There was nothing else I could say.

Lisa and I were left alone, and I saw her slip the rock into the pocket of her thin raincoat. 'You didn't go home?' I asked her.

She cast her eyes down. 'Dad took my key away. I forgot to put the washing on yesterday, see. He says I can't be trusted.' So she had nowhere to go, on a blustery grey evening.

'What time do they get back, your parents?'

She was chewing her braids again. 'Six,' she mumbled.

I wasn't about to leave a child on her own to mooch about the village for three hours.

'Alright, Lisa, come with me.'

It wasn't right to take her by myself, especially after I'd made such a fuss about Jeffries doing the same, so I was relieved to see Lucy and Grace hanging round the school gate still. Up to no good, probably.

'I'm going to Janna's!' Lisa boasted. Poor girl.

'You can both come too, if you like,' I offered casually. I saw the flicker of interest – they always wanted to know about the secret life of teachers. Lisa's face fell slightly – she wanted to be special. But it would do her good to make friends with the other girls, not be as strange and lonely as I was as a child, if for different reasons.

Grace shrugged, in that pre-teen way she already had. Not that she would ever make even her eleventh birthday. 'Alright. Nothing else to do, is there.'

◆ ◆ ◆

We trailed up from the village, Lisa bobbing along beside me, demanding my attention, the other two girls cooler, like cats, wanting it as well but too proud to beg. I found I was thinking of the Pied Piper of Hamelin, and what a sinister story that was. They didn't pay him, so he stole their children. What the hell?

'Now, girls, I hope you won't make too much noise – my mother isn't very well, you know.'

'What's the matter with her?' said Grace, always the ringleader.

That was a good question. Officially Mother had MS, but it was my opinion that the loss of my father, after years of his violence and anger, had broken something in her. I knew there were bad days, when the pain twisted her like a cruel hand. But other days, I saw her look almost wistfully out the window at the sea. I'd offered to take her there over and over, though pushing her chair up the hill would have been tough, but she wouldn't countenance it. She had given up on life, and there was nothing I could do to bring her back.

Mother was still alive when I went to prison – I never saw her again after my arrest, and about a month after I was sentenced, I learned she had died. From neglect, no doubt, from pain, from sorrow. It can kill you faster than cancer.

That day, I gave the girls orange squash, diluted from the tap, and realised I had no biscuits or snacks in. I didn't like that kind of thing, and with my lack of appetite recently, I increasingly just ate whatever Mother had, which wouldn't feed a bird. I was losing weight, too much weight. If I didn't take care, my own heart would give up.

The girls roamed the garden with their drinks, curious about everything.

'Miss, is it true you make potions?' said Lucy, who was starting to develop already. I felt for her – Innocence is so quickly lost. So little time to be a child when your body is turning into a woman's.

'Not potions. Medicines. It's just herbal healing, it's no different to what the doctor prescribes you, not really. Same chemicals.'

Except mine were freely given, yielded by the earth, and theirs had been synthesised and copied and made for profit.

'Can we see?'

'Alright.' I didn't see the harm in teaching them a few things. I opened the cellar door, pulling on the cord of the faint bulb, and let them look at the brown bottles, the mortar and pestle, the drying herbs, my collection of knives. 'Don't touch anything, girls, whatever you do.' There was enough poison in my collection to kill them several times over.

'Wow!' They were actually impressed, and maybe I was a little flattered. Adam Jeffries had done a number on my self-esteem, reminding me I was only a teaching assistant, with no real qualifications or power. But this I could do.

Grace said, 'Miss, can you make love potions? Like, to make people fancy you?'

I laughed. 'That isn't possible, Grace. You can stir up mixtures that might make someone feel a bit more confident, that's all. And you can strengthen the heart, with various different plants. Sometimes it's all we need, a little boost. But you can't make someone love you if they don't.' All the same, I had started to gather some of the ingredients to make one for Morag – rosebuds, hawthorn. Why would I do such a thing? I felt guilty, I suppose. I owed her.

'Can we try some?' Grace was examining the labels on the bottles.

'Absolutely not. These are made for adults, way too strong for you. Now come on, let's go outside and get some fresh air.' I ushered them up and locked the door behind me, dropping the key into a little pot on the kitchen windowsill.

Out in the garden, the girls fanned out, running like young colts in the wide space, the sea glinting in the distance. 'Miss, can you tell us what these plants are?' Lisa was feeling bolder away from school, I could see. Her excitement was almost palpable, that maybe Lucy and Grace would be her friends now, maybe she would be magically popular after today and life would change for good. I don't know why people are so sceptical about magic – everyone seems to believe in it in some form. In change, in luck, in love.

Thinking I could show them the basics of herbalism, I named some of the common plants in my garden. Rosemary, spiky and fragrant; wild garlic; lavender, for comfort and rest. Lisa was keen, asking questions long after Lucy and Grace had drifted off to play on the old swing some long-ago relative had hung from a big willow tree. Probably my grandfather, he'd been a kind, soft man. A mystery why he'd married Granny Tresallick. My mother had inherited the softness, Granny had said. But not me. She saw me as her heir, and I had little choice in the matter.

'Be careful, girls, the ropes are very old.'

They ignored me. I admired their confidence, so I let them be. It was in short enough supply for girls.

'What's this one?' said Lisa, kneeling down to a plant that grew in the shade of the big oak. There was always a flourish of plants in that particular spot, a rich crop of mushrooms in the autumn.

My voice was sharper than I intended. 'Don't touch that one. It can be poisonous.'

Henbane. Dark-green leaves, a yellow-white flower with mottled petals, like something dead, around a dark heart. Innocuous enough, but a little sinister growing so close to the house. I remembered Granny planting this one, nurturing a cutting she'd found deep in the woods. The Devil's Altar, the kids called the clearing where it grew, though it was really just a flat rock. No occult significance at all, but it made a good story. I had learned that stories were even more powerful than plants, and could not be controlled no matter what you did.

I left Lisa to potter about with the flowers – it was something I'd loved to do at that age, a lonely child myself – and went over to the other girls. I could see they were bored. Grace was standing on the seat of the swing, twirling the ropes around on themselves, and Lucy was pushing her in lazy circles.

'Are you enjoying school this year, girls?'

They exchanged a look and shrugged.

'It's school,' said Grace. 'It's not supposed to be fun.'

'You like your new teacher?'

I tried to ask it casually, scraping at the bark of the tree. It could be made into a tea that soothed period pains, something these girls would soon have to deal with, the blood and the agony. It didn't seem fair. I would shield them as long as I could from that adult world. Especially Lisa, who was nowhere near ready.

'He's OK. He's always helping Lisa, though – just because she's so behind.' This was Lucy, and they both cast a bitter glance at their classmate, who had picked a bunch of common mallow and was examining it with childish curiosity.

'Girls, try and be nice to Lisa. You two are – well, you're good friends, and things are easy for you.' I meant they were smart, and would be pretty, and had parents who cared for them and didn't send them out in unmatched socks with holes in them, like poor Lisa. But they were too young to understand me. Animal cubs, with no perception of kindness or altruism.

'We *are* nice to her,' said Grace. 'We let her play with us, don't we?'

'Well, that's very good of you.' I didn't believe it for a second. 'When Mr Jeffries helps Lisa, does he have the door shut?'

'Yeah,' said Lucy, seeing no significance in my question. 'He takes her out of class and we have to just read our books. It's boring.'

Grace, though, Grace understood what I was asking. She flashed me a wary look. If I pushed her, I might find out more.

'For a long time?'

'Yeah, for like an hour sometimes. It's not fair, why does she get all the attention?'

I had to choose my words very, very carefully. I looked over at Lisa, playing among the flowers, a picture of innocence. 'Does that upset you at all, girls? Scare you maybe?'

Lucy looked confused. 'What? No, it's just not fair.'

I tried to catch Grace's eye, but she looked away, her fair hair falling over her face. She was going to be so pretty in a few years' time – I worried for her.

Suddenly, Lisa gave a short, sharp scream.

'What is it?' I ran to her, thinking maybe she'd cut herself on a thorn.

She was sobbing and pointing into the longer grass at the edge of the trees. 'It's dead. It's dead!'

I hurried over, and found that my snare had caught a little rabbit, its eyes dark and glassy, its fur still sleek. It had died in terror, suffocated, and I felt sick. I forced myself to be the grown-up.

'Lisa, you live in the countryside, surely you know that people trap rabbits.'

'Dad says they're pests,' said Grace, wandering over, entirely unperturbed by the small dead thing. 'They eat the crops.'

'But they don't deserve to *die*,' said Lisa passionately.

Grace rolled her eyes. 'You eat meat, yeah? It's the same thing.'

I agreed with her, of course, that we should be ready to kill anything we were going to eat, but all the same it hurt me to see it, and I wasn't at all sure I would be able to skin it to cook for Mother. I nudged it with my foot behind some grass.

'Come on, let's make some sandwiches, shall we? You must be hungry.'

It was after five now, and I could soon send them on their way. I hurried them away, hoping Lisa might forget about the rabbit with some food in her.

Later, at the trial, much was made of this day, why I had taken the girls to my house, when exactly they had come into contact with the bottle of 'poison', as it was called. Anything can be a poison, if given to the wrong person or in the wrong dose. I'm sure it wasn't then – I would have noticed them taking it from the cellar, though they might have seen me put the key in the pot on the kitchen windowsill and sneaked back sometime. Perhaps I was reckless, showing ten-year-olds where I made my preparations, but it hadn't occurred to me they would steal from me. I was too busy watching for the bigger evil, the one I had to protect them from, that I failed to understand everyone is capable of bad acts, no matter how young, or how powerless.

◆ ◆ ◆

In all my time in prison, I've barely had a single visitor. I didn't want anyone to see me like this, and most of the village had turned their backs on me anyway. Also, I'd noticed what it did to the women, how broken and chaotic they were after seeing their families, especially the ones with small children. But today, I was going to see someone. It was a visit I'd put off for a long time, but I was ready to know the truth, I told myself. All the same, I was ashamed to feel the uncertainty in me, fear, when I'd long trained myself not to feel any, not to attach to anything so I could never be disappointed. I sat on my bed for hours, watching the light shift through the window, unable to settle on a book or project. Then I heard it – the shift and rattle that announces visiting time. Doors opening, women talking loudly, feet shuffling on the noisy floors. Usually, I stayed in here, listening to the sounds change, but today I stood up with the rest and joined the queue. I saw them noticing, nudging each other – *look, Janna has a visitor*. At long last.

I'd not been in the visiting room for so long that I didn't realise they had a whole row of new vending machines, and I felt a momentary pang that I'd been missing out on these different snacks, salty and sweet with artificial chemicals. How small my world had become. There was a time when I wouldn't have let any of that stuff pass my lips. That's the true poison, if you ask me.

Across the room, a man stood up. He looked like I had imagined – a middle-aged man in a raincoat, scruffy beard, upper-class accent. He was ex-army, I knew, had moved into this type of work after an injury on the front line. It was so long since I'd been this close to a man, it made me nervous. His left leg was stiff, and I wished I could give him something for it. Chamomile, perhaps, for muscle relaxation, or peppermint oil.

'Miss Edwards. Hello, it's good to meet you.'

You don't hear that often when you're a convicted murderer. 'Do sit down.' We scraped out our chairs. 'It's Mitchell, yes?' Mitchell Hargreaves. A private detective, who I had written to several weeks ago, in anticipation that I was finally, after almost thirty-six years, up for parole.

We sat on the plastic chairs, the noise of the room pressing in on all sides, children crying, everyone shouting to be heard, the irritating whistle of the coffee machine I saw they'd also installed, so drinks could be purchased for two pounds fifty, which seemed a lot to me. This room made me nervous, the way the boundaries blurred, the outside was allowed in. 'So did you . . .'

He nodded. 'I have all the information you asked for.'

'You found them – everyone?'

'Of course. It's quite simple to find people. Even closed adoptions are no longer secret.' He took a scrap of paper from his pocket – innocuous, just a list of names and numbers. Nothing he couldn't take through the metal detectors, although I knew from the other women they would strip you of surprising things, watches and lip balm and headphones. 'You asked me to find several people. Margaret Jeffries, as was. Lisa McSweeney, Susan Bodger, Denise Jenkins, Nancy Dunne. And the main one, George Sanderson.' George Sanderson. A stranger's name, as if he had nothing to do with me at all. 'He never tried to find you, from what I could gather. I doubt he knew the truth of his birth, beyond that he was adopted.'

'No. I expect they thought that was best.' His adoptive parents. I imagined them safe, solid. Dull. For his sake, I hoped they were dull, filled with boring, everyday love.

183

'Then he took possession of the keys to the house in Cornwall, several months ago.'

I knew this from the solicitor who had handled it. I had made the place over to him as soon as my mother died, some desperate attempt to keep it in the family. It was up to his new family to tell him about it, if they chose to, if they wanted him to know his history. Probably it had sat empty all these years, my lovely house, going to ruin. What had prompted him to move now? How much did he know about me – had they finally told him the truth? 'He's living there?'

'Yes. With his wife.'

His wife. I hadn't imagined that somehow. 'Tell me about her?'

He checked the piece of paper. 'Helen Gillis is her name. She was a doctor until quite recently. Aged thirty-seven.' I studied his face – there was something he wasn't telling me about this unknown woman, this cipher my son had married.

'What else?'

'Something I didn't quite understand. Perhaps I was confused. When I looked into the background of Helen Gillis, I discovered she had the same former address as someone else on your list. A house in Devon, Okehampton. One of those people was Margaret Jeffries – she's changed her name now, remarried – she's Margaret Keown.'

'I don't follow.'

'I didn't either for a time. It seems that this woman, your son's wife – Margaret Keown is her mother. Gillis was Margaret's maiden name.'

I didn't follow at all. Helen. Yes, there had been a Helen, hadn't there? The little girl with ginger curls. Margaret's child. Who would have been two when George was born, almost three . . . my mind blanked, and then I had it. But that couldn't be true. I gaped at him. 'You don't mean . . . ?'

He shrugged. These were just names to him, after all. 'It seems he's married to Margaret Jeffries' daughter, yes. You didn't know?'

'No. No, I didn't know.'

How. How could this happen? They had moved away, after the trial. It made sense Margaret would change their surname, go back to her own name. But . . .

'I don't understand how this could have happened. George grew up in Reading, she was in Devon – you're telling me it's just some huge coincidence they met and married?'

How could that be? That the two children involved in this case, my son and Adam Jeffries' daughter, had even met in the first place?

'I don't know. What else could it be?'

That's what I would have to find out. And once I got out, I would be able to track them down and do so.

◆ ◆ ◆

So we've come to it. Those final few days, when everything suddenly unravelled. I've had a lot of time to think it over, imagine what I could have done differently, if there was any way to prevent what unfolded. I could have taken Lisa to my house, and kept her safe there. I could have gone to the police – but I'm not convinced that would have changed anything, as no obvious crime had been committed at that stage. Or I could have left the village, gone far away, avoided my fate. But I'm not the kind of person who could have done that, even without Mother. So there was perhaps no way to avoid my fate after all. That should be more of a comfort than it is.

As we approached the end of term and Halloween, I had begun to dread going into school, worried about Lisa and what Jeffries might do next. I hadn't noticed him spending time alone with her again, and watched carefully each day to make sure she went home rather than meeting him after hours. He too seemed to leave on time, to be picked up by Margaret. I hadn't seen her since the day I gave her the lotion, and was sad for it – I had the feeling we might have been friends, in a different situation, and I worried for the little girl with the bright curls and inquisitive expression. But maybe I had been wrong. Maybe it was all over, whatever Adam Jeffries had been doing, or perhaps nothing had even happened in the first place.

One day, Lisa was again loitering outside the school building, already tearful, biting her lip and scuffing her old shoes in the dirt. One was beginning to come loose from its sole.

'Lisa. Are you alright?'

She nodded unconvincingly. 'Dad took my key again. It's – it's really cold to wait outside, miss.' The temperature had dropped, an autumn chill in the air.

'Do you want to come to my house?' I couldn't leave her here by herself, upset and alone.

'Yes, please.'

We walked away, and as we climbed up the hill I began to hurry slightly.

'I'm sorry, Lisa. I don't feel very well.' I barely made it into the downstairs loo, throwing up and shivering on my knees. I looked up to see Lisa at the bathroom door, watching me with curiosity. 'It's just . . . something I ate maybe.' I wanted her to leave, but couldn't kick her out, and she hadn't been taught enough manners to suggest it herself.

'Can I look in your cellar, miss?'

'Of course not. You know, there are dangerous things in there, Lisa. That can kill people in the wrong doses. It's not safe for children.'

'I'm not a *child*. And I'm careful.'

'Well . . . maybe later. Perhaps you can play in the garden for a bit – pick me some different herbs? I need to lie down a minute.'

I climbed the stairs weakly, wondering what on earth was wrong with me. For a mad moment I had the idea Jeffries had poisoned me. But no, it was only me who was crazy enough to mess with such things.

Mother was sitting up in bed, reading a book – one of her old Jackie Collins paperbacks. A good day, then. 'What's the matter with you?' she said, taking in my grey face.

'I don't know. Something I ate.'

She tutted. 'You haven't been wearing your gloves, have you?'

'Well. No.' I was slack about doing it when I worked with herbs, a careless practice since they can be absorbed through the skin.

'She warned you about that.' No need to ask who *she* was – it was always Granny, who loomed large in our lives despite having been dead for twelve years.

'I know.'

'Come here.'

I went in and sat on her bed, breathing in the stale fug of illness and disappointment, and she put a cold hand on my head. It felt nice, to be mothered for a moment. I'd had to mother myself for most of my life. 'Hmm. No temperature.' She looked at me keenly. 'Your grandmother would say you were expecting, looking peaked like that.'

I flushed and turned away. 'Well, obviously I'm not.' I always thought Mother was a helpless invalid – did she see more than I realised? I stood up and opened the window. 'Let's get some air in, since you're feeling brighter.'

'That girl's here again.'

Lisa's thin voice drifted up, singing a song. Something about Xanadu.

'She's nowhere else to go.'

'You don't have to save the whole village, Janna.'

But I did. Who else would do it? 'I better go down to her. There's dangerous plants in that garden, if she picks the wrong one.'

'Janna. I know your gran taught you to meddle in everything, but she didn't know it all. She did things that weren't right and you know it. Don't you?'

I nodded reluctantly, looking out the window to the old oak tree. I could have said I was only trying to help. That I felt evil was being done, though I had no real proof of it, and I was trying to stand between the children and harm. But why was I doing all this? I wasn't Lisa's mother, I wasn't even her teacher. It needled me, that Mother had seen through my pathetic attempts to make a difference. To interfere. What if I was making it worse somehow?

I dragged myself out into the fading afternoon light, gulping in herb-scented air and trying to settle my jangled nerves.

'Are you alright, miss?' Lisa stopped twirling. She had made a crown of daisies, like a woodland princess.

'I think so. What about some sandwiches and squash?'

'OK.' She bent to pick something, a pale purple flower. 'Look, it's an autumn crocus. He showed me this. In the woods.'

'Who?' I wasn't really listening to her, just trying not to be sick again.

'Mr Jeffries. He takes me to the woods, you know – it's where we meet, outside of school. Since we can't go in the storeroom after you told on us.'

'What?' My senses leapt to high alert. 'Lisa – what do you mean? Did Mr Jeffries do something to you? Because if you tell me, I can help you.'

She was examining the flower up close. Her voice was dreamy, remote. 'He asks me to meet him by the big rock, the Devil's Altar. It's our special place.'

I tried to stand up and found my legs crumpling under me. As I looked closer, I saw that she had pulled out every petal of the flower, and thrown them to the ground.

◆ ◆ ◆

'It's really happening, Martin.' I couldn't think of anyone else to talk to, so the next morning, very early, I had knocked on the pub door, praying Morag didn't answer, and made him come down to the shore-front with me. 'Lisa said he's been meeting her in the woods. Jeffries.'

'And did she say what he . . . did?'

'She clammed up again after that, wouldn't say any more. But she's showing all the signs of abuse. I know it.' I was pacing on the hard sand, the wind blowing my hair to a tangle, gulping in lungfuls of cold sea air but still gasping for breath. 'What do I do?'

Martin thought about it. It was one of the many things I liked about him, that he took his time. 'You shouldn't have to deal with this alone. Is there no one at school who's in charge of it, like?'

I barked a laugh. 'He's the child protection lead. And no one else seems to see it like I do.'

'What about her family?'

'I haven't gone to them yet. They're not home very often.'

'That's what we should do first. I'll come with you and we'll talk to them.' There was such great comfort in his support, I could hardly describe it. To not be alone facing whatever this was.

It was early, barely seven. My favourite time of day, when the beach was empty, swept clean by the tide, the birds scavenging in rock pools. 'Now might be a good time.' I knew Lisa's parents left for work at seven, and she was often alone in the house for hours. It wasn't right, but what else could they do? The rural economy was stagnant, with some of the lowest wages in the country.

Martin and I traipsed through the village, him in his jeans and T-shirt, me in my trailing purple dress, wet around the edges with seawater, my hair wild. We must have looked strange, and I was aware of people glancing at us from doorways and windows as they started their days, fuelling the gossip, no doubt.

The McSweeneys lived in the little crescent of council houses just outside the village, depressing grey ones with pebble-dash walls and unpainted doors. I went up to number eight, noticing the abandoned child's bike, one wheel missing, on the overgrown front lawn. Several dog poos as well, and when I rang the bell a chorus of barking started up. I've always been afraid of dogs – something in my energy seems to upset them, and I looked to Martin. I was so thankful he was there, his forearms solid from lugging barrels, his expression grim. I had never known whether it was more painful to be near him and not allowed to have him, or to not see him at all.

The door was opened by Lisa's father, a red-faced tank of a man who carried with him an indelible smell of fish. He was already wearing his rubber boots, and I saw he was about to leave for the boats in Newlyn.

'What?'

The noise of barking went up, a snarling mongrel appearing at his feet. The house smelled of fried food and animal fur.

'Hello, Mr McSweeney – I work at Lisa's school?'

'I know you, yeah. What is it?' His eyes flicked to Martin, no doubt wondering what this had to do with the local pub landlord. John McSweeney was in there a lot, I heard.

'I wanted to talk to you about . . . well, about Lisa.'

'What's she done?'

'Nothing, nothing. I'm just a bit worried.' I could see this wouldn't work. The dogs, the doorstep, his mood – none of it was right. 'Is there a better time when I could come to talk to you, or your wife?'

'We work, love. No time for chatting. Say it now, I've to be on my way.'

'It's just I've noticed Lisa seems withdrawn, and . . .' How to say it, that I thought her teacher, our esteemed headmaster, was doing things to her?

'Li-SA!' He leaned back and yelled, making the dog bark louder. Oh no – this wasn't what I wanted at all.

She appeared, her school uniform on but hair unbrushed, a look of terror on her face. The look of someone who'd been caught out.

'What's this about you being in trouble with school?'

I cut in. 'No, no, she isn't in trouble, I just wanted to chat to you and Lisa's mum, see if we can help her at all.'

'Fallen behind, has she? Thought that London fella was giving her lessons.'

'Yes. So that's what I wanted to—'

'Very good of him, and no charge too.'

'Well, the thing is, he shouldn't really have—'

'So if she's still crap at school, there's no hope for it, is there? Just not very bright. Nothing wrong with an honest job, factory or farming or whatever. Serving in a shop.'

I tried again. Lisa was making herself as small as possible, her eyes darting like prey ready to run. Behind her I got the impression of several older children, her siblings who were working or at the secondary school in Penzance, their mother shouting at them to hurry up and get dressed.

'Lisa, is there anything you want to tell your dad? About what we discussed yesterday? Mr Jeffries?'

Her dad frowned. 'What are you on about?'

Lisa stammered, 'N-nothing. I don't know what she means.'

Betrayal. But then, I had betrayed her too, by coming here. I could see it in her eyes.

He sighed at me. 'Look, love, I don't have time for this. And why you've brought Martin with you I've no idea.' Martin had thrown him out of the pub once or twice, I knew, so there was no love lost there, especially as he was an outsider and John McSweeney seventh-generation Cornish. 'If Lisa's done something, take it up with her mother. I've to get to work. Some of us work hard for a living, we don't start at lunchtime.' A hard look at Martin.

I could see it was hopeless, but I couldn't just leave. 'Lisa, please think about telling your parents. Maybe then we can help you.'

Lisa raised her chin. 'I don't know what she means, Dad. I'm fine. I'm not in trouble, I got ninety per cent in my spelling last week.'

Martin met my eyes, a quick warning. 'We'll leave you be, John. Janna was just wanting to offer her help, that's all.'

'Yeah, and I know what kind of help she gives. Herbs and potions and all that muck. Now, I have to go.' And he shut the door in our faces.

'They think I'm a witch,' I said, half-laughing. 'Who's going to listen to my advice about child safeguarding?'

Martin nodded slowly. 'People like him round the village, Jeffries. For all he's a Londoner. And you – love, there's a lot of people who don't trust you.'

I was stung by that. 'I've been here all my life! He's been here five minutes!'

'Well, and so have I. Sometimes folk turn on their own.' And there had been plenty of people I'd declined to help over the years. Refused that which would do harm, told them their illness was more serious than I could fix with plants, or that they had to stop drinking if they ever wanted to feel better. Affairs I knew about. Secret pregnancies, infections, judgements I had passed. There would be more than a few who'd want to see me fall.

Martin went on, 'And your grandma . . . people were afraid of her.'

'Well, yes, she was terrifying. But I'm not her.'

'They say you look just like her.'

I sighed deeply. 'What can I do? Leave town? I've got my mother to care for.'

'I think, love, you might have to let this one go. Unless one of the kids complains, like, or tells you for sure he's doing something.' But then I would be as bad as everyone else, closing my eyes to terrible things until they smacked me right in the face. Until it was too late to stop them. And that would make me a different kind of person, one I wasn't sure I could live with.

We had started to walk, and again I was aware of the bristle of eyes from every window. As we reached the point we'd have to part, he stopped for a moment, caught my elbow. 'You're sure about this, Janna? The girl – that something's happening to her.'

'She's never said for definite. But . . . yes.' I just was, with every instinct I possessed. 'What can I do about it?' I needed his advice, because I had no idea what to do.

'Leave it with me for now. I can have a word with Jeffries too, I've nothing to lose there.' Meaning he had no child who could be barred from the village school, whose life could be made difficult. And despite the herbs I had given his wife, a large part of me hoped he never would, or at least not with her. Perhaps that explains what happened to her next. Granny always said that actions done with a clouded heart turn out badly. My hands had made Morag good medicine, but my heart had only wished her ill.

◆ ◆ ◆

Later that day in school, Lisa's face told a story – a large black bruise, purple round the edges, as if someone had struck her across the cheek. I saw her trudging to the gates and horror filled me.

'Lisa? Are you alright?' Her father had done this, I supposed because of my meddling.

She gave me a mute look, and pushed past me into the building. I saw Jeffries greet her at the door, where he was waiting to welcome the kids in. I saw him touch the bruise, lightly, intimately, and I saw her let him. Close her eyes to receive it, even, holding up her face. He looked at me over her head, smug and cold. And I knew that, like someone cursed from Greek mythology, I had somehow caused to happen the very thing I had been trying to avoid.

I got through the day, working mainly with Susan, though my eyes kept straying to the wall, wondering what was going on in the next classroom. If I'd known that would be the last normal day, I might have paid more attention to the small details of it, the life I hadn't realised I loved until I lost it. The sunlight coming in the window, stepping out into the playground and smelling the sea, feeling it on the air. Walking on the shore, checking on my plants in the garden. The children, their chatter, their swooping joy and sudden sorrows, like flocks of birds wheeling in flight. Watching them grow and change. Even Mother, though I sometimes resented her, she loved me. She brushed my hair and stroked my forehead when she was able to. In prison, no one ever touches you with tenderness and it's one of the things you miss most. And Martin. Even the scraps of him I had, how much more precious they were. I have never seen him since, of course. I didn't let him visit me after the trial, for obvious reasons. It was for the best, for everyone. That doesn't mean it didn't hurt worse than anything.

◆ ◆ ◆

It's not easy, in prison, having a reputation for being a poisoner. I could never work in the kitchens, for example, and whenever a woman falls ill to her stomach, they all look to me, as if we're in *The Crucible* instead of a crowded space with food often well past its sell-by date. It's always a risk you run when you make herbal medicine, but no one had ever accused me of poisoning before Morag.

I first learned about it on the last day of term before the holidays. I walked to school slowly, for once not keen to get there and see the kids. I felt rattled, afraid, helpless to protect them. The sea wind was whipping my hair and I could see the pub sign creaking ahead of me in the village. I was thinking of asking Martin to take me out on his boat during the holidays, though I knew I couldn't, not really. But it was a nice dream. Just the two of us, the autumn sun golden on the water, the sounds of wind and waves drowning everything out, salt on my skin, the weight of the boat bearing us up.

'You've a nerve, you have.'

I blinked – a woman had stepped out on to the narrow pavement in front of me. She must have come out of the church hall – it was Alison Moncrieth, the vicar's wife. Not a position well suited to a hinge-tongued gossip, but she couldn't help herself. A thin, pinched woman, her dark eyes ablaze with the joy of some drama, an accusation to sling. She was wearing leggings and a pink sweatshirt with an embroidered peacock on it.

'I've no idea what you mean, Alison.'

'Morag's been telling everyone you poisoned her.'

'What?'

'You gave her some herbs, didn't you?'

'Well, yes, because she asked me for them.' My mind was racing. There were certain contraindications with the herbs. Maybe she had mixed them with the wrong thing . . . 'Are you saying she's sick?'

'Been throwing up for weeks now, then she took a turn for the worse last night. I thought maybe she was in the family way, but

Dr Smith says no, it's poisoning. Told her to drink milk and wait for it to pass.'

At least her life wasn't in danger. 'But that shouldn't happen. She must have taken too much, or . . .'

'I said, that's the last thing we need, a woman who deals in poisons working in our children's school!' Alison was the mother of Damian and Hannah, both dull, dumpy little things, the life scolded out of them.

I tried to stay calm. 'That's a very serious accusation, Alison. I'm a herbalist, and my family have been doing it for generations. If people don't take things correctly, don't follow my instructions, well, it's just like medicine – they can get sick, yes. I'll go and check on her.'

'Oh, they won't want you there! Sniffing around.'

I had moved past her, walking towards the pub, but at this I whipped my head around. 'What?'

'You heard.'

My heart was sinking – I'd thought I had hidden it so well, the things I thought about Martin, the way I looked at him and he looked back when no one else was around. Clearly, I hadn't.

I turned and went back up to her, pressed my face close to her thin one, till I could see the hairs on her upper lip and the smear of pan stick on her nose. 'Listen, Alison. Your husband has an important role in this village. And as his wife, if you're dealing in gossip and, quite frankly, slander, it's not a wise move. I have a reputation, and I will protect it if I have to.'

She blinked and stepped back at my tone of quiet fury. 'Well . . . maybe you should be more careful what you give people.'

'You were quick enough to take that mixture for your own little problem, weren't you?'

She'd forgotten that, the time she came to me with what was plainly crabs. I saw it cross her face – fear. Like the vicar and the

196

doctor, I knew things about this village, and I would use that knowledge if pressed.

'I just . . . I'm just telling you what people are saying,' she faltered.

'And I'm sure you'll tell them that they're wrong. Now, I must go and see my patient.'

With a confidence I certainly didn't feel, I walked on to the pub. I could feel every eye in the village on my back. I would be late for school, but I couldn't worry about that now, I had to fix this.

At the side door of the pub, I met Dr Smith coming out. An old and rotund man, he had semi-retired down here in order to drink a lot of wine and paint the sea. He could patch up small injuries and prescribe obvious treatments, but his diagnostic skills were rusty and out of date.

'Janna,' he greeted me. His face was grave.

'Is she . . . ?'

'She'll be alright, I hope. Did you really give her black cohosh?'

'She asked me for it. For fertility. Did she take too much? Or she mixed it with something maybe?' My mind was running over what I knew about the herbs I'd given her.

He looked past me, and I knew he hadn't bothered to get to the root of what was wrong with Morag. 'I told her to stop taking it immediately and rest up, drink milk and eat bland food. It'll be out of her system soon – but Janna, I have to advise you not to make these mixtures. You could be criminally liable, if something goes wrong.'

I was annoyed. If he prescribed the wrong drug to someone – as he had with beta blockers and the Olsens' asthmatic daughter last year – he would be protected by the NHS, the General Medical Council, his professional insurance. I had nothing and no one behind me. Perhaps I would have to get patients to sign something in the future if they came to me, but I really didn't want to do that – it would put off the many, many people who came in secret, ashamed of their maladies.

'I've been doing this for years, Dr Smith.'

'I know, and your grandmother, I remember her, she was extremely skilled in some ways. But with plants, we can't control the dose of active ingredients.' He patted my shoulder clumsily. 'I'm trying to help you, my dear.'

Dr Smith would testify at my trial that I had only good intentions, though he was even older by then, and the young prosecution lawyer ran rings around him, so I ended up looking more guilty than before.

When he'd lumbered off, I knocked hard at the door of the pub. After a while, it was opened by Martin, in his shirtsleeves. He just looked at me and I couldn't, for once, read his expression.

'Is she alright?' I asked.

'Throwing up non-stop.'

'There's a few things I could—'

'No. Janna, come on. No.'

'She asked me to give her medicine!'

I didn't want to say what for. He must know.

'Why didn't you tell me she came to you?'

'It was confidential.' And I was too ashamed, to talk to him about his wife.

'Aye, but you're not a doctor, are you? Not bound by any oaths? And she's my wife and you're—'

He stopped. Because what was I to him? Neither of us had a name for it. I wasn't going to beg, no matter what. I put my chin up.

'What I gave her was safe, if she didn't mix it with other medicines or take too much. I was trying to help, even though – even though it hurt me to. I'd have thought you would have understood that.'

I paused for a moment more, which I hated myself for – waiting for him to take me in his arms or declare himself or any of the stupid things I'd been imagining ever since he moved to Little Hollow.

'Martin. You know I didn't do this on purpose.' But did he know that? He was looking at me like he didn't recognise me. 'Please,' I whispered. Breaking my own rules. Begging.

'I think you should go, Janna. You've done enough damage.'

Walking through the village and down to school, the wind at my back, I felt more alone than I ever had before. When I arrived at school, breath coming fast, the children had already gone inside and the building was quiet. I was late. He would have something to say about this, I was sure.

When I opened the front door and stepped into the corridor, Nancy stuck her head out. 'Janna. Can I have a word?' Nancy and I had always been on friendly terms – if we clashed sometimes, it was always done from mutual respect. I'd never seen her like this, so cold and formal. 'If you'd just come into my office a moment.'

'Is that what we're calling it now – an office?' Normally we just called it the Broom Cupboard, after that show on kids' TV.

Nancy didn't laugh, just ushered me into the tiny room, and shut the door behind us. I could immediately feel it in my throat, the lack of light, the enclosed walls.

'What's going on, Nance?'

'Sit down.'

I didn't want to sit down. But I made myself.

'Mr Jeffries has asked me to speak to you about some rumours he heard in the village.'

I knew which ones. I sat back, folded my arms. 'We're dealing in rumours now, are we?'

'Janna. We've known each other a long time. I know that you – what you do in your spare time. The plants and things. And Mr

Jeffries, and the governors, they're a bit concerned about whether that's – safe for the children.'

I sat back, winded. 'I've worked here for years. Have you ever known me to harm a child, in any way?'

'That's not the point. We can't exactly wait until it happens. We have to make sure they aren't around anyone who could hurt them.'

Me. They thought the person who would hurt the children was me, who had only ever tried to protect them.

'So what, he's firing me?'

'Well, he can't do that without consultation. So he's going to start doing that. He asked me to inform you, officially.'

I stared at her and she squirmed.

'I'm sorry, Jan. I'm just doing my job.'

'Who's he consulting with, exactly?'

'The board, the parents. Me, Susan, Denise Jenkins . . .' Great. I knew exactly what Susan's opinion of me would be. 'Also, he thinks you're a bit too friendly with some of the kids. He saw you hugging Bobby Jackson the other day.'

'Do you know *why* I hugged Bobby? He slapped him. Your precious Mr Jeffries. Hit a child right in the face.' I was being unprofessional, and I saw Nancy's face change at my tone.

'It's in the guidelines, Janna, you know that. We aren't supposed to touch them unless really necessary. You've been having them to your house as well, I hear.'

I felt it boil up in me, that dangerous rage, a black river of tar. 'If anyone's been inappropriate, it's him. You know he's been giving the year six girls private lessons, in his store cupboard? With the door shut? That he's been meeting kids in the woods?'

She frowned. 'What are you saying, Janna?'

'I saw him.'

'Saw what?'

'Him. And Lisa McSweeney. In that space alone, after the school day. I raised it, if you remember, but no one seemed to care.'

Nancy was frowning intently. 'Are you saying something was going on in there? You want to make an official complaint?'

'Well, I didn't see it, but . . .' I could hardly say I just knew things, sometimes. And I knew this wasn't right. 'It wasn't appropriate. And there are things that she's – said, hinted, that make me very concerned.'

She frowned deeper. 'That's a very serious allegation, Janna.'

'I'm not making an allegation.' I hated myself for backing down. 'But if I shouldn't take a child to my house, when they're left out in the rain, surely he shouldn't be shut up in a small room with them.'

'No. Perhaps Lisa was just . . . perhaps the door blew shut or something. We can't ever be alone with them, you know. There are safety concerns.'

'I'm very aware of that, Nancy. That's why I brought it up in the first place.'

It hung between us, that I wasn't qualified. I might know everything I needed to for this job, I might be capable of doing it in my sleep, but I didn't have a piece of paper to say so, so it counted for nothing. It meant I was paid a third of what Adam Jeffries would be on – and even that I couldn't afford to lose. It ran through me suddenly, that my self-sufficiency was an illusion. I could grow all the vegetables and catch all the rabbits I wanted, but I still needed to pay for electricity to keep Mother warm and heat the bathwater, keep the lights on. We both needed clothes and her incontinence pads were expensive too. I couldn't make her go without – the loss of dignity would I think kill us both. So I had to keep this job.

I looked at Nancy with naked fear in my eyes. 'What should I do?'

'Look, we have to investigate, but there's nothing to find, is there? Just keep your head down for a few months. Enough of the parents will vouch for you, won't they?'

'I mean, I hope so.' I had been vocal, over the years, if children were being hurt at home. A cold mother who mocked her daughter. A father with a temper. Parents who left their kids alone every night to go to The Green Man. I would challenge them all, and of course they didn't like it. 'Everyone seems to love him, don't they?' I said bitterly.

She stiffened. 'He's a very effective teacher. The children have really responded to him, and the parents are keen, the governors too.'

Because he was charming. But abusers often were. I had to find some proof, I knew. Of the seeds of suspicion that were germinating in my mind.

'Alright. Thank you for the warning, Nancy.' I could see that was what it was. She smiled weakly, grateful I'd given her an out, probably.

'That's alright. I'm on your side, you know. I'm sure this will all blow over, don't worry.'

I went out to find Susan waiting furiously in her classroom. 'I need you to set up the AV equipment, Janna. Where have you been?' I scurried to it. Turning on a television, surely she could manage that. But I had to justify my presence here, clearly.

Small towns can be lonely when you're on the outside. Where was there for me to go aside from the house? If I lost my job, as I might after half-term, there was only the pub, and that was obviously off-limits. An occasional café in the village hall was also out of bounds after my run-in with Alison, who made the teas. I certainly wasn't welcome at the church, and hadn't been inside it since I was a small girl, and Angie made the post office unwelcoming as well. I began to feel the town had been safe before outsiders came. Martin and Morag, to an extent, and later, a more shadowy couple, Margaret and Adam Jeffries. In fact, it was as if Adam Jeffries was the source of all my ill-luck. To be thirty and full of life like the plants at high summer, but trapped in a damp, settling house, caring for my peevish and confused mother. In love with a man I could never have, and now suspected of poisoning his wife. And locked in an unnamed conflict with my boss, the person who could take away the one thing that was mine, my job with the kids. Looking back, it's really no wonder I felt so stuck. There was no other option left to me, or none that I could live with at least.

What else did I do on the final day? I arranged the Harvest table, helped the children make Halloween masks – a fact not lost on the media, who unearthed pictures of the 'chilling' tokens I had apparently crafted. Flat things of paper and glue, nothing scary there. The kids were in a good mood, ready for their break – it was a half-day for them, an occasion for joy. I clapped along as we sang various hymns in our end-of-term assembly, my heart heavy. Watched Adam Jeffries, every moment, every movement. He didn't treat Lisa any differently in front of the others – they had noticed her bruised face, of course, and there was a lot of nudging and whispering. I wonder if anyone told the police about that small detail, that just before the murders a girl had come in with injuries. Maybe it didn't seem important, after what happened next. Lisa would not have seemed like an important player in the story, after all. I'd made sure of that.

That day – it must have been a Friday – he had assigned me the normal tasks, beating out dusters, setting out the craft materials, helping those who struggled. At lunchtime, he stood up and clapped his hands together for silence. Large hands, a man's hands, strong and capable.

'Class, I want to let you know I'm going to be starting my one-to-one lessons again after the holidays. For anyone who needs a bit of help, or might want to try for a scholarship to the grammar school.' His eyes raked the room, and I could feel Lisa tense all the way across it. She had begun to wilt as his attention turned away from her, an unwatered flower.

'The next person to have lessons with me will be Lucy Fillane.' A murmur went through the class. Lucy flushed red then white, bit her lip. Grace was staring at her, puzzled. Lisa's face had fallen. Shock, and fear, and maybe a touch of anger.

Oh no, I thought. It wasn't over at all, as I had hoped. If anything, it was going to be worse.

'That's all,' said Jeffries, dismissing them. 'You can all go off home. Enjoy your break, and happy Halloween.'

Lisa hovered by her desk, and I saw she had that same stone with her, the one shaped like a heart. She was holding it in front of her in both hands. Jeffries looked up once, tidying some papers. 'Off you go now, Lisa,' was all he said. As if he'd never spent any time alone with her at all.

Later, much was made of the murders and their proximity to Samhain, that Celtic festival. Normally, I would perform my own rituals for the turning of the season. That year, I didn't have the heart. I could barely smile at the children as they raced past me, shouting *Happy Halloween, Janna!* I didn't know then how much I would miss that too, their childish voices, their puppy-like enthusiasm, their mess and noise. It has been years since I've even seen a child.

I waited till the last kids had cleared out. I had to say something. 'Mr Jeffries – do you really think it's wise? Teaching the girls like that?'

He glanced at me, as if he hadn't known I was there. 'I don't see that it's any of your business, Janna. You're not a teacher here, though you seem to forget that sometimes.'

'But – the child protection policies . . .'

He gave a short, nasty laugh. 'I was the child protection lead at my last three schools, Janna. I feel I probably know more about it than you do, wouldn't you say?'

I didn't know what to do. The other teachers had taken his side, and the governors were unlikely to listen to me, the lowly TA. 'I just – we need to keep them safe. It's our job, it's why we're here. And they're so vulnerable at this age.'

He perched on the edge of the desk. Had I noticed his camping gear stacked in the corner of the classroom, ready for him to head off to the woods? I don't know if I did or didn't. When it came down to it, there was no point in me arguing I couldn't have known how to find him later that day. Everyone knew he camped there often. I had followed him from school, perhaps. It would have been easy for me. 'After the break I think we need to have a serious discussion about your role here, Janna. I'm not sure you realise exactly who is in charge.'

Then he looked at me, and I knew – I just knew – that he realised what I'd done with the lotion. And he was telling me here, with that very public announcement to the children, that I could shield Lisa if I wanted, she meant nothing to him. There were other girls he could move on to. That he could do whatever he liked, and I couldn't stop him. Had I in fact made things worse by my actions? Would he have moved on to Lucy if I hadn't made such a fuss about Lisa – had I sacrificed one to save another? I've never known.

'I do realise that, I just – I . . .'

'I gather Nancy spoke to you earlier.'

'Yes.' I didn't meet his eyes, just focused on stacking the reading books, the comforting smell of old paper and dust.

'I couldn't help but hear some of the gossip that's been going round the village. About certain ... potions you might have made?'

'Medicines.' My voice was dry. 'I make medicines, I've always done it.'

'People are also saying that the husband of the woman you gave it to – you and him – well.'

My face was burning. If only I had been strong and pure, totally above accusation. But I had fallen.

'That's my private business.'

'Well, it isn't, I'm afraid, when you work with children. I'll be honest, I don't know if we can have someone working here who isn't qualified, who's known to dabble in poisons, whose morals have been called into question. And look at your appearance, how you dress. It's hardly appropriate.' He waved a hand, taking in my loose hair and flowing purple dress, not the drab greys and browns the teachers wore. He went on: 'Not to mention how difficult and obstructive you've been to me. I know it was hard, losing the power you'd gained under Mrs Critchley, but you were never qualified or entitled to run this school.'

I just stared at him. I didn't have a leg to stand on. How had this happened? How had I let myself be cornered like this?

'I'll be conferring with the governors over the break, Janna, but I don't want to give you false hope, or suggest this isn't extremely serious.'

'It's not true. You know it's not true.'

'Not true that you gave her the potion, and now she's ill?'

I swallowed hard. 'It would have been fine if she'd taken it properly.'

'Regardless, it's simply too dangerous to have you around the children, and I feel confident the governors will agree.' He stood up, straightening his trousers. 'You can go, Janna. I'll finish the rest myself.'

I felt sick. Nausea filled my body as I groped down the corridor, almost holding on to the walls in my shock. I saw a figure outside, silhouetted against the autumn sky.

It was Lisa, hanging about in the playground when everyone else had gone. Why, I could only guess. The bruise was still livid across her cheek. 'Lisa,' I croaked, my voice dying in my throat. She turned away.

'What happened to your face, Lisa? Please tell me.'

She flashed me a look. 'My dad called me a liar. Because of you.'

'I'm so sorry, Lisa. I was just trying to help you.'

'I don't want your help. You took him away from me! He won't meet me any more now because of you. Only Lucy.'

I knew what *he* she meant. She shouted it, and one or two straggling children looked back. Lucy and Grace, I remember, whispering together as always, their kitten-bright eyes taking it all in. Again, I don't know if anyone reported that to the police, Lisa's comment. Perhaps it didn't seem important. And of course Lucy and Grace would not be able to report anything.

'Lisa, I just – I know it might seem nice, that Mr Jeffries wanted to help you, he pays you attention, but believe me, it isn't.'

'I don't care. It's all your fault! You spoiled everything.'

Lisa ran then, and I let her go. I was too weak to catch up to her.

Adam came to the door of the school, his rucksack on his shoulders. I could see the difference in how he looked at me now. Brighter, colder, harder. Morag's illness had tipped the power balance, given him the excuse he needed to be rid of me, and the only thing stopping either of us from saying it was the ice-thin layer of convention. The need to keep a fragile peace, at least for a few more days until he could be sure of my downfall. It didn't seem far off.

'Her father,' he said, looking the picture of a concerned teacher as Lisa ran off. 'It's not right.'

'Perhaps we should call the police.' My voice wavered, cracking when I should have been strong, threatened him in return for the way he'd threatened me.

'Well. I'm not sure it's come to that, Janna. I hope you haven't been intervening again? You aren't trained in these matters.'

But what did you do when the person in charge of keeping the children safe was the very one hurting them?

'No,' I said, cowed.

'Well then.' He ran his eyes over me. 'You should go home. You look terrible.'

I dragged myself away without wishing him a happy holiday. I had a week to work out what to do. I could fight back, contact the governors myself and tell them my suspicions. Or I could just leave before I was pushed, use the time to look for another job, maybe in London. I could take Mother with me, if I really had to.

But Martin.

It might be wise for me to leave Martin behind as well, though I was doing my best not to admit it.

I was at home for about two hours, I think. I have retraced my steps many times, those last hours of freedom. I brought Mother up some cheese sandwiches. She was tired again, barely able to manage a few bites. I dusted her room and let some fresh air in, though she said it hurt her skin. I made a lesson plan for Remembrance Day in November, which I would never see taught, and Adam Jeffries would never teach. I drank a cup of tea. Feeling sad and helpless, I realised the only thing to do was go to the cellar and consult the book. Perhaps there was some remedy in the section I rarely looked at. The spells for love, revenge, cursing. I didn't entirely believe in those. But I was desperate.

I unlocked the door, taking the key from the pot on the kitchen windowsill, and descended into the gloom under the house. This was where my grandmother had made her potions and cast her spells, and she had believed in them, even if I didn't. This was also where she'd made the remedy that rid us of my father, that handsome man who liked to see his wife and child cry when he struck them. I was only five, but I had understood what she'd done when he collapsed after dinner one night, when my mother wept and screamed, when I crouched at the top of the stairs listening to Granny drag a body. A strong woman, she had done it all herself. Mother would have been no help, and she had never recovered from what happened that night.

Where's Daddy? I had asked in the morning.

Don't worry, Janna, my grandmother said. *I dealt with it. When there's a problem, that's what we have to do. Tresallick women, we deal with things.*

Feeling her influence on me, her dark approval, I took down some jars. What did I have that would stop Adam Jeffries? More henbane. Belladonna. Death-cap mushroom, just coming into season. Digitalis. Could I really do this? With no proof but my own fears and some vague comments from a child? I didn't know, was the answer.

But wait. Something was wrong. I ran my gaze around the dark space, and realised a bottle was gone from my stores. The gap in the middle of the row was like a missing tooth. It was a bottle of the 'love' potion I had started making at Morag's request – a stupid thing, just herbs and plants, like everything. I had only done it to assuage my guilt, not that it had worked. But it could be deadly in the wrong hands, if too much was ingested. I wondered who could have taken it – Lucy or Grace, that first day? Lisa, on the several occasions she'd been back? I remembered her earlier comment, that I had taken him away from her. The way he had dismissed her, turned to Lucy instead. She was just a child. Was it possible she might be so desperate for his attention, without knowing what it entailed, that she would try to use the potion? Oh God. I had to stop her from taking it – it would poison someone of her build and age. She was so young, so neglected – she might think she wanted something from him. But not this, never this.

A thought occurred – something else was missing from my workbench too. What was it? The knife. The sharp one, Granny's knife, that I used to crush tough stems and open seed pods. Was it really Lisa who'd stolen my things? More likely to be Lucy and Grace, surely, much bolder, less afraid of punishment.

I ran upstairs, panting for breath. 'I have to go out, Ma! I won't be long.'

That wasn't true, as it turned out. I would never see my mother again. As I sped from the house, my eye was caught by the oak tree. The luxurious growth of grass and daisies underneath it. No one had ever come looking for my father, content to believe he had simply left us, but the truth was he had never gone. He had been with us all this time, under the tree. Because Granny had handled it, and I had to do the same now.

I hurried down the hill to the village, the sun starting to shed golden rays over the huddled houses and shops. Not much life about the streets at that time, just after three.

No one home at Lisa's, the door locked, washing flapping on the line. I ran to the other end of the village, reaching Grace's family's bungalow first. There was no answer at the door, and I was about to leave when I heard a high, childish laugh. I went around the back of the house and the girls were sitting at the picnic table, Lucy and Grace. I remember they had glasses of orange squash, and a packet of Party Rings open on the table. They stopped laughing when they saw me, puzzled.

I was out of breath. 'Girls, is Lisa here?'

'Why would she be here?' Grace bothered with manners even less outside of school.

'You're friends, aren't you?'

'Eh, no.' They both laughed again. 'She'll be off with him, won't she?'

'Who?' Even though I knew.

'Mr Jeffries,' said Lucy. 'I dunno why but she hangs about with him all the time. In the woods and that.'

The woods, near the Devil's Altar. Like she had told me. 'He's still – I thought he wasn't teaching her any more.'

There had been so much I didn't know. Lucy shrugged. 'They just meet up. I don't think he teaches her now.'

I didn't have to chase after Lisa. I could have gone home, or I could have told the girls to be careful, I could have emptied their orange squash on to the ground so it all drained away, harmless, but of course it didn't occur to me. I had no idea what was going on.

As it was, I left Lucy and Grace without a backwards glance, not knowing I had been seen running along the street, visibly agitated, by two different neighbours who would testify at my trial, and I made my way as fast as I could into the woods.

I'd grown up among these trees, loving as a child the way the light fell through them, the ancient hush, the moss that made the ground so springy. The secret plants and flowers Granny knew where to find. But on that autumn day, sunny as it still was, they seemed foreboding. Adam Jeffries had come and spread his malign influence over everything I loved. I would not stand for it any longer.

It took me about half an hour to reach the Devil's Altar stone, deep in the heart of the forest. I saw no one else during that time – it was a weekday, still working hours, and the other children were too afraid to come in here by themselves. The secondary-school ones did, judging by the rankly sweet smell of old alcohol, the bottles piled up here and there and patches of burnt earth, but their bus hadn't come in yet. It was just me, Lisa, and Adam Jeffries. The key actors in this drama, which I saw now had been playing out for weeks. I remember I pushed aside a branch, the leaves sweeping my face like my mother pushing back my hair, tender, warning, and then there they were.

Here is the part I never told anyone, not at my trial, not in my police interviews, not any of the journalists or lawyers who've tried to get my story since. When they asked if I had killed Adam Jeffries, followed him into the woods or lured him there and murdered him, I had at first said yes, then tried to change my story, though by then it was already too late. But I offered no other credible explanation for who had done it. He'd hardly cut his own throat, after all, his body splayed out on the wide, flat stone. His tent nearby, a little fire smouldering still, a Thermos of tea still warm. He had knives too, sensible Swiss Army-style ones, that would have done the job if necessary. There had been no need to steal mine and bring it here, damning me in the process because it looked like premeditation. Here's the truth: when I arrived he was still alive. He was lying down on the stone, his breathing harsh, his eyes shut.

'What did you give him?' I was out of breath, hectic and dishevelled.

Lisa was standing over him. She was in her school uniform, and she'd let down her hair, which was shiny and long. She looked almost pretty, I remember noticing. She glanced up, not surprised to see me, gasping and covered in scratches and leaves, my long skirt catching in brambles.

'The potion.'

I saw the brown bottle there, cast aside in the weeds.

'You swallowed it?' I tried to remember exactly what was in the bottle. Strong poison, if ingested all at once. 'No. You gave it to him.'

I glanced at the Thermos. Easy to slip something in when he wasn't looking. Perhaps she had even made the tea for him, playing the little housemaid. He would have liked that.

'He didn't want me here. I could tell when I followed him today. He was annoyed. I thought it would help – but it didn't. Nothing's going to help, is it? He doesn't like me any more. He just – he *used* me. I don't mean anything to him.'

My mind was racing. Adam was still alive, if I could get him to be sick, throw up the poison . . . Then I saw Lisa had the knife in her hand. My knife, taken from my house. As I watched, horrified, she drew the blade lightly over his cheeks. But it was razor-sharp, as I always kept it, and blood welled up even at a stroke.

'Lisa, we don't have to do this. You've got your whole life to live, sweethcart. I can help you. Just give me the knife, OK?'

She was ten years old. Ten. I hadn't believed she could do it, even now after she'd poisoned him, stolen from me. But while I was still five paces across the clearing from her, she caught hold of his chin and ran the knife across his neck. Quite a light stroke again, but the knife was so very sharp that blood immediately gushed to the surface. Adam started making a noise, a gurgle, then he arched his back. He was half-waking up from the pain. He would have known he was dying; he would have felt his own blood flow down his throat. If I could stop it – I was already in motion, and I put my hands on him, his blood running over my wrists and down on to my dress, pooling there. I could feel the warmth of it through the material. I wasn't thinking straight – she still had the knife, and I had just seen her use it, but I could only focus on saving his life.

'Lisa, help me! Give me your jumper, or look for a cloth or . . .'

She just stood there. I remember she was smiling slightly, as if she had no idea what was going on. This was in the days before mobile phones, although I doubt there would be a signal in the woods even now. I knew if I ran for help it would be too late, and I would come back to find Lisa alone with a corpse. There was nothing to be done for him, and so as I pressed down futilely on his wound, gaping like a second mouth, I watched the life ebb from his eyes. I was sorry for him, in that moment, whatever he might have done. No one deserves to die like that, drowning in their own blood.

Lisa had not a drop on her, since I'd pushed her out of the way the moment it began to well up. I was drenched in it, all over my hands, embedded in the whorls of my skin, soaking my skirt so it stuck to my legs, on my feet and even in my hair. Lady Macbeth. Every inch the murderess, and the knife even belonged to me. Lisa was still holding it, and for some reason I knew exactly what to say next. What to do. My mind was as clear as water.

'Lisa.' I would have grabbed her except I was covered in blood. 'Go home right now. If anyone asks, you were always there. I'll tell them – I'll say I did it. But you need to tell them what he was, what he did to you.' Had he even done anything to her? She had never told me in so many words. 'Do you understand me, Lisa? When the police ask, you weren't here, but Mr Jeffries did – hurt you. Did bad things to you. Just tell the truth about that part and not the rest. That way we'll both be OK. Alright?'

She nodded. She still had that faint smile on her face. 'Yes, miss.'

'Now go home. Give me that.' I took the knife from her – blood on its tip – and wiped her prints off on the mossy ground. She turned away obediently. 'What about the girls?' I suddenly thought. 'Lucy and Grace – they know you come in here with him.

Will they tell the police?' I had to be sure there were no loose ends, though I could hardly think, stunned and stuck in the moment.

Lisa turned, and I remember the light falling gold over her face. 'Oh, they won't tell anyone.' And she was gone.

I had a moment alone with what had been a man, what was now just meat. I laid my hands on his chest and said sorry. That I had not prevented this, what happened to him, as well as whatever he might have done to the girls. I thought about running, I'll admit, for a moment. But I had no car, and I was covered in blood. I would never get away without someone seeing me. And someone had to take responsibility for this, because the headmaster was dead with his throat slit, and he would be found soon. Someone had to have done it. So I made my decision. It was easy in the end. I could see nothing else to do.

I walked down to the road, knife in my hand. It was very uncomfortable as the blood dried on my legs, becoming tacky and chafing. I wondered who the first person I met would be, and as it happened, it was a man named Bob Marks, a labourer on his way back from a job, walking along the road with his backpack, his hard hat dangling from it. He knew me, of course – I'd treated his wife for polycystic ovaries, and now they had twins.

He nodded to me, then as I came closer he did a horrified double-take. I staggered over.

'I've killed him,' I said. My voice was high in my ears. 'I'm sorry, but I've killed him. Will you call the police?'

No mobiles in those days. Bob had to run home to make the call, and so there were five or ten minutes where I just sat down at the side of the road, right there in the grass. One or two cars passed, I remember, faces looking out at me in curiosity, though no one stopped. Later, they would all be interviewed and give their testimony.

When I heard the first sirens, I knew it was Stephen Brady, the local police officer – the only one for the whole of the west of Cornwall – on his way from Penzance. He'd been two years above me in school. As I heard him coming, the noise echoing off the trees and deep into the woods where the body lay, I prepared what I was going to say.

I stood up as he pulled over, in his uniform, his face showing the same mixture of shock and confusion as Bob's had.

'Janna? What the hell?'

'I killed him,' I said, as calm as I could. 'I didn't mean to, but I had to.'

'Him? What him? You mean . . . The girls – did you do that too? Why, Janna?'

'What girls? What do you mean?' I thought of Lisa, hoped she had made it home to her empty house, no one any the wiser she'd been out.

Stephen got out, and I saw that he was grey with shock. 'Lucy Fillane and Grace Monkton. I've just been to the house, Janna – they're dead.'

Lots of things happened after that, of course. There are many steps between a murder and going to prison for it. There would be the months I spent on remand in a prison near Bristol, the strange limbo when I could technically still be set free, found not guilty. My lawyer, a patronising middle-aged man, had told me that was unlikely, given I'd been arrested with Adam's blood all over me and carrying the knife that killed him. There were the days of questioning before I was charged, a confused nightmare of no sleep and windowless rooms, more and more senior officers being brought in from as far as Portsmouth, all of them stumped by this case. The twenty-four hours before they could find a forensics person, during which I wasn't allowed to shower and had to sit there with Adam's blood drying and flaking off my hands and feet, stiffening my hair to my scalp. My attempts to take back my confession, say I hadn't done it after all, without revealing who had. The appeal I would launch after five years, dismissed by the court within hours. The almost thirty-six years I would spend behind bars.

All of that was ahead of me. But when I stepped forward and let Stephen arrest me, from that moment on I was never free again. He didn't put handcuffs on me, though maybe he should have. I got into the back with no protest and he drove me in silence to the small station in Penzance, where I was booked in by another officer, and brought into a windowless interview room. I was given a plastic cup of water, but I was left in my blood-stained dress. Outside, I heard them discussing what to do about me.

'Maybe someone can bring her clothes from home,' said Stephen. The sad thing was I couldn't think who I could even ask to do that. There was only Martin, and I couldn't involve him in this. Then came my first interview, and I knew how important it was to get my story straight from the start. But I had not anticipated the final sting in this tale, and my mind could not make sense of it. Stephen recorded that I hadn't seemed to know what happened to Lucy and Grace. I was in a sort of shock by then, I think. I didn't really believe it.

'But you went there, Janna – the neighbours said you were the last person to see them, that you ran away from the house?'

'Yes, but I – I wanted to make sure they were OK.'

'Why?' He was baffled, way out of his depth. Usually he dealt with stolen farm equipment and drunken punch-ups on a Saturday night.

'I was worried about them.' How to broach the whole story of what had happened? 'Mr Jeffries – he'd been . . . hurting the girls.'

Had he even? I'd been so sure, but what if I was wrong? What if I'd misinterpreted all the hints and rumours I'd heard? 'How did they . . . I'm sorry, I'm very confused here. How could they have died? I just saw them.'

In my head at this point, I had decided it was all a misunderstanding, owing to my fevered brain. He couldn't have said they were *dead*, could he?

'It looks like they drank poison, Janna. It matches what was in Jeffries' Thermos, and we found the bottle in the woods.'

I opened my mouth and shut it again. The bottle from my shed, left in the weeds at the murder scene. I had forgotten to take it with me or to hide it. They would find it all – my writing on the label, my prints, the gap on the shelf in my cellar. A trail leading straight from Grace's house to the woods, connecting the crime scenes.

'I . . . they were at my house the other day. Maybe they took it then.'

He wrote that down. 'It was yours then? The bottle?'

'I . . . don't know. I imagine so.' I remembered the glasses of orange squash, the biscuits on the table. Had they put it in their drinks? They'd wanted to try a love potion? I didn't understand. Was it my error, allowing them access to it, a fatal carelessness? Why had these things happened on the same day, at the same time?

Suddenly, it hit me how much trouble I was in. 'Listen, Stephen, this is important. The reason I did it – Jeffries, not the girls, I would never, ever hurt a child – it was because he was hurting the kids. The girls. You need to talk to Lisa McSweeney about it.'

'John's girl?'

'Yes. She'll confirm it – what he was doing. I had to stop him, you see. I didn't mean to – this wasn't supposed to happen. I went to talk to him and he just – he attacked me, so I fought back, but I didn't mean to hurt him. It was self-defence.' I was frantically trying to remember what I knew of the law around murder. If it wasn't premeditated, if he had struck first, that was less serious, wasn't it? But the knife had come from my house, so it would look as if I'd brought it with me. And I could hardly have bumped into him in the woods by sheer coincidence. I had clearly gone after him. And I'd been poisoning him too, they would surely find that out soon. A noose had closed around me, and I hadn't even noticed it. In the end, my patronising lawyer wouldn't even let me speak in court. There was no evidence of anything I claimed, he said. Better just to stay quiet. 'Please. Just talk to Lisa.'

He nodded and went out, his brow creased with worry. I feel sorry for Stephen, a simple man who got caught up in one of the most notorious murder cases of the decade. It changed him, I think, as it did so many people. I heard he died a few years ago, barely sixty-five.

After he'd gone, another man interviewed me for a few hours, the same questions over and over. I forget how many people I spoke to in those first hours, although I know that not one of them was a woman, and all of them were older than me by at least fifteen years. I could see it in their eyes what they thought of me, my blood-soaked hippy dress, my long fair hair, the witchy silver jewellery, the charms I carried on my person to protect against evil (hilarious in a way, that). Stephen returned around ten, and I was so pleased to see him. I had the idea that it could all be solved now, that they would, if not thank me, at least understand why I had done what I'd done.

'Well? Did you talk to Lisa?'

He hesitated. 'Janna, I don't know if I can . . .' He didn't know how to deal with me, his old schoolfriend, an accused murder suspect. 'She didn't know what I was talking about. She was in bits, poor girl. Her teacher and her little friends at the same time! She said all the kids really liked him. So.'

It's amazing how we cling to hope, long after we should. I think it's how the mind works, to shield us from going mad. Lisa was ten; she probably wouldn't want to tell the truth to a male officer her dad drank with.

'I need a lawyer,' I said.

They would tell me what to do, maybe put Lisa on the stand if it came to a trial, get the truth out of her about the abuse. Unearth Adam Jeffries' past, the reason he had left London. I still had hope that Lisa would come through for me, in return for me taking the blame for the murder. If I made one mistake in all of this, it was that I didn't see her for who she was, what she had been made into. It was that I didn't understand what children can be capable of.

'Of course. We'll get you a lawyer, Janna. Miss Edwards. That's your right.' He was trying to distance himself from me, though he'd be taken off the case the next day anyway. Too close. When Stephen left the room, someone else came in, a female officer that I didn't recognise. Older than me, solid and no-nonsense. They must have brought her over from Truro or somewhere.

'Janna, is it? Your man here didn't book you in properly, so I'll have to do that now.'

She took my fingerprints, leaving me inky and smudged, and catalogued the possessions I'd had on me – the knife, my rings, and charms, that was all. I didn't carry door keys and I'd gone out without any cash, in my haste to stop something terrible happening. There were no pockets in my light dress. She asked about medications and any health conditions I might have, any dependants. Promised me someone would check on Mother. I could hardly imagine how she would take the news. It might be the thing that pushed her over the edge, and I felt the worry dimly, through my bubble of shock.

Then she said, 'Now, I have to ask this of every woman we take into custody, Janna – is there any chance you could be pregnant?'

It was a routine question, and she had her pen hovering already over the 'no' box on the form. But I swallowed hard and made myself face what I had been ignoring for weeks. That morning with Martin, very early at the beach almost two months ago now, and I had barely allowed myself to think about it, that it had happened again, the thing we had promised not to do. Though it was like torture to stay away from him, I couldn't stand the betrayal. The sickness ever since, the odd unsettled feeling. The fact my blood hadn't come, and I'd pretended to myself I was just stressed, not eating enough, though nobody knew their body better than me. I had to admit it now, because it was the one thing that might save me from this trap I had walked right into.

'Well. Actually, now that you mention it . . .'

I couldn't settle after the private detective's visit. I joined the ranks of the other upset women in the prison, though I wasn't crying or banging my head off the wall.

In the past, when I felt like this, I would have taken down my Tarot, the old cards that had been Granny's, and run them through my hands, feel which one called to me. In here, they aren't allowed, though I've asked repeatedly. It's at the governor's discretion, and she's a Baptist, I've heard, so likely thinks them the work of the Devil. I had made my own, drawing the images as far as I could remember on to bits of paper. There was a book in the library that showed them, an encyclopaedia that must have slipped past Governor Holiness's gaze. The light bits of paper would never have the same impact as my own cards, heavy and well used, but they would do. I closed my eyes and ran my hands across them. For a while after my arrest, I had lost faith in these practices. Then, one day, I had found myself tearing up the paper and tracing the

221

designs, and even if I didn't believe it with my whole heart, there was something in it. If only a way to read my own thoughts, based on what I saw in the cards. Reach into the murky pond of my mind and dig about.

The Tower. I shivered to recall the image on that – a burning building, lightning in the sky, people plunging to the ground. It could mean a disturbance in living situations, not always bad. A move. Or trouble with a house. It could mean imminent danger. Well, I knew what that was. The Page of Cups – a young man, innocent, to be protected. George, maybe. That made sense too. The last one made me laugh out loud. Justice. A female figure with her scales, dishing out just deserts. Did that mean I'd face mine? Or that someone else would?

My son was married to Adam Jeffries' daughter. How could this have happened – did he know? Did she know? Back then, finding myself pregnant and facing a life in prison, I had turned to Margaret for help. I had asked her to look out for my boy. It was possible in adoptions to keep a family link going, not that Margaret was family, but she was the only one who might have helped. Perhaps unsurprisingly, she had never answered, never even seen George, as far as I knew. So how had this happened? Had Helen somehow tracked him down? Did Margaret know too? Was any of this remotely possible?

I knew that it was. It was exactly the kind of thing I would have done.

◆ ◆ ◆

Later that day, I had my appointment with my case officer. Julie is a nice enough woman – perpetually sniffing from an allergy she seems to have to the plants on this vast plain. I always want to offer her a tissue, or better yet a remedy, but of course I have neither.

It's one of the hardest things, seeing what could be healed and not being able to do it. As if anyone would ever take medicine I made again anyway.

'So, Janna.' She was chewing on the end of a cheap, leaking biro. Behind her was a calendar set to July – last year – and a dying pot plant. 'How are you feeling about your upcoming release?' It was up to her to give the final go-ahead.

It was hard to believe I was getting out of prison, finally, at last. That my years of appeals had finally borne fruit, and they were letting me off the final fourteen years of my fifty-year sentence – generous of them.

I smiled at Julie. 'Good. I think I'm ready.'

'And you're planning to go and stay with your son, once your post-release conditions are met?' She read from her notes, with no sense of the story behind those words.

'That's right.'

'This is in the same village where your crimes took place? Do you anticipate any fallout from that?'

'It was thirty-six years ago. And the family of the . . . man . . . they've long since moved away, I believe.'

I couldn't say *victim*, even after all this time. Julie could not know that Adam Jeffries' family might have moved away, but one of them at least had come back. Why would this Helen return to the village her father had died in? Perhaps she knew I was getting out – Margaret would likely receive a letter about my release, as the widow of my 'victim'. But why had Helen married George in the first place? I didn't understand any of it. 'And the girls. Their families have gone too, I believe.' I'd had to give up my insistence that I didn't kill the girls. It would not have counted as rehabilitation otherwise.

Julie was tired, she had a lot of people to see. She wanted to fill in her boxes and send me on my way, out of this place and no longer her responsibility.

'Janna, would you say you feel remorse for what you did?'

I did feel remorse, of course. Not for killing Adam Jeffries or the girls, because I didn't do it, but for all the rest of it, the accidental damage, my failure to prevent a disaster I saw coming before anyone else. For all the pain and loss and suffering that I was unable to stop. So I was able to smile sadly at Julie, and say with absolute sincerity: 'Oh yes. I'm more sorry than I can ever express.'

She stamped something. 'Alright, Janna. I see no reason why we can't proceed with your conditional release next week. Here's a list of the rules you'll have to follow.' She passed me a badly copied sheet of paper.

'Thank you.' I stood up, taking the paper. I had hardly dared hope for this, and I wouldn't believe it until the gates of the prison shut behind me. But it was time, after thirty-six long years. I would be free, and now I could finally track down the people who'd put me in here, and settle my scores.

Helen

George was more upset than I'd ever seen him.

'I don't understand,' he said. 'Who are you? Explain. Now.'

I'd been sitting on the bed in our room, still surrounded by boxes and bags, when he stormed in, after being out for the best part of the day with no contact at all. I carefully set down my book. 'You seem really agitated. Where've you been?'

'I . . .' He was pacing. 'Look, we really need to talk. There's some things I haven't told you, and there must be things that you haven't . . . it just doesn't make sense! And she's gone, she's not even there!'

Word salad. I tried to get on top of it, remain the calm and rational one, as I had always been, although my lungs seemed to be closing up and my hands were shaking. I put them under my crossed legs.

'Babe, you aren't making any sense. Who are you talking about?' I could guess, but I needed to bluff this out as much as possible until I could see what he knew.

'You know. You do, don't you? That I . . .' He trailed off, staring at me wild-eyed. An ocean of unspoken words between us.

'Are you talking about Janna?' I offered, reaching across to him. 'You know about her. Right?'

'Well, yes. I found out why people are so hostile to us here, why they shun the house, that it used to belong to a murderer everyone thinks was a witch. I do know that, yeah. Did you think I wouldn't find out?' I was annoyed he'd thought me so stupid.

'I . . . was going to tell you.'

'This book, that's what it's about? Buying the house of a murderer?'

He was still staring at me. 'I have no idea what you know right now. I just – I don't even know where to start. It's like you're a total stranger.'

I was doing the same calculations myself. Did he know what I knew? He couldn't. How would he have found out?

'Why don't we just tell each other the truth?' Not that I meant it. Not the whole truth.

He took a deep, juddering breath. 'I didn't buy this house.'

'Well, yes, I guessed as much.'

'I inherited it. From my mother.'

Again, my mind went to Ruth in Reading, and I was baffled – but that wasn't what he meant. He meant his birth mother.

'Oh,' I said. Of course. Everything fell into place. It was as I'd suspected, though I hadn't wanted to believe it – he had found out the truth at last.

He stared at me. 'You know, don't you? Who my mother is?'

I could have lied, said that I didn't. But there is a space in a marriage, between the two of you, where everything is known on some level. Where the breaking of a trust can be felt. And I couldn't lie directly to his face. Not after all this time.

'Yes.'

'And your father – he was Adam Jeffries.'

How did he find that out? My mind raced ahead, framing more lies, denials. But I couldn't do it, so instead I just said, again, 'Yes.'

'My mother killed your father.'

'Yes.'

It was all I could think of to say. He was still standing over me, and I felt his confusion, the house of cards tumbling around him. Truths I had known for years suddenly hitting him. There were other things I didn't know – how he'd learned who I was, why he'd lied to me about the house, when he'd discovered his mother's identity, and where the money went if we hadn't actually paid for the place – but these were small compared to what he was just now finding out.

He said, 'How – how long have you known this? That we were . . . connected in this way? I mean – how could it happen? I don't understand.'

I sighed. May as well keep pushing on with the truth – we were drenched in it now, swimming hard against the current, and another lie would pull us under.

'George, I've always known.'

That wasn't entirely true, of course. For the first eighteen years of my life, I didn't know the name of my real father. Mick had come along when I was nine, and before that we'd gone by Mum's maiden name, Gillis. I hadn't even realised this wasn't my father's name – you don't ask about these things when you're a kid, and if I thought it was strange we didn't see any friends or relations, I didn't question it too much. Then, I was nineteen and coming to the end of my gap year – there hadn't been the money for me to go straight to uni – all set to go to medical school in Durham, when one day my mother said we had to talk. I remember it was mid-June and I'd just come back from my job at the hospital, where I worked in the cashier's office, trying to get together as much cash as I could, desperate to kick the dust of this town from my feet. Mick had gone out fishing for the day, and I was alarmed by the way Mum sat down opposite me at the kitchen table, making intense eye contact. We didn't do that kind of thing, she and I. I hoped this wasn't about sex because I was well aware of that (and had been doing it quite happily since I was fifteen).

'Helen. There's something you need to know, about your dad. What happened to him. I'm telling you now because you'll have that internet at university, and you might . . . see stuff.' She had always refused to get the internet at home, and my primitive Nokia didn't allow for such things.

But what she said next I had never even suspected. My father was a man called Adam Jeffries, and in 1986, when I was two, he had been murdered.

'A woman named Janna Edwards went to prison for his murder,' was how she phrased it. Careful.

It didn't feel real. 'Who was she? Someone he knew?'

'They worked together. At the school.'

I knew he'd been a teacher, a headmaster.

'Were they . . . ?'

'No,' she said, very firmly. 'He wasn't involved with her. People said that, but it wasn't true. Don't ask me again, Helen, but I'm sure of it.'

My mother was rarely so forceful, so I paid heed. I was nineteen, wearing bootcut jeans and an Adidas sweatshirt, my hair straightened to within an inch of its life. I wasn't ready for any of this. 'So – she's still alive? His killer?'

'She got fifty years. So, unless she wins an appeal, she'll stay in prison till she dies, most likely.'

I wanted to ask everything. All the details of how it happened, how she killed him, and above all why. But I could see how every word cost my mother dear. Her face was frozen with the effort of forcing them out.

'And – you knew her too?'

'I had met her a few times. This was in Cornwall. We lived there when you were very little. Just for a few months.'

'What?' For some reason this shocked me most of all. A part of my life I'd had no awareness of. 'I was born in Cornwall?'

'No, you were born in London. We left there so he could take the job, and then we lost him, so I moved here.' Devon. Close enough, but not so close I'd ever heard about this murder. 'We were only there a few months before it . . . happened.'

'Oh.'

'I know this is a lot. You can look it up on the world wide web if you must – you'll find out lots of nasty details. Two girls died the same day. Ten-year-olds.'

'She killed *children*?' I couldn't believe all this. How had I never known I was connected to such a grisly case?

Mum bit her lip, her eyes glassy, as if looking into the past. 'I don't think we'll ever know what happened that day. But the girls died too, and she was convicted of the three murders. That's why she got so long in prison.'

I sat back. I remember the grain of the cheap wooden table, the ugly raffia place mats we'd had all my life. Had my father sat at this same table, used these? I had no sense of him at all, bar a few photos of a handsome man in outdoor gear.

'Well. This is – kind of mad. Is there anything else you can tell me?'

'There's a lot, obviously. Whether you need to know it or not, that's another matter.' Then she pushed the box across the table to me – the same one I later found again in the attic. 'I kept some things about the case, in case you wanted to know one day. Cuttings and that. You can read what you like, but I can't talk about it any more. I just can't. Is that understood, love?'

What else could I do? She was saying, this story is yours too, go and learn if you must, but I won't be a part of it.

'Alright. Can I just ask one thing?'

Her face tensed. 'What?'

'Where was I? When it happened?'

Had I been nearby? Did it take place in our house, with me in the next room? Had I seen my father die and not remembered it?

She tutted, as if annoyed by the question. 'You were with me, of course. At our house. It was a few miles outside the village, nowhere near where it happened. It was hours before anyone even came to tell me.'

My father had been murdered. Murdered! I could hardly believe it. I was part of a whole story, and I hadn't known it. After that I took the box to my room, and Mum and I have never spoken about it since.

The newspaper clippings told me a fair bit, and I went to an internet café in town and paid for several hours of use, clicking and clicking until they kicked me off. I saw her picture, Janna Edwards. Blonde and beautiful, smiling in the images before the murder. Afterwards, as she was snapped going to and from court, I saw the knowledge of it on her face. Terror, shock. And one thing stuck out above all, searching as I was for my place in this story – a mention about the victim being a 'father of one'. I was that one.

There was a picture of my mother going into a police station that looked to have been taken by a paparazzo. She was tight-lipped, a scarf over her red hair – where had I been then? She hadn't attended the trial at all, apparently.

I learned that the murder had taken place at a slab of rock called the Devil's Altar, in some woods not far from Penzance. I suppose I would have read the name Little Hollow then, but the Devil's Altar was the one that stuck in my mind. Later I found out the villagers did their best to promote that, keep their home out of the press. A lot of the reporters didn't check details anyway, called the area Penzance or Lamorna or even just 'Cornwall', as if they couldn't be bothered to learn the exact spot.

I found out that she had cut my father's throat, this woman, and tried to poison him first. That the girls had died from drinking poison the same day, poison that was traced back to a potion she'd made in her cellar. That she was considered locally to be a witch, that people speculated my father had been killed as part of a satanic ritual. That he'd been a respected member of the community, a valued teacher. That no one could understand why she would kill him, except that he had raised some concerns about her work and conduct, that she might be fired soon. Was that enough to murder someone – a man with a young baby? Did she even think about me as she took his life? A child who would grow up never even remembering her father?

As well as spending all my money in the internet café, I went through the box of cuttings again and again, finding out the what and who and when, but never the why. Maybe there was none. Certainly she had never given a motive in court. She had pleaded not guilty but not offered a defence, not even given evidence herself. No one else had been there at the time, and he'd hardly killed himself. It was an open-and-shut case.

Then I saw it. A long white envelope stuck in the flap at the bottom of the box, which had once held Tunnock's Teacakes. It had the postmark HMP Longacre. The letter had been sent from prison. My heart began to hammer – I remember I was in my childhood bedroom, with its built-in white chipboard wardrobe and Blu-Tack from my A-level revision notes still clinging to the striped nineties wallpaper. I opened the envelope.

At first I was confused. There was no letter, just another envelope, torn open, and a letter inside that. That letter had been sent *to* Janna Edwards, not from her. Had Janna forwarded it on to my mother? Had there been a note of explanation with it, now vanished? The address on the first envelope was in Cornwall, and had a mail-forwarding stamp stuck over it.

My main question – why, why, did Janna send this to my mother? It made no sense at all. Just to taunt us, to torment Mum even more? Hadn't she done enough, killing my father in cold blood before I could even remember him? And had Mum meant for me to find this, or just forgotten it was in there? I didn't dare ask. It was a mystery I have still never solved.

The letter had been sent from someone called Ruth. No surname. In it she was thanking Janna for allowing her to adopt a baby. Janna's baby.

We're going to name him George. I hope he will have a happy life. We live right near the Thames, and there's a boat club next door, a cricket pavilion two streets over. The letter was dated July 1987.

Frantically, I started pulling out the rest of the news reports. There was nothing in the press about Janna being pregnant at her trial, and in the court drawings and the brief news shots of her being bundled to and from court, no sign of a bump. But she had been arrested in October 1986, and the trial was not until the following June. She could have been pregnant while on remand. And of course they'd take her child away – you couldn't have a baby in prison.

The murderer had a son, and she'd given him up for adoption – or been forced to. This child would be almost three years younger than me. I knew right away that I had to find him. I had no idea what I'd do when I did or what I was looking for – revenge, amends, healing, justice? I just knew I had to do it.

A George who'd grown up beside the Thames. I spent hours looking for him online, which was a lot less easy in 2004. This boy would be seventeen now – maybe he had a place at university already. I trawled through what felt like most of the internet before

I found one – George Sanderson. Grew up in Marlow, right by the river, in a pretty cottage. Played cricket for the school team. Edited the school paper, hence his name was all over their website. It was a nice school. Mine didn't even have a paper, let alone a functioning website. I would click on his pictures for hours, zoom in obsessively. Was this him? He had dark hair, not like Janna. Wore glasses. In a rather dull article about where the upper sixth were going to university, he alluded to the fact he had chosen UCL, so he could live in 'the Big Smoke', and he poked fun at those headed to posher enclaves. Oxford, Cambridge. St Andrews. It was impossible to tell if it was the right boy or not, but that day I told Mum I was withdrawing from my place at medical school.

'What?' She just stared at me. 'Helen, this is your future.'

And that was my past. 'I need time to process it. Everything you told me.'

'But – what are you going to do?'

'I'll work for another year. Save up money.' And wait for George Sanderson to start university. 'Maybe I'll transfer somewhere else. Durham's bound to be full of posh people, after all.' I'd already be twenty-one by the time I started, old for my year, but I didn't care.

You know the rest of the story. I got into UCL with ease, after spending almost two years working in the same hospital. I watched George around campus for a few weeks – he was prominent, always hosting debates or getting into political arguments with people, and one night I approached him in the student union, when he was absolutely smashed. I could see no trace of his mother in his kind, open face, the scruffy beard below piercing blue eyes, the ubiquitous hoody. Was this really him, Janna Edwards' son? If I could find out his date of birth, I would know for sure. He would have had to be born sometime before the trial, in the May or June of 1987.

He was too drunk that night in the student union, so the next day I followed him to the student canteen, where he always ate before his early tutorial, and I struck up a conversation. I could tell that he liked me, and it gave me a surge of power, something I'd been missing since I learned what had been done to my father. But what was I going to do, now I'd found him?

Panicking, I almost cancelled the date I'd agreed to go on with him in a fit of foolishness. The whole thing was ridiculous – how could I date the child of my father's killer? But I still didn't know for sure. I told myself I'd get to know him a little more, just to see if I had the right person. I went to the gig, which I didn't enjoy – it was crowded, and the music bored me. But it was easy afterwards to get back to George's room, which was filthy, full of guitars and CDs and socks on the floor, a carton of milk left out to spoil. He had photos Blu-Tacked to his walls and I examined them closely.

'You don't look like your parents,' I observed, even though that wasn't noticeably true.

'Oh yeah. I'm adopted.' He was struggling to open a cheap bottle of wine.

'Oh?' It had to be him. It had to.

'It's no big deal, I was only a baby, so I don't remember.'

'You ever wanted to find your birth mother?'

'Hmm, I'm not sure. Sometimes I wonder about her, what she was like. If she had my eyes or liked writing or hated peas like me – seriously, *never* offer me a pea. But I've got a mum, the best. So I don't know. Why rock the boat?'

'I think I would want to know.' So he had no idea who he really was. He had grown up without any contact with Janna.

'Maybe I will one day, I don't know.'

'My dad's dead,' I said, impulsively. 'He was killed. When I was a baby.'

George's expression changed. 'Oh my God, I'm so sorry, Helen. Do you remember him at all?'

'No. In some ways that makes it worse.'

'So – it was a long time ago?'

'1986. Halloween that year.' That was risky – what if he looked it up? The date didn't seem to mean anything to him.

'I'm really sorry. I mean, Halloween is bad enough with kids on a sugar rage and guys off the rugby team competing to find the worst bad-taste costume. The Twin Towers, I heard someone did last year.'

His little joke gave me a moment to wipe my eyes, and I was grateful. I didn't want to cry in front of him. 'A two-person costume, or one?'

'God knows, not sure those guys can even count to two. Anyway, let's get drunk. Ta-da!' He'd got the cork out, leaving several bits floating in the murky red liquid. 'For madame we 'ave the finest vintage, would madame like to taste?' The first time I experienced his French waiter voice.

'Why not?'

He poured me a dribble into an Oasis mug, and I swallowed it. 'Oh, no, no, madame, you must speet it out! Barbarian! You must not swallow ze wine!'

I played along. 'I'm getting notes of cork . . . more cork . . . would this be the 2004 Tesco?'

'Madame is quite the expert!' He filled the mugs, clinked with me. 'Cheers.'

'Cheers.'

'I really am sorry about your dad.'

'Thank you.'

We talked for almost two hours, about music and our courses and life. The time just seemed to melt and slip away, he was so easy to talk to, so funny. He didn't find it odd I was older than him – I muttered something about glandular fever, then spent the next eighteen years worrying that he'd bring it up in front of Mum. Of course, I could have had no idea then that finding Janna's son

235

would not be a passing whim. That I would marry him, and my lies would haunt me for years. At one point, just to be really sure, I asked him casually when his birthday was. Perhaps I was hoping he'd say a different month or year, so we didn't have to be connected in such a terrible way. So we could just be strangers who kind of liked each other. So I could explore the weird feeling I had that we'd always known each other – *oh, it's you*.

'Star signs,' I smiled, by way of explanation.

He rolled his eyes. 'Of course you're into star signs. Girls! Eh, I have no idea what sign I am. It's June fourteenth though.'

'Gemini then,' I said, having learned them before. It was him. It had to be him. I wonder if George has ever thought how out of character this was for me to ask about star signs, since I've never showed any interest in them again. He was pretty hammered, so he possibly doesn't even remember. My heart was pounding as I swallowed the horrible wine. This was him. This boy, so funny and smart and fun, was the son of the woman who'd killed my father.

And the worst part was, I liked him. I really, really liked him.

Now, almost twenty years later, George looked like someone whose world had crumbled.

'You tracked me down? You stalked me?'

'I just – wanted to see you. I thought, I don't know, since I couldn't see her, maybe it would help me understand. Why I lost my dad. Why she killed him.'

'So . . . that first night we spent together? The gig, the kiss . . . all of that was nothing? Our *marriage*?'

'Of course it wasn't nothing. For God's sake, George. The only thing you didn't know was how I found you in the first place. Once we met I . . . well, it was real after that.'

I'd told myself he would never know who he was, or who I was. And my mother would never know either – would never make the connection between my scruffy, cheerful husband, and the murderer Janna Edwards. Even if she had read Ruth's letter to Janna, which I wasn't convinced she had, or she'd never have left it in the box for me to find, I didn't think she'd figure it out. Who would imagine George and I could meet by coincidence, fall for each other, marry? It was unthinkable. Over time I came to believe it was true, that his real mother was Ruth anyway, kind and flustered, always making sandwiches just in case anyone was hungry. That it wasn't George's fault who his birth mother was, and he didn't deserve to know his dark legacy. So I had never told him. I just kept on living my life, loving him, convincing myself the secret would never come out, and now here we were. I had never even googled the case again, not once since I was nineteen. I'd made a promise to myself that I would try to forget the past, that I would never even think about it in front of George, in case he should uncover my lies. I couldn't bear that, you see. For him to look at me differently, like I wasn't perfect, and special, and brilliant.

'When did you find out?' I asked. 'About her?'

'Oh, they told me at eighteen I was adopted, I could find my mother if I wanted. You know that. I never wanted to, so they didn't tell me who she was. Trying to protect me from it, I suppose. Then you and me – well, we needed to move, so I asked Mum and Dad for help, and I suppose they realised they had to tell me about the house.'

'Janna made the house over to you.'

'Years ago, apparently. When my – when her mother died. So it's just been sitting empty.'

'And you decided we could just come and live in it.'

'It seemed a good solution. Not far from your mother. And – there's a story here.'

I understood, at last, why he had kept all this from me. 'That's what you're writing about. Finding out that your mother was a murderer, moving into her house.' It was a good idea for a book, I could see that. I just had never realised George was so ruthless. I'd thought it was just me.

'Yes.' We were so cold with each other. Just an exchange of facts, nothing more. 'Extra twist for me here, finding out I'm married to Adam Jeffries's daughter. That's a bestseller right there, that is.' He was so bitter.

'Weren't you upset? To find out your birth mum is a killer?'

'Well, I don't know, Helen. Think back over the past year, did I seem upset to you? When I couldn't get off the sofa, couldn't shower or so much as make a cup of tea?'

He'd never spoken to me like this before, not even in the depths of misery. So cold and contemptuous. I hadn't realised his latest depression was caused by something in particular. There had been many periods like this over the years, and anyway, I'd had other things to think about during that time, caught in the undertow of my job, fighting to stay afloat. We had both lost sight of each other.

'You lied to me. About buying the house.'

He scoffed. 'I hardly think you're in a position to throw stones here.'

'I didn't lie to you. I just . . . tried to protect you. I thought Ruth and Gerald would never tell you about Janna, if you didn't look for her. There was no reason for you to ever find out.'

'I suppose they decided the truth was better than lies after all. Though I'm not sure that's right.'

A thought occurred to me. 'Wait. So if we didn't buy this place after all, where did all the money go?'

We'd put down almost two hundred grand, or so I'd thought, all our savings over the years.

George blanched. I hadn't thought he could go any whiter, but here we were. 'Oh. Well, yeah, about that . . .'

I put my head in my hands. Who was this man I had married? I'd thought him innocent, lovely, sweet and funny and not quite strong enough for the world, someone who had to be shielded at all costs from the truth. And here he was, lying to me for months, and quite probably he had spent all our money without telling me.

'What did you do with it?'

'I was out of work for two years, remember,' he said stiffly.

'I thought you were freelancing.'

'Huh. Yeah. A hundred quid for a thousand words, less for blogs . . . I couldn't tell you, I was so ashamed. And plus, I – well, it's expensive, looking for work.'

I didn't know what he meant, but then I remembered the research trips he'd gone on over the past year, the new laptop, the piles of books he apparently needed to read, the training courses in new software. None of it leading to any work or any money.

'You took out a loan?'

'A loan, credit cards, overdraft. Then there's repayment fees, and interest, and – it's a scandal, really, how they trap you. It just keeps mounting up. And then we got this free house, and it seemed like the perfect way to start over. Clear the slate.'

'By using all our money. *My* money.' I hadn't wanted to say it, but it was the truth. Our savings had mostly come from my salary, my sweat and tears at that hospital. I couldn't help bursting out with: 'Christ, George. That money would have been for IVF, you know. If we needed it.'

'Funnily enough, I don't think that's top of our priorities right now. Given that you've been lying to me the entire time I've known you.'

There are things between people that, once said, cannot be taken back. Damage that can't be healed. George and I sat in our shattered home, facing each other across the battlefield of lies and secrets. Who had come out the worst? Me, for lying with good intent, though I had stalked him in the first place, tricked him? Him, for lying now? Defrauding me?

'What are we going to do?' he said, after what felt like a long time.

'I don't know. I really and honestly don't know.'

How could we go on like this, knowing the truth of each other? Mum would be broken by it, if he wrote his book, if the secret came crashing out. Everyone would know what I'd done in marrying him.

Then he said something that shocked me: 'You've never considered there's a chance Janna didn't do it?'

'What?'

'People had doubts at the time. There was no real evidence, after all – no witnesses.'

'She confessed, George!'

'At first, yeah. But then she changed her story, pleaded not guilty.'

'The poison was hers.'

'It wasn't poison – well, anything can be a poison, I suppose – and anyway, that doesn't mean she gave it to the girls. Does it?'

I sighed. 'They sentenced her to fifty years. That means they were pretty bloody sure she did it.'

'I know, but . . .' His face was so naked, so vulnerable, and I loved him so much still, despite all the lies between us, it almost made me gasp. 'She's my mother, Helz. I have to at least hope she's innocent. If there's even the smallest chance.'

Was it possible? I had spent my life thinking her the worst person in the world, someone who had robbed me of the life I should have had, taken my father from me. 'You really think so?'

'I – listen, there's something I haven't told you.'

'Oh God. What now?'

'I called the prison earlier. The one she's been in all this time. I had an idea – I might try to visit, at last. But they told me – well, she got out already.'

I stared at him. I had never countenanced a world where Janna Edwards did not die in prison. 'But – she still has years to serve.'

'Parole, I guess. It was a very long sentence she got – a lot of people thought it wasn't fair. Apparently they'll have written to your mum to tell her, victim impact and all that. But yeah, she got early release.' Mum would likely never have seen such a letter. Mick often let the post pile up for weeks.

'So where is she?'

'I have no idea.'

'George – someone has been watching us, since we got here. I've seen shadows – someone in the trees.'

He nodded reluctantly. 'I saw them too.'

'So where's she going to go if she's out? She'll come back here. To her house.' I suddenly thought of the hole in the wall, the rattling, insecure doors. We were so isolated and unprotected. 'What do we do? We have to get out of here.' He said nothing. 'You really think she didn't do it.'

'I don't know! I have no idea if she's wrongfully convicted, or some – brutal killer who's on her way to us. I need to find out.'

'So – what's your plan?'

He sat down finally, on the bed beside me, pulling a notebook from the stack of papers and books on his side. 'I've already spoken to most people involved in the case, if they're still alive. Martin from the pub, I'm pretty sure he thinks she's innocent, though he's keeping schtum. Nancy, the school secretary, she was a character witness; and the other teacher, Denise Jenkins, she vouched for Janna too. There was a girl from year six who lives locally still, Lisa McSweeney – she was a bit vague but she seemed to think Janna didn't kill the girls at least. The policeman who first arrested Janna is dead, unfortunately, and then of course there's . . . well, your mum.'

'She can't exactly tell you much,' I said tartly.

'No. I wouldn't ask. But there's the other teacher at the school, Susan Bodger. She would have witnessed most of their interactions, Janna and – Adam.'

My dad. Maybe it was easier to talk of them as strangers. 'You spoke to her?'

'She put the phone down on me. But I've a feeling she must know more. Just something she said.'

'She's still local, in Cornwall?'

'Not too far. Gweek.'

I nodded, as if I had already thought all this through, as if years of believing Janna was pure evil had not been overturned by the terror that I might lose George. I still didn't think she was innocent, but I was willing to humour him at least. 'Alright then. Tomorrow, you should go. We should. I'll come with you.'

'Do you mean that?'

'If you really think Janna isn't guilty, you need to try and prove it.' Myself, I could hardly believe it. I'd seen the evidence years ago, and it was compelling. But if there was a way to save my relationship, for me not to be married to my father's killer's son, then I wanted to find it. Because we couldn't go on after this, both of us knowing who we really were. I could see the truth of that. I had been able to live with knowing whose child he was, but he couldn't live with knowing the same of me. 'Either way we need to know what we're up against. If she really is back here, and if she's the one who's been watching us.'

'Alright.' He looked stunned by all these revelations.

'I'm going to bed,' I said, getting up to brush my teeth. 'There's nothing else we can do tonight. Go down and check all the windows and doors are locked.'

'You do know there's a hole in the wall.'

'Yes, I'm very well aware! What else can we do? We'll put a chair against the bedroom door.' Janna would be in her sixties now, and had been in prison over half her life – could she really be a threat to us? George was right, we had to find out what we could before we decided what to do.

George hesitated. 'Can I – there's nowhere else to sleep. No sofa.'

There was no reason we shouldn't share a bed. Nothing had really changed between us, not on the surface. We were still George and Helen, still in love. Just finding out our whole marriage was built on a bedrock of lies. 'Like you say, there's nowhere else.'

When I came back from the bathroom, he had turned the light off and was lying on his side, away from me. I felt his weight in the bed as I climbed in, and I knew he was awake, but neither of us said a word.

◆ ◆ ◆

After the night at George's room, back at university, I could no longer deny it – this was the son of my father's killer, and he seemed to really like me. I was a sensible girl, despite my mad actions in following him to UCL. I knew I should leave it there. No good could come of pursuing it. And so I did leave it. I stopped answering his texts, buried myself in work, avoided the students' union and the nearby pubs. Ate in my room instead of the cafeteria. My mind kept throwing up funny and sweet things he'd said that night, him pushing my hair back from my face with awkward affection, making wine come out of my nose with an impression of Liam Gallagher, getting me to test him on the name of every single Bowie album in order (of course he got them all right). Lou, who lived next door to me, thought I was mad. 'He's really into you and he's cute, what are you doing?'

'I have to study. I don't have time for boyfriends.'

Lou looked sceptical. She was studying hard too, for a law degree, and still managed to snog at least four boys a week. 'You don't have to marry him, Helen.'

But I stayed firm, even if I found myself thinking of him during dissections and in lectures and scanning the room on nights out, just in case he might be there. And I would have stuck to this. I would have forgotten George Sanderson in time, I'm sure. Married a nice cardiologist or something. But a few weeks later, Halloween was approaching. Most of my friends loved it, the chance to dress up and go wild – the medics really liked to party. But for me, it was the season of my father's death. Of a loss I would never be able to heal.

And George remembered. On the day of the murders – Halloween itself – he was outside my room, leaning awkwardly against the wall with a bunch of wilting daisies. No one had ever bought me flowers before and I was touched, despite everything. 'Hi.'

'Hi.' He cleared his throat. 'Um, look, I won't stay. I don't want to bother you, if you're not interested. But I remembered what today was – and I thought you might be feeling – well. Here.' He thrust the flowers at me, and I could see he was nervous, sweating. He had remembered that today was the day my father died. He was innocent – he knew nothing about who his mother was or what she'd done. He was just George. Just the nicest, sweetest, funniest boy I'd ever met.

I unlocked my door, holding the limp flowers in my other hand. 'Are you coming in then?'

'Oh. I don't know – um, it's OK if you don't . . .'

'George. I'm asking you to come in.'

So he did. And we've rarely spent a night apart since. I didn't know who I'd be without George, and I hoped I wasn't about to find out.

◆ ◆ ◆

The next morning George was up before me, something that was practically unheard of. Usually he would try to pull me back into the warm pit with him, and it would take all my self-control to leave his solid arms and face the chilly morning air. Maybe all that was over now, the part of our lives where we'd been happy. I washed as best I could in cold water, since we still had no functioning boiler, and brushed my hair, pulled on old clothes. Everything felt dirty in this house, as if its corruption had seeped right into our skin. He was downstairs drinking coffee, and I could see he hadn't made me a cup of tea, another shift in our dynamic.

'We should go soon,' was all he said. 'It's an hour's drive at least.'

'Alright.'

I had to content myself with a glass of water from the tap – or rather, a mug of water, since all our glasses were either dirty or unpacked. The bread I'd bought a few days ago was already mouldy.

We drove in silence for the hour or so towards where Susan Bodger had moved, a small town on an estuary called Gweek. I twitched at every movement, straining to look at every face we drove past. Janna Edwards was out in the world, something I had never imagined. What would she do – where would she go?

The landscape was different here, jungly and overgrown, though the coast was very near, as it always is in Cornwall. George pulled up by a riverside cottage, painted white and blue, the garden kept very neat and regimented, with red begonias nodding outside.

'Shall I come in?' I said.

'I suppose. Might seem less threatening that way. She didn't want to talk to me at all on the phone.'

I undid my seatbelt, and we crunched over her pebble drive to her blue door, which had a porthole in it, nautical style. There was no answer to the first few knocks, and I would have given up, but George's final try was emphatic, and the door opened slightly, left on the latch.

'Hello?' he called. 'Miss Bodger?' Cautiously, he took a step inside, and then he exclaimed, 'Jesus Christ!'

'What?'

Then I got it too. A thick smell of blood, ripe and meaty. I darted away as a cloud of flies buzzed out the door, some brushing my face.

'Oh my God.' George stumbled back – he was pale in the bright daylight. Inside, the house was dark and shuttered, so I couldn't yet see what had so alarmed him. 'She – I think she's dead.'

I peered inside past him. On the floor of the living room lay a body. A woman who looked to be in her sixties, judging by her grey hair and clothes – walking trousers, fluffy slippers – but her face was obscured by a torrent of dried blood. This time, I did not hesitate, did not find myself rooted to the spot. Perhaps because she was so clearly dead, I could be no risk to her. I had to certify it though, and I was already moving towards her to feel for a pulse, when George stopped me with a hand on my arm.

'No, Helen. You can't leave any DNA.'

'But—'

'She's dead. Her throat's been cut. And there are – marks.' He made a compulsive gesture against his cheeks. 'Someone's . . . cut her.'

I could see from across the room she was stiff and pale, likely dead a few hours only. No lividity yet. 'It was recent.'

I could hear a wheezing in George's chest. His asthma always got worse when he was upset. 'They'll think – Christ, Helen, we'll be the ones to find her. They'll think we did it. And I'm *her* son. And it's the same way, the throat.'

He wasn't making any sense. 'George, we have to call the police. They'll need to send an ambulance, there'll be an autopsy at least for a suspicious death.'

This was murder, though, wasn't it? If her throat was cut. The cause of death was clear.

His eyes were wide. 'I can't go through it again. Being in the news. I can't.'

'But it's not the same at all, George! You're not making sense.'

He clutched my arms, and I could see the whites of his eyes. 'What if it was her?'

I didn't understand for a moment. 'Janna?'

'Susan gave evidence against her. Janna's finally out, so what if she's taking revenge on everyone who sent her to prison? She lost so much – her whole life. Me.'

Seconds ticked by, and I felt frozen where I stood. I was a doctor, I should have been checking the woman's vitals, even if it looked hopeless. I should have called the authorities already. Instead I just did nothing. Shock, maybe.

Janna was out of prison. And one of the key witnesses against her had just been murdered, her throat cut just like my father's had been. If Janna had done this, who would she come after next?

I ran through the list of witnesses George told me about. Nancy, the school secretary, who lived far away. Martin, but he'd never testified. 'You should call people – everyone you spoke to. Warn them they could be in danger.' Then I realised who was most at risk from a newly freed Janna, bent on revenge.

'Mum,' I said. 'I think Janna wrote to Mum when you were born – it's how I found out you existed. She sent Mum a letter she'd got from Ruth, about your adoption.'

George looked as surprised as I'd been. 'What? Why?'

'Honestly, I've never understood it. I'm thinking they must have been friends or something, but she couldn't have expected Mum to help when she'd killed – after what she did. It doesn't make any sense.'

'You really think she'd go after your mum?'

'I don't know.' I was already moving. 'Come on, get in the car.'

'The police?'

'There isn't time to wait. I'm driving.'

There was no answer to the phone at Mick and Mum's house. I made George run over our story as we drove towards Devon, in case the police did track us down. We had turned up at Susan Bodger's door, but she was already dead.

'You didn't touch her?' I asked him for the third time.

'No – I just . . . I ran back out.'

He would likely still have left hairs or fibres, fingerprints on the door. But they wouldn't know who to look for and of course he wasn't on the system. Then I realised I perhaps wouldn't know if he was.

'Have you ever been arrested?' I said bluntly.

'What? Of course not!'

'Just asking. It seems there's a lot you weren't telling me.'

He just raised an eyebrow at that, and it was true, I was a hypocrite.

I thought of another problem then. 'OK. There's the car though. That'll be picked up on ANPR, so they can probably trace us and find out we drove to the area.'

'Um. You know, I don't think I ever updated the address with the DVLA.'

'George, that's against the law!' Honestly, I couldn't trust him with anything.

Another eyebrow raise, and I conceded the point. 'Alright, so they'll go to London first. But they'll find us eventually. So what will you say when they do?'

'That I was going to interview her about this case, because I'm writing a book on it. I'm a journalist, that's all. I didn't have an appointment, it was just on the off-chance.'

An old-fashioned doorstopping, because she likely wouldn't have agreed to see him. That also helped us, since she wouldn't have told anyone we were coming.

'Did anyone see us run back out?'

'I don't think so, no. The house is kind of isolated.'

'Right. So maybe they won't even know a car was there, if we're lucky. Will they recognise your name – that you're connected to the case?'

'I can't see how. Unless they looked way back into the adoption.'

And me, I had a different name now. I was sure they would find us soon, but maybe not today. For now we just had to keep us both away from the police and figure out what was going on.

'You really think she did this? Janna?'

'God, I don't know. I'd hoped she was innocent – but it was the exact same method of killing. Even the – cuts. The face.'

Mutilations, he meant. Like my father. I realised I had also allowed myself to hope for a moment that George was right, that Janna somehow hadn't killed him, that we didn't have this between us.

'So what's her goal here?'

'She probably blames Susan for giving evidence against her. Maybe she's . . . chasing down people involved in the case.'

And in the meantime my mother might be at risk. 'Try Mick again.'

George held the phone to my ear as I drove, and this time Mick picked up the landline. He'd likely been out at the shops for his daily paper.

'Mick? Is Mum OK?'

'Helen, is that you? She's fine, love, I was over there an hour ago.'

'And she didn't have any other visitors today, anything like that?'

'No, why?' He was baffled.

How could I explain this? 'Mick, you know what happened to my dad, yes?'

We'd never spoken about this. 'Well, yes, love. The basics.'

'The woman who killed him – she's out of prison. I'm worried she might come to see Mum.' I was playing down my fears, partly to spare him, partly because George was right and we had to keep this to ourselves for now until we worked out what was going on.

'Oh. We should call the police then, love!'

'No, no, it's nothing serious like that. I don't want Mum upset, that's all. With the memories. I'm going over there to check on her now.' Calling the police would only draw attention to us, the fact that we had fled a murder scene.

Where could Janna be? She would hardly have much money if she'd just got out of prison – and wouldn't she have to check in with a parole officer or something? And did she know I was married to her son? How I'd tracked him down and lied to him for years? If so, it might well be me she was coming for.

'But Helen, love—'

'Please, Mick, don't ring the police. I have this under control. I'm on my way there now.'

'If you say so.' He must have been confused. I hardly knew what to do myself, just praying Mum would be alright, and counting the minutes on the drive through twisty, shaded lanes, on to the motorway and surging east. The care home seemed just as usual, calm and brightly lit as I threw myself into reception.

'Is she OK? My mum – eh, Margaret Gillis? Margaret Keown, sorry.' I was getting mixed up. She had used Mick's surname for years now.

I didn't recognise the nurse behind the desk, who looked at me in puzzlement. 'She's absolutely fine.'

'Sorry, sorry. I'm her daughter. Helen. I was just worried about her.'

'I don't understand. Did she call you or something?'

'No, of course not.' Mum hadn't been able to use a phone for months now. 'I just . . . it's hard to explain. Can I see her?'

'She's asleep now, I'm afraid. It's outside of visiting hours.'

'I know, I just – need to see her. Look, there's an old friend of hers who wants to visit her, but Mum wouldn't want her to, if she could speak. If someone comes here, could you promise not to let them in?'

The nurse was looking down her nose at me, in my dishevelled, incoherent state. It's not every day your marriage unravels and you also learn your mother-in-law might be on her way to kill your mother, in my defence.

'We can't bar people. Unless your mother gives an explicit order to that effect.'

'Right. It's just – it would upset her very much, to see this person. Can you at least make sure she understands who it is? Give her a chance to communicate before you bring someone in?'

'We would do that anyway.' Her tone was extremely frosty.

'Thank you. I know this sounds mad – can I please just look at her for a second?'

'Do you have any photo ID on you?'

'Oh God. Is this really necessary? Wait.'

I fished my driving licence out of my wallet. I didn't have the same surname as Mum, since I'd never taken Mick's. Or George's, which wasn't even his own. I wondered what his surname might have been, if anyone knew who his father was. Nothing I'd ever read had mentioned Janna being in a relationship. The nurse stared at my ID for a long time, accusing.

'Alright. Just a minute, don't wake her up. She had a difficult night.'

She led me along the long corridor with its smell of rubber and urine, to Mum's room. A small lamp burned by her bedside, the curtains drawn against the daylight, but she was asleep, peaceful even. The pain ironed out of her face in rest. Ignoring the nurse, I stepped forward and smoothed the grey hair from Mum's forehead. She'd once been so careful about dyeing it, in the hairdressers' every Friday. Then I spotted something on the bedside table, beside the lamp and tissues and framed photo of my wedding. She'd had a picture of Janna's son all this time and not known it.

'What's this?' I asked the nurse in a harsh whisper. It was a small brown jar, and when I unscrewed it, a strong smell of herbs came out. Some kind of lotion inside.

'Oh, I don't know.' She was looking at her watch. 'I do need to get back . . .'

'Did someone drop this off for her? So someone did visit?'

'I'd have to check with the night staff.'

A cold feeling was running through me. Janna had made potions like this for her victims, my father, those girls. To be consumed or absorbed through the skin, often using a compound called scopolamine, found in plants like henbane. In the right dosage it could cause hallucinations, convulsions, and death. Those symptoms, in a stroke patient with aphasia, would likely not be detected, as no one would think to run the tests. My hand felt itchy where it had touched the glass, likely a psychosomatic reaction, but I put it into my bag, thinking I would try to have it tested. Although who could test for a thing like that?

'I'm taking this away,' I said to the nurse. 'She shouldn't have unprescribed medications.'

She was puzzled. 'Isn't it just hand cream?'

'I don't know. But please, don't give her anything new, or let anyone in to see her. Or else . . . You'll find yourself facing legal proceedings. You know I'm a doctor myself.'

I hated to say it, and saw how her face stiffened up in irritation as she nodded. But I felt I had no choice. Had Janna come here and tried to poison my mother?

◆ ◆ ◆

A large part of me wanted to stay with Mum, but the staff wouldn't allow it, and I knew there was a chance I'd draw Janna there if I did. As we drove home, having given strict instructions that she wasn't to be left alone, the jar in my bag lying there like a snake, it came on the radio: *A woman has been murdered in the Cornish village of Gweek. She has been named locally as Susan Bodger, a retired teacher. A murder investigation has been launched . . .*

I tensed, digging my nails into the material of the seat. It was real. A woman was dead, and we had found her body. George and I didn't look at each other but I was sure we were thinking the same thing. How long before they worked out that the woman Susan helped put away had been recently released from prison? Would that then lead the police to us?

The next news item was a warning about a storm coming in.

'That's all we need,' he said, fear strangling his voice. 'Where should we go? Is it even safe in Little Hollow?'

'I don't know.'

Wouldn't Janna gravitate there, to her old home? Our insecure house, that had a hole in the wall, loose roof tiles, windows that rattled in their panes? I so much missed our safe London flat, even the black mould that grew in the shower, no matter how much I squeegeed and sprayed it.

'Where else can we go?' He shook his head – there was nowhere that wouldn't draw her to people we loved. If she was even coming – I still found it hard to believe, that she could be out of prison and bent on revenge. We drove the rest of the way in silence, two people in an uncomfortable temporary truce. I couldn't think what to do, my thoughts fuzzy and jangled. Had we already missed our window to call the police? George's reaction to the idea had been so vehement – was he hiding other things from me?

It was already raining when we reached The Gables, and I had never found it more foreboding, black against the darkening sky, the surrounding trees whipped to a frenzy. No lights on to welcome us back, and when we made a dash for it through the rain, coats held over our heads, the cold draught blew through the wreck of our living room. I still had the jar from Mum's care home in my bag, and drew it out, unsure where to put it. How could I find out what was in it? I settled for putting it in the half-destroyed kitchen, washing my hands thoroughly after touching it, though it looked so harmless, just a little brown jar with a screw-top lid.

The living room was freezing and filthy. I couldn't face it a moment longer, the dusty house with the abandoned tools, the kitchen with its jars and charms, the very walls full of Janna's malice. How stupid I had been, to walk right into this. To chase down her son, and let myself fall for him, to lie to him, and think I could get away with it. I'd imagined she would die in prison, I suppose. And now she was free, the blood of at least three people on her hands, perhaps four. The house was freezing – the builders still hadn't come to turn the boiler back on. The only place with any warmth at all was bed.

George and I barricaded the house as best we could, locking doors and windows, piling furniture in front of the gap in the wall. The builders had keys, of course, which I deeply regretted. We'd been so naive, handing them over to people we barely knew and couldn't trust. I should have known, with my past, to be more careful.

All that night there was such a terrible banging. The storm moaned and wailed, and though I am a rational person, brought up to not believe in any of the superstitions and witchery that had contributed to my father's death, I was frightened. George and I lay together in the big bed, neither of us sleeping. Not sure what to do, or where to go for help, or what would become of our marriage now. I had never felt so alone – I could no longer talk to Mum, I couldn't burden Mick with the truth, and Lou also felt a million miles away. Even if I had the reception to call her, she would be bewildered, insist we rang the police, left the house. Something was stopping us. Maybe some impulse to believe George, hope we were wrong about Janna. Maybe the need to finally know the truth.

'What's that?' I said, after several sleepless hours, straining to hear a noise.

'I don't know. The gate maybe.'

There was a rhythmic knocking, as if something was banging to and fro in the wind.

'Can you go and see what it is?'

How primitive this was. A man and woman, human animals, lying in the dark listening to the sounds of the storm. Wanting him to keep me safe, in our cave, our shelter.

'It's tipping it down.'

'I know! But something might blow away.' My mind was racing ahead. The shed roof, the porch tiles, the tarpaulin and chipboard protecting our living room . . . 'Please, George.'

He tutted in the dark. 'What does it matter if something blows off? I think we've got more serious problems, don't you?'

'But what if . . . well, the house isn't exactly secure, with that hole in it.'

Another sigh. 'If someone's coming after us, there's nothing we can do to stop them.' So he wasn't going to do it. He would not protect me, when it came down to it.

And I found myself thinking: *At least we don't have a child.*

The banging continued. Bang, bang, bang, bang, bang-bang-bang. It must be changing tempo with the wind. I could hardly hear anything else over the storm's fierce roar, the windows rattling, the house almost swaying in it, like we were on a ship at sea. It even sounded like a person shouting at times, as it roared through the trees and whistled at the gables that gave the house its name. I couldn't stay here any longer. Tomorrow, I would get out and find somewhere else to stay. If George wouldn't come with me, I would go alone.

I must have fallen asleep, because I woke up some time later with an even louder banging, and the ring of the doorbell.

'Someone's here.' My heart was thudding in my chest, adrenaline flooding my system. George was snoring lightly; I prodded him hard with my foot. 'Someone's *here.*'

'Alright! Jesus.'

He got up, fumbling for his glasses, and I switched on the lamp. The clock read just after four. Who would come here at this time? Would Janna bother to ring the bell, at her own house?

I followed George downstairs, my bare feet light on the bare and dirty stairs. There was a black shape at the door, illuminated against the occasional flashes of lightning.

'Don't just let them in!' I hissed, as George advanced towards it.

'What else am I supposed to do?'

'See who it is.'

Not Janna. A man.

'It's Martin,' he said, short with me, and undid the chain. Pointless to have it when the house was so insecure, but it was at least a gesture against the danger.

Martin was indeed on the doorstep, soaking wet, rivulets running down his hair and over his black anorak.

'Is she here?' he barked.

'Helen?' George glanced up at me hovering on the stairs in my pyjamas.

'Janna.' Martin barged in, bringing a gust of cold air and dripping water on to the rug. 'Did she come here?'

And I realised from seeing his outline in the door who had been watching us those times, from the treeline in the garden. Martin, not Janna.

'It was you,' I said out loud, and he glanced up at me. 'You've been lurking about here. Spying on us.'

'You weren't safe,' he said. 'I tried to tell you not to stay here. Now answer me, is she here?'

'No!' George ran his hands through his hair. 'Look, we don't know what's going on. I didn't even know she was getting out of prison, and now I find she's maybe killed someone else, and Helen's mum had some weird medicine left at her care home, maybe it's poison, and I just don't know what the hell's happening, OK?'

Martin frowned. 'You think Janna had something to do with Susan Bodger's dying? I didn't know she was out either until they sent my last letter back. I wrote to her, all these years, though I never heard a word from her.'

George frowned back. 'She's only just out of prison, and look what's happened – a major witness against her gets their throat cut.'

George should not have known details like that, how the woman had died, but it was too late to stop him. 'And how did you know I meant Susan Bodger, anyway? What's going on, Martin? What's your role in this?'

But I had finally figured it out, seeing the two of them together, as I never had before, the way they both stood with their shoulders cocked, as if ready to flee. It was like looking at George older, without the glasses and beard.

'Oh my God,' I blurted, and they both whipped their heads to look at me, and the effect was heightened even more. Their faces were equally blank and confused.

Janna had already given birth before the trial, she hadn't allowed anyone to visit her in prison, Martin had been married at the time . . . maybe he didn't even know she had been pregnant. Certainly not that it was his child.

'What?' said George, irritated, but he wasn't really paying attention to the look of pale shock on my face, he was too agitated. 'So what do we do? She'll come here, I suppose. Where do we go?'

Martin sounded irritated too. 'Janna won't hurt you, lad, for God's sake. She never would. It's her I'm worried for. She's definitely not here? Didn't sneak into the house without you noticing?'

'There was a banging,' I said, hugging my arms to myself. 'Some strange noise, it's been going on all night. It sounds like maybe it's under the house.'

'The cellar,' he said grimly. 'Did you look there?'

'Um – no.' I had been too spooked to go back down after the incident with the dead bird.

'I heard noises,' George said, looking pale. 'A few days ago. But there was nothing.'

Somehow the idea chilled, of a void beneath my feet, holding secrets in its dark corners.

'What if she's down there?' I voiced my fear. It was plausible. The walls were thick, and we'd learned to ignore the creakings and groanings of the old house.

Without speaking, the three of us moved to the cellar door. As we did, the sound of banging grew louder still.

I was more frightened than I'd ever been in my life, and I acknowledged this, attempting scientific interest. Oh, there's my heart whirring like a motor. There's my mouth dry and clenched. My hands shaking as I braced myself against the wall of the hall, its paint marked by generations of other hands, other bodies brushing against it. Janna, her house all around me like a chrysalis.

Martin got to the cellar door first and reached for the handle. 'It's stuck.'

George frowned. 'It must have swollen from the damp. Help me push.'

The moments stretched on as they rattled at it, while I shivered in the hallway on the bare boards, the noise below coming and going all the while.

Eventually, with the two of them pushing, and me standing back, clutching myself in fear like a pathetic woman in a horror film, the door gave way with a clatter, stiff from years of rain and heat, the building pressure of the storm. The steps led down into darkness, only the upper three pooled in weak light – we'd never replaced the bulb. All I could think was: *I'm so scared. I'm so scared.* It was ridiculous – even if my mother-in-law was a murderer and even if she had come after us, she was still a mortal woman, and I didn't believe in witches. But I did believe in evil, and it was evil that had killed and mutilated my father, and now Susan Bodger. Poisoned those little girls.

'Hello?' George called, voice wavering in the dark space.

Martin shot him a scornful look and pushed past, his heavy boots ringing on the bare wooden steps. I was glad to have him here, this no-nonsense man. The kind of father I'd never had, one who protected without question. Mick had tried to be that, but I'd never let him.

I should have put on slippers; the stairs were jagged and splintered. We creaked down, and George turned on his phone torch and shone it in front of us, illuminating the shadowy corners. There was the workbench, its jars and knives and the old spooky book. The walls of the house exposed, beams and insulation like sprouting fungus. Collections of old broken furniture, dusty luggage. Ahead, attached to the back wall, was the smaller room with its low white door only a child could have fitted through. The door was shut, and I could see what had happened – a plank of wood had fallen from a stack left by God knows who, and wedged it shut.

'That's the boiler cupboard,' said Martin. He seemed very familiar with the house, which made sense if I was right that he'd fathered Janna's child.

My mind was dull with the series of shocks it had absorbed over the last twelve hours. Was there something about a boiler? It came to me – we'd asked the builders to come and look at it. Oh, God.

I clutched George's arm, relieved to have him there, despite all our differences. 'I think someone's in there! One of the builders – maybe they came to fix it after all.'

Martin was already there, moving the plank of wood, crouching down to open the little white door. A few seconds went by, no more. Then he shouted, 'Call an ambulance. It's the young lad Ciaran, he's out cold.'

'George – call the ambulance!' He had his phone out already, stabbing at it, lighting his face with a ghoulish glow. I couldn't stop talking. 'It's carbon monoxide poisoning, has to be, that's why the pilot light wouldn't stay on, why the boiler kept going off . . .' I should go to Ciaran. I should check him out, give CPR if needed.

But I couldn't. I found myself rooted to the spot once again. The fear, that terrible dread of hurting someone, it was back.

George shook his head at his phone. 'No reception down here.'

'I'll go.'

The horror of it all dogged my steps as I ran upstairs, catching my bare foot on a nail, a burst of pain. The builder, that young boy, barely twenty, had crawled into the small room to check the boiler, a job of a few minutes, and become stuck. Not much air in a tiny cupboard, filled with fumes. He'd been down there all night – all night! – while we lay in bed, ignoring his pitiful bangs, thinking it just the wind. As if the house itself had attacked him.

Where the hell was my phone? I raced upstairs, found it plugged in beside the bed. Dialled 999, thinking surreally I had never actually done this before. I was a doctor myself, it had never been necessary. The connection was patchy, and I couldn't hear what the despatcher was saying.

'Hello? Yes, we need an ambulance, please.' Was there even a hospital near enough with facilities? He might need the air ambulance and there was no hope of that getting out in the storm. He was still alive though. I had to cling to that. 'Yes, hi, can you hear me?'

'. . . service . . .'

'I'm sorry, the line is so bad. A workman's been injured at our home.' God, the second time for that too. The place was cursed.

'. . . madam . . . available . . .'

'It will take too long.' Martin had appeared in the doorway behind me and I jumped. 'I'll drive him over to Penzance.'

'They have an A&E there?'

'A small one. Have to just hope the road's passable. It flooded for three days in the last storm.'

How vulnerable we were, far from the things I took for granted in London, hospitals and transport and help.

There was no choice. 'I'll look at him. I was – I'm a doctor.'

I had sworn no one else would ever die under my hands, but here we were. With Martin at my back, I raced back downstairs, my feet complaining at the cold floors, and found George in the cellar, crouching over Ciaran. They had pulled him out and draped a coat over him where he lay on the bare floor, beside the broken frame of an old bed. He was grey, not moving. I could do this. Just check vitals. I didn't need to give treatment. I wouldn't have to cut into him.

I steeled myself to kneel down on the cold floor and I checked his airways and pulse – a faint flutter.

'He has acute carbon monoxide poisoning, I'd say. No surprise if the boiler's been leaking it all this time and he was stuck in there overnight.'

I tried to think what I knew about that condition. People who thought they had been haunted, often that was due to hallucinations caused by carbon monoxide leaking from old appliances. Like gas fires, or boilers. Did this explain everything, my dark suspicions, my fears of the past few weeks? My horror at the poppet, which was after all just a doll? I compressed the man's chest, noticing how slight he was, still a boy really. I pressed my lips to his cold, blue ones, trying to pump in air. How intimate this act was, and yet I'd done it to dozens of people, trying to bring them back. He could not die under our roof. He coughed under me, his pulse erratic but still there.

'Take him upstairs, he needs more air.' The irony of what he was suffering from did not escape me – so much poisoning in this story. My father, the girls, an attempt on my mother's life too. I couldn't think about that now. I just had to keep this boy alive.

Between us, we dragged him up and lay him on the dining table. Was there some colour in his cheeks, or did I imagine it? I kept working, hammering oxygen and life into him. His own breath was raspy, laboured, each gulp of air hard-fought. He had been sick on himself, I saw.

'Quick, get the windows open. I don't know if the ambulance despatcher even heard me. Martin thinks we should put him in the car, but he might go into arrest on the way.'

'It's his only chance,' said Martin gruffly. 'I'll ring his mother, tell her to meet us there.' His mother. He was so very young.

Then another voice said, 'Have you tried charcoal? It can help expel poison from the system.'

I straightened up and saw a woman standing in the hallway. Of course, we had left the door unlocked after Martin came in. She was in her sixties, with long silver-grey hair, wearing an ankle-length print dress that was wildly unsuitable for the weather. She was wet through, dripping on the floor, like a selkie woman. My heart rate, which had never really dropped, ramped up again. Her eyes, a stunning turquoise, moved over us.

Janna.

'Martin,' she said. A smile softened her face.

He seemed for once speechless.

Her eyes turned to me. 'You must be Helen. We met once, but you were very little.' She moved over to us, pressed a hand to my husband's face. He seemed frozen, as we all did, including the near-lifeless man on the table. 'George. There you are at last. I'm sorry we're meeting in these circumstances.'

She turned now to Ciaran, rolling up her wet sleeves in the same gesture I'd seen consultants use on the wards. Assured, in control. She pressed slender fingers to his neck, bent to listen to his breath. 'He's in a bad way. What happened?'

'The boiler must be malfunctioning, and he got stuck down there. He needs oxygen,' I said. 'Pure oxygen, probably in a hyperbaric chamber, though I don't know if they have one round here. Maybe there's a diving school?'

She glanced at me, nodded once. Approving. 'Would an oxygen tank work – if someone has emphysema for example?'

'It could definitely help, till we get him to hospital.'

'Martin, is anyone in the village on oxygen?'

He finally found his voice. 'Where have you been – you've been here since you got out?'

Janna frowned. 'What? No, of course not. I had to sign into the place they sent me first, dreadful hostel-type thing.'

George cleared his throat. 'I heard noises – there were noises in the cellar. We thought . . .'

She tutted. 'Honestly – you thought I'd hide in the cellar, like an animal? Birds were always getting in down there. There's some hole in the chimney breast, I think. So no, I've only just arrived. By rights I shouldn't have come, but I just had to see you all. It's been a long time.' I saw her gaze fall on George. He looked stunned, breathing hard in a way I didn't like. I could do without two patients, if he went down with an asthma attack.

Janna was looking at me now. 'Helen. Tell us what to do – you're the doctor.'

How did she know that? And was I even, any more? I had given up, because a doctor who freezes in terror in a crisis isn't much use. Every time someone's life was in my hands I panicked. Yet here I was, still giving CPR because there was no other choice. I bent to blow in more air, then came up, gasping for breath myself. 'If we can find an oxygen tank, that would buy some time to get him to Penzance. We'd need a mask too.'

Janna nodded. 'Martin, see what you can find around the village. George, dear, you keep trying the ambulance and hospital. We can at least warn them we're bringing him in.'

My head was reeling. She had simply walked in, the woman we were terrified of, and taken control. Had she really killed Susan Bodger? And my father, and the girls? She was so attuned to healing, even of this total stranger, that I could hardly believe it. She had the manner of a senior consultant, who knew their mere presence in a room could save a life. Once, that had been me.

George was floundering. 'But what are you . . . What's going on? Why are you here? I'm so confused, I can't deal with this.'

Janna cast him a look. Tender, but brisk. 'I know it's a lot, dear, but I don't have time to explain now. Your father can fill you in on some of it.'

Even in the midst of all this, I almost enjoyed the look of sheer thunder on both Martin and George's faces, as they figured it all out.

Martin left to find the oxygen, and I didn't envy him going out in the lashing rain and wind. George made several calls on his phone from the porch, where reception was strongest, and I could hear his voice rise and fall, but I couldn't make out the words. All the while, Janna and I worked on Ciaran's limp body, rubbing his feet and hands, massaging his chest, sometimes blowing into his mouth. Keeping him alive as best we could. It reminded me of how it had been at the hospital, working in tandem with people you'd sometimes only just met, all of you totally focused on the patient. But I had so many things to ask her.

'So – you and Martin . . .'

She shot me a look full of quick intelligence. 'I was in love with him, yes, but he was married. You know how it is. I was stupid, is the truth, and careless. Not thinking of the consequences.'

'And you got . . .'

'Yes, I found out I was pregnant the day I got arrested. I suppose I knew before that, on some level. We often do, women.' Another look, and I was starting to see why people had called her a witch. How could she see into me, a stranger she'd presumably last met when I was two, and know all my secrets? 'Maybe I even wanted it, secretly. The body is very powerful that way. Then I thought they'd be lenient with me, because of the pregnancy. That they wouldn't separate us, perhaps that I'd even get away with it. Self-defence, or some other excuse. Now that was very stupid of me. Instead, I gave birth in shackles and I never even got to hold him.'

'I'm sorry.' But she had murdered my father. Could I really feel sorry for her?

'The situation isn't much better now – there's only sixty-four mother-and-baby places in all the prisons in this country.' Janna spoke like an activist, not a convict. Prison had not broken her. 'I'd never have confessed if I'd known what they'd do to me. Naive.'

I wasn't sure what she meant. 'What do you . . . ?'

She tutted again. 'Oh, for goodness' sake, you don't still think I did it, do you? I'm a healer, Helen. I don't kill people. Certainly I would never hurt children – I'd have died first.'

'But . . . the poison . . . They found the bottle in the woods. It was yours.'

'It was mine, yes. But that didn't mean I used it. To be perfectly honest, I might have given him something, if things had progressed further. Perhaps that's another reason I confessed. I had the intent, maybe. But I didn't actually kill him.'

This was my father she was talking about, and I faltered for a moment, letting Ciaran's arm fall. It hit the floor, limp as a noodle. He was barely alive; we had to get help for him soon.

'Janna, I don't understand. None of us knows what happened in the woods that day. Does Martin?'

'I never told him, to keep him safe. One more sacrifice, I suppose. I was very deep into it by that point. But I really never thought they'd take my baby. And the girls . . . that was very unfortunate timing. Of course, I didn't know about them when I confessed, but perhaps I was responsible in a way for that too. I think he's going to need a tracheostomy.'

I blinked at the reversal. 'What?'

She nodded to Ciaran, who had grown grey again, lips blue. 'He's still not breathing by himself. I think he's aspirated vomit, we need to clear his airways.'

'Right. OK.' I tried to take this in. She was saying I had to cut him, into his vulnerable throat. The very same procedure I had not been able to perform that time, that terrible time. No. I just couldn't.

Janna was motioning me forward. 'You'll have to do it.'

'Me?'

'You're a doctor, aren't you? I'm not qualified, I might hit the artery. But I'm sure you've done dozens of them.'

Oh God. Here it was, the awful responsibility I had avoided by quitting my job, giving up the only thing I had ever loved to do. The moment where someone's life would be in my hands, where their blood would run over my wrists and I would wrestle with death and maybe lose.

My voice was very small. 'I can't.'

She looked at me, steady and calm. I just couldn't believe this woman had murdered my father, I couldn't. I tried to think of him, handsome and tall, but I had no memories of him at all. He'd liked camping, the outdoors. He was a good teacher, people said. But what did I know? He was a complete stranger to me.

'What happened to you?' she said. Her tone was gentle. 'Why are you afraid?'

'I – someone died. During the pandemic. I was cutting into them and . . .'

It all flooded back to me. The teenage boy, his skin pale and blue-tinged. Covid didn't affect children, they said, and so when

267

he started coughing his family didn't come to hospital, thinking it safer at home, away from all the germs. Until his mum went to call him for dinner and he wasn't breathing. And everyone else was off sick and there was only me, the sole doctor in the ward that night, to save him. I had tried ventilation, CPR, intubation. His parents were on the other side of a curtain and I could hear his mother screaming, actual sharp yelps of terror. The nurse was watching me. A young Somalian man, I couldn't remember his name. *Doctor, what do we do? We have to act now, Doctor.*

His life in my hands.

I'd said, 'Bring me a trach kit.' And it appeared under my trembling hands and I picked up the scalpel and placed my fingers on the boy's throat, so pale and delicate, and I cut.

'He died?' said Janna, still working at Ciaran, pumping his chest.

'I cut in the wrong place. I – yes, it didn't work. His oxygen was too compromised by then. It was too late.'

Idris Pelota, that was his name. I would never forget it.

'You gave up medicine?'

'I couldn't do it any more. We lost so many in the pandemic and we just – there was this sense we were alone, that the government didn't care how much it had broken us, and two of our nurses got Covid and died, and it was just . . . untenable.'

'But it's who you are, Helen. You heal.'

'I used to.'

'I thought I'd never do it again, save a life. After what happened, so much death and loss. But in prison people are sick all the time, they have heart attacks or overdose or try to hurt themselves. I saved a few, and I realised it would never really leave me, that need to heal. The ones you lose or even harm, it hangs in the balance with the ones you save. In the end the reckoning comes out.'

The ones you harm. She meant the murders, surely – because she had killed my father, and two little girls. Hadn't she? And here I was confessing my secrets to her.

'I . . .' I stepped back. 'I can't do it.'

Any of it, I meant. Be in a room with her a minute longer.

'He'll die if you don't, Helen.' Her voice was clear and firm.

And there it was. I could act, or not act. It was as simple as that. I nodded. 'Alright.'

Janna was as brisk as any ward nurse. 'Are the knives in the same place? Top drawer?'

'I – yes.'

She went into the kitchen and came back with one, long and pointed, 'You should keep these sharper. I used to whet mine twice a week.' And then she had used one to kill my father. Cut his throat. 'There. Feel for the windpipe.'

I could do this. I had learned, I had done it a dozen times before Idris Pelota. My fingers crept on to Ciaran's throat, and I poised the knife tip over it, where weak breath stirred the skin. I looked up at Janna and she nodded – *go on.*

And I did. I pressed down, saw the bright well of blood and heard the hiss of air that means a tracheostomy has worked.

I panicked then. 'I need something to put in it!'

She had thought of that – a drinking straw, still in its wrapper. Left over from one of George's takeaways. I guided it through the skin, and now air was getting into Ciaran's lungs. I saw red suffuse his face immediately, and the rattle of his chest eased a little. She had been right, his airway had been compromised, probably from when he'd been sick in the cellar. I should have seen it. There wasn't even much blood on his neck, and Janna quickly cleaned it with an anti-bac wipe she had taken from her bag. We all had those around these days.

'You did it. Well done.'

I could have wept. She had given me this gift, this woman who'd destroyed my family, this cold-blooded murderer. She had allowed me to save a life again, to set against the one I had failed to preserve.

I might have said something then, challenged her, asked who did kill my father then if she was innocent, and why the hell she had come back here, but the door slammed and Martin came in, soaked and grim, with an oxygen tank in his arms. George was behind him, phone in hand.

Martin said, 'I remembered Maureen Brandon had one for her lungs. All ready to go.'

George said, 'I got through too. They won't send an ambulance out in this, but A&E has a bed if we can get him to Penzance.'

Martin looked at Janna, as I busied myself with the tank. 'You'll be alright here if I drive him in my van?'

'We could take our car,' I said. 'So we can all go.'

He threw me a look. 'It'll never make it there. Road's half-flooded.' I remembered my thought that we would need a Jeep out here – I'd been right.

What was going to happen? I couldn't just . . . hang out with my father's killer, who also happened to be my mother-in-law. I was going to lose my mind.

'We'll be alright,' said Janna. 'When you come back we can sort everything out. George, can you find a blanket for the poor young man?'

George went, snapping to her orders like we all had, as I fixed the mask to Ciaran's face. Before, I had been irritated by his presence, but now a strange wave of tenderness swept me, and I pushed back his hair, glad to see him breathing more easily.

Martin was saying, 'Why didn't you tell me, Janna?'

From his tone, this was a private conversation, but I knew what he meant. Why hadn't she told him she was pregnant?

'Oh, because it was too late for me by then. I thought you could at least move on, make a life with Morag.'

'But I could have taken him, all these years! Looked after him!'

'I thought I'd done enough damage, and you and her – maybe there was still a chance. Did you ever – have any of your own?'

Any children, she must mean.

'No,' he said shortly. 'We split up not long after you left. It was all too broken.'

A moment of pain crossed Janna's face, then she rallied. 'Left is one way to put it.'

'But Janna, why didn't you tell the truth? When you knew there was a baby coming? For God's sake, why did you take the blame?'

'I tried to change my story. I thought they'd be more lenient on me, to be honest. Let me keep him at least a while. Or even acquit me – I thought they'd see there were mitigating circumstances. But then there was no evidence in my favour. Who else could I say had done it? And I'd already confessed. So it was too late, really.'

They looked at each other significantly, and I knew I was missing something, but there was no time.

'Shouldn't I come with you to hospital? In case he crashes on the way?' I said.

Perhaps I could get away from here, to the relative safety of a hospital, the familiar beep of machines and hush of plastic curtains. Maybe then I would feel more sane.

'No room to go safely in the van,' Martin said, glancing round as if he'd forgotten I was still there. 'Not in this weather. Best you stay here – the roads will be bad. I'm used to them, at least, but I can't risk having you injured. There's cars jackknifed from here to Penzance, I hear.' He looked at Janna again. 'I tried to ring Cara – that's my niece, she's staying with me for a while – but she's not answering the phone. Would you check on her, if there's a break in the rain? Power might be out and I wouldn't want her frightened.'

'Is she your brother's girl?' said Janna. 'Callum had a daughter?' Cara would not even have been born when Janna went to prison.

'Aye, she's Callum's lass. She's a good girl, works in the pub with me.'

'Are you talking about Cara?' said George, coming back down the stairs with a blanket. I was mildly surprised he knew where to find one. 'Is she OK?'

'We'll go and check on her,' said Janna. 'You just drive safe, and get him the help he needs.'

I saw the look that went between her and Martin. So much love had been there, still remaining, and yet they'd been separated for over thirty years. We helped Martin carry Ciaran to the front seat of the van, settling the tank beside him, getting soaked in just those brief moments outside, and then he was gone, screeching off in a spray of gravel and water, leaving George and me with Janna.

◆ ◆ ◆

There were bloodstains on the table, from where I had cut into Ciaran. Opened his flesh to the light, arrogant enough to fight with death.

Janna saw me looking as she tidied away the towels. 'He'll be alright. You did your best for him.'

I just nodded. There was so much I wanted to ask I didn't even know where to start. *Did you really not kill them? And why are you back? What do you want from us?*

'There are things we need to discuss,' she said, calmly pushing back her wet hair. 'Helen. You must have so much anger against me, if you believe the stories in the papers, what was said at the trial. You must have always thought I was guilty.'

'Aren't you?' I blurted.

She smiled, wearily. 'In a way. No one is innocent in this world. I played my part in the deaths of your father, and those poor girls. But not in the way you think.' She glanced at the window, the rain still rattling against it. 'I want to explain it all – if you're able to hear it.'

'Of course I am!'

'Really, Helen? Even if you find out your father wasn't who you thought? Even if it ruins his memory forever? Sometimes the truth is the worst pain of all.'

I swallowed. My life had been built on this belief, that Janna Edwards had robbed me of something. 'I want to know.' I was a doctor, after all. I would always look for the inconvenient truth.

'Alright then. I'll tell you everything. But first we should do what Martin asked, and check on his niece. She's young?'

'About twenty. She's been . . . helping me look into your case,' said George, sounding embarrassed. 'You know young people now, they're so obsessed with true crime. And she's . . . something of a trainee witch. That's what she calls herself anyway.'

Janna smiled, rolled her eyes slightly. 'How nice to see the traditions handed down. Now, do you have your car keys?'

We all trooped outside, the rain lashing at our hair and clothes, like a physical force pushing against my body. George put the lights and wipers on full beam, and started the engine.

'Drive very carefully now,' said Janna, who had settled in the front without asking. Already she was acting like his mother.

We progressed very slowly through the black, wet night, the windscreen wipers barely coping with the onslaught, the car buffeted by gusts of wind. We saw not a single other car, but tree branches were down all over the road, scattered bin lids and recycling tubs. There would likely be power cuts tonight. Martin lived behind the pub in an attached flat, and Janna let out a sigh as we parked up. 'It's exactly the same.'

I looked at George to see how he was processing the news that Martin was his father. Nothing I could read in his face. That meant Cara was his cousin – what would it be like, if you were adopted, to suddenly find so many blood relatives? I couldn't imagine.

Janna went ahead of us as we struggled to shut the car doors in the wind, but she turned and walked back, pale beneath her hair. 'The door's open.'

'Unlocked?' I didn't understand.

'Open. Look.'

It was ajar, banging to and fro in the wind. A cold feeling slid down my spine like a raindrop.

Janna pushed on the door. 'Cara? Hello, are you here? I'm a friend of your uncle's.'

'Cara?' George went in after her, and I followed. 'It's George, are you OK?'

Inside, the flat was in darkness, and I reached to flick on a light.

The light revealed carnage – furniture tipped over, a broken glass of water on the floor, red liquid soaking into the sofa. Wine, I thought. Not blood.

I said, 'What's happened? Burglar?'

Janna stood very still, looking round at the mess. I saw she was staring at something on the coffee table, a small stone in the shape of a heart. She turned to George. 'Cara was helping you with your book?'

'With some background, yeah, she really knew about true crime and—'

'Did you speak to Lisa in your research? Lisa McSweeney?'

'Of course, yeah, she's still based just outside town.'

Janna closed her eyes for a second. 'She must know I'm back. That stone, it belonged to her. The prison – she'd have got a letter maybe, telling her about my release. She was a witness in the case, though she never gave evidence. She'd have known I would go to Martin when I came back. This, taking the girl, it's a sign for me.'

'I called Lisa earlier,' said George, wincing. 'Because of – after Susan Bodger was killed. I left a voicemail. I thought maybe she was – that she might be in danger.'

'From me? You thought I hurt poor Susan? Oh, George, my dear. You've got this all so very, very wrong.'

George's eyes went wide. 'You mean it was her who . . . ?'

Janna cocked her head. 'Who else could it have been?'

'I wondered, but it seemed so crazy that I just . . . I mean, she was, what, ten?'

'Children can kill, if put under the right amount of pressure. Anyone can.'

I didn't understand. 'Can someone explain what the hell's going on? What has Lisa to do with all this?' The slightly batty massage therapist? She'd only been a child when the murders happened.

The wind whistled through the open door, as if to illustrate how creepy this was, the dark, ransacked house, the girl gone.

Janna sighed. 'I'm sorry you had to find out this way, Helen. I would have taken it with me to my grave, if not for this. After all, I'd already lost everything. She must have thought I'd come for her, finally, and so she's gone after leverage. You two were out, I suppose, when she came.'

I was losing it. 'Can you stop all these . . . riddles and just tell me what happened? Who killed my father, if it wasn't you?'

'There isn't time.' Janna was moving towards the door.

'Lisa,' said George briefly. 'It was Lisa who killed your dad. And Janna took the blame for it.'

I ran out after Janna, shouting over the rain. 'But why? Why would you do that, and you were pregnant as well?'

'I didn't know I was pregnant when I confessed. It was a split-second thing – I wanted to protect her, she was so young, and I felt I had failed her. And then, well, I thought they might go easy on me, because of the pregnancy. I thought Lisa would tell them why I . . . what he'd done to her, and that they'd understand why I did it. I imagined, like a fool, I might serve only a few years. Or none, even, if the truth came out.' We were at the car now. 'George, you should drive Helen home. I know where Lisa has taken Cara, I think. She's luring me there.'

'We're not letting you go alone, in a storm!' he cried. 'Between the three of us we can stop her. I'll call the police and—'

'No. It would be too late by the time they got here, and anyway, this is between Lisa and me. If she's taken the girl, it's just for collateral.' She opened the car door. 'Get in then, if you're coming. We likely don't have much time.'

I got in, mind still grasping at the pieces of this puzzle. 'You're saying Lisa, a primary-school child, was really the one who killed my father? What about the girls?'

Janna buckled her seatbelt. 'I've never really known what happened there, but I'm fairly sure she gave them something she stole from my cellar. In their orange squash, I imagine. You see, the bottle had my prints on it, my writing on the label. And the knife, that was mine too. Lisa was at my house all the time, it would have been easy for her to take them. I don't know if she actually set me up on purpose – she was a child, after all – but the evidence all pointed to me.'

I didn't know if I believed a word of this. I braced myself as George started the car. 'Where am I going?' he said.

Janna seemed oddly calm. 'The woods. The Devil's Altar.'

The place where my father died. Of course. George bumped the car off, the wind as strong as ever.

'Why didn't you tell someone?' I said, struggling into my seat-belt in the back. 'I don't understand. You went to prison for something you didn't do?'

Her eyes met mine in the mirror, chips of ice. 'I did change my story, once I realised I was pregnant. But think how it looked, Helen. Your father and I had a very public disagreement, he was trying to have me fired, and it was my poison and my knife, I was on the scene with his blood soaked into my clothes. And I had confessed. Thinking I was saving Lisa, thinking she would save me, too, by telling them what he did to her. But she wouldn't speak up, so they locked me away, and they took my boy and I . . .' For the first time I saw her lose composure. Her throat moved as she swallowed hard.

'But what did he . . . ?' Did I even want this question answered? 'Why? I don't understand why either of you would want to hurt my father.'

She glanced back at me. I remembered her words: sometimes the truth is the worst pain of all.

'I can take it,' I said. 'I just need to know.'

'You have to understand that in the eighties, the idea of grooming was not understood at all. Even at ten, eleven, a girl might be assumed to want attention from a grown man. Especially a lonely girl, one neglected at home, who'd latch on to a kind, handsome teacher offering her help. No one else even realised it was wrong, I don't think. They just saw a pillar of the community, being nice to a vulnerable child.'

My father. Always spoken of as handsome, charming, clever, a devoted teacher. She was saying he . . . 'He abused them. Is that what you mean? The girls?'

'I was as sure as I could be. There were signs.'

'You believed it enough to think about poisoning him.'

'Not to kill him. I just wanted to . . . neutralise the situation. I was very afraid of him, actually.'

Was this true? My noble father? 'Did Mum know?'

Janna turned back, and I saw the lights gleam in her eyes for a second. 'No one knew, I don't think.'

'Do you still believe it? That he . . . did things to the girls?'

'Yes.' No hesitation. 'I watched Lisa cut his throat, Helen. A ten-year-old girl. That wasn't for nothing.' I felt sick. The bumpy car ride, the terror of the night, and this choking truth, it all welled up in me. Did I believe it? I had no idea.

'We're here,' said George, who had remained uncomfortably silent throughout this conversation, eyes on the road. The entrance to the woods looked terrifying, dark trees thrashing to and fro, rain lashing on the windows of the car. 'You should stay in the car, Helen.'

'No. I need to see her. I need to know if it's true.'

My father's real killer perhaps was within these woods. And maybe, though I didn't want to think about it, Cara would need medical attention when we found her. I couldn't shirk my duty any more. If people needed help, I had to be the one to give it. It was what I'd trained all my life for, and Janna had given it back to me tonight.

We got out, leaving the warmth and dry of the car for a night so wild it tore the words from our mouths. Huddled into our rain-coats – Janna didn't even have one – we trudged towards the top of the path, and started our journey into the woods.

When I'd been here before, it was peaceful, green, full of the sounds of birds and the gentle rustling of trees. In the storm it was a very different place, with the howl of the wind and branches whipping right in our faces. The ground underfoot was marshy, and my train-ers were soon caked in mud, wet through to my toes. Janna must have been freezing in her light dress – one of hers from years before, I gathered, which still fitted her perfectly – but she marched on ahead of us, pushing aside trees and bushes, her shape wavering in the light of our phones. Janna had no phone, of course. She was like a time-traveller from the eighties, frozen at the moment she'd been arrested. George was wheezing a little, and I wondered when we'd last seen his inhaler. Had it ever been unpacked? He wouldn't have done what I'd suggested, put it into a separate bag for the move and keep it near him at all times.

'Are you alright?' I asked him, shouting over the wind.

He coughed and nodded. 'Keep going.' The damp would be getting to his chest, I knew.

The clearing – the Devil's Altar, as they called it – was about fif-teen minutes into the woods. No hikers here tonight, no dog-walk-ers or rowdy teens. I wondered if I had been there as a child, perhaps with my father, who'd liked to camp here. No tents now, no sign of anyone, and I was beginning to think we'd tramped all this way for nothing.

Then Janna froze. 'There,' she said, very quietly.

Up ahead, a faint light, as if from a head torch, and indeed that's what it was. From that light and the dim glow of the sky, I could see a woman, sitting on the altar stone, swinging her legs. She was more sensibly dressed than any of us, in welly boots and a grey raincoat, a bobble hat. It was Lisa. Beside her, lying on the rock, was a crumpled figure – I caught a flash of green hair and round glasses. Cara.

'You came,' Lisa said, running her eyes over us. 'Hello again, Helen. I couldn't tell you before, but I saw you once, you know, when you were a baby.'

I couldn't speak. She seemed so normal, a youthful-looking woman in her mid-forties. Could she really be a multiple murderer?

Janna said, 'I came. So let the girl go, Lisa. She's nothing to do with this.'

I was trying to assess Cara from a distance – was she breathing? She was certainly unconscious. Maybe I could creep around to her while Lisa was distracted.

'She knows things. She's been digging about. With *him*.'

Him was George, who now said, 'Lisa, let her go. She doesn't know anything, I promise.'

'That just isn't true now, is it? She was at my house a few times, asking me all kinds of questions. I tried to find her notes at Martin's place, but they must be in the cloud or something, I don't know. I imagine she sent them to you already. I imagine you know everything, or you think you do.'

'No. I don't know what happened that day. No one knows, not all of it anyway.'

She cocked her head at him, as though trying to work out if he was lying. 'But I know all about you, George. Why you lost your job, what you did. And I know about poor baby Helen, too, what she grew up to be. The kid you killed at the hospital.'

I flinched. How did she find that out? There had been a small inquiry, that was all, which had cleared me of any wrongdoing. It might have been available online as a short news item, if you knew what to look for.

Janna stepped further towards the faint light, rain on her face, her hair blowing loose. 'Helen was just a baby when it happened, and George wasn't born. It's nothing to do with them. Cara wasn't even thought of. It's me you want. What's the matter, Lisa – did I not give you enough already? Going to prison for something you did, that didn't cut it?'

At that Lisa threw herself off the rock, landing in the mud with a splash. I saw for the first time she was holding a knife, a long one with a black handle. 'It was you who made the poison, Janna. The one that killed people.'

'But I didn't give it to Grace and Lucy! I would never do a thing like that. And I don't think they stole it either.'

'Why not? They were nasty little girls, always lying and thieving. You should have heard the things they said about you.'

'They were children. And so were you. You didn't know what you were doing, so I took the blame. It was my fault, in a way. I should have protected you better. From your dad, from the bullying at school. And from him.'

'I didn't need protecting! You made him turn away from me – so he picked her instead. Lucy. Like I just didn't matter any more.' A child's voice was coming out of the woman's mouth.

George caught my eye, and I could still read him enough to get the message. *Go.* I pressed myself back against the edge of the clearing, trying to get to Cara.

He stepped forward, clearing his throat. 'It must have been hard, Lisa. If you felt Adam was the only one who cared for you, and he stopped paying you attention.'

'He was. And she made him drop me. I couldn't bear it. It wasn't right, what he did – just using me, then moving on like I meant nothing. And it was all *her* fault.'

She was trying to rationalise it, drawing a knife across a man's throat. It was almost impossible to imagine, and even now I didn't really believe she had done it.

The altar was just a few metres away on my left. I thought Lisa must have drugged Cara to get her here – she'd learned all of Janna's herbal tricks, and more besides. Maybe it wasn't fatal, if we could pump the girl's stomach or make her sick. The wind lifted

Cara's hair, but her skin was pale and I couldn't tell if her chest was moving.

'That must have been really tough,' said George, soothingly. 'I'm sorry you went through that.'

'It was all her fault. She deserved to take the blame.'

Janna said, 'And I did, didn't I, Lisa? Even though I was pregnant, and they took my baby from me. I said I'd killed Adam because you were just a child, and I thought you would tell the truth. About what he did to you.'

I wanted to close my ears to this part, because he was still my father, after all. I took another few small steps.

'I don't know what you mean.' Lisa's voice trembled.

'Yes, you do, Lisa. I saw him with you. It was grooming, we'd call it now. And it was more than that, wasn't it? When you came up here with him those times, and his tent?'

Lisa was shaking. I wondered if she would drop the knife, and maybe that was George's plan in moving closer, to grab it from her. Another few steps. I could almost reach out and touch Cara now. She wasn't dressed for the freezing night, wearing only a T-shirt and ripped jeans. Lisa must have drugged her at the house. A needle, probably. An oral mixture wouldn't have worked fast enough. That meant throwing up likely wouldn't help her. I tried to think what to do.

'He loved me. He said I was special!'

'Lisa, that's what predators say when they want to abuse children. You know that, deep down. That's why you killed him.' Janna was so calm.

'I didn't kill him! You did!'

'I stood here and watched you cut his throat. I tried to save him – I was covered in his blood. I sent you home, no one even knew you were here. And when it came down to it, you wouldn't tell the truth about him, to help me. But Lisa, I don't blame you.

You were only a child, you were likely traumatised. And who knows, I might have killed him myself, had things gone on. I certainly thought about it. But you took the matter out of my hands.'

'It's not true. You're a liar.' She was crying now, like a child, putting up her hands to hide her face, as if forgetting she held a knife in one. 'I didn't . . . I never meant . . . he didn't care about me any more!'

I should have moved then, got to Cara, taken her pulse, administered CPR. But part of me just had to know for good if Janna had killed my father or not, and so I waited long enough to hear Lisa whisper: 'I didn't mean to do it.'

So it was true. She was the one.

Then I sprang forward, scrabbling up on to the flat surface. It was cold and hard under my knees, as I searched Cara's neck for a pulse. A faint one, a shallow breath, her lips blue like Ciaran's had been, her skin pale and clammy. Yes, she was almost certainly drugged, and she would die of exposure if we didn't get her out of here. I started wrestling with my coat to put it over her, so wrapped up in my medical haste I forgot about the murderer with the knife for a moment.

Until I felt it pressed against the base of my skull.

Lisa's voice was in my ear. 'And what do you think you're doing? You think I'm stupid, is that it?'

'I'm just trying to help Cara. It's freezing, she could be hypothermic already.'

'I don't care.'

Her voice was so cold. I had thought her nice when I'd last met her, friendly, a little woo-woo maybe, but in a warm way. Now I saw what was just under the surface. Someone who had, at the age of ten, murdered three people, including my father. What had been done to her, to make her like that?

I wasn't sure I wanted to know the answer.

Carefully, keeping my head forward, I sat up on my heels. 'What do you want, Lisa? Why are we here?'

She seemed to calm a little at the question. 'I want to know she's going to keep her mouth shut. That no one ever decides to reopen the case.'

'So that's why you – Susan? Miss Bodger?'

'She knew too much as well. I couldn't risk it.'

'How could they reopen the case? The evidence at the time all pointed to Janna – no one even knew you were there.'

'It was your father. Surely you'd want justice for him.' I felt the knife press harder and gasped for breath.

Forgive me, Dad.

'It sounds like maybe my father wasn't who I thought, Lisa. I don't remember him, to be honest. So come on, hasn't there been enough hurt done? Janna served time for it – more than half her life, Lisa. Thirty-six years. No one's coming after you.'

Lisa jabbed the knife in Janna's direction, and I felt my whole body sag as the blade was removed from the delicate base of my skull. Calculating all the nerve endings there, the brain matter, how easy it would be to paralyse me or strike me forever dumb, like Mum. Janna was standing about three metres away, rain falling straight on to her face, but she didn't close her eyes or blink at all.

'I don't trust her,' said Lisa. 'She'll do something to me. An ill-wish, a curse. Maybe she already did. I bet that's why I never met anyone, why I couldn't have children.'

Janna said, 'Lisa, I gave up my life so you could have yours. Why would I want you to suffer?'

'Because I – I didn't do what you asked.' She was faltering. 'I didn't tell them what you said. About – about him.'

'You were just a child. You were ashamed, maybe, or in denial or shock. I shouldn't have expected it of you.' She held out her hand. 'Give me the knife, Lisa. It's going to be OK. We can put all this behind us now.'

I almost believed it, and Lisa might have believed it too, because she did lower the arm holding the knife, and take a step away from Cara and me. So it might have been alright. But somehow it went wrong, and I still don't really know why. I spent a long time piecing it together afterwards, that split second in the clearing, under the stormy sky. My breath loud inside the hood of my anorak, the cold skin of the girl under my hands as I sought her pulse to check she was still with us.

Lisa seemed to think of something, and she wheeled around until she was in front of George, pointing the knife at him. 'But he was working on a book. With the girl. Investigating.'

I could hear George's wheezing breath over the wind and rain. 'I don't . . . I didn't come to any conclusions . . .'

'You're lying. You'll have written it down somewhere, that maybe Janna didn't do it after all.'

'I had no proof of that. Look, there were a lot of things I didn't know.' He gulped, and fear ran through me. I'd seen him have an asthma attack in the wilderness once before, on our first camping trip in Scotland. An hour from a hospital, he'd forgotten to refill his inhaler and I'd had to drive him all the way there while soothing him, getting him to blow into a paper bag that had once held scones, keeping him alive as best I could, as his face turned blue and terrified. 'I – I had no idea about any of this. I only found out about Janna a few months ago. And Helen – I didn't even know who her father was, I swear.'

'You've sent bits of the book to people already, I bet. Your editor or something. I saw your messages to *her*.' Her being Cara in this case, I assumed. 'Or some friend or something. You've told people what you found out.'

'N-no . . . I don't have an editor. No one knows anything.' He was lying, that was clear. His skin was getting paler by the second. 'Lisa, I can't . . .'

'He's having an asthma attack!' I shouted. 'We have to get him out of here – both of them.'

Where was his inhaler? Back at the house? Too much to hope there was one in the car, as I'd suggested so many times? *Oh, George, why do you never listen?*

I had to leave Cara. I crossed the ground, my feet sticking in the mud. I walked right past Lisa, trying not to look at the knife in her hand, and I caught George as he sagged to his knees, making a horrible choking sound. 'Come on, relax, relax. Imagine your chest loosening.'

The horror in his face. Like when someone knows they might die – like Lisa's victims must have felt. Like Idris that day, dying under my hands, fighting to get air in his lungs, eyes growing wide with terror. 'George, come on, breathe for me. You can do this. Take sips of air.'

The sound of his chest was unbearable. I couldn't see what was happening behind me, as I fumbled with his coat and jumper. His lips were blue.

Was Janna going to watch her son die? Was I going to fail to save my husband? I couldn't allow myself to think about that, let the fear in. *Just do it. Just do the job.* I placed my lips over his and blew, tasting the familiar tang of his skin. Breathing him in, breathing for him.

It wasn't working. I was losing him, and I could see in his eyes he knew it too.

In despair, I shouted in his ear: 'George – I'm pregnant, OK? I think I am, anyway, I'm almost sure. Finally it happened. So you need to breathe, alright? Because I can't do this on my own. You need to stay with me.'

The secret I'd been keeping for weeks now, afraid my marriage was imploding, not knowing what to do. Like Janna, I had barely wanted to admit it to myself.

I saw he had heard me. His breathing cleared slightly, perhaps from the surge of adrenaline, like someone clinging fast to a rope. If he could just get enough air in to stay alive, if we could get to the car, if Lisa would let us go . . .

I pounded on his chest. I blew air into his lungs, nothing like the kisses I'd given him so many times, noticing how blue his skin was.

'George, breathe. *Breathe.*' That terrible, terrible wheeze.

Distracted, I dimly heard a noise like something falling in the mud, and felt a hand on my shoulder. I flinched, but it was only Janna.

'Where's his inhaler?' she said quietly.

'There's one at the house, but I don't know where.'

He was so careless. I thought helplessly of having to hunt through boxes and bags.

'Come on, let's get out of here. An ambulance won't make it, not tonight. We'll have to drive him to hospital.'

'But . . .'

Lisa. Where was Lisa? I turned and there was something curled up on the ground, in a muddy pool of water and blood. Her body, the knife plunged deep in her stomach, red spreading out on to her coat. Eyes open to the rain.

'J-Janna . . .'

'It's alright.' I had never seen anyone so calm. 'She can't hurt us any more. Come on, Cara and George need our help right now. You get him.'

'But what will we – what can we tell people?' She'd be arrested surely. Sent right back to prison.

I watched then as Janna rolled up the sleeves of her dress, and drew the knife over her own flesh, leaving welling cuts on the pale skin. I gasped, but she didn't even flinch. 'I should have done this last time. Now, come on.'

Janna was strong – she had spent her years in prison working out, so she was able to support Cara's slight body through the forest, half-carrying and half-dragging her. George staggered beside me, leaning heavily on my shoulder. I thought of nothing but getting them to safety, and putting one foot in front of the other in the dark of the woods, mud and branches underfoot. I didn't think of the dead woman we'd abandoned in the clearing. I didn't think about the fact that Janna really was a killer now, or that everything I'd known was wrong, so wrong. I thought nothing for the dead, my father, the little girls, even Lisa, left alone in the mud. I only thought of saving lives. The thing I had been born to do.

Margaret

There are lots of things I would like to tell my daughter if I could. I didn't know I would be robbed of my voice in my sixties, of course. I could manage to write to her, perhaps – my hands are a little better from the ointment Janna made for me – but somehow it doesn't feel right. There's too much complexity, too many shades of grey. I don't know if she will ever really understand.

Helen came to see me the day after what happened to them in the woods. I'd slept right through it, senseless from kind herbs, and had no idea that she'd found Janna's gift and jumped to the wrong conclusion. Janna had come to see me, of course, and knowing about my stroke, brought me what relief she could, as she'd done in the past. My biggest regret was the way she took the blame for what happened back then. That I didn't speak up for her when I could have, that I was too afraid of being arrested myself, too guilty at my role in it. She said she forgave me, but all the same I'm not sure I can ever forgive myself, not really. My failure to act, my lack of courage when it mattered, these are all things I will carry till I die. If I could, I would tell Helen I didn't know for sure what happened to her father, but also that I should have trusted Janna more. That poison and cure are often the same thing.

Helen and Mick came to see me together, and in the corridor I saw him put his arm around her, rub her shoulder, and she laid her head briefly on his and I was glad. One of the things I would tell her if I could is how much better a father he is than her actual one, how much better a man. Maybe she can see it now. She told me what had happened, that it was that young girl Lisa who'd killed Adam and her schoolfriends, not Janna after all, that Lisa was dead now because Janna had stabbed her in the woods. To save George, who was having a severe asthma attack, and a girl named Cara, who apparently is George's cousin. I remember Martin, his father, from the pub back in the day. Another thing I didn't know, that he and Janna were in love.

I hadn't known Janna was pregnant either, of course; she never told anyone until it was too late. In case we talked her out of her decision, maybe. If I'd known, would I have done more to help her avoid a prison sentence? If I'm being honest, I'm not sure. I was too afraid, too guilty. When Janna wrote to me, asking me to keep an eye on her boy, I ignored it. I burnt her letter to me, terrified someone might find it and that I'd be arrested as well. Accessory to murder, conspiracy to murder. Those are crimes I am technically guilty of, after all. I couldn't bring myself to destroy the letter from George's adoptive mother – it was not mine to burn. And so Helen discovered the existence of a child, and tracked him down, and married him. It had never occurred to me my daughter would do such a thing, go to such lengths. That my son-in-law was Janna's boy, the one I had failed to help.

Helen told me George would be alright after his asthma attack. She told me she was expecting a baby, at last. My daughter has not often confided in me, but I knew there was trouble in that department. I could see it on her face any time we were out and a small child toddled past. I'm glad. She told me Janna had been arrested for killing Lisa, but they were confident she wouldn't be charged, since Janna had injuries to her hands and arms, classic defence wounds, and the knife had Lisa's prints on it, and of course Cara could testify that Lisa had drugged and abducted her. When Helen said all this, it had the feeling of a rehearsed story, but that was alright. I wished I could have squeezed her hand to show I understood, but it felt impossible, as if the message just couldn't get through to my nerve endings.

She told me they would give Janna back her house, haunted for them now by the near-deaths of two builders under their roof – although the men will be alright as well. She told me their contractor, Bob, was almost bankrupt because of the pandemic, which explained why he was the only one who'd take the job at the witch's house, and why he had threatened to sue them, out of sheer desperation. That's all sorted now, and Cara is out of hospital too, after treatment for mild exposure. I hope Janna and Martin will finally have the time they deserve, denied to them all these years.

Helen told me she and George might move back to London, since the countryside hasn't worked out for them, that George wouldn't write the book now, so he'd have to find something else to do with his life. Even if he can't get the kind of job he wants, he'll have to move on, adapt. It's what people do. And Helen will be busy once she goes back to work – a doctor can always walk into a job. I knew she couldn't stay away from it for long – it's what she was born to do. So different from her father and from me. So full of courage, when I never was.

There are more things I could tell my daughter, but I don't think I ever will. What good would it do? She didn't say as much, but I could tell she knew something of why her father died, the things he did. It would be called abuse today. Never proven, never overt, nothing so crude as skin on skin or mouths or hands, that whole sordid world. Or maybe it was, and I closed my eyes to it as well. I don't blame Lisa for not speaking up back then – it's a lot for a child of ten, to accuse her headteacher. And she had wanted something from him, affection maybe, even love. Just not that. Never that.

I could also tell Helen the reason The Gables was familiar to her when she first arrived on that day several months ago. About how I took her there, a child of two, pushing her buggy up the hill and over the gravel drive and up the stone steps to knock on Janna's door, one day after school when I knew she would be home, when Adam was working late, or whatever horrors he was really up to.

Mummy, where this house?

We're going to visit a friend. Be a good girl now.

And Janna had answered the door, in her floral dress and apron smudged with sap, her face flushed and hair loose. How pretty she was – still is, after thirty-six years in prison. How I started to cry and her face changed, how she ushered me in. How she left Helen in the living room, cluttered and old-fashioned even then, with a biscuit, and took me to the kitchen.

I could tell Helen how I tried to explain why I'd come. That I was afraid of my husband – not what he'd do to me, but of who he was. Of what monster I had helped to hide in plain sight. About the last two schools and why we'd left London, the allegations of the children, the tears and shouting, the girl he was caught driving with in his car, all of eleven years old, and both of them drunk, so he'd lost his licence. About the parents who were more believing than Lisa McSweeney's, the father who had punched him in the play-ground, thrown him to the ground and injured his shoulder. How the police were never involved because no one in charge entirely believed it, the governors taking his word over that of young girls and working-class parents, fathers known to drink. But how all the same we had to move, because that kind of rumour will follow you around like a stink, and soon your friends won't bring their children to your house, and before you know it your life has eroded under you like a rotten floor. How I tried my best not to believe it either, to take his word that all these girls were little liars, brought up to it by their class and background. Sluts. Flirts.

I could tell Helen how I leaned against the kitchen counter that day and wept into my hands.

I don't know what to do. I'm so afraid – I saw him with that girl. And he's been out so many nights, camping, he says. I see how he looks at them in the playground. And I have a daughter. A little girl.

That was my main fear, wasn't it? For Helen. What would happen when she got to whatever age he liked best. Nine? Ten? I couldn't bear the idea of it, watching them both for the rest of Helen's childhood. I wouldn't live like that, but I was too afraid to leave.

Janna was very calm. She was by the sink, running the water to pour me a glass, which I gulped down. I remember it was very cool and sweet.

Do you want me to help you, Margaret?

How did I know what she was capable of? I'd heard the village rumours and perhaps I had already guessed what was in the lotion she'd given me for him, telling me not to say it was from her. Perhaps I knew she could go further, if I asked her to.

Was that what I'd wanted? I could pretend otherwise, I could lie to myself, but the truth is at the time I knew exactly what she was asking me. I thought of Helen, of the little girls I had seen in his class, so young and fresh, on the edge of something they couldn't understand yet.

Yes. Please help me. I have no one else to turn to.

I'm glad to know, after all these years, that I didn't damn her, that she didn't strike the fatal blow in the end, that the years in prison were to some extent her choice – though she couldn't have known she had asked too much of Lisa, or that they would jail a pregnant woman for so long. I remember then she took my hand with her cool one, and held it against her chest. George was already growing there between us, though neither of us could have known. She may have suspected, perhaps.

We need to deal with this, Margaret. It's not safe. For any of the children.

And I nodded. *Yes. You're right.*

She paused a moment. The sun was bright on her hair. *You can't know anything about this, if they come to ask. It's a crime, to even have this conversation. You understand?*

Yes.

I don't know how far Janna went with her plans. Poison, she would have meant, not the brutal slitting of his throat, the blood soaking her clothes and hair. She would have done it differently. Quietly, discreetly, so no one even knew what had happened. Later, afterwards, I took her warning as a sign to stay out of the investigation, avoid the trial, pretend she was nothing to me but my husband's killer. I wonder if that was the right thing to do, or if I was just fooling myself, if my testimony could have saved her. But it might have meant damning me to prison alongside her. Helen an orphan, adopted like George was, lost to me. I can't tell myself I would make a different decision this time round.

On that day in 1986, all the while we had this conversation, Helen was in the next room, singing to herself, dropping biscuit crumbs, playing very carefully with what I later learned was a curse doll, the kind you put in the wall to deflect evil intent.

I could tell her all of this – how I arranged her father's murder because I was too afraid to leave him or denounce him, how she was with me when I did it, how I did it all for her, to keep her safe, how I let Janna go down for it without speaking up, how I lived with the guilt all this time. But as she sits on my bed now and hugs me close, her smell of body lotion and shampoo, my daughter, my only child, with her own child growing inside her, I realise that I never will.

BOOK CLUB QUESTIONS

1. Helen allows George to buy them a house without her even seeing a picture of it. Is that something you would ever trust a partner to do?

2. Apart from the killer, many people blame themselves for the events in 1986 – Janna, Margaret, even Martin. Who do you think was to blame for everything that happened, and how much?

3. Helen and George are both guilty of lying to each other. Is either of them justified in what they do?

4. How does the 'witch hunt' George experiences on social media compare to Janna being accused of actual witchcraft and murder?

5. Do you believe in anything 'other-worldly', such as the remedies and spells Janna uses in the book?

6. Could Janna have done more to stop Adam? Should she, when no one believed her?

7. Do you agree that people moving 'down from London' can ruin small communities and drive up prices, or is it necessary to keep villages alive?

8. Should Janna have told Martin the truth about George? How might things have been different if she had?

9. Should Margaret have told Helen the truth about her father? How might this have changed the story?

10. Do you feel any sympathy for the character of Lisa? Why, or why not?

ABOUT THE AUTHOR

Claire published her first novel in 2012, and has followed it up with many others in the crime fiction genre and also in women's fiction (writing as Eva Woods). She has had four radio plays broadcast on the BBC, and her thrillers *What You Did* and *The Other Wife* were both number-one bestsellers. She ran the UK's first MA in crime writing for five years, and regularly teaches and talks about writing. Her first non-fiction project, the true-crime book *The Vanishing Triangle*, was released in 2021. She also writes scripts and has several projects in development for TV.

Get your free collection of short stories now at www.clairemcgowan.co.uk – just sign up to Claire McGowan's newsletter to receive this. You will also receive occasional news updates, exclusive short stories, and be entered into giveaways just for subscribers. It's all free and you can opt out anytime.

Join now at www.clairemcgowan.co.uk

Follow the Author on Amazon

If you enjoyed this book, follow Claire McGowan on Amazon to be notified when the author releases a new book!

To do this, please follow these instructions:

Desktop:

1) Search for the author's name on Amazon or in the Amazon App.
2) Click on the author's name to arrive on their Amazon page.
3) Click the 'Follow' button.

Mobile and Tablet:

1) Search for the author's name on Amazon or in the Amazon App.
2) Click on one of the author's books.
3) Click on the author's name to arrive on their Amazon page.
4) Click the 'Follow' button.

Kindle eReader and Kindle App:

If you enjoyed this book on a Kindle eReader or in the Kindle App, you will find the author 'Follow' button after the last page.